DOCTOR SCANDALOUS

J. SAMAN

Cover Design: Lori Jackson

Photographer: Rafa Catala

Model: Christian Balic

Editing: My Brother's Editor

Proofing: Danielle Leigh Reads

❀ Created with Vellum

1

Oliver ♥

I'm walking toward the gates of hell. And they charge for admission.

"Oh, Oliver..." Christa Foreman greets me with a slow once-over, her pastel-pink lips curling up into an impish grin. She's aptly named, because our senior class president was no joke when it came to strong-arming and manipulating her fellow classmates into getting what she wanted. "It's so good to see you. Wow. I mean, I see your pictures in magazines and on social media every now and then because I follow you, but you're way better looking in person than I remember from high school."

"Um. Thank you?" It comes out as a question, my head tilting in her direction.

"Sure. No problem." She licks her lips, her long, fake eyelashes batting faster than a butterfly's wings at me. "Are you here alone tonight?" She giggles as a flush creeps up her cheeks. She's married. Can we just say that? "I'm only asking because I need to know how much to charge you. I got stuck collecting money until the event coordinator can get her shit together." She huffs out a flustered breath, rolling her eyes derisively. "Anyway, it's a hundred per person. Should I put you down for one or two?"

And this is where I hesitate. Not over the money. The money is not an issue.

"Just give me a second."

Christa stares longingly at me, licking her lips. "Sure. I'll give you all night."

"Right." Because I have no idea what else to say to that. I don't remember Christa being so overtly interested in me when we were in high school. Then again, that was ten years ago, and I was most definitely taken. Which is both the main reason I don't want to be here and the main reason I came. But now I'm starting to reconsider everything.

I have nothing to prove by being here.

Not to *her*, her douchebag husband—my former friend—or anyone else.

I should just go. Maybe meet up with Carter, who I already know is going to our favorite bar, and get lost in a night of fun. Nothing about this hellhole will be fun. And in truth, I could really use a drink. A quiet one. It's been a shitful week. Too many patients. Not enough time. Oh, and finding out that your mom's cancer is back is always a winner.

I slip my phone from my pocket and shoot off a text to my best friend, Grace.

Me: Sorry, babe. Not gonna be able to make it.

The message bubble instantly dances along my screen. **Grace: It's not a choice, honey pie. Everyone is already asking when you're going to get here. Everyone.**

And instantly I'm tempted to ask if *she's* asking. In fact, my thumbs, who seem to have a mind of their own, start to type that very question until I tamp them down and rein them under control. Of course, she's asking. That's what she does. She continues to hunt me down with terrorist-level determination, even all these years later.

She's likely giddy at the prospect of rubbing her picture-perfect life in my face without even caring that she's the last person on the planet I want to see tonight or any other night. Hence why now is the perfect time to leave.

Me: Don't care.

Grace: Yes, you do. Come on. I know you're already dressed for tonight. Carter sent me a text.

Carter. My traitorous brother.

Grace: Just come inside the hotel. Come up to the reunion. Have a drink with me. See the people you haven't seen since high school who will fall at your feet the way they did back in the day. Oh wait, they still do.

Me: You're doing a shitty job of selling it there, sweetums.

Grace: Everyone will think you're a pussy if you don't come.

Me: Nice gauntlet drop.

Grace: I thought so. Now get your ass over here!

I growl out a slew of curses under my breath, still seriously contemplating fleeing for the sake of my sanity, when I catch sight of a short, curvy redhead in a tight, backless black dress, higher than high heels, and fuck-me red lips that match her hair walking up to Christa. She's as late as I am, and before I know what I'm doing, a smile cracks clear across my face.

I know her instantly.

Even if it's been ten years since I've seen her. A guy never forgets the girl who gave him his first boner. A first-ever boner in class, I might add. We were twelve and she bent over to retrieve her fallen pencil when a flash of her training bra caught my eye. Instant erection.

I was pretty smitten after that moment, as you might imagine.

"Amelia," Christa greets her, her face now lacking any of the warmth it had when she was talking to me. "I had no idea you were coming."

What the fuck? You'd think in the ten years since we graduated from our annoyingly prestigious prep school that the rich girls would get over the self-created, mean-girl bullshit they had with the scholarship kids.

Amelia turns redder than her hair, and she takes a small step back before straightening her frame and squaring her shoulders. "Well, I'm here. Graduated same year as you. I even received the invitation in the mail. Must have been an error on your part," she finishes sarcastically.

"Uh-huh. It's a hundred-dollar entrance fee," Christa snaps, taking far too much pleasure in announcing that sum as she purses her lips off to the side, giving Amelia a nasty-girl slow once-over.

"A hundred dollars?" Amelia asks, though it comes out in a deflated, breathy whisper.

"Yup. Sorry," Christa sneers with a sorry-not-sorry saccharine sweet voice. "No exceptions. Not even for the kids who were on scholarship."

And that's it. Before Christa can say anything else that will make me want to throttle her, I walk over to Amelia, wrapping my hand around her waist. "Sweetheart," I exclaim. "You made it. I was starting to get worried."

Amelia jolts in my arms, her breath catching high in her throat as she twists to face me. Then she looks up and up a bit more because she's about a foot shorter than I am even in her heels. Suddenly, two sparkling gray eyes blink rapidly at me, and my heart starts to pound in time with the flutter of her lashes, my mouth dry like I've been eating sand all night.

"I'm sorry," she says, confused, her parted lips hanging just a bit too open for us to be selling this. "I think you must—"

I lean in, my nose brushing against her silky red hair that smells like honeysuckle or something sweet and I breathe into her ear, "Just go with it."

She swallows audibly as I pull back, staring into her eyes and wondering how a color like that is even possible when she smiles and robs me of my breath. *Whoa.* That's unexpected.

"I didn't mean to worry you..." She trips up, biting into her lip like she's searching for a suitable term of endearment. Or maybe my name? I guess it is possible she has no idea who I am. We didn't exactly run in the same circles, and I just came up to her and wrapped my arm around her. "Oli," she finishes with, and I blow out the breath I didn't even realize I was holding.

"It's fine. I just didn't want to go in without the most beautiful woman in the world on my arm."

Amelia gives me that stunning smile again, this time with a blush staining her cheeks, and I marvel at how it makes her eyes glow to a smoky charcoal. Goddamn, she's fucking sexy.

"Wait," Christa interrupts. "You're with her?" She points at Amelia.

"I sure am," I declare without removing my eyes from Amelia's because those eyes, man. They're just too pretty not to stare at. "I'm a lucky bastard, right?"

"You're with him?" She turns that finger on me.

"So it seems," Amelia replies, her tone a bit bewildered, though there is a hint of amusement in there, too.

"But. You're. You. No. You're Oliver Fritz," Christa sputters incredulously. "And she's Amelia—" Her words cut off when I throw her my most menacing glare, already knowing the exact nasty nickname she's about to throw out. Why certain women feel the need to degrade and belittle other women, I'll never understand.

I slip two one-hundred-dollar bills from my wallet and toss them at Christa. "Have a good night," I say instead of what I'm really thinking. My fingers intertwine with Amelia's, and then I'm dragging her past Christa, down the long corridor with the paisley rug and gold walls, toward the ballroom.

I guess I'm going to my high school reunion after all.

The second we're out of sight of Christa, Amelia yanks her hand from mine, stopping in the middle of the hall and turning to stare up at me. "You remember me?" she asks and then shakes her head like that's not what she meant to say.

"Amelia Atkins. You were in most of my classes from the time we were in sixth grade or so, on."

"Right. What I meant to say is, thank you for stepping in back there, but it really wasn't necessary."

"Maybe not. I'm sure you can handle yourself with women like Christa. But it felt wrong to stand there and watch that go down, doing nothing. I can't stand women who feel the need to hurt others just to make themselves look and feel better."

She folds her arms over her chest, giving me a raised eyebrow. "And yet you dated a woman who did exactly that all through high school."

Touché. A bark of a laugh slips out my lungs. "Can't argue with that. Hell, I dated that same vicious woman through college too. Adolescent mistake. What can I say?"

Still, at the mention of that particular woman, an old flair hits me straight in the chest. My fingers find my pocket, toying with the large diamond solitaire set in a diamond and platinum band I stuck in there tonight. It's *the* ring. The one I nearly gave to said woman who was screwing around on me with my friend, Rob. A lesson in betrayal I've never forgotten. It's why on certain occasions, I carry it with me.

A reminder to never get too close again.

"Sorry," Amelia says, withering before my eyes. "That was insanely rude of me. I don't even know why I said that. Christa got my hackles all fired up, and I just took them out on you instead of her, like I should have. Damn, some women seriously suck, right?" I can't stop my chuckle, though I think she was being serious. She stares down at the rug, shifting her stance until she's leaning back against the wall opposite the closed doors where the reunion is taking place. "Look, I wish you hadn't paid for me. Money and I aren't exactly on speaking terms at the moment. It's going to take me a while to pay you back. But I *will* pay you back. I just don't have that kind of—"

My fingers latch on to her chin, tilting her head back up until our eyes meet. "I don't care about the money. And I don't want you to pay me back." She opens her mouth as if to argue with me, and I shake my head, cutting her off again. "I mean it."

She huffs out a breath. "Well, thank you. That's very generous. But if this is how this night is already starting off, I'm thinking maybe I should just go. Hell, I shouldn't even have come here in the first place. I don't know what I was thinking. My sister talked me into it, and I thought..." She shakes her head. "Never mind. It's stupid."

I prop my shoulder against the wall so I'm facing her, folding my arms while I stare at her because I can't seem to help myself. "Why is it stupid?"

"You really want to know?"

"I really want to know."

Those big eyes slay through me, slightly glassy with emotion. "Because no one in there wants me there. You heard Christa. I was fooling myself into thinking that I could waltz in here ten years later and everyone who treated me like garbage growing up would finally see me for me. That they'd finally realize we're all on an even playing field now that high school is over. It was going to be like putting all my old bully nightmares to rest once and for all. Only, nothing has changed. I'm still the girl wearing thrift store digs who couldn't even afford to pay the entrance fee."

Wow. That's...

"Can I tell you something?" I ask.

Her hands meet her hips. "You mean something to rival the way too personal verbal diarrhea I just spouted at a man I haven't seen in a decade?"

She's trying for brave and strong, and even sarcastic. But she's sad. I can see it in her eyes that bounce around my face, almost as if she's not sure she wants to know what I'm about to say. No one wants to be slammed back into their high school nightmare. She wanted to walk in there and make all those assholes eat their words.

I want that for her too.

I like Amelia. I always have. There was something about her that just got to me on a weird level I never quite understood. She was sweet and nerdy and quiet and reserved. So understatedly beautiful. Her hair was all wild with red curls. Her glasses a touch too big for her face. Her body small with her ample curves hidden beneath her ill-fitting prep school uniform.

And looking at her now, after hearing what Christa was saying to her...

In truth, I do remember people being that nasty. Though now I'm positive it was a lot worse than I knew about if Christa's reaction to her tonight is anything to go by. I only heard comments here and there that I didn't pay much attention to, nor did anything to stop. Even if I never directly contributed to it, by not stopping it, I was part of the problem.

That's on me. And it's not okay. I should have done more to protect her. I should have said something.

"Something like that. You told me yours. Now I'll tell you mine."

"Alright."

I step into her, bending down like I'm about to tell her a secret when really, I just want to be closer to her. Smell her shampoo that makes my cock jump in my slacks. Feel the heat of her body as she starts to blush from my proximity.

"I don't want to be here either. I got talked into it by my friend, Grace, and now here I am."

Her eyebrows knit together. "Why wouldn't you want to be here? You're a doctor. You were the most popular guy in our class. Captain of the football team. Everyone loved you. Still do, if the tabloids are anything to go by."

I suck in a deep breath, ready to tell her something only my family and Grace know. "My ex is not only in there with her husband, my former friend, but she's pregnant. Likely going to be delivered by either my brother or my best friend since she sought them out to be her OB. How's that for irony?" I roll my eyes. "The only saving grace I have when it comes to Nora is that she never knew I was about to propose. I had the ring in my pocket, ready to drop down onto one knee, but before I could do anything, she told me she was in love with Rob and that we were over."

Amelia sucks in a rush of air, her eyes flashing. Her hand shoots up, covering her parted lips as she stares at me with a combination of shock and sympathy. "God. That's awful."

"The real kicker of all that is I had made a lot of sacrifices for her. A lot. Nearly everything I wanted I had given up for her with the exception of medicine. But I chose NYU to be with her instead of playing ball at Michigan. I finished college in three years instead of four because she said the sooner I can complete med school and residency, the better. Then, on the fucking day I got into Columbia for med school and was set to propose, she informed me she had been cheating on me for the better half of six months."

Six. Fucking. Months!

"Jesus, Oliver. I'm so sorry. I never heard anything about that."

"That's because no one knows, so if you wouldn't mind keeping that to yourself, I'd appreciate it. The last thing I want is for that to hit the press next."

She reaches out her hand, touching my arm and giving me a squeeze. "Of course. I'll never tell anyone. I don't blame you for not wanting to go in there. It seems we both felt like we had something to prove by showing up tonight."

That's not the reason I came tonight. But Nora is the main reason I didn't want to go in. I've successfully avoided seeing her for years. In truth, I've been over her for a long time, just not over what she did to me. Most of my bitterness and resentment is on me. I should never have made those sacrifices for her.

I gave up pieces of myself I can never get back.

But Amelia deserves more. She always has, and she never got it. She deserves to have people look at her and treat her with the respect they never did. They owe it to her. Hell, I owe it to her. I don't want her to leave tonight the way she is now.

"I only wish it had turned out better for us," she continues. "But I think my carriage has officially turned back into a pumpkin and I should just cut my losses and head home. Tonight can't possibly end the way I had envisioned it."

Like a bolt of electricity flowing through me, suddenly I'm giddy with an idea that is quite possibly the most ridiculous idea in the history of ideas. Christa nearly swallowed her tongue when she thought Amelia was my date. So maybe everyone else will react the same way if that's what they see. Bonus for me—I'll have a hot as hell woman on my arm and maybe Nora will leave me alone.

More than that, I *want* to go in there with Amelia. I want to spend more time with her tonight. And if they don't like it or think less of me for it, well, I don't give a shit.

But Amelia being my date isn't enough. Not with my reputation.

They'll just assume I'm using her, because ever since Nora and I split up... I've been somewhat of a player. A fact the media loves to report on. Hell, my face is splashed across the internet every other week, showing me with a different woman each time. Not in the last few months or so, but it's been the standard of my life since Nora. It's the way I keep from getting hurt again.

And the media reporting on it all? Well, that's the standard of all my brothers' lives. It comes with being a Fritz and living in Boston. We own this city. We're royalty. For better or worse, that's how it is.

But if Amelia and I really want to make an impact tonight... if I really want to make all those assholes who hurt Amelia choke, and Nora—who still calls me to tell me *all* her 'happy' news—realize that I've finally and officially moved on from her... it needs to be more than just people thinking I'm dating Amelia.

They need to know she's something special. Believe she's something special *to me*.

My fingers dig back into my pocket, locating that ring. Looking at her... plotting this insane idea... I'm hit with the fact that I know it will change everything. Both for her and for me.

A deviously crooked smile curls up at the corner of my lips.

Yeah. I have an idea, alright. And I think I can get Amelia to go for it. It's only for a few hours anyway. What could go wrong?

2

Amelia 🖤

No matter how many things I checked off my list, nothing could have prepared me for the night ahead. But at the time, it'd given me a moment of false security.

Long red hair down in thick glossy waves? Check.

Makeup a bit much for me but completely flawless? Check.

Black dress a lot too tight, a little too short, and has zero back to it? Check.

Sexy, sophisticated, confident goddess? Check.

Well, at least I was until Christa Foreman sunk her talons into me. She knew just where to strike. Exactly how hard. Her and her pack of vultures always had a thing for making me feel like roadkill. Taking me down, especially at my most vulnerable state. In a matter of seconds, I was reduced to that girl again tonight. The one I was in high school.

The one always too afraid to speak up for herself or fight back.

I'm so pissed at myself for it too.

I wasn't going to come. I left Wilchester Prep ten years ago and never looked back. Hell, I practically sprinted from that place the moment that diploma was in my hand. Then two years later, my life fell apart around me.

Everything changed.

My dreams, gone. My heart broken. My life, onto a new plan. A new reality.

But when that invitation for the reunion showed up, my fourteen-year-old sister not so kindly reminded me that I haven't had a night out in a long time. And we're talking a *long* time. Like so long I wouldn't be shocked if my vagina was growing cobwebs.

"It's a night out, Amelia. You need to take this. Show all those assholes who said you were too poor to amount to anything what you've become since high school. A hot babe of a woman. A kick-ass nurse. Show them that they didn't beat you."

She dragged me down to the thrift store and we spent money I don't have on this dress and these heels—sky high to compensate for my Hobbit stature. Layla did my hair and makeup to painstaking perfection.

And when I walked in here tonight, I felt good. Like really freaking good. No, I felt fucking amazing.

I started to let Layla's words sink in.

I stepped into a role, one where I'm not the eternal wallflower watching from the sidelines. Where I'm not drowning in so much debt I can't even keep my head above water. Where I'm not essentially a single parent, raising a teenager. Where it hasn't been so long since I've had sex that if I didn't occasionally see penises at work, I'd forget what they look like.

Then Christa Fucking Foreman had to ruin all that in the blink of an eye.

Now here's Oliver Fritz, staring at me with those gorgeous green eyes of his, towering over me with his tall, perfectly built body, and smelling like every bit of the sexy god he is.

I'd be lying if I said he wasn't on my mind when I agreed to come tonight. A girl never forgets her first crush and much like everyone else we went to school with, he was mine. From about the age of twelve on. But it was always from afar. I've known him nearly my whole life without actually knowing him at all.

Before tonight I think I've said maybe two dozen words to him.

We had moments. Brief interludes that meant a hell of a lot more to me than they did to him, no doubt. He even touched my shoulders once. I know, right, total swoon and completely pathetic.

It's likely why I've been staring at him like a mindless fool, stuck in some horror show of spewing every word and thought as they spring to my mind. I think it's because I'm unable to wrap my head around what he did for me. The fact that he even remembered me. How his hands feel on my body when they touch me.

How unbelievably *hot* he is, especially up close.

And when he stepped in back there, I'll admit, I had some Cinderella fantasies going on. A few heart palpitations when he wrapped his arm around my waist. A ton of giddy butterflies when he held my hand. But hearing his story about what Nora did to him?

What a stupid, stupid woman to let someone like Oliver Fritz go.

I mean, did she not see his smiles? Like the one he's giving me now. It's kinda mischievous and a little dirty and possibly a touch flirty? I don't know about that last one. It's been too long since a man has flirted with me other than my boss and that doesn't count as flirting. That's more leering with overtly suggestive undertones.

"Amelia, I don't think you should go home," Oliver states. "I think you should stay and go into the reunion."

I'm already shaking my head at him before he can finish. "If Christa back there is any indication, this won't get any better for me. Seriously, reliving shitty high school memories while a bunch of women sneer nasty things at me is not how I want to spend my night. I should have known it would be like this. It was stupid of me to think otherwise. My life is not a John Hughes film."

"But what if they didn't sneer nasty things at you? What if they did look at you and speak to you the way they always should have?"

"Are you going to sprinkle them with anti-bitch pixie dust or something? Because otherwise, I don't see how anything like that is even remotely possible. I don't want to go in there, Oliver. I'd rather just go home, take a bath, and eat my weight in chocolate."

And now I need to shut up. Again. What is wrong with me? It's like my brain-to-mouth filter just up and quit at the sight of him.

Shockingly he doesn't laugh at me. Instead, he just runs a hand across his jaw, still smiling kind of manically. "What if you didn't go in there alone?"

I tilt my head, folding my arms over my chest so I'm not tempted to touch him again. I press further back into the wall. "How do you mean? Like walk in there at the same time?"

"No. Like walk in there together. As a couple."

"Um. I'm not sure I understand."

Oliver takes a step into me, slamming my senses with the delicious scent of his cologne, his warmth, his proximity. My neck cranes to meet his green eyes that are swirling with devilry. His hands land on my biceps, his thumbs brushing back and forth as his face dips down, inching in even closer. Goose bumps erupt across my skin as sparks of electricity zap up my spine and through my chest, quickening my heartbeat.

He licks his lips as if he feels it too before his words tumble out in a rush. "You're going to think I'm nuts. But I'm not. This makes such good sense; you have no idea. It's genius really. So genius, we absolutely have to do it just so we can see all their faces."

"Oliver, you're starting to freak me out."

"Neither of us wants to go in there alone, right? So what if we don't? What if we go in there together? As a couple. But not just any couple..." One hand abandons my arm, plunging into his pocket and a second later, he produces a wowzer of a diamond ring that he holds up directly in front of my face. "An *engaged* couple."

"Oh my god. What the hell is going on? Where did you get a freaking diamond ring from?!"

"It's the one I never gave Nora. I brought it with me tonight as a reminder."

"A reminder of what?"

He shakes his head dismissively. "It's not important. But it couldn't be more perfect that I have it with me. Let's do this, Amelia. I *want* to do this. With you. What do you say? Wanna be my fiancée for the night?"

"Jesus, Oliver. This is too much. You barely know me and you're going to put that massive thing on my finger that likely costs more than I'll earn in a lifetime? Why would you do this?" I ask, my eyes playing some sort of intense round of ping-pong, whipping back and forth between the diamond and his eyes.

His grip on my arm tightens, his handsome features growing more urgent. "Because then nothing and no one can touch you, Amelia. Don't you see? You will be invincible. No one will dare say anything nasty to you because you'll be with me. My fiancée. It's like you said, I was the most popular guy in school. Loved by everyone. For better or worse, let's use that to our advantage."

"Oliver..." I'm at a loss.

"If you won't do it for you, then do it for me. If you're with me, Nora won't try to rub in the fact that she's happily married and about to have a kid."

"She actually does that?"

"She does. All the damn time."

"Wow. She's really something."

A smile lights up his face. "That's one word for her. She likes to leave lengthy voice mails since I don't pick up her calls. I even blocked her, and she changed numbers. What kind of psycho ex does that? With any luck, she'll avoid me like the plague, and I can get away with a simple head nod or something instead of having to talk to her and dickhead Rob McQueen. Don't you see? It's a win-win for us."

"It's a lie, Oliver. All of it."

"I know." He cups my jaw, his eyes intense and laser-focused on mine. "But it's just for tonight. Just for a few hours or so. You're still you, Amelia. Beautiful. Smart. Funny. You're the whole package. You always have been and I..." He puffs out a breath, his eyes fluttering shut for a moment before they reopen with steadfast determination. "I'm sorry people were so cruel to you. It was wrong. In truth, if no one saw how incredible you are back in high school, then that's on them. It's their loss, not yours. And truly, you have nothing to prove to anyone. But I'd love to see those who were ever mean to you swallow their tongues. And they will. You know they will. You heard Christa before. It'll be like that."

I think I'm impersonating a goldfish. I open my mouth, but no sound comes out.

"Besides, it could be fun," he continues. "Our little inside joke and secret. A prank we're playing on the world. A delicious form of revenge."

"I don't know. It's…"

Tempting. It's tempting, is what it is. For a lot of reasons.

He's right. I don't have to prove myself to anyone. I am very likely a better person for not having those women as friends or in my life. But his words. The things Oliver just said to me. Him wanting to do this for me. The idea of walking in there on his arm.

Even if just for tonight…

Tonight, a night I was supposed to come out of my shell. To remember what fun feels like. To be reminded, even if just for a short while, that I'm still young and there's more to life than what mine is presently comprised of.

"Say yes, Amelia. Please do this with me."

Say yes? How does a woman ever say no to him? Especially when he stares at them like that?

Before I can answer, Oliver drops down onto one knee, that mammoth diamond raised in the air. "Amelia, I-don't-know-your-middle-name Atkins, will you make me the happiest man on the planet and agree to be my fake fiancée?"

An incredulous laugh bursts from my chest, but also—and I know this is stupid—I start to get choked up. Because no one has ever proposed to me, fake or otherwise. And they sure as hell haven't stared up into my eyes the way he's staring into mine. Like he means it. Like it's somehow sincere even when we both know it's anything but.

My hand hits my chest as I try to suck in air. My face is heating up by the second and something about that makes an irresistible smile spring to Oliver's lips.

"God, you're sweet," he says. "Come on. Don't leave a man hanging on one knee."

Oh hell. It's only for tonight. Just a few hours, like he said. What's the worst that could happen?

My teeth dig into my bottom as I try to contain my almost giddy smile. "Yes, Oliver. I'll be your fake fiancée."

His eyes sparkle as he slides the ring onto my fourth finger and all I can do is stare dumbly down at it. It's cold, heavy, foreign. But so beautiful it looks like it was made just for me. "It fits."

"Perfectly, I'd say."

He stands up, taking my hand and drawing my knuckles up to his lips. With his eyes on mine, he kisses each one, lingering on the finger holding his diamond. My knees just about buckle at the feel of his lips on my skin, and I have no idea what's happening here. I am not this woman. The one who breaks all the rules and flies by the seat of her pants and receives fake proposals from gorgeous billionaire playboys.

It makes me seriously wonder if I passed out and hit my head and now I'm in a coma. Or dead, even. In either case, right now, I don't care. I'll take it. This is fairy tale, fantasy caliber shit right here. But for real, who suggests something as hair brained as getting fake engaged to get through a reunion? Oliver Fritz, apparently. I swear, only he can pull something like this off. His charm knows no bounds.

Oliver takes the hand he was just kissing and loops it through his elbow, twisting until he's beside me. "Are you ready to do this, future Mrs. Fritz?"

Oh god. What the hell am I doing? A sudden rush of nervous doubt bolts through me. "Everyone's going to know this is fake."

"No way. Only Grace and her fiancé will, and they won't say anything. I don't exactly talk to anyone else from high school all that often."

"Except you're Oliver Fritz. Everyone knows you. The media stalks you and your family like you're a Kardashian. I'm sure everyone in there follows you on social media. Your face and dating life are very public and obviously no one has photographed us together before."

He shrugs like it's not a big deal. "We'll just tell them we've kept a low profile. That we only recently met again, but we knew instantly it was right."

"Everyone is going to think I'm a gold-digger."

"Nah. They'll know you're head over heels in love with me."

I get a wink and a cocky smirk and just like that, I'm out of time as he throws the doors to the ballroom hosting our ten-year high school reunion open. At the exact moment when one song ends, and another is about to begin making the sound of the heavy door closing behind us sound like cymbals crashing through the room.

All eyes swivel in our direction and if I thought my heart was racing before, I was wrong. Every single woman in here is glaring at me and trust me when I say, that is not just my imagination.

"Have you ever seen the movie *Carrie*?" I murmur, trying not to fidget or chew on my lip or, God forbid, look down. "You know the prom scene?"

He laughs. I don't.

"No one is dousing you in blood."

I'm not so sure about that.

"If they do, you have my permission to go all *Carrie* on their asses. Hell, I'll even help you do it."

"Oliver—"

"Just smile. You look gorgeous. More than gorgeous. You're a siren in this sea of boring. We've got this. Fun, remember? Try to relax and enjoy this for what it is."

Right. Fun. Relax. I can do that. I never have before, but how hard can it be when faced with a room full of people who used to bully the hell out of me?

Oliver guides us through the room that looks more like a wedding than a reunion with the way it'd decorated. Lots of cream, silver, and red against the glow of twinkling lights and votive candles.

I ninja grip Oliver's arm, all the while he nods hellos and heys to people we pass without stopping to talk to anyone. We reach the bar, and he orders a glass of champagne for me and bourbon for himself. I don't argue with his choice. I barely ever drink, so champagne is not only a treat but also probably a hell of a lot safer than hard alcohol.

"A little liquid courage," he offers, handing me the flute filled to the brim with golden bubbly liquid. He holds up his glass. "To a night of unexpected turns."

"I'll drink to that."

"Good. Because here comes the circus."

3

Amelia ♥

When Oliver said circus, he wasn't kidding. By the time I finished half my glass of champagne, we were nearly surrounded. Everyone wanted their shot with Oliver. The king of our high school. The celebrity if for no other reason than his family's wealth. I teased him quickly about being an influencer and he simply rolled his eyes, but it's true.

If one of the Fritzes is photographed wearing something, by the end of the week, every male in the city is. The women they date get their fifteen minutes of fame and bragging rights to their friends. It's a Boston condition, but I know their faces reach national status. I saw Oliver's eldest brother, Kaplan, in a copy of *People Magazine* once and I'm pretty sure Oliver himself has been in some national tabloids too.

Oliver doesn't let me get far. Instead, he holds me close, introducing me to everyone as if I never went to high school with them while he toys with the bare skin of my back, eliciting uncontrollable shudders and chills with every pass. The looks I get are something else. Women want to talk to me, like somehow Oliver will rub off me and onto them. They want to know where I got my dress. Who did my hair?

I had to laugh at both of those.

But their eyes are filled with envy and awe and yes, there are still some sneers, but it's nothing like Christa. Not even close. There is reverence and respect and while that should never come from being on a man's arm, right now, I'm still riding my who cares high. I'm not seen as charity case Amelia Bedelia. I'm seen as me, Amelia Atkins. My opinions listened to, my presence valued instead of teased.

Finally, after what feels like hours though I know it was only about one, it's just us with Oliver's best friend Grace and her fiancé Tony. Grace Hammond and I were mathletes together. She was an academic nerd in high school but floated in her own world with lots of friends, the best of which was Oliver. Girls were jealous of her like mad because of it. She's smart. Beautiful. Funny.

And had the devoted attention of Oliver.

Still does, by the way they hug and instantly start in with the automatic teasing. We're lingering by the bar, my new favorite place to be since I'm now officially on my second glass of champagne. The first having gone down so quickly and so smoothly, I hardly noticed. Grace is wonderful, so much fun to catch up with. That is until Oliver takes my hand—the one boasting the ring—and kisses it, making sure Grace and her fiancé Tony notice it.

Tony snickers, covering his holy shit laugh with a fake cough and a long sip of his drink.

Grace, on the other hand, looks like someone electrocuted her, complete with eyes bugging out of her head. "Oliver?"

That's as far as she gets.

The others who saw the ring oohed and ahhed. Grace looks like she's about to pass out. In a good way, I think.

"As my lifelong best friend, Grace, it means so much to me that you and my stunning fiancée have grown so close. I know in the past, my significant others have tried to throw you off the pedestal I hold you on, but not this one. She is perfect, wouldn't you agree?"

Another kiss on my knuckles.

I open my mouth to say... something, only to realize I have absolutely nothing to say. All I can do is offer her an awkward grin and sheepish half-shrug. What felt so crazy and spontaneous out in the hall and with all those other people now feels ridiculous.

I must look ridiculous to her.

Grace's eyes volley back and forth between us before holding Oliver's gaze for a very long few moments. Some sort of nonverbal conversation passes between them before a delighted smile breaks free across her face, her blue eyes glimmering.

"Oh, Oliver. You have no idea how happy I've been since you decided to settle down with Amelia. You're right, she is absolutely perfect."

"Um... but..."

Then she grabs me, hauling me into her chest and making me nearly spill my champagne all over her designer dress. "Don't fret, darling," she whispers in my ear. "He's a cocky bastard, but he has a heart of gold. I don't know what game he's playing, but I'm loving the hell out of it."

"You know it's fake, right?"

"A best friend can dream, Amelia. Let's not ruin that. Besides, it'll be fun to watch the expression on psycho Nora's face. She's been asking about him all night. And for real, I've been dying to watch that albatross she likes to keep around his neck get lost in the ocean of I've found someone way better than you. Fake or no, that's you." She pulls back, winking at me. "Cheers. Now drink up. You're going to need it to get through this shitshow."

Ain't that the truth. We clink glasses and I down the rest of my drink, loving how the flavor and bubbles explode in my mouth. A delicious little buzz plays with me, tilting a lazy smile up my lips.

"Here." Oliver hands me another glass, and I eye it warily before glancing up at him.

"You're trying to get me drunk," I accuse.

He chuckles. "I'm trying to get you to let your guard down. You're still very stiff." His eyes soften as they take me in. "You don't have to worry. I've got you tonight and I won't let anything bad happen. Promise. Just enjoy yourself. Enjoy being with me. This was meant to be fun."

"Do you know I legit cannot remember the last time I had fun? Like real, I'm only twenty-eight years old, fun?"

"That's insanely tragic. We're changing that up right now. Drink and dote on me. That's fun, right?"

I laugh, already feeling a little lighter.

His thumb brushes along my cheek as I stare up at him. Marveling at how his simple touch breathes life into places that have been dormant so long, I wondered if they were extinct. Green eyes gaze into mine, a captivating kaleidoscope of shades I swear I could get lost in. And you know, Oliver is right. Tonight was supposed to be fun for me. All of this was.

"I've got this now," I tell him. I might also be a bit drunk, so that helps. I take a hearty gulp, loving the warm tingles as they flow through my veins, my mind growing light and giddy with every beat of my heart.

"That's my girl. How about we go and—"

"Oliver?" an impatient voice snaps behind us, interrupting him.

Grace mutters something under her breath that I don't catch, and beside me, Oliver stiffens. Both he and I turn, coming face to face with Nora, who is standing alone, looking polished, gorgeous, and brilliantly flustered. Oliver's arm wraps around my waist, his hand clutching my hip. Nora's eyes zero in on the action, clinging to his hand as her cheeks flush and her lips purse.

Placing a hand on her small but obviously round belly, she forces her gaze back up to his. "It's nice to see you. It's been such a long time." She gives him a lingering look. "You look wonderful. Better than ever."

Oliver rolls his eyes, but I don't catch any anger behind it. "Thanks," he mutters dryly.

He moves to turn back around to Grace when Nora makes some sort of clicking sound in the back of her throat, stopping him. Her eyes caustically dance back and forth between us, then back down to his hand still on my waist.

"Christa texted that you're here with *her*, but I didn't believe it. Then Trisha Jordan said you were in love, but I knew that couldn't be true." She glares at me with ice-blue eyes before immediately returning to Oliver.

"You should have believed it," Oliver states without even a hint of an edge, though a subtle smirk bounces up the corner of his mouth. "I am most certainly here with Amelia and yes, I love her."

Sipping his drink, he twists to face me. His fingers abandon my hip and find the hand with the ring. The ring that at one time had been meant for Nora. Oliver toys with my finger, rolling his large diamond back and forth, but not saying anything else as he continues to smirk at me with a bemused expression.

"Is she still there or did she leave yet?" he whispers to me out of the corner of his mouth, and I can't help my giggle.

Nora gasps shrilly. Then two other people sitting at a nearby table do as well. They start to whisper and instead of being nervous or afraid of what they're saying, I'm smiling stupidly up at Oliver.

"She's still there," I inform him.

"Dammit. I was hoping she would take the hint and go."

"Oliver," Nora hisses. "You can't be serious."

He shrugs, but I swear a sparkle hits his eyes as he says, "What can I say? When you know, you know."

Nora scoffs derisively. Loud and harsh. "You mean with charity case Amelia Bedelia? You cannot be serious," she repeats, her voice rising as she slams her hand on top of a cocktail table, rattling some of the half-empty glasses abandoned on it. "Look at her." Her hand shoots out in my direction, dismissively waving up and down. "She's a mess in ragtag clothes and frizzy hair with too many freckles on her face. Can't you see someone like her is just using you for your money and fame."

Oliver's spine goes ramrod straight. His fingers clench around mine, squeezing me as fury blazes a path across his face. But before he can verbally eviscerate Nora, I do.

I meet Nora's gaze head on. "You'd think that, right? That I'm using him? I mean, the girl you just described was exactly who I was in high school. The janitor's daughter on a scholarship wearing a second-hand uniform. Well, the dress is still second-hand. But who knew a little hair product could make you go from frizzy to fabulous?" I wink at her, which only seems to boil her blood further. "I'll be honest with you. At first, I never thought Oliver and I would work. Our differences are so great. Then I slept with him. Even though I told him we were just friends, and it was only one night, the man pursued me like a hunter pursues his prey. Relentlessly."

She squints at me, looking like she just swallowed a bug.

"I couldn't deny him," I go on. "I was just as crazy about him as he was about me. And keeping my hands to myself where he was concerned?" I shake my head, laughing sardonically. "Pfft. Totally impossible. The man seriously knows what he's doing in bed, though I suppose I don't have to tell you that."

Nora grits her teeth, her complexion turning redder by the minute. She clutches the end of the table she's practically leaning against.

"Anyway, it wasn't long before we became something so much more and I couldn't let him go. Now we're addicted to each other. Completely head over heels in love." I turn to meet Oliver's eyes, noting the small crowd around us as we hover by the bar. "We just clicked so perfectly. Right, Oli?"

"Definitely," Oliver agrees, his darkening eyes roving all over me. "Totally addicted. So in love. In fact, right now, I'd like nothing more than to drag your gorgeous ass into one of the rooms upstairs in this hotel and show you just how grateful I am for you."

My tongue thickens in my mouth, making it impossible to swallow.

He must read this because he grins, dipping into my neck and asking my flesh, "Later then?"

"Um. Sure. Later." My empty core clenches in staggering disagreement with not jumping him here and now, while my brain reminds me he's just playing a part. That none of this is real.

Oliver grins, pressing his lips into my neck, trailing up along my jaw until he finds the corner of my lips. My knees buckle on cue, and I audibly sigh. In fairness, I haven't been touched by a man who knew what a clitoris was and where it was located in eight years. He hasn't even gone near my pussy, but his voice and words certainly have with surprising precision.

I clear my throat, turning back to the woman who no longer has color in her face. I smile endearingly. "I hear you're married to Rob. And expecting. Congrats. How lovely."

"Oh. Yes. I am." She recovers quickly. Her hand rubs along her belly as she glances somewhere out in the fray in the direction of her husband, I presume. "I called Oliver to tell him the good news." Her gaze snaps back to mine. "You know, so he wouldn't have to hear something that might be painful for him from anyone else."

My eyebrows become one as I tilt my head in mock contemplation. "It's sweet that you were worried about him like that, but if memory serves, he saw your number and figured it was spam."

Nora gasps, her hand clutching her chest. "Spam?"

"Spam," I confirm to her before looking back to Oliver, who is pressing his lower back into the edge of the bar as he leans casually against it like all he's missing right now is some popcorn while he watches the show I'm putting on. "But I'm sure you would have called her back to congratulate her if you had listened to the entire message before deleting it?"

Oliver shrugs indifferently. "Probably not. As you know, that ship sailed a long time ago."

Grace snickers, trying to mask it as a cough and Oliver lets out a small half-chuckle with it, the two of them exchanging looks I can't decipher.

"So, this is for real?" Nora asks, her lips curled in dissatisfaction. Possibly a touch of jealousy and heartache too.

Oliver grasps my jaw in his hand, holding my face, so we're staring into each other's eyes. He tugs me closer to him, my body angling against his. My heart that had been lazily beating in my chest thanks to the champagne kicks back up into high gear.

"Definitely real."

"So real."

He grins. "The realest."

"That's not a word."

"Run with it, Red Hot."

My head launches back in a laugh. "Red Hot?"

"Sexy. Hot. Spicy. A fiery temptation. Am I missing something here?"

"Oliver." Nora stomps her red-soled heel, pounding on that table again, this time succeeding in knocking over a few glasses that were thankfully empty. "You can't do this with her. That's your great-grand-mother's ring."

Oh shit. His great-grandmother's ring?

He must read the shock on my face because suddenly his lips hit mine. Not a kiss. Not quite that. But a press. A definite press. "Relax. It's not a thing," he murmurs into my ear so only I can hear.

"But Oliver—"

"Relax," he repeats, and right. Fake. It's not like he actually gave me his great-grandmother's ring for real. "And it fits her perfectly," he says louder for everyone to hear. That's when Nora storms off, nearly smashing into the table of people who were blatantly listening while trying to pretend they weren't directly behind her.

But by now, we've drawn a bigger crowd. All eyes are situated right on us and it's weird that I'm not freaking out about that. Espe-cially considering about eighty percent of those people made fun of me growing up. But instead of having a panic attack or even being worried about potential nasty comments like the ones Nora and Christa made, I feel oddly empowered. Brave.

It's like I'm having some sort of out-of-body experience. It's the ring, I think. I'm like the Green Lantern from the comics with his magic ring. I'm transformed into someone else completely. Someone who isn't worried about every small detail. Who isn't stressing out about absolutely everything.

The champagne might be helping that along as well.

The next song starts and Oliver squints down at me. "Dance with me, beautiful?"

He doesn't give me the choice. Both of our glasses are set down on the bar he was leaning against, and he takes my hand, intertwining our fingers. He mutters something to Grace and Tony and then leads us straight to the middle of the dance floor.

Lifting our joined hands over my head, he twirls me in a circle before settling me right in against his chest. I snake my hands around his neck just as his find the line between my bare back and my dress —his favorite spot to play for most of the night—and everything about this feels like a dream. Like any second, I'll wake up and be so disappointed that none of it was real.

"I have no idea what I just said back there," I tell him.

He laughs lightly, pressing me in closer. So close we're touching. My soft breasts to his muscled chest and my heart flutters with anticipation at the idea of us like this without the barrier of our clothes.

"You were brilliant," he says. "You basically told Nora I'm a sex god and that you couldn't keep your hands off me and that we're crazy about each other. Half the room, I believe heard you as well. It took everything in me not to laugh my ass off."

"Oh god." My face plants into his chest and when did I become comfortable enough with this man to do all these things? His lips have touched mine. His hands have been all over me. His eyes too. "I don't even know who I am right now."

And that's the God's honest truth.

"You're a breath of fresh air, is what you are. I have to admit, I was nervous about seeing Nora for the first time after all these years. But having you with me, I didn't care about her or anyone else. Listening to you tell her all those things, it was... fun almost. Just watching you was so much fun."

"It was fun. Kind of crazy and definitely out of character for me, but fun. What kind of woman am I right now?"

"A woman who is driving me absolutely insane with the way I want you." His fingers find the ends of my hair and I feel him wrap one of the long strands around his fist. "I love your hair." He leans down by my ear to whisper. "I always have. The color, I think, is what I first noticed about you. It's like a brick red. Deep and rich and beautiful as hell."

"Oliver. What are you—"

Only my words cut off as his lips meet the base of my neck. He takes a deep inhale of my skin, groaning into me, trailing up to my ear. I shudder in his arms, my teeth sawing a path of destruction on my bottom lip so I don't moan.

Swallowing hard, I grip his shoulders, praying I don't collapse right here on the dance floor. What on earth is he doing? Is this real or an act? I can't tell, I just know how it feels.

"We're in love, remember?" he murmurs into me. "Engaged. So wild about each other we can't keep our hands to ourselves."

Oh my god. What have I done?

And how will I ever recover from having Oliver Fritz's lips on me when tonight's over? I'll be going through batteries like mad with all the self-play I'll have to do. Good thing Costco sells them in bulk.

Another inhale, another kiss, and I just about lose my mind.

"Damn," he hisses into me. "I'll admit, this was certainly not how I expected this night to go, but I'm definitely not complaining. You smell like sweet candy and taste even better. I wonder if you're this sweet everywhere."

Jesus. My eyes roll back in my head.

He pulls back, the intensity in his gaze making my stomach flip with nerves. With excitement. Hell, with so much arousal, my panties are most definitely wet. Trembling hands find the nape of his neck, my fingers twirling into the ends of his hair as we continue to sway gently to some slow song I've never heard before. His eyes lock on my lips, holding there. Mine do the same to his, desperate for him to close the small distance between us and kiss me.

Kiss me.

I can't go home with him. Can I? I've never left Layla alone all night. She's only just fourteen, but the look in his eyes tells me that even though this was not how he expected this night to go, he has a very real vision of how he wants it to end.

With me in his bed.

Eyes on mine, his head inches in, dipping down, getting closer, testing me out. My heart rate skyrockets as my thoughts scatter.

This is a fantasy.

A fantasy I'm going to wake up from any second.

Oliver's bourbon-tinted breath hits my lips, and right before I succumb to wherever this night will lead us, the fire alarm blares through the room, jolting both of us apart and snapping me back to reality.

I guess this means it's officially midnight and the ball is over.

4

Oliver ♥

The blare of the fire alarm almost feels personal. Like someone pulled it just to stop me from kissing Amelia.

The overhead lights flicker out just as flood lamps above the exit doors flash on, creating an eerie glow in the room. All around us, people start screaming and running, trying to get out, though there are no obvious signs of smoke or fire in the room. The music sharply cuts off and the DJ's voice breaks through, asking everyone to quickly and calmly head for the exit just as Amelia's body starts to slip away from mine.

My gaze snaps away from the chaos of the room back down to Amelia. Her back is to me, her hands in front of her body as she wiggles around, struggling to do something I can't figure out.

Looping my hand through her elbow, I spin her back around to face me. "We need to get out of here."

She lets out a hopeless sigh, her hands dropping to her sides. "I think the ring is stuck."

I shake my head. "We can worry about that later. Come on."

Before she can protest, I drag her along until we're funneling out of the ballroom, through the building that is now overflowing with hotel guests, all looking stunned and curious when everything around us appears fine.

I wonder if someone pulled the fire alarm as a prank or something else and again, my thoughts flicker to Amelia, to our almost kiss.

The front doors part with a mechanical hum, and I immediately march us over to the side where the valet guys are standing listlessly. "Hey, can one of you get my car for me?"

They exchange glances like they're not sure what they're supposed to do. "Uh. I guess we could."

Fantastic. I hand one of them the blue slip and he stares at it for a second before pulling my keys from a hook. "Oh. Hey, man. We kept your ride out front. We do that with the nicer cars. Makes the place look good, right?" He points behind him toward the circular drive where there is a line of expensive cars. "Do you want me to get it for you?"

I grab my keys and hand him a hundred. "I've got it. Have a good night."

"Yeah. You, too. Wow, thanks for the tip, man."

Amelia has been silent this entire time, but that doesn't mean her mind is. I can see it all over her face. I don't know Amelia all that well, but I don't have to to know she's excessively cautious and, unfortunately for right now, an overthinker. Especially as I open the passenger side door for her, and she hesitates.

"Oliver, I don't think—"

"Come home with me tonight," I interrupt.

She gawks, speechless. I don't think she expected me to just blurt it out like that, but if I don't, she'll run. She already tried when we were upstairs, and the alarm went off. I saw it. It's why she had her back to me. Why she was trying to tear the ring from her finger.

I can't let that happen.

"How were you going to get home?" I ask when she doesn't answer, changing tactics because there is no way this woman is ending the night anywhere other than in my bed.

She shifts in her heels, staring out into the dark night and away from me. Out of the corner of my eye, I notice they're ushering everyone back inside, but the reunion is done as far as I'm concerned. We did what we intended in spectacular form. She faced the assholes of her past and I faced Nora. Deed done; we can check all that shit off our bucket list.

Past dealt with. Check.

"The bus," she finally replies so softly I have to strain to hear her.

Oh, hell no.

"Come home with me, Amelia," I repeat.

Hands fall to her hips as she shakes her head, a burst of a humorless laugh escaping her lungs. Her head falls back, her long hair with it, and she stares up at the night sky as if she doesn't know what to say or what to do with my second proposal of the night.

My heart beats painfully in my chest as I watch her, desperate for her to say yes. I want more time with her. Real time. Not fake. Even if nothing happens tonight, I want her to come home with me. I'm not done with her yet.

Then I inwardly laugh. What am I doing? This is insane. It makes no sense. I don't bring women home with me just to spend more time with them.

I should let her go home. Just drive her there and leave it at that. Let the night end and wake up tomorrow and go to my parents' compound for Sunday dinner and deal with that. I have enough going on in my life and the last thing I need is to get entangled with someone like Amelia. She's not a fling. The opposite of casual material.

I don't have to know her to know that about her.

I'd be doing us both a favor by ending this now. But...

She angles in toward me. Not a lot. Just a couple of inches, but it's enough to drag me in with her. A magnet helpless against her pull, I reach out, covering her hand with my own and it's like that action snaps her back to me. Her chin drops and her eyes fall upon mine.

"Oliver."

And that's all it takes. My name slipping through her lips in that sexy rasp whirls through my head like a spell. Before I can second guess myself, I'm combing my fingers through her hair, adjusting her face until it's lined up perfectly. Then my lips meet hers, similar to the way they did earlier. I rest them there for a beat, giving her the chance to push me away, breathing in her taste, but it's so goddamn sweet I instantly lose control.

"God, you're fucking sexy."

My lips meld to hers, pressing in deeply. The hand that was covering hers wraps around her waist, drawing her firmly against me. My other grips her hair, tightening my hold as I open her lips with mine. Our tongues meet and she whimpers hungrily into my mouth like this is exactly what she's been waiting on all night.

Like she can't get enough of the way I taste either.

"I want you so bad," I murmur into her.

Her hands skirt up, cupping my cheeks, her fingertips tickling the stubble along my jaw, making my skin tingle with an electric current. What was meant to be something of an introduction—a tease with a taunt of more to come—quickly turns heated as I devour her, my mouth scraping down her neck, sucking and licking, my hands all over the silky skin of her back.

She shudders against me, my name pushed out on a breath compelling a growl to sear past my lips only to have me jarred away from her for the second time tonight when yet another alarm goes off. This one belonging to a car.

Goddammit! Can't a man catch a break here?

Only with that alarm do I realize we're still in the parking lot, my car door open, waiting for Amelia to make her decision. She's breathing heavily, her lips red and swollen, some of her lipstick smeared, very likely across my own face.

My forehead drops to hers, my thumb wiping away the streak of red from her chin. "Come on, let's get out of here."

She nods on a resigned breath.

In a flash, I tuck Amelia into my car, shutting the door behind her and racing around to my side. Starting up the car, we pull away from the hotel and out into the Boston night. It doesn't take long to get back to my place and since Amelia didn't say a word about driving her home or where she lives or the fact that I was very obviously driving her here, I'm taking that as my green light and going with it.

Still, I'm not sure how I feel about her silence when she's been nothing short of verbose, speaking her mind at every turn all night.

"Good evening, Dr. Fritz."

"'Evening, Gerald."

The doorman opens the door for Amelia, helping her out.

"Thank you," she says demurely.

He tips his hat at her. "My pleasure. Enjoy your evening, ma'am."

I grab her hand, holding on tight. She was quiet on the ride here. Too quiet. And for once, I didn't know how to fill the silence. I knew she was contemplating all the ways this is a bad idea. I knew she was trying to talk herself both into and out of coming home with me.

Her face isn't hard to read.

And maybe part of me was hoping we'd pull up, and she'd say, you know what, never mind, just take me home. But she didn't. She let Gerald help her out of my car. She's holding my hand now. We're walking side by side toward the elevator that will lead us up to my place.

"You live in the Ritz."

She's so deadpan I half-chuckle, blowing out a breath I had no idea I was holding. "I do. It's the residences, but we get hotel amenities. Why, you interested in a spa treatment?"

"Oliver, in my entire life, I've never had a spa treatment. What am I doing here?"

I frown before I can stop it. This woman has never had anything special, has she?

It fills me with the weirdest of sensations. Things I cannot understand float through my mind. I've gone out with dozens of women. And I never cared. I mean, not really. Not since Nora. I made sure of it. And I don't exactly know Amelia. It's been a decade since I've seen her and it's not like we were besties back then either.

So why do I care that she's never had a spa treatment or feels out of place in my place? Why do I care that I want the Noras and the Christas of the word to see her the way I see her? Like a goddess.

I don't know her.

I just want her. That's all this is, I convince myself.

I press her body against the elevator wall, leaning in and hovering over her. "You're here to be with me. Tell me how to pleasure you and I will spend the entire night doing just that."

Her breath catches. She grins, almost as if she thinks I'm kidding. I'm not. Not even a little. I want to eat her pussy till it drips all over my chin. I want to have her hands rip at my hair while I do it. I want to fuck her until she's screaming out my name and the name of whatever god she prays to. I want her breath. Her cries. Her words. Her pleasure.

All of it. All of her.

And after I've done all that, I want to do it again. Slower. While possibly looking into her eyes because that gray, man. It knocks me out at the knees. Especially up close like this. And her hair is this red. This really pretty red. A red I want wrapped around my hands and all over my bed.

"Oliver."

My name again. Only this time, instead of filled with lust, it's indecisive. It's unsure. But it's my fucking name on her lips and no one else's.

"Do you want me to stop?" I breathe against her only to get silence in return. "If you want me to stop, you have to tell me, Amelia. There will be no misunderstandings between us. Tell me you understand."

She swallows thickly and nods.

"Do you want me to stop?"

A headshake this time, and that's my go.

I step in front of her in this elevator because it's slow as shit and for the first time ever, I'm glad for it. My face dives into her neck, inhaling deeply. She gasps, making some kind of squawking noise as she jerks back into the wall.

"Oliver."

Again, with my name. This one has a lot more reprimand to it. Lucky for her, that turns me on. My hand slides up her dress, bunching it up over her panties, hips, and ass. Then my fingers dig into those soft globes, guiding her out of the elevator as the doors part. I knead her, staring down and watching myself work.

And fuck, she's hot. I mean, this ass is just perfect.

It has me unzipping her dress right here in the hallway, knowing there are no cameras or eyes watching. A strangled gulp hits the air just as my fingers slide the barely-there straps on her shoulders down but not off. No bra, so my hands come around, finding her full breasts and hard nipples. But it's not enough. I want to see what my hands are feeling. I want to taste what my fingers are teasing.

I whisper, "You feel good in my hands," into the shell of her ear.

"I don't do this." Her voice trembles with nerves.

"I know. But you will tonight."

She moans, her ass pressing into my straining cock as I unlock my door for us, all the while my hands greedily explore her body within the confines of her dress. But the second the door shuts behind me, I'm done with being nice.

Spinning her in my hands, I rip the top from her shoulders, falling to my knees and sucking on her tits because they're right here. She's short and I'm tall, and it's fucking perfect like this. My hands go nuts, unable to be controlled as they squeeze and lift and pinch and claim. My lips and tongue too. For such a small-framed woman, she has surprisingly large breasts and I think I want to fuck them. Not tonight. Next time for sure.

But for now...

The hem of her dress glides higher and higher, the perfect peep show attraction as I bunch it around her waist, and suddenly I'm face to face with black panties. My hands reach around, grabbing her ass, thrusting her into my face. Her breath hitches, fingers getting lost in my hair. I peek up. Into those eyes that slay me every damn time.

A foreign sensation squeezes my chest, making it hard to breathe and for the longest moment, I can't do anything other than gaze at her.

Her lips twitch. "Problem down there? You're staring awfully hard."

I clear my throat, the sensation along with it. "Just enjoying the view. It's quite something from where I'm kneeling."

I kiss her mound over her panties and her body jerks forward, nearly toppling us both over, my hands somehow managing to stabilize her hips.

"Wow," she exclaims on a breathy laugh. "Okay. I can't do this standing up."

In a flash, I'm on my feet, scooping her up in my arms bride style —because she's still my fiancée for at least the next few hours—and then I march down the hall in the direction of my bedroom.

"Thank god. My knees were killing me."

She laughs and it's the sweetest sound. Light and playful and... happy. It has me grinning from ear to ear in return like a triumphant warrior while I inwardly fist pump the air. I not only made her almost fall over by barely touching her, but I made her laugh too.

Her first genuine laugh of the night, I think.

I set her down on the bed and immediately strip her dress off. Her panties next. And when she's totally naked before me, sprawled out, I take a moment to appreciate just how fucking stunning she is like this. Her hair all wild and splashed across the duvet. Her full beautiful breasts begging for attention. The landing strip of red hair directing me to the paradise between her legs.

Maybe it's been too long since I've been with someone. I was slowing down the amount I was screwing around. Or maybe it's just her. Amelia. Because I can't stop staring at her like a man on the verge of coming undone.

She doesn't cover herself despite the flush taking hold of her chest and face. Instead, she quietly observes me ogling her. The dark lusty fire in her eyes no doubt matching my own. Then something catches my eye. The diamond on her hand. *My* diamond. Weird how that doesn't make me want to throw up.

Bizarre how that only seems to make my dick harder for her.

Before I can think too deeply on that, I climb on the bed, prowling toward her on all fours, spread her legs open wide, and then dive in. Her fingers instantly find my hair, pulling and tugging as my lips and tongue French kiss the hell out of her pussy. Desire crashes over me as I ravage her, my lips growing hungrier and wetter the louder her cries get.

"Oliver."

What is it about my name falling from those pretty lips?

"Yes. Say it again," I growl into her before I can stop it, my tongue flicking her clit as I pump two fingers into her.

"Oliver." This time it's a piercing cry as she writhes against me, thrashing on the bed.

How long has it been since a man did this to her? Savored her? Consumed her? Gave her pleasure like this? It's messy and wet, dirty, and I'm loving every second of it.

"Holy. I'm. *Yes!*" She comes hard, ripping my hair and driving my face deeper into her. My fingers pump her through her orgasm, my cock leaking with anticipation over the way her pussy clenches around me.

I swear, I've never been this turned on in my life.

Trailing back up her body, I nip and lick at every inch of sweet skin I can, kissing and sucking and on her breasts and nipples, until I reach her lips. My tongue pushes in, letting her taste herself on me, and then I'm up, quickly undressing and grabbing a condom from the nightstand.

She watches me the entire time, her eyes wide and her breathing ragged.

"You still okay with this?" I ask. Suddenly I'm not sure she is.

She licks her lips and nods. Again, with the nods. I took that as a yes before, but now, with this...

"Amelia? You gotta tell me, baby."

"I... yes. Yes, I want this."

I raise an eyebrow, stroking my cock lazily. "You sure?"

"Positive. I do. I'm just... like I said, I don't do this. But I want to. I want tonight."

Tonight. A frown inadvertently wrenches my lips down before I just as quickly shake it off. I climb on top of her, kissing her, tasting her lips before I roll us. I want her to be in control. I want this to be on her terms. At least to start.

She straddles my thighs and with her eyes on mine and my hands on her hips, she sinks down on me. A grunt presses past my lips before I can stop it, my neck arching back, straining. Damn. She's *tight*. And so fucking good. My hands glide up her smooth stomach, cupping her tits.

There is so much rough desire swirling between us I'm already high with it and she hasn't even started moving yet.

Slowly she rocks forward then back. Forward then back. I just about lose my mind and then she slides up and down. Up and down.

"Fuck," hisses out. The sensation. The pace. It's killing me. Her movements. When I wanted her to have control, I didn't think it would be like this. *So* controlled. "Let go, Amelia." Sitting up, I put us face to face. My hands framing her cheeks while my lips consuming hers. "You're so beautiful. Pleasure yourself on me. I want to make you come again. I want to feel you come all over me. Watch as you lose your mind with how good this feels."

She moans into me, finally relaxing her muscles and moving. And when I say moving, I mean moving. She's bouncing up and down, using my dick like a trampoline, and holy hell. This woman is a fucking firecracker. Her hands meet my shoulders, her nails digging into my flesh as she lets go completely. My hips thrust up to meet hers.

Deep, pounding, powerful strokes that make me dizzy.

My arms wrap around her, pressing her soft breasts against my chest as I climb up onto my haunches, her legs over my thighs, and then I slam up into her. Over and over, I take her as she cries out, her head thrown back in ecstasy, propelling her breasts up and into my face. I suck her tits—because I might just be a tad obsessed with them—as we lose ourselves.

Sweaty and loud and so goddamn good.

My thumb finds her clit and seconds later, she detonates. Her face on my shoulder as she clings to me, riding it out with profound, resonating shudders. I follow her over the edge, bellowing out her name before I can stop the bastard from getting free. A smile on my face, the likes of which I know has never been there before.

"Was that the fun you needed?" I whisper.

She giggles, forcing my smile to grow with the sound of it. "Mmmm."

"I'm taking that for a yes." I kiss her bare shoulder, holding her tighter.

For the longest moment, we just sit like this, breathing heavily, mind spinning, heart racing. And all I can think is... wow. This woman. Because that was just... absolutely fucking earth-shatteringly amazing. Like, I want to do it all over again and then again and then again. So, we do. I take her again, this time against the shower wall before we pass out for the night, my arms wrapped around her body where I fall into a deep, blissful sleep.

The next morning, I wake up with a voracious hard-on that has her name on it only to find my bed cold and empty. My great-grandmother's engagement ring sitting atop my nightstand. No note. No phone number. No thanks for last night it was the best sex of my life.

Nothing. Just gone.

The ring left behind with no way to contact her.

And no matter how many times I tell myself I should be relieved, I'm anything but.

Dammit. That's not how this was supposed to go.

5

Amelia ♥

I shouldn't have left like that, and my mixed emotions about last night are compounding my exhaustion. With a yawn I check the underside of the pancake, getting ready to flip it when a "Hey, you're up early," startles me so bad the spatula jerks and the pancake goes *splat* on the floor. "Sorry," Layla says, going for the paper towels, taking off too many sheets and balling them up to the point where I grimace for both the waste to our planet and the cost of new paper towels. "I didn't mean to startle you like that."

"It's fine," I tell her, taking the paper from her hand and cleaning up the mess I just made. "I just didn't hear you come in. How'd you sleep?"

Layla folds her arms over her shirt that says, 'all the cool kids are reading', her eyebrow raised pointedly in my direction. "Nice deflection. How was the reunion?"

"Oh. It was good. You know, nothing crazy."

"Uh-huh. I didn't hear you come in last night. Must have ended late. So late, in fact, you're wearing your sacred Red Sox T-shirt inside out."

Am I? I glance down. Dammit, she's right. And because I can't jinx their amazing four-game win streak right now, I quickly whip it off over my head and fix it.

"You must have not only gotten in late but been either so tired and distracted or you know, the world exploded. Amelia, when have you ever put on anything Red Sox inside out unless it's a rally hat? What happened last night?"

And now I blush. A lot. Because there is nothing like having a night of unbelievable sex and sneaking out to do the walk of shame home in your dress, heels, messed up hair, and then having the doorman of the guy you just slept with offer to have the residence car take you home and you're too broke to say no because an Uber would have been like thirty bucks, and then having to hide it all from your much younger sister.

Which is why I go back to pouring more pancake batter into the pan. Because pancakes are Layla's favorite breakfast and I'm feeling a bit guilty I was out so late, and a lot confused and conflicted about last night with Oliver.

"Amelia?"

"Huh? Oh, yeah. It ended late."

"That's it?" she whines, sagging back against the counter. "You're too boring with the details. Give me something good. Something juicy."

"The fire alarm went off."

"Amelia!"

"What?" I squawk. "It did."

Her eyes roll derisively before narrowing as she goes about taking out plates and silverware from the cabinets in our tiny kitchen, setting them out on the table.

"You're so boring. I want details. I want to know if those hags tripped over their Louboutins when they saw you. I want to know if you drank expensive champagne and ate canapes. I want to know if you danced with someone."

Cue the blushing again. I'm like a robot with an on-switch Layla keeps hitting. "No one tripped in their heels over me. It was the same with those girls. Nothing's changed with them and that's fine because they're not people I would want in my life anyway. I did sip on some champagne. No canapes and the alarm went off before the dancing could really get going."

"Still," she sighs dreamily, "it was a night out. I was hoping you'd land a hot date out of it."

I choke on my sip of coffee, sputtering while it drools down my chin. Awesome.

"You okay?" She pats my back, making sure I'm not about to die. I wave her away, giving her the universal I'm fine thumbs up. She opens the fridge and then groans. "No OJ."

Thankfully Layla moves on quickly.

"It wasn't on sale this week."

"Milk?"

"Milk."

And coffee. I'm already on my second cup because after I got home around three this morning, I tossed and turned. Uneasy. Obviously insane if I put on my beloved Sox tee inside out. I was debating and second-guessing my move to run out after he fell asleep. But I had to get home before Layla woke up and since she's not a normal teenager who likes to sleep in, I didn't have a choice. I figure it saved us the awkward morning after, last night was fun and maybe I'll see you around some time conversation.

I don't think I could have looked into his eyes as he gave me the universal brush-off speech I knew inevitably was coming.

It's not like Oliver and I were going to start dating or anything. He's a notorious player. A heartbreaker. A billionaire. Men like him don't date. And if they do, it's certainly not women like me. They break hearts not keep them, and I don't have the luxury of going through something like that.

I'm too damn busy trying to juggle a life I'm not so great at juggling.

I plate up two large pancakes for Layla and one for myself since my second one already hit the floor, and then I join Layla who is strangely quiet, staring at her phone at the table.

"You have your interview at Wilchester in a couple weeks. You still want to do this?"

"It's the best shot I have at getting a scholarship for college," she says absently.

I nod, taking a bite of my pancake and forcing myself to chew and swallow. I know why Layla wants to go there. She's smart. Gifted even, and she deserves the best shot at going to the college she wants. Her current high school just isn't cutting it for her. She needs a scholarship to get into Wilchester, which they don't give out all that often and only partial ones at that, but since I'm an alumnus, and our dad worked there, they're willing to meet with her and then make a decision.

We're keeping our fingers crossed. Her, that she gets in. Me, that she has a better experience there than I did. Oh, and that they'll bend a billion rules and give her full tuition otherwise, I have no idea what I'll do.

I do my best. I earn a good salary as a nurse working for a prominent plastic surgeon—it's why I took the job instead of working in the hospital as a floor nurse. But life is expensive. Life in the city is expensive—even in a not-so-nice apartment in a not-so-nice neighborhood.

Plus, there is how we survived for the first two years after my parents died.

On my student loans and credit cards. A debt so thick I'll be paying it off until my dying day at this rate. So, by the end of the month, things get tighter than they already are. I save what I can for Layla's college, but it's nearly impossible.

All of this is.

I was in my sophomore year when my parents died and just like that, my medical school dreams were gone. The guy I had been with for over a year—the guy I was endlessly in love with and who I thought was in love with me—wasn't. I transferred back here, finishing at a community college to be a nurse instead of a doctor, grateful I had all my prerequisites under my belt.

I had debated dropping out entirely and just finding a job, but I knew graduating with a degree in nursing was my best shot at job security and a decent living for us, so I trudged through for both of us. Those two years when I was in college full time and unable to work were the hardest of my life.

I don't regret the sacrifices I had to make when my parents died.

I don't regret giving up on med school and becoming a nurse instead.

I don't regret taking care of my sister, who was only six when my parents died—the baby they had always tried to have after me, who finally became their miracle after multiple miscarriages. No, I don't regret any of it, not even losing the guy.

I just wish it was easier.

Layla continues to swipe through her phone, somehow managing to scarf down her pancakes one-handed. "Hey, I was thinking since the weather is nice today that maybe we could—" She freezes mid-sentence, fork full of pancake in one hand, phone in her other. "Um. Why is there a picture of you with your arms around Oliver Fritz's neck and he's about to kiss you?"

"What?" I shriek. I don't even ask how she knows who Oliver Fritz is. Everyone in this city does.

"It's all over Twitter." She drops her fork with a clang and starts attacking her phone with both thumbs. "Amelia, there are like dozens of pictures of the two of you."

"*Dozens?!*" Oh my god. My stomach flips.

She keeps working and then suddenly stops on something before screaming at the top of her lungs, "Oh my god, you're engaged to him!"

Shit. "It says that?"

"Yes! Look!"

She flips her phone around just as I fly out of my seat, hovering over her. Sure enough, there's a picture of me dancing with Oliver, both of us staring into each other's eyes, smiling. And right there, front and center, is his great-grandmother's diamond ring on my hand. The caption reads, "Oliver Fritz, prominent Boston Billionaire Bachelor suddenly off the market."

The color drains from my face as my knees start to give way. I think I'm going to pass out. How did I not anticipate this? People taking pictures. Them ending up online.

I fall back into my chair, covering my face with my hands. "Oh god. This cannot be happening."

"Amelia, you're freaking making out with him in this one. What the hell happened last night?"

"Watch your mouth," I grumble through my hands, my stomach churning all over my barely digested pancake that's suddenly threatening to come back up.

"Right," she snorts. "Okay. Sure. I'll watch my mouth when you start telling me the truth from yours."

My hands fall to my lap, my mind swirling with what to tell my teenage sister. "I got to the reunion and Christa Foreman was there collecting money. It was a hundred dollars, which I hadn't realized, and she was being nothing but nasty. Oliver stepped in and told Christa he was with me. He paid for me, and then he and I talked. He told me some stuff and I told him some stuff. Then he suggested we go in together as a fake engaged couple. It was meant to be our private joke. A way for us to show up the people who had hurt us in the past. It was all pretend, Layla." I shake my head, my teeth biting my lip so hard I'm shocked I'm not drawing blood. "I had no idea people were taking our picture."

"But you're kissing him," she protests, flipping her phone back around for me to see. It's us standing by his car mauling each other, hands all over, lips pressed, tongues in each other's mouths. Lovely. It's one step below porn and my sister is looking at it.

I don't know what to say. I can't tell Layla that I went back to his place and had meaningless sex with him—even if it really didn't feel meaningless to me at all—and then ran out.

"It wasn't real," is what I go instead, because it wasn't, was it? "We just got swept up in the moment." Because that's all it was. A night of make-believe that got out of hand. "I'll likely never see Oliver again."

But even as I say the words, they hurt. I had fun last night with him. Too much fun. So much fun I started to like him. Again. Stupid, I know.

"But. So..." She stares at me with wide, unblinking, slightly devas-tated eyes. "You're not dating him or whatever? I mean, I know you're not actually engaged, but..."

Have I mentioned my sister loves to read romance novels, same as I do? We even read the Twilight series together last year. Sweet Valley High before that, and any other young adult romance series she can get her hands on. Even in Harry Potter and The Hunger Games, she swooned over the romantic undertones.

I already know she's not going to let this go lying down. Case in point, "You haven't had a real date in years."

"So you like to remind me," I grumble.

"I'm not a baby anymore, Amelia. You can go out on dates. You can't let what that jerk face did to you in college keep you from meeting someone and giving them a real chance."

"I give them a real chance."

She laughs. Actually laughs. "You'd have to date someone first for that to happen and anyone you have ever gone out with has never made it past the second date."

I huff out a breath, really, seriously, desperately not wanting to get into now after last night. "I don't have time for dates and where would I meet a guy anyway?" One who is into a woman with more debt than she can handle and is the guardian of a teenager. Men see that and run as fast as they can—trust me.

I work five days a week, eight to five. I come home, make dinner while Layla does her homework. Then we watch a little TV or read before bed and somewhere around ten, I pass out only to wake up and do it all over again. My weekends are spent doing laundry, cleaning the apartment, and grocery shopping. And when I'm not doing all that, Layla and I hang out because neither of us has that many friends.

Me because everyone else my age is either living the single life of bars and hookups or has a significant other. I don't have money for restaurants, clubs, or bars. Layla because she's never really connected with other girls her age. She's hoping the honors program at Wilch-ester will change that. Again, my fingers are crossed those girls are good to her and can look beyond the scholarship she comes with. That obviously never worked out well for me.

"Still, Oliver Fritz is hot. Like so freaking hot. Amelia, you kissed him!"

I hum something out of the back of my throat as I get up to start doing the dishes. Layla joins me, helping me dry off everything before putting it away and mercifully letting the topic of Oliver Fritz drop.

"How about we go get lost in the Museum of Science today? Bring a picnic down there since it's nice outside and then check out the new Bodies exhibit."

Best part, my boss is a lifetime member and huge donor of the museum, so we get to go for free. Layla wants to be a doctor, like I did. And hell on earth, I will make sure she reaches that dream.

"Sure," she says. "That sounds fun."

"Good."

But I can feel her wanting to say more about Oliver. A point she proves when she asks, "Was he a good kisser at least?" Her voice is soft, kinda sad almost.

I peek over at my sister who looks so much like our mom it sometimes takes my breath away. Whereas I have my dad's gray eyes, she has our mom's bright blue. I got the red hair, and hers is honeycomb blonde. She's also already taller than me by a few inches, lucky girl.

I smile wistfully. "He was an amazing kisser."

She sighs, sagging against the counter, a small, dreamy smile on her lips. "He looks like it. I know you say it was all pretend, but who knows, maybe he'll come looking for you. Want to take you out for real."

I scoff out a little at that before I can stop it, already knowing that will never happen. Oliver's likely already forgotten all about me, though I do have to wonder what, if anything, he'll think about those photos and headlines of us.

"I don't think so. That only happens in fairy tales." And I am no Cinderella.

6

Oliver 🖤

"What the hell have you done?" my brother Carter bellows, walking into my apartment uninvited and unannounced.

He thinks because he lives in the same building as I do that he can do that whenever the hell he wants. I think it's time to have a small chat about that.

I hold up my finger, indicating that I need a minute, not even bothering to face him as I down my cup of coffee like it's a sports drink. I set my now empty mug on the counter, wipe my mouth with the back of my hand, and turn to find Carter.

Only Carter isn't alone.

He's with two of my other brothers, Luca and Kaplan.

"What did I do now? And I thought we said you'd pick me up at four to head over to Mom and Dad's? It's not even noon."

"You're in a crappy mood," Luca comments dryly. "You must have already seen it."

I am in a crappy mood. That's what happens when a girl you have no business wanting to stay runs out on you before you wake up. Wait... "Seen what?"

"Is there something you want to tell us, baby brother?" Kaplan smarts, his voice dripping with sarcasm. "You know. Like maybe how you got engaged last night to some woman we've never met? How she was wearing our great-grandmother's family heirloom diamond? Ring any bells?"

He's the eldest of us, so he thinks he can get away with that baby brother shit. Even though the joke's on him. He's the one with the babyface. So much so that he's been called Doogie Howser his entire career and that includes in med school.

I snort out a half-laugh, half-groan. "People in this city really need to get a life and stop bothering with ours." I go back to my espresso maker, readying to make myself another double because it seems like it's going to be a day and I haven't even had breakfast yet. Probably because I was planning to eat Amelia for breakfast before I cooked something special for her.

Yep. I'm officially bitter.

No one has ever run out on me before. Well, except Nora, but that was obviously different. Evidently, it's wounding my pride, *hard*. I mean, that's all this feeling is, right? Just ego? It's not like I actually like her or anything.

"Oliver?" Luca snaps, dragging me from my thoughts. "Have you even checked your phone?"

"Nope." I pop the p sound just to annoy him, especially since he absolutely has no business saying anything to me when it comes to hitting social media. The man's face is practically pinned to the top of every damn post out there. Kaplan's too.

The espresso machine hisses, the scent of excessive caffeine filling the air as precious black liquid starts to fill my mug.

"It's everywhere, Oliver," Carter continues. "And I do mean everywhere. Even *The Boston Globe* picked it up. No one seems to know who the woman is, but pictures of the two of you with her wearing your diamond on her hand are already viral."

"What?" *The Boston Globe?* I turn to face them, Carter's hands are on my counter, Kaplan's on his hips, Luca's folded over his chest. All fucking serious, no bullshit glares. My eyebrows hit my hairline. "It can't be as bad as you're saying."

Truth, I expected one, maybe two pictures at that. It's not like we were at the reunion all that long or like we went out on the town flashing the ring about after. Plus, most of the people who were in that room I didn't think cared about things like tabloids and media. At least not enough to post anything.

"No, you're right," Luca drawls. "It's not as bad as we're saying. It's actually fucking worse."

"It wasn't real," I assert, staring each one in turn, suddenly bewildered as I explain to them what happened. I tell them everything. Every last detail. Well, with the exception of what happened between the hours of ten p.m. and three a.m.

"This is a problem," Kaplan declares, picking at a piece of pizza he's hardly touched. Carter took it upon himself to order up our usual while we hashed this out at my dining room table. And while we've been here, I've heard my phone go off no less than ten times. I don't have it in me to check or pick up for anyone.

Because what they said is true.

It's everywhere.

It's viral.

Oliver Fritz is officially engaged. Only I'm not and what the hell do I do now? I can't exactly come out and say, oh no, wait, hold up, it was all fake. Just a trick and a game we were playing to piss off my ex and show up a bunch of nasty women who made bullying an art form.

I'll look like even more of an asshole than I typically do where the media is concerned.

"It gets worse," Luca says, talking with his mouth full of pepperoni and mushrooms.

"Worse?" I bark out. "How on earth can this get worse? Did I knock Amelia up too?"

Then I pause... no, we were careful. But damn... that's a heart attack waiting to happen.

"No," he says like I'm a moron. "Mom's in on it. Who do you think is blowing up your phone in there? Mom read the news, saw her grandmother's ring on your mystery girl, and went crazy. And when I say crazy, I mean, good crazy, Oliver. The woman was just told her breast cancer is back and suddenly her baby boy is engaged. She's insanely fucking happy."

"Shit."

Kaplan points at me. "Yeah. Shit. She called each of us this morning in tears over it. She said you'd never put that ring on someone's hand if you weren't seriously in love."

"Fuck."

"Fuckity, fuck," Carter agrees. "This isn't just some small thing you can blow off."

My mom's cancer is no joke. I mean, not that cancer ever is, but recurring breast cancer is especially scary. She was diagnosed a little more than three years ago and at the time, it was in situ, meaning it hadn't spread anywhere. They only needed to do a lumpectomy and a round of radiation for good measure. No chemo. No mastectomy.

But now that's all changed. She's set for surgery in two weeks. Chemo shortly after that.

And while our baby sister, Rina, is the only one of us in a relationship, she and her boyfriend Brecken are nowhere near talking about marriage, per her report. Bonus, it's always been our mother's dream to see her children happily settled. In love the way she and my dad are.

This is going to hit her hard.

"What do I do?"

"You find Amelia and talk her into being your fiancée again."

I stare at Carter like he just grew another head right before my eyes. "Come again?"

"You know, that's not a bad idea." Kaplan leans back in his chair, rubbing at his smooth jaw as he ponders this.

"You want me to find Amelia and somehow talk her into staying my fake fiancée?"

"Yes," Kaplan states, still rubbing his jaw, his mind visibly working. "That way, you don't look like a total dipshit to the press and drag our entire family name along with you through the mud. Mom is still happy. Everyone wins."

I shake my head, incredulous. "You want me to lie to Mom, who is about to undergo surgery and chemo?"

"Not forever. Just for a while," Luca chimes in. "A few months and then you and the girl can come out and make a public statement that says it just didn't work out, but you're parting as friends or whatever."

I shoot out of my chair, taking my plate with me, setting it on the counter when what I really want to do is smash it against the quartz. "Even if I were considering this, which I'm not, you're forgetting Amelia ran out on me. She's not going to agree to this."

"You'll have to make her an offer she can't refuse."

I roll my eyes at Carter. "Thanks, Don Corleone, but it's not that simple. If she wanted to see me again, she wouldn't have left the way she did."

"You said she's poor, right? Couldn't even afford the entrance fee into the reunion?" I stare at Kaplan as he says this. "Pay her."

I shake my head. That's so wrong, I can't even stomach it.

"She's not a whore," I growl at him, my fists balling up.

He smirks at me, noting the fury in my eyes his words just caused. "Not saying she is, brother, but this is a mess you have to clean up and you have to do that with as little scandal as possible. Besides, you obviously already like her, so it shouldn't be so hard to come up with a plan to get her to fall in line. You're known as the charming one."

"Yeah, and you're the asshole."

"No," Luca says, tossing his arms behind his head. "That's me. Kaplan is just a dick. Carter is the serious guy. Landon, the broken man. But you're the nice one. The charmer."

"Whatever." I shake my head. "I can't do this. Last night was meant to be harmless and now look."

"Right. The harm is already done," Carter acknowledges. "Now we have to clean up the mess without causing *more* harm. What's the damage in letting Mom stay happy about this for a couple of months? By that point, the media will be over it and Mom knows us enough to understand that weird shit happens to us when it comes to women."

"It's a lie," I grit out. How do you lie to your sick mother? Wouldn't that make me a monster? Or is it palliative? Something that takes her pain away and is good for her soul when she needs it the most.

"So was last night, but that didn't stop you. You even said it was your idea."

I flip Kaplan off. "She hasn't even met Amelia. If I'm engaged to someone, that means I've been dating her for a while. Mom and Dad know nothing of this."

"You've kept women you were sleeping with a secret from them before," he says.

"Except I'm supposed to be dating her. Not just screwing around with a random woman."

"You can say you were blindsided by how quickly it all took over, and you were planning to introduce her to them today, but the media caught you first."

"I—" My phone rings again and this time, I pick it up, seeing it's my mom and answering it. "Hi, Mom." I meet each of my brothers' eyes.

"Oliver. Oh, my goodness, Oliver," my mother pushes out in a gust of rushed air. "Why didn't you tell me you were seeing Amelia Atkins? I always liked her. Such a sweet girl. Tragic what happened to her parents." *Her parents?* "I remember when we approved her scholarship. She had such potential. And now you're with her? *Engaged* to her?" My mother giggles. "I should yell at you for not telling us anything, but that's so like you, I can't even say I'm surprised. In the years since Nora you haven't told us about a single woman. Not one. We have to read about them on the internet, same as everyone else. Oh, remember when you were ten and you didn't even tell us that you had broken your fingers playing basketball until they were so swollen you were afraid they'd turn gangrenous and fall off?" She laughs. I don't. She's absolutely manic with this. "Anyway, now that the secret is out, bring her for family dinner tonight. I can't wait to see her. I'm just so happy about this, Oliver. I feel like lately it's been one bad thing after another, but this is such a bright spot for our family. Of course, this was not how we should have announced your engagement to the press, but too late for all that now. We'll have to make a formal announcement about it later. It's expected of us, you know."

My eyes close on a heavy breath.

"Mom. I... Amelia." Fuck. Just fuck. A hand hits my shoulder and my eyes snap open to find Kaplan right in my face. He gives me the look. The you have to do this look. The it's not just to make my mom happy, but it's for all of us look. If I come out and say it was all a lie, I'll be the most hated man in the city. I'll lose the respect of my friends and colleagues. Hell, I'm a doctor. A resident. Who will want to go see a doctor who publicly lied like that? Who will want to hire me when my residency is up in a few months?

I have to do this.

I have no choice.

I shouldn't have done it in the first place, but even with everything that's subsequently happened and the predicament I find myself in, I can't find it in me to regret it. Amelia last night was a sight to behold. A flashfire against the night sky.

"How did this happen, Oliver?" she continues to my silence. "How did you reunite? How did you propose? You gave her the ring." She sniffles. "I'm your mother. I'm entitled to details."

I swallow hard and then clear my throat. I guess I'm in this now. "I'll be sure to tell you everything when I bring Amelia with me tonight when we come for dinner."

Then I hang up because I may have been secretive as a kid—I was the youngest brother of five brothers, the second youngest of six, so who can blame me—and I may be secretive about my love life now—because I haven't met a woman worth sharing with my family—but I hate lying to my mother. My sick mother at that.

"I'm a piece of shit."

Kaplan shrugs. "Better you than me. She'll forgive you. I'd likely be written out of the will and lose the foundation. Being the baby has its benefits. Being the oldest sucks."

"My heart's bleeding for you, Kap," I deadpan. "Now, can you guys help me find Amelia and convince her to do this with me?"

"Find her," Luca scoffs, "we can do. Convince her to stay fake engaged to your sorry ass, no. You're on your own with that one."

"Thanks, dick."

"Sure. What are brothers for?"

I flip him off, my face dropping into my hands. I have no idea how I'm going to be able to convince her to do this with me. I'll be asking her to lie. Not just to the media, but to my parents. Likely the people she works with. Her friends. Family.

Her family. My mom mentioned something happened to her parents. I don't even know about this because I know nothing of her life. I don't even know her.

"How will we ever get away with this?"

"You'll have to figure out a way," Kaplan says.

"She'll never agree."

"Only one way to find out. I found her address," Carter announces. "She lives in Mission Hill, so if you want to convince your new fiancée to say yes to you, you better go shower and get a move on. You're expected at the compound before five. Oh, and Oliver?"

I meet Carter's brown eyes.

"Don't forget the ring."

7

Amelia ♡

I can't stop thinking about all that happened last night. So much so that I don't hear Layla talking until she waves her hand in front of my face. "Are you even listening, Amelia?"

"Hmm?" I dart my gaze to her. "Yeah, you were saying... ummm..." God, what was she saying?

"Ugh. That I want to be a surgeon," she provides for me as we hop off the green line and make our way up Mission Hill toward our apartment.

Oh. That's a big deal. I force myself to focus on that instead of the other person on my mind. The one who's already a doctor.

"What kind of surgeon?" I pry because Layla declares a new specialty every week. When I was in college, I had dreams of being a surgeon too. I wanted to be a trauma surgeon. Now I work in plastic surgery, because ED nurses earn crappy pay and work horrific hours. Not exactly something I can do, though the dream is still alive somewhere inside of me and once Layla is grown and in college, we'll see if I can make them come back to life.

"I don't know," she muses. "I still want to have a life, you know? I want to be able to read and maybe have kids one day."

I laugh lightly. "You can do all of that and still be whatever surgeon you want to be. It's all a matter of scheduling and priorities. I know plenty of female doctors who do all the doctor things and have time for their families."

"Okay." She taps her chin as we huff it up the hill, turning the corner onto our street. "What about general surgery? They have the widest variety of patients. The most flexibility with their schedules. Their residencies also aren't as crazy as neuro or cardiothoracic."

"I think general surgery is fantastic. But I also think you should wait until you're in your fourth year of medical school to make the final determination."

"Probably. When you were in college, did you—" Layla's words cut off, as do her steps. In fact, she comes to a screeching halt, her jaw unhinging itself from her body while her eyes bug out of her head. "Holy prince popsicle on a stick."

"Layla? What? Are you..."

And then my words die on my tongue because I follow her gaze and discover Oliver Fritz patiently waiting on our porch. He looks so out of place here, sitting on our worn, paint-chipped steps in his designer dark jeans, crisp blue button-down shirt rolled up to the elbows, and Vans like those casual sneakers somehow urbanize him and makes this prince among mortals more human. His brown hair is styled with a small wave in the front that curls back off his forehead just so. His green eyes pierce into me, taking me in from head to toe as a smirk hits the corner of his lips.

Cocky bastard gives me a wink once he meets my eyes again and then cools his features as he turns that magnetic gaze onto Layla.

"If you're looking for advice on medical school and specialties, I can certainly help you with that. Having been to medical school myself and being a doctor along with all of my brothers and my father, we can most definitely answer any question you have."

"Where did you go to medical school?" Layla challenges instead of asking the obvious question: What the hell are you doing here?

"Columbia. Where do you want to go?"

"Dartmouth."

A smile lights up Oliver's face. "My eldest brother Kaplan went there. He's your man if that's the program you're interested in."

"What are you doing here?" I ask since Layla is no help.

He rises on the steps, his eyes holding mine. "I need to talk to you."

"Now might not be the best time for that." My hand swings in Layla's direction.

His smile is undeterred. He steps down onto the sidewalk, extending his hand to my sister. "You must be Layla. Your sister told me all about you last night."

Only I didn't. He's just fucking charming.

"Hi." She shakes his hand, glancing in my direction for a hot beat before turning back to Oliver. "It's nice to meet you. I heard about you too. I think this is the moment where I'm supposed to go inside."

"I'll be up in a few," I offer.

"And I won't be listening from the window," Layla retorts.

Oliver chuckles under his breath and I think one slips from me too. The front door shuts behind Layla, and a few seconds later, I hear the window in my bedroom opening. I inwardly sigh.

"Can you take a walk with me?" He glances up at my apartment and then back to me. "Please?"

"Yeah. Sure."

"No. Don't do that," Layla groans. "I won't be able to hear you then and she won't tell me anything."

"Layla," I holler. "Close my window and go finish your homework."

"Already done."

I growl. "Then go see what we have to make for dinner."

"Fine," she grouses under her breath and a second later, the window closes with an irritating squeak.

Oliver twists to face the same direction as I am, and we start meandering along. I don't say anything, he's the one who sought me out, and for a few moments, neither does he. We just stroll side by side, trapped in some version of awkwardness. The problem is, I'm happy he showed up. And I'm also not happy he showed up. I'm lost in some weird dimension, stuck between stupidly giddy and tragically terrified.

I was already thinking about him too much and now he's here.

"It's just the two of you, right? What happened to your parents?"

I'm not sure why, but for some reason, I didn't expect him to just come out and ask. Probably because no one ever does. People always tend to dodge the uncomfortable, but Oliver isn't one of them.

"Yes. It's just Layla and me now. My parents died in a car accident when Layla was only six. She was in the back seat but completely unharmed. My dad died on impact and my mom the next day in the hospital."

"That's... horrible. I'm so sorry. For both of you."

"Thank you." I pause once we're a few houses over and look up at him, fighting the sun that's shining down on us. The suspense is killing me, and I can no longer play this cool. "What are you doing here, Oliver? Are you here because of the photos on Twitter?"

"You ran out on me," he says instead of actually answering me and the hurt note to his voice rocks the shell I'm trying so hard to keep in place.

I point in the direction of my house. "Now you understand why. What was I supposed to do?"

"You could have told me."

I shake my head at his despondent tone, my hands meeting my hips, my gaze snapping down to the cracked concrete. Opening up to him wouldn't have changed the outcome, it just would have made me more vulnerable to him.

His hand cups my jaw, lifting it until I'm forced to meet his eyes again. It's a move he did a few times last night, and I realize Oliver likes it when I look at him. I don't know if it's so he can read my expression or so I can read his but looking at him likes this is dangerous. He's gorgeous and sexy, yes, but he's also commanding, and I can't help but be drawn to him.

He's magnetic and engrossing, especially close up, and every time I look at him, I feel something I know I shouldn't. He strips me of all my armor and defenses, leaving me bare to infiltration. I can't allow that no matter the temptation he presents.

My heart won't survive it.

"Do you regret it?" he asks when I don't respond.

"Regret what?"

"Last night. Being with me."

"No," I admit on a shaky breath. "I don't. I had a wonderful time with you despite the madness of the reunion and the subsequent pictures it produced. But we both know the reality of this, and I didn't see the point in prolonging something that I knew wouldn't be prolonged."

His features harden. "You didn't give it the chance to."

God. Is he even serious about that? Doesn't he know his reputation? The things he told me? Not once did he indicate he wanted something beyond last night. No, it was easier to leave him before he left me. Necessary even.

"I'm sorry I ran out and didn't tell you beforehand. You're right, I shouldn't have done that. But the reality of our situation is unchanged."

His hand cups my cheek as he stares deeply into my eyes. "That's actually what I'm here to talk to you about."

I blink a few times, my eyebrows pinching in. "I don't understand."

He grins. "You said the same thing last night when I proposed a fake relationship and I'm actually here today with the same offer."

I take a step back and his hand falls to his side though his gaze doesn't waver. I cup my hand over my eyebrows so I can see him better as I fight the sun. "What are you talking about?"

He blows out a breath, scanning the sidewalk and other than a guy mowing the small lawn in the front of his house across the street and two houses down, it's pretty empty out here. "You saw the press, right?"

I nod. "I saw what Layla showed me on Twitter."

"Well, it's a hell of a lot more than just Twitter. We're in every major Boston publication as well as some national entertainment rags."

A gasp hits my lips that I just as quickly stifle with my hand. "Why?"

"Because I'm an Abbot-Fritz, Amelia. My family is the twelfth wealthiest in the world. The Abbot foundation owns more of this city than I can even think about and funds about sixty percent of its charities. All of my brothers, as well as my father, are prominent doctors, and my sister is an ICU nurse. People follow us, especially my brothers' and our dating life. Me getting engaged to a woman they don't know about is big news."

"An influencer."

He throws his hands up in the air. "For better or worse, that seems to be the case."

"Can't we just say it was all a joke?"

He shakes his head immediately. "Think of how that will look. The scandal that will create. What that will do to my family and my reputation as a doctor. I can't come out and tell the world it was all a lie." He grabs my waist, dragging me in a few inches and leaving his hands there. "Amelia, there is more to this than just the media and I'm about to ask you for a huge favor you're not going to want to do."

I swallow, nervously licking my lips. "What? Just say it."

"My mom is sick. She has recurrent breast cancer that is now stage three. She is set to undergo a double mastectomy and chemo. When I spoke to her this morning, she remembered you from high school and was so overwhelmingly ecstatic that you and I were engaged. I had put my great-grandmother's ring on your finger, and she believes that meant it was the real deal because when she gave me the ring to give to Nora, I promised her I would never put that ring on someone's hand unless I meant it."

"Jesus, Oliver." I scrub my hands over my face and back through my hair. "What are you saying?"

"I'm saying I fucked up. I'm saying I put us in a not-so-favorable position. I'm asking if you would consider being my fake fiancée just a little longer. A few months maybe and then we can come out and say it just didn't work out between us."

I stare up at him, flabbergasted. "So you want me to *lie* to your mother and the media for a few *months*?"

"I know it sounds bad—"

"Bad?" I bite out incredulously, shoving him back and off me. "It's ridiculous. I don't like lying. I don't want to lie to your mother. When I was applying to Wilchester, she was nice to me. She's the one who approved my scholarship. Not only is it wrong, but no one will believe we're engaged. We don't know anything about each other. We're complete and total opposites. Your mother will know instantly that it's a lie. I'll be painted as an opportunistic gold-digger. This will never work."

"Calm down."

"Calm down?!" Is he kidding me with that? How on earth can I calm down? Doesn't he realize what he's asking of me? What pretending to be engaged to him for a few months will do to me? How easy it is to get attached to someone like him and I cannot get attached to him. My heart can't take the inevitable loss. Not again.

"Yes, you're freaking out. It will work because they'll want to believe it." His steady hands grip my twitching hips as he grabs me again, his gaze imploring. "What can I give you to convince you to do this for me?"

"You're trying to buy me off?"

He has the grace to wince. "There has to be something you want or need."

Wow. That seriously stings. "Yeah. For you to fuck off."

I shove against his chest, pushing him away and storming off toward my apartment, ready to leave him standing here and never look back when he stops me dead in my tracks. "What about Layla? If not for you, what about her?"

I idle in the middle of the sidewalk with my back to him, my eyes shut and my breathing ragged. I'm so angry and confused and scared. God, I'm so scared. It's all I ever am, day in and day out, and this just made my chronic low bubbling fear ratchet up a million degrees. Some days I have no idea how I'll make it through.

Now I have no idea how I'll make it through him.

His hands meet my shoulders, and my teeth sink into my bottom lip. His touch already undoes me. I don't want to take his money. If I take his money, arrangement or not, it makes me feel sleazy. But the truth is, Layla needs this chance at Wilchester. The one I can't fully provide for her.

And if she doesn't get it, she'll be crushed.

She's already lost so much in her life I can't bear for her to lose this too.

"It's just a few months, Amelia. You'd make my mother so happy during a time when happiness is in short supply. We'll go in public on a few dates. Hold hands. Kiss for the cameras. I'll shield you from my mother as much as I can, so we keep the lying to a minimum. I know you don't give a shit about my money. If you did, you would have reacted very differently to my offer. But if there is anything I can do for you or Layla, I'd really like to help. Just name it."

"Wilchester," springs from my lips before I can stop it.

"What?"

"Layla has an interview there in two weeks. She wants to go for their honors program. She's gifted and the school she's in now..." I trail off, shaking my head, my face falling toward the ground, hating the words as they spew from me, one after the other. "She needs a full ride for tuition. I can figure out books and uniforms for her, but they don't do full rides, only partial. When I went, I was able to go because my dad worked there, and I had a partial scholarship to make up the other half. That's not the case anymore. Given Layla's grades, my academic history there, and the fact that our father worked there, they're willing to meet with her anyway to see if we can work something out."

Like a payment plan that will sink me even deeper into a hole with no escape.

"You want Layla to get a full ride to Wilchester for high school."

It's not a question, but I nod all the same. "Yes." I spin around in his arms and stare up at him. "If I agree to do this with you, I need Layla to get a full scholarship for all four years of high school. I don't want your money, Oliver. You're dead-on right with that. But I know you have strings you can pull—"

"Consider it done," he interrupts.

My eyes pop out of my head. "Seriously? Just like that?"

"Yes. Just like that. Layla will not pay a cent for anything at Wilchester. Her tuition, books, uniforms, nothing. I promise."

A strangled sob catches in the back of my throat and my body starts shaking so uncontrollably, I can hardly continue to stand upright. Oliver wraps his arms around me, his face planting in my neck. And for a moment, he just breathes me in, holding me so close and so tight. Keeping me from collapsing to the sidewalk beneath us.

"Is that a yes?" he whispers against me.

"Yes," I reply, my voice hoarse, cracking on the end. There is no other option now. If he can do this for Layla, then I'll do whatever he asks of me. I still don't like it, but if it's only for a few months, I can do that. In fact, I'm getting a hell of a lot more out of this than he is. "Thank you."

He chuckles, his hot breath brushing along my exposed skin. "Don't thank me. I've gotten us into quite a mess."

"I think we both did that. If this is going to work, we have a lot to talk about and figure out."

"We do," he agrees, planting a kiss on my neck and making me shake again, only this time it has nothing to do with Layla going to Wilchester. "Bonus, I think we've got the physical part of this fake relationship down."

I grin into his chest, inhaling the addictive scent of him. "I didn't say I was sleeping with you again. Not a whore, Oliver."

"Not a whore, Amelia. I get it. But that doesn't mean I'm not gonna try for more time with this sexy body of yours." He plants another kiss on my neck, pulling back and cupping my face. "There's a lot to discuss, but unfortunately, we're expected at my parents' place for a family dinner in about an hour or so."

"*We're* expected?"

"Yup." He grins impishly, taking my hand and sliding the diamond back on, both of us staring at it as it sparkles like fire against the sun. "You're officially my fake fiancée again, Amelia. Time to go meet your future in-laws."

Oh my god. What did I just agree to?

8

Oliver

Amelia doesn't know this, but her request is the easiest side of this arrangement. I've been sitting in their tiny kitchen for the last fifteen minutes while Amelia freaks out about meeting my family. She's changed her outfit at least a dozen times and I think she's finally onto her hair and makeup. In the meantime, it's just Layla and me.

And let me tell you, Layla is fucking smart.

Not just that, she's fun. A lot like Amelia was last night.

Not the high-strung woman she is now, but given the situation, I can't exactly blame Amelia for that. It's obvious her life isn't simple or easy, but she does whatever she can for Layla.

Amelia's a good person. An honest person. A person I admire and respect.

So getting this kid a full-boat ride to Wilchester is total cake. My mother isn't on the board any longer, but our family still gives a lot of money in endowments to the school. It will seriously just take one phone call to the admissions office, and it'll be done.

Bonus for me, I get to have a hot as sin woman on my arm for the next few months. Having a fiancée, fake or otherwise, also takes a lot of the dating pressure off me. I can just focus on my mom and finishing up my residency without any of the added pressure that comes with women trying to get into my pants and my wallet.

So, there's that.

But I'd be lying if I said I didn't want to spend more time with Amelia. I'm strangely more comfortable being myself with her than I have been with anyone else with the exception of my family and closest friends. I was in her presence for ten minutes last night and I spilled the entire Nora beans without so much as a blip of concern that she'd run off to the press about it.

Being with her is fun. It's easy. She's hot and smart and I haven't stopped fantasizing about her mouth all damn day. Whether it's screaming my name or reprimanding me or just sassing the hell out of me, I can't get enough of it.

But meeting Layla is a game-changer. I can't imagine all Amelia deals with being alone while trying to raise a teenager.

It makes me want to do more for them.

Maybe get them a nicer place where the furniture isn't older than all three of us combined and the walls aren't sagging. Preferably a place with AC because it's only the end of April, but it feels like July up here on the third floor. I already know Amelia would never go for any of that. She doesn't want my money or my help.

She's only doing this because like my brother said to do, I made her an offer she couldn't refuse.

"How are you gonna play this?" Layla asks, resting her chin on her linked hands, staring at me like she's getting ready to fuck up my whole world. "What are you going to use for your meet-cute?"

"Huh?" I rasp out, my eyebrows at my hairline.

She rolls her eyes at me like I'm a moron. She's been doing that a lot since I sat down with her. No one makes you feel stupider or more outgunned than a teenager.

"Everyone is going to ask how you and Amelia met. You need a story."

"We met in high school."

She rolls eyes at me again and I've treated enough teenagers to know she's only warming up. "Yes, Oliver. I'm aware. But it's not like you and Amelia have been in a relationship since high school, have you?"

Yep, Layla definitely thinks I'm a moron. "Clearly not."

"So, what's your story for how you reunited?"

Oh. That.

"You obviously can't say you met up last night. You need a story. And it has to be good because people love good love stories. You can't go with you met at the grocery store or something lame like that unless you make it funny. Like Amelia accidentally knocked over an entire display stand of toilet paper and you came to her rescue."

"Um." Yeah. I'm at a loss.

"You could try saying you met at the hospital. Amelia's in the OR at Brigham and Women's two days a week. Where do you work?"

"The OR?"

"Oh my god. Are you for real?" Her hands fall to the table as she gapes incredulously at me. "How do you expect this to work if you don't even know where your fiancée works?"

Shit. I don't even know what my fiancée does for a living, let alone works. "Help me out?"

Layla levels me with her blue eyes. "She works for Dr. Mike Saggingballs."

I choke out a strangled laugh.

"Layla!" Amelia admonishes from the other room. "I've asked you to stop calling him that. I nearly said it to his face the other day at work."

I can't fight the smile that explodes across my face as I try desperately not to laugh.

"Fine." Another eye roll. "Dr. Mike Sagginalls. He's a plastic surgeon. She's his nurse."

"You're a nurse?" bellows past my lips because shit. That is not good. Not good at all.

"She wanted to be a doctor, but well, yeah, so now she's a nurse."

I close my eyes, falling back in my chair that creaks under my weight. "I date nurses."

Layla snorts, her tone mocking. "Yeah. We know. Everyone knows. But why do you look like I just kicked your dog?"

"Because I serially date nurses." More like take them out for dinner and then sleep with them, but who's keeping track.

"You've got a type," Layla says like it's not a big thing. "Now you've met your match. Work with it."

My eyes fly open, and I take in the kid before me. "How old are you?"

She sits up a little straighter, pinning her shoulders back. "I turned fourteen eighteen days ago."

I can only shake my head at that. She doesn't look like Amelia at all. Layla is tall and skinny as a rail. Her hair is blonde, and her eyes are cornflower blue. She's pretty like Amelia though. She's going to break a ton of hearts one day. Guys will flock to her, and she'll eviscerate them with her smart mouth.

Same as she just did me.

"Alright, Sprite. Tell me, how should Amelia and I have met?"

Layla opens her mouth like she's got it all mapped out when Amelia steps into the room, her heels clicking against the ancient linoleum floor. She's wearing a navy-blue dress that hugs her gorgeous body to perfection without being tight or inappropriate, and matching navy heels. Her red hair is down, similar to how it was last night, and her makeup is minimal. Just some shimmery stuff on her eyelids, mascara, blush, and crimson gloss on her lips.

Oh, and my diamond on her hand, which shockingly only seems to be adding to her beauty. Odd that seeing it sparkle on her hand isn't giving me palpitations. It didn't last night either, which I still can't figure out. Maybe because I know it's fake? That has to be it.

But goddamn, she takes my breath away. "You look..." Words fail me. Words have never failed me. Not ever. "Stunning," finally manages to escape.

I think I'm sweating, and it has nothing to do with the subtropical climate of their apartment. Holy Jesus, my fiancée is fucking hot. And crazy if she thinks I'm going to be able to keep my hands to myself. The greedy bastards are already twitching, begging to be set free on her. I'm going to fight heaven and hell to get her back into my bed again.

That's for damn sure.

"Do I look appropriate to meet my fiancé's parents?" Her face falls to her hands in shame and she sighs, shifting her weight from one heel to the other. "Layla, since the day you were born, all we've ever told you is that lying is bad and now you're watching me do just that. I'm a terrible role model."

"If it helps, I would have done it too," she exclaims, chewing on her thumbnail. "I think it's awesome and super cool. Like a prank on the planet."

We haven't told Layla why Amelia's doing this. Amelia didn't want her to know about the scholarship unless she has to.

"Dude, that's almost *exactly* what I said last night." I fist bump Layla, who is giving me a thousand-megawatt smile.

"Thank you. I don't know if that helps or hurts." Amelia's hands fall to her sides.

"You could always wear your tattered Red Sox shirt," Layla dead-pans though there is mischief in her eyes. "Oh, or your pajama pants that are meant to look like baseball pants. Show off your fan-girl Red Sox nation side of things. That'll really get the future in-laws jazzed about you."

"Ha. Thank you for settling my nerves instead of hiking them up."

"I'm only teasing. You look beautiful. Perfect."

"Wait. You're a Sox fan?" I interrupt.

"Not just a Sox fan," Layla exclaims. "A psycho Sox fan. You should see her room. Her clothes. She's like a twelve-year-old boy with this stuff. Trust me on that one. She has a particular seat on the couch she has to sit in to watch them and only certain foods she'll eat during the game."

"That's not true," Amelia squawks indignantly and I think a little embarrassed. "It doesn't have to be the same every time."

"Oh, you're right." Layla holds her hand up. "If they're losing, you mix it up. I forgot."

Amelia hisses something under her breath before reluctantly meeting my gaze. "Should we go? We should go. You said an hour. I don't want to be late."

"No way. I need to know more about this Sox obsession." Because it's adorable and unexpected and I love seeing her embarrassed and flustered. Plus, I might just be a diehard Sox fan myself—though clearly not as superstitious as she is—so if she has cool paraphernalia in her room...

"No. I don't want to be late to meet them. Please. This is too important."

Oh boy. She's nervous as hell. And a little sick. Nothing about what I'm asking her to do sits right with her. She's doing it for Layla, which I think officially makes her my hero because it doesn't take a genius to understand all the sacrifices Amelia has made in her life for Layla without even blinking an eye or second-guessing them.

She takes care of Layla, but who takes care of her?

I stand up and clasp her hands, even with Layla no doubt watching us like a hawk. "Relax."

"You said that to me last night, Oliver, and look where it got us."

She has a point.

"Listen, it won't be as bad as you think. My brothers already know. My sister Rina too because we're very close, and if I tried to pass this as real, she'd call me out in a hot second. My parents are great and will love you. Plus, my niece Stella will be there, and she just turned thirteen, so I think she and Layla will get along well. And if the shit hits the fan, I'll take full responsibility and keep up my side of things regardless."

She tilts her head, studying me. "Why would you do that?"

"Because I can and the whole fake engagement thing was my idea to start with." I cup her face. Her skin is so soft, and I have the biggest urge to kiss her sweet lips, but I won't dare with Layla right here and Amelia still so unsure. "You still with me?"

She sighs while staring at me with something similar to fear in her eyes before she steels her features. Finally, she says, "Yes. I'm ready. Lord baby Jesus, I'm sweating like a preacher in church. If I start to smell, will you tell me?"

I chuckle. "Absolutely not. That's how lesser men get hit. But you're perfect. Just as Layla said. You've got this."

Helping the ladies up into the Wagon, I listen as Layla goes crazy over it. I have two cars. One is a vintage Porsche 911 Carrera GTS—it's what I drove last night. The other is my Mercedes G-Wagon, because this is still New England, and it likes to snow its balls off from time to time.

But if Layla's going crazy over this car, I'm excited for her to see my parents' place. Maybe it's the family doctor in me who likes treating his pediatric patients more than his adult patients. Maybe it's the fact that I'm the 'fun' uncle with Stella. Maybe it's just that I really fucking like Layla a lot. But whatever it is, I have the biggest desire to spoil the kid rotten.

"Layla, have you ever ridden a horse?"

"A horse?" She cackles. "Yeah. Every day right after afternoon tea."

"Layla," Amelia admonishes. "Rude."

"It's fine," I tell Amelia before catching Layla's eye in the rearview mirror. "If you're interested, my parents have a stable with horses. My mother loves to ride and now Stella is starting to get into it. If you want, I bet we could get you up on one today."

"You're for real?"

"I am with this."

Amelia smirks at that, shaking her head as she stares out the window.

"Then hell yeah," Layla screams excitedly. "I'd love to go riding."

"Awesome. I'll make sure you get set up when we get there. We won't eat until around six-thirty, so that will give you plenty of time."

Layla squeals in the back seat and Amelia turns to look at me, a soft appreciative smile on her lips. I catch her eye and she mouths, *thank you.* I toss her a wink back, my chest filling with some kind of strange sensation I have no name for or experience with.

I can't even tell if I like it or not.

Whatever it is, it has me lifting her hand and kissing her knuckles before intertwining our fingers and holding her damn hand as I drive us to meet my parents. This feels like a date. But not just any date. Like a seriously important date. Like there is a lot riding on it, more than just the lie I'm about to tell that I'm trying damn hard not to think about or dwell on.

"I recognized you," I say out of nowhere.

Amelia's head flies in my direction. "Huh?"

"I saw you out with Layla..." I pause to think this through. "At the Barnes & Noble in the Prudential Mall. I was walking by, headed to grab a bite since I work at Hugh Healthcare in Copley, and I saw you. You were both in the romance section and I couldn't take my eyes off you. I approached you and we got to talking. I convinced the two of you to have lunch with me and we started quietly dating after that because you don't like media attention."

Amelia makes a snorting noise. "Well, that part is true. Still, I like it."

"I love it," Layla whispers wistfully. "It's sweet and romantic, believable even. How long have you been dating?"

"I checked into that," I tell them. "I was last photographed with a woman about four and a half months ago. So, let's say then. We kept it quiet because it came out of nowhere and took us by surprise with how fast and how hard we fell in love."

"How long have we been engaged?" Amelia asks.

"I proposed to you the night before the reunion."

"How did you propose?" Layla pushes, leaning forward from the middle seat, desperate to be in on the action. She likes this lie more than Amelia does. Amelia is a mask I can't read, though she's staring into the side of my face like her life depends on it.

How did I propose? I was going to propose to Nora at dinner. I had made reservations for us at a very expensive high-end restaurant in New York. It was under the pretenses of celebrating my acceptance to Columbia for med school, but I had the ring ready in my pocket.

Then she gutted me like a fish before getting up and walking out on me right there before dessert was served.

So... not like that.

"You did it on your balcony," Amelia says, breaking the silence, her voice a note above a whisper. "We were watching the sunrise, both of us needing to get ready for the day but stealing an extra moment together. Layla was still asleep in your guest room because she likes to sleep at your place. You put your arms around me from behind and whispered it in my ear."

A rush of air invades my chest, my voice thick. "I like it."

And I do, which really sucks. Something about that feels more intimate and genuine than getting down on one knee. It feels more romantic than all the grand gestures you see and hear about. Worst of all, I can picture it in my head. The way Amelia's hair would look burnishing against the morning rays of the sun. The way her color-less eyes would glitter. How her body would feel pressed against mine. The way she'd smile and tear up.

The way my heart would pound for her.

I lick my suddenly dry lips, trying to swallow when my mouth is like a desert. I release her hand, bringing it back to the wheel.

What am I doing?

I don't get involved. I don't date seriously and I sure as shit don't get engaged by whispering words of love and forever into a woman's ear. That will never happen. I don't *want* it to happen. I spent years of my life with a woman who I sacrificed everything for. Then she took all my love, all my devotion, all my fucking sacrifices, and threw them in my face.

Hell, I should have wrung her neck last night for all that she did to me.

But in severing my heart from my chest, she also did me a favor.

She taught me the hard lessons.

Live your life for yourself and no one else while guarding your heart against those who wish to use it against you.

I like Amelia. I always have. Last night with her was fantastic, and she's helping me out now. I'll play my part. I'll be the doting and in love fiancé. But that doesn't mean I'm about to let any of this turn real.

Three months.

That's what we agreed on. And after those three months are up, Amelia will be gone, and my life will return to the way it's supposed to be. It has to.

9

Amelia ♥

The rest of the car ride is eerily quiet. At least it is between Oliver and me. Layla, if she feels the tension, isn't bothered by it. She's chatting away about this, that, and the other thing. All the while, my mind is in a tailspin. It's stuck on some weird acid trip, stranded between parallel universes.

One real.

The other fake.

I want Oliver's parents to like me. I want his family to like me. I want them all to like Layla.

But it would be SO much easier if they hated me.

I feel like all of this would be easier if I hadn't slept with him. If I had never had a crazy, useless crush on him growing up. If I had just met him last night, none of this would be a problem. But even though I didn't exactly know Oliver growing up, I watched him. I daydreamed about him. I fantasized. I admired. I desired.

Then last night happened and now...

I keep having to tell myself that it's pretend, and there is a very real and important end game for me. Problem is, I shouldn't have to already tell myself this on day freaking one. My plan is to mentally and emotionally detach. I will treat this clinically. Play it off as some sort of whacked sociology experiment and nothing more.

I don't have time or space in my life for the likes of Oliver Fritz. If I let him, he'd plow through me like a tornado, over in the blink of an eye and destructive as fuck. I can't allow him to annihilate what little Layla and I are already clinging to. I've lost enough already.

I knew that last night and now it's become my mantra.

Especially as we pull into his parents' compound. And compound is absolutely the correct term for this place. The grounds are massive and meticulously maintained. There are gardens—both flower and vegetable. Stables as previously mentioned. A guest house and staff house, tennis courts, and an Olympic-size swimming pool complete with a grotto and whirlpool.

And that's not even including the main house, which is the size of a hotel.

Layla's jaw is completely unhinged, her eyes have officially fallen out of her head.

"Believe it or not, I've been here before. Once."

Oliver nods at me as he drives along the gravel path up to the circular drive that leads to the front of the house. "My graduation party. I remember."

My head whips in his direction. "You do?"

"Yep. You wore a black bikini that made your alabaster skin glow, but your shoulders were getting a little burned. I brought you—"

"Sunscreen. You brought me sunscreen."

His eyes meet mine briefly, and the small frown that had been sitting on his face for more than half the drive here is suddenly replaced with a wicked grin. He puts the car in park. "I believe I even offered to apply it for you."

I grin back at him, relieved that whatever tension had settled between us after the engagement conversation now seems to be dissipating. "You did. I believe I tripped over my tongue and then you did it anyway when I couldn't say yes or no."

"That would be correct. Too bad Nora didn't see me do it. Or know what I was thinking. Would have saved me a lot of years of bullshit." He gives me another wink and then hops out of the car. Now my jaw is unhinged, but I quickly rein it, and my racing heart, back in.

"Oh, he totally likes you."

"Zip it, Layla."

She laughs at me, hopping out of the car without waiting on Oliver who comes around, opening my door for me and helping me down. He threads our fingers together, offering me a charming smile. "You ready?"

"No."

He laughs. "Me either. But we'll get through it together. With Layla as a buffer, of course. Good thing we decided to bring the Sprite along with us."

Layla groans. "God, that's gonna stick, isn't it?"

"Yup." Oliver tosses his arm over her shoulder and shakes her. She laughs and tries to duck out from under him while I watch on nervously. She already likes him. And what's not to like, right? He's fun and perfect. He's offering to help her learn how to ride horses and is currently suggesting she can come back another day when it's warmer to swim.

She's going to get her heart broken when this is over, and I have no idea what to do about that. Our dad died when Layla was so little. Her memories of our parents are spotty at best, though she does remember the accident that took them from us. It's been just the two of us for so long. Layla was right when she said I don't bring men into our lives.

For this very reason.

We get attached. They leave. We're alone.

And now Oliver is messing with that all over a stupid lie that should never have started.

Will he be yet another person we lose? Another heartache to survive?

The heart is resilient, but it's not indestructible. Once it's broken, it never reforms to its original state. There is always a scar left behind. Even when it fades, it's never fully gone.

Loss creates the ugliest and slowest to heal scars of them all.

Before I can go any deeper down the rabbit hole, the front door of the house opens and there stands Dr. and Mrs. Fritz. Oliver looks a lot like his father with his tall, broad frame and dark hair, though he has his mother's green eyes.

They smile at us, and my heart starts to thunder in my chest as my palm grows sweaty against Oliver's. He must feel it because he gives me what I assume to be a reassuring squeeze.

"Mom, Dad, this is Layla." He points to my sister who offers them a polite wave and a slight hello. "And this is my Amelia." Oliver plants a kiss on my cheek and I'm relieved he called me his. I'm definitely not that either, but it feels like less of a lie than fiancée.

"Welcome. My goodness, I'm so happy to see you." His mother, who has a perfectly coiffed blonde bob wearing a pink dress and heels—in her own home on a Sunday—comes barreling down the front steps practically at a sprint. She throws her arms around me, and I have to release Oliver's hand to catch her. "Oh, Amelia. You're so lovely. I don't know if you remember me, but we met years ago when you were applying to Wilchester."

"Yes, Mrs. Fritz, I remember. I'm so happy to see you again. Thank you for having us here today."

"I didn't give Oliver the choice." She laughs against me, holding on for dear life. "And please, we're going to be family. Call me Octavia."

I inwardly wince, knowing Dr. Fritz is watching us, even as he talks to Oliver. Octavia pulls back and meets my eyes, staring intently at me for a very long moment. Nearly to the point where I'm desperate to shift or look away from her scrutinizing gleam.

Then she takes my hands in hers. "Yes, I think you just might be the answer to my prayers for Oliver."

Oh, holy hell.

I clear my throat, a half-beat from breaking down into tears when Dr. Fritz comes in for a handshake. Thankfully he's not a hugger like his wife or I'd really be done for. Especially as Octavia narrows in on Layla, fussing over my sister like she's one of her own. They're already talking horses as Octavia walks Layla in the direction of the stables, leaving us here alone with Dr. Fritz.

"It's a pleasure to meet you, Amelia," Dr. Fritz says. "Unfortunately, in typical Oliver fashion, he hasn't told us anything about you. I'm hoping you'll be able to fill all the pieces my son seems to have left out."

I blink up at him because he's damn tall, and in his eyes, I see everything his words are saying and everything they're not. Every inch of judgment and skepticism he has for me. I'm poor and Oliver is rich. He's an Abbot-Fritz and I'm a nobody. Oliver never mentioned me, so therefore, I must be pregnant or blackmailing his son.

Oliver wraps his hand around my waist, drawing me into his side. "Back off, Dad, before you scare her away. Now you know why I like to keep my love life a secret. We wanted to be sure before we told you guys. You saw Mom. Every time a woman's name is anywhere near mine, she goes crazy."

His father holds my eyes as he says, "If Amelia is the one for you, Oliver, I doubt she'll scare off easily."

I have to grin at that. At the challenge behind it. "Absolutely not. Every moment I've been with this man has been like trial by fire and here I stand." I glance over to Oliver. "Then again, sometimes I think I'm the lucky one of the two of us. I'm a lot to take on."

"It's true." Oliver's eyes dance about my face before locking on my lips. "You do have a mouth on you that never fails to put me in my place. Maybe it's a redhead thing. Or maybe it's our mutual love of the Sox or all things medical that binds us together." Then without warning, Oliver leans in and presses his lips to mine. Right here in front of his father. It's not overly passionate and there's no tongue, but it's not a quick peck either.

It's his way of standing up for me to his father, and even though I shouldn't, I like it.

My hand meets his arm, giving him a squeeze. Hand on my hip, he squeezes right back.

A warning. A warning for what I'm not sure, but I decide I'm on his territory here, so all I can do is follow his lead and trust him.

Layla wants Wilchester and Oliver is her ticket there. That's all that matters to me. It's the only reason I'm doing this.

Last night is done and needs to stay that way. So all the hand-holding and touching and kissing and looks—those fucking looks—are nothing.

Because that's all they can be.

They're not breaking my world open.

They're not throwing me off balance. Readjusting things I need to always stay aligned.

No.

It's all part of the ruse, I convince myself even as the kiss ends and the smile tugging up his lips makes my belly flutter in an impossibly inconvenient way. Luckily, we're saved from further—I don't even know what you call what just happened with his father—as a fleet of luxury cars all seem to arrive at once.

Doors open only to slam shut just as quickly. One gorgeous man after the other crunches along the gravel drive in our direction. Only Oliver's father hasn't removed his gaze from me. If anything, his eyes are harder than they were before the kiss and it makes my stomach roil. His father clearly doesn't like me. Not only that, he doesn't trust me.

And he's doing absolutely nothing to hide it.

I don't know any of Oliver's brothers as they approach us. I think I've only seen one or two in person before, but none of that matters. I know their faces by headlines. It's like meeting a horde of celebrities, because that's exactly what they are.

With the exception of Rina, who has perpetually kept a very low profile. I met her at the graduation party I mentioned in the car though it was a quick conversation. I doubt she even remembers me.

But whether she does or she doesn't, she's putting on a hell of a show, greeting me first with a smile and a twinkle to her green eyes that match her brother's. "Amelia!" I get a tight hug. "God, I know we just saw each other a week or so ago, but it feels like a lot longer. I can't believe he proposed!" She lets out a girlish squeal, squeezing me again and grabbing my hand as if she's anxious to see the diamond sparkling there. "Wow. Gorgeous. The slug didn't tell any of us he was even planning on doing it." She reaches out, smacking his shoulder.

"Because I wasn't," Oliver says simply. "It just happened. I saw her, and I just knew I had to do it."

A blush creeps up my cheeks, especially as Oliver plants another kiss on me, this one on my cheek.

"Your sisters and brothers knew all about Amelia, but not us," his father states flatly.

"Probably because every woman any of these guys brings home, you stare at the way you're staring at Amelia and Mom immediately wants to indoctrinate them into the family. If that's not reason enough to keep Amelia a secret from you, I don't know what is. You did the same thing with Brecken the first time you met him."

Oliver throws Rina a grateful grin for that. At least now I know it's not just me his father looks at this way.

But before I can get swept away with that, his brothers distract me by coming around us one by one, giving me hugs and making sure to somehow drop their names in conversation, making it natural. As if I didn't already know them, though Luca and Landon are difficult to tell apart—identical twins is really identical in their case.

Yet I can't help standing here impossibly quiet. Overwhelmed. Still hung up on the displeasure pouring off his father in waves.

Oliver gives me a pointed *get your head back in the game* look. Right. I totally suck at this. I don't want to be awkward or weird. The girl always quiet and plastered to wall so she'll stay invisible.

Oliver takes my hand, kisses my knuckles and tucks me back into his side. A place I'm far more comfortable being than anywhere else and that troubles me worse than Rina hugging me like we're ancient besties and his brothers teasing me like they've been doing it forever when this is the first time they've ever set eyes on me.

It's as though I've made a deal with the devil and all his friends. Only I'm stranded in some purgatory I can't climb out of. His father's discerning eyes are all over me, watching my every move and twitch. We haven't even made it inside yet. Layla is off riding horses with Landon's daughter, Stella, whom I have yet to meet.

I can hardly breathe through my nerves, and I think I need a drink. I came here to help Oliver sell a lie to his parents and I'm worried I'm doing a shoddy job of it.

"You okay?" Oliver whispers in my ear as if reading my mind. He sweeps his hands into my hair, pressing his forehead to mind. His lips dip in, kissing mine softly, sweetly, so tenderly I whimper. It's like with this kiss, he's imparting everything that's going through his mind. All the turmoil with what we're doing. The relief and gratitude that I'm here with him. The fear over how quickly and irrevocably everything between us has changed. He deepens the kiss, his eyes closing, and I can't stop myself from questioning, is any of this real?

No. Of course, it's not.

Thankfully Rina comes over and snakes her hand around my arm. "Enough making out. It's gross." She gives me a yank. "Let her go, Oli. You're always hogging her and it's my turn."

Oliver, as if on cue, pulls away only to immediately kiss me again. We're going to have to have a discussion about all this kissing because it's doing things to my mind—and body—I don't appreciate.

"We'll eat in about an hour," he tells me. "You doing okay?" he asks again, likely because I didn't answer him the first time. His eyes search mine and I can tell he's genuinely asking.

"I'm great." I get an eyebrow from him. "Okay, I'm nervous. But I'm good." And because I know his father is still within hearing distance, I say, "I just want them to like me." It's true. It's absolutely not even close to a lie. But it's also not something I would have admitted without an audience either.

Oliver laughs. "My mother ran in heels to hug you. It's a sight I've never seen before."

Now I feel worse instead of better, a frown hitting my lips.

Mercifully Rina gives me another tug, drawing me away, and before I know where the hell I am—this place is absolutely mammoth—I find myself in a lounge of sorts sitting in a chair that costs more than my life while Rina shakes us up a couple of martinis at the built-in bar like a professional.

"I'm making you what I like and I'm making it strong," she tells me. "But only because that's seriously all I know how to make, and you look like you could use it."

"I'm not picky. I can't tell you the last time I had a martini."

"Oliver really put you in this, didn't he?"

I glance down at my hands. "It was my fault too. And I agreed."

"Well, Oliver is my favorite brother, so that makes you my favorite sister, if not my only one. I'm a nurse too, so I get it. I truly do. I may be this—" She waves her hand around the room "—But I'm also that if that makes any sense to you."

I glance up and meet her green eyes with a grateful smile. "It does. And thank you for that." I laugh under my breath, sagging back into my chair, feeling so lost and out of sorts. "I don't have many girl-friends. I wouldn't mind having one."

"Didn't you hear? I'm not just your girlfriend, I'm your sister. And I have a pack of sisters who will fall in love with you too. We'll plan something for this week. You'll see."

"Can I ask you a very rude question?"

Rina chuckles, handing me a green concoction in a heavy cut-crystal martini glass. Jesus, even their glasses are fancy. "Sure. I don't get butt-hurt easy."

"Why are you being so nice to me?"

Now she laughs. Kinda loud. "You won't like my answer."

"Try me. I don't get butt-hurt easy. At least not anymore," I add with a shrug.

"I saw the pictures, same as everyone else has. That and when my mom called this morning, she was elated and keeping her that way and her spirits up is the name of the game for her right now."

I shake my head, not fully understanding what she meant by she saw the pictures, same as everyone else, but before I can ask, she holds up her glass to me.

"Cheers. To doing the wrong thing when it feels right and doing the right thing when you're pretty sure it's wrong."

I snort out a laugh, though there is no humor in it. "I'll definitely drink to that." We each take a sip and it's delicious. Tart and strong, but smooth and cold.

She sets her glass down, angling her body in my direction. "For what it's worth, my brother likes you. My mother and the press aside, if he didn't, you wouldn't be here, and he'd be able to keep his hands, lips, and eyes to himself. But I will have to warn you because I like you. Since Nora dug her talons into his heart, he hasn't been the same. And he's sworn to never put himself out there like that again."

I appreciate her candor, so I decide to return the favor. Even if it stings.

"I've been hurt myself, so I get it fully. You don't have to worry because I have no intention of putting myself out there again either. Your brother likes women, Rina. And he's as charming as it gets. I know all too well that what we're doing is fake."

I'd be a fool to allow myself to imagine otherwise.

10

Oliver 🖤

The ride home from my parents' place isn't long enough to keep this night going. Even when I know it's not headed where I want. With Amelia back in my bed. But still, tonight was unexpectedly perfect. Everything went off without a hitch.

Which just makes me all the more certain this can't last between us. Because the other shoe always drops, and if I let things with Amelia and I get real, the pain when it all falls apart will be real, too.

Layla hasn't stopped talking. Not once. She's told us all about riding Frosty and how awesome it was. Then all about how my mom invited her to come back whenever she'd like to ride. Then came everything about Stella. The two girls hit off famously and already made plans for next weekend.

Plus, Rina and Amelia seemed to have formed a fast friendship as I knew they would.

I'm happy about that. About all of it, really. Layla deserves this. Amelia deserves this.

And maybe I should feel more guilt about what Amelia and I are doing, but I don't. My mom was over the moon tonight. Lit up with more smiles than I've ever seen on her. My dad, however, was a different story. He thinks I'm being taken for a ride by Amelia. He didn't say as much, but I can see it in his cool, assessing gaze. I can hear it in the undertone of his barely polite words.

Maybe that's the irony of all this.

I've finally met a woman who doesn't care about my money, who sees something else when she looks at me, but I'm not actually dating her. I know she feels like a fraud. That she hates lying, especially to my mother. I also know she liked the way my family embraced her as one of our own tonight. She laughed and relaxed—though I'm sure much of that was thanks to Rina's cocktail and the wine with dinner. But when was the last time she had that?

People on her side? People who have her back? Just people?

And what will it be like for them when this charade is done?

My hand grips the wheel a little tighter as I glance in her direction, her expression soft and a little lazy as she talks to Layla, answering her about something I missed completely. As if she can sense I'm looking, Amelia turns, catching my eye and blindsiding me with a smile. My heart trips clumsily in my chest and I quickly turn back to the road.

"I'll be sure to get dinner going tomorrow if you're home late. It's not a problem." Layla shifts in her seat, tapping Amelia on the shoulder. "Hey. Now that you're engaged, maybe Dr. Saggingballs will finally stop asking you out all the time."

"What?" flies out of my mouth like a heat-seeking missile as my grip goes from tight to white-knuckling the steering wheel. A hot trickle of jealousy creeps through me, blindsiding me once again. I don't get jealous, and I never care. But that thought doesn't stop my jaw from clenching either. "What do you mean, Dr. Saggingballs asks you out?"

Amelia angles herself in our direction, rolling her eyes at Layla. "First, that's not his name. Second, he stopped doing that years ago."

"Right," Layla snorts. "That's why he still calls you like five times a night to 'talk about patients who don't need talking about'." She puts air quotes around those words. "It happens nearly every night. And I hear him because he speaks louder than God talking to Moses on top of whatever mountain that was. The man bellows. He always asks what you're doing over the weekend or that night. What?" Layla's hands fly up in the air. "Stop glaring at me like that. You know it's true. He calls to make sure you're not out on a date or with a man."

"You're exaggerating," Amelia says dismissively, sitting forward again and folding her arms over her chest. "It's not like that. He's my boss, Layla. He can call me to discuss a patient."

Not after hours and not if she's not on call, he can't.

"I am not exaggerating."

"It's not a thing, Layla. Just drop it. Please."

"He harasses you?" I grit out. Fuck that. I will hook Dr. Sagging-balls on a line and cast his scrotum out to sea for the fish to nibble on painfully slow.

"No," Amelia says while Layla simultaneously says, "Yes. But he's in plastics, so he pays her well and her hours are bomb, so she puts up with it," Layla continues. "I see you wince every time he calls right before you pick up."

"Layla," Amelia snaps in a tone that's demanding she drop it.

"You think because he pays you well and you have decent hours that gives him, your boss, an excuse to make you feel uncomfortable? To call every night and ask what you're doing in your private time? No. I don't fucking think so. Not any woman and certainly not mine."

And I said that aloud. That she's mine. Even when she's techni-cally not. Something I'm painfully aware of as the car grows inter-minably silent. But screw it, I'm not taking it back. Amelia is my fiancée, fake or otherwise, until this thing is over and I will protect her accordingly. I will stake my claim and make my presence known because that's what a man does for his woman.

I pull up in front of her house and Amelia turns to Layla, handing her the keys. "Can you go on upstairs? I need to talk to Oliver for a minute."

"You mean I have to miss this and the goodnight kiss?"

"Layla."

She groans. "I hate missing all the good stuff," she grumbles under her breath. "Fine. Later, Oliver. Today was the best."

"'Night, Sprite. Catch ya later."

And with that, Layla hops out of the car, skipping up the front steps. I watch her go in, making sure the door shuts behind her, and then I swivel back to Amelia who has those gray eyes pinned on me like a vise I don't mind being strangled with.

"It just came out."

"That's not what I'm upset about," she says. I tilt my head, not buying that for a second, watching as she works her bottom lip with her teeth. "Okay, not entirely. That took me a bit by surprise. I think that's why for this to work, we need rules."

"Rules?" I parrot, because that sounds awful. And I'm still hung up on Dr. Saggingballs calling her every night. And asking her out. What a sleazeballs. I'm legit having homicidal thoughts. I want to leave a nasty red hickey on her neck, so he knows. She. Is. Mine. Not his, motherfucker.

I take in the smooth, pale slope of her. So delicate. So pure. So sweet. I bet it wouldn't take much. Her skin is so fair and so quick to redden and—

"Oliver? Did you hear me?"

I blink, snapping away from her neck. "No. I was thinking about where I can purchase a brand at this hour."

"A *brand*?"

"Not for you. At least not that kind. Maybe a prod is what I meant? Something sharp, and hot, and metal that will hurt and burn his flesh."

She smirks at me, amusement dancing across her pretty features. "It's not all that Layla says. She likes to exaggerate."

Yeah, I'm not buying it, sweetheart.

"So Dr. Sleazeballs doesn't call you every night?"

She huffs out a breath, her smile slipping. "I don't want to talk about him. I want to talk about us. We need rules, Oliver. My head is spinning like a top and I have no idea which way this will fall."

Us. That's all I heard. What is happening to me that I like the way that sounds coming from her lips? It's her boss. Her damn boss thinking she's his when she won't ever be. It's messing with my head, and I can't get it under control. I keep picturing some douchetard touching her. Cornering her in the hall...

I growl. *Fucking growl.* I'm losing my goddamn mind here. I decide to let the conversation of her boss drop. For now. Though I certainly intend on doing my own research on him. I cool my shit, thinking about what she's saying. Hadn't I demanded distance and emotional detachment for myself, promising corporal punishment for allowing anything else? She might not be a Nora, but that doesn't make her safe or me interested beyond what we have going.

Which is why I find myself wisely asking, "What kind of rules?"

"Maybe expectations is the better term? I want to know what I should expect from this. How long do we plan to do this? Like drawing up a contract so lines don't get blurred."

I ponder that. How smart that is to do. "I think three months should be enough. At least one to two dates a week, whether in public or at one of our places, is a necessity because people need to know and see we spend time together. Kissing and touching should absolutely be allowed on those dates."

She squints at me. "I'm not sleeping with you and the kissing has to be kept to a minimum and only when we're out in public."

"Don't burst my bubble, Amelia. The idea of fucking you senseless is what got me through dinner tonight."

She turns the exact shade of crimson as her lips and hair. "That's not a good idea."

And because I'm kinda feeling sour, I ask, "Why? Because you're afraid of how good it will be, and you'll never want to stop, or because you're afraid of how good it will be and eventually we will have to stop?"

She glares at me. Rightfully so. I'm being a dick. Did Layla have to mention that her boss hits on her? Jesus.

"I think you need to wear the ring at all times, especially when you're at work and we'll agree not to date or sleep with anyone else." Because obviously, I'll kill a motherfucker if he tries.

She smiles, relieved at that and I don't know if it's because she was worried I'm the sort of bastard who would claim to be engaged while still screwing other women or if she likes the idea that I'll only be with her. Who am I right now?

"Anything else you want to add?" I ask, reaching out and toying with a wisp of her silky red hair before tucking it behind her ear. Her body trembles as my touch slips past the shell of her ear and damn, I want to kiss her. For real. Without an audience. I want to hear her breath hitch right before my lips press to hers because she does that every time. I want to taste the crème brûlée she had for dessert on her tongue and feel her body press against mine.

I want to slip inside her, feel her clench around me while moaning *my* name. I want her nails raking down *my* back because she's just as fucking greedy to claim me as I am to claim her. Her skin, soft, pale, delicious, is mine for the taking.

I can't stop wanting this woman, even after I've already had her.

I clear my throat, forcing my hand to fall away from her just as she shakes off my touch.

She squares her shoulders, creating space between us. "No sex," she forces. "I already told you that, and I meant it. I'm okay with everything you said, but when we're not out in public, hands to yourself. This is a business arrangement, and I'd like to treat it as such. Physical intimacy blurs lines."

I stare into her eyes, tracking their anxious shift. It manages to twist something up inside of me. Something that drags painfully under my skin. I'm with her and it's like everything inside me short circuits. I forget all the lines I'm not supposed to cross. The words I'm not permitted to say. The thoughts I'm not allowed to have. The way I'm no longer authorized to touch her.

It's like something else takes over and I'm just along for the ride.

Which is exactly why I right myself.

"You're worried about getting attached?"

She licks her lips. "Sex confuses things and I have no time or space in my life for that. There is a lot at stake here. For us, yes, but also for Layla and I'm not just talking about school for her. She's already lost so much."

And what about you, I think. *How much have you already lost,*

Amelia? Who looks out for you? I would say that's me, but that's not the case. She doesn't want either of them to get attached. It's smart. It stings, but it's smart. I don't want to get attached to these women either. And I can already see how easy it would be to do that.

Then something occurs to me. "Who hurt you?"

She starts at that, drawing back close to the door, her eyes growing glassy. "How... did Layla say something?"

"No. But I can tell." It's like looking into a mirror with that.

"I... Yes, I've been hurt. Badly. And as I told you last night, I don't have one-night stands or even meaningless sex. So please, Oliver, let's just keep this as simple and easy as we can. The last thing either of us wants is another broken heart."

I give her a steadying look. "I like you. I like Layla. And I'll never do anything to hurt either of you. Whatever you need me to do, I'll do. Three months. Just business. Not a problem."

***

After a shitty night's sleep where the past twenty-four hours with Amelia compounded by our conversation slammed through my head on constant repeat, I walk through the doors of Hughes Healthcare for my shift. This is what I need to get my head back on straight. To stop thinking incessantly about Amelia. A shift. Helping patients. Saving lives.

Only I barely make it three steps down the back hall before I'm inundated with a barrage of questions and congratulations, and we never thought you'd ever get engaged flying at me from all sides. My colleagues are worse than the press.

If I wasn't second-guessing this decision last night after my talk with Amelia, I sure as hell am now. I stop to chat with everyone, ignoring sneers from women I've had encounters with in the past and trying not to wince every time a lie exits my mouth. Thankfully my boss and friend, Jonah Hughes, comes to my rescue, slapping a hand on my shoulder and guiding me away from the fray.

"You alright, mate? You're looking a little sallow."

"Thanks," I mutter dryly, following him into his office, where he shuts the door. I've worked here through my residency and now that I'm finally finishing in July, Jonah didn't hesitate to offer me an attending position. Jonah's wife, Halle, and I are also good friends—were before she even started working here as a nurse practitioner and met Jonah because she is best friends with Rina. It's all very incestuous, but somehow it works out well. Probably because Halle and Rina's other friends are among the few nurses I haven't slept with in this town.

"Love life getting to you then?" He gives me a smug grin. "Oliver Fritz, self-confirmed lifelong bachelor, is finally off the market. Not just that but engaged. I have to admit, I never thought I'd see the day either. Nurses everywhere are in mourning."

I take a seat, falling back in my chair and rubbing my bleary eyes with my fists.

"Is it true then?" he continues when I don't take his bait.

I can't lie to Jonah. As I said, he's a friend and his wife and Rina are close. "It's fake," I admit and then launch into the whole story, forcing his secrecy along with it.

"Christ, Oliver," he mutters, bewildered. "I understand your position and why you felt the need to do this, but it's risky as hell. You're already creating quite the scandal. You're all over the internet. Pictures of you with this woman are everywhere. Halle was going on about it, teasing how woman-loving Oliver has met his perfect match."

I groan. "There's no such thing as a perfect match and it's not real. Amelia is in on this and it's only three months until my overly joyous mother is over the hump with her breast cancer and the media has forgotten all about us. We can make it through."

We have no choice.

Jonah looks like he's sucking on a lemon. "Right." And that, right with his posh accent, tells me he's not buying anything I'm saying. "Ironic she's a nurse, yeah?" he teases. "Considering those are the woman you typically go for."

"Har. Har." Though for the first time today, I'm smiling. Nurses aren't the only women I go for, just the ones I tend to sleep with most often because they're the ones I meet and see on a daily basis. But speaking of... I sit up, dropping my elbows onto my thighs and leaning in Jonah's direction. "Hey, do you know Dr. Mike Sagginalls?"

"Sure. Brilliant plastic surgeon. We occasionally send him some of our pro bono cleft pallet cases."

That catches me by surprise. "We do?"

"Yeah. Why?"

"That's who Amelia works for."

And instantly Jonah's curious expression falls as he shuffles papers around his desk that don't need shuffling. "Oh."

"What does 'oh' mean?" I press. He looks down, picking a non-existent piece of lint from his scrubs. "Jonah?" I press.

"He has a reputation with his nurses, is all," he tells me, still on that lint. "Similar to yours though, I've heard things that make you sound like a saint in comparison."

My jaw clenches, and I swear, between last night and today, I can feel the enamel on my teeth wearing thin. "What do you mean by that?"

Jonah shakes his head, finally meeting my eyes. "Nothing really. It's mostly old gossip."

"Stop being a cagey bastard and tell me."

Jonah sighs, leaning back in his office chair, tossing his arm back behind his head. "He's a ruthless flirt and philanderer. Very arrogant. He was married for a bit but had so many affairs his wife eventually left him. I haven't had much contact with his office other than the sporadic email here or there that I send directly to him about a patient. But he had a reputation for hiring young, pretty nurses to work for him, promising them the moon and stars to get them to sleep with him. Then he grows bored and forces the woman out, either paying her off or making her miserable at work until she quit. But like I said, that gossip is mostly old. It's likely nothing to do with your bird."

"Shit."

"How long has your Amelia been working there?"

I ignore the point about him twice referring to her as mine. "Few years, I think. She hasn't slept with him. At least that's not the impression I've gotten, but it sounds like he tries very hard to change that."

"Hmmm. Well, then it seems she can handle herself if she's been working with him that long."

"Would you want Halle working for him?" I challenge.

He smirks at me. "You mean Halle, the woman I'm actually married to?" I give him a dirty look and he chuckles. "No. Of course not, but obviously Amelia's getting on well without help. And anyway, is it your place to interfere?"

I think about that. "Probably not." I have no business interfering with her job. With her livelihood that she seems to desperately need. She's essentially a single parent and I can already see she doesn't have much. Plus, effectively our business arrangement, as she called it, will be over in a few months. There is no more kissing. No more touching. No more flirting.

At least in private.

She made that damn clear last night.

Still, I can't stand the thought of that asshole treating her like that. Cannot. Fucking. Stand. It. I can't sit idly by and do nothing. I just can't.

"Then you best let it go."

"Not possible. But I don't have to interfere to make my presence known or felt."

A grin springs to my lips, already knowing my idea will piss Amelia off something fierce. Jonah is right. She is more than capable of handling herself. But seeing the fire in her eyes at what I plan to do might be half the reward. She may not want me to blur the lines between us, but it seems I already can't help myself.

11

Amelia 🖤

I t's exactly what I feared would happen.

"You look familiar to me. Why do you look familiar to me?" the woman who is three months pregnant and in for an initial rhinoplasty (nose job) consult asks with a tilt of her head as she studies me.

"I must have one of those faces," I deadpan, knowing damn well it's because she saw me in the tabloids. *Please don't remember where you know me from, lady.* "I've been getting that all day." At this point, I at least have a sense of humor about it. She's my tenth consult of the day—I see all new patients regardless of what they're coming here for —and every single one that I saw recognized me within a matter of minutes.

At first, it annoyed me. Especially with the subsequent line of questions that had nothing to do with why the patient was seeing me and everything to do with Oliver. Now I just take it for what it is, Oliver Fritz engagement hysteria. I even got a call from *Boston Magazine* asking to do an exclusive photoshoot and interview about our engagement.

Thankfully I missed their call, but they left all the details in their message.

I feel like it's one thing to know something and another to see it and live it and that's what's happening now. I knew the Fritzes were a big deal in this city. I knew the tabloids and media love to follow them—hanging on their tragedies and swooning over their love lives. I just had no idea the storm would be this big and continue to grow.

"No," she continues. "I definitely know you."

I'm giving her another minute before she connects the dots.

"As I was saying, we will have to wait until you've delivered the baby before we can perform a rhinoplasty."

Suddenly she's back to business. "But I want my new nose for my pregnancy photo shoot."

"I understand that, but the anesthesia is not good for the fetus, not to mention the procedure itself can be taxing on the body. Dr. Sagginalls has a very firm policy with this."

She huffs, folding her arms over her chest, nonplussed. "And he can't make an exception?"

You'd think the whole not good for the fetus line would have thwarted her, but no, it didn't, and it rarely ever does. The patients who come in here are used to always getting their way under every circumstance.

"I'm sorry, but even if he were willing to do that, which I'm positive he's not, we're booking more than seven months out for procedures anyway."

She's aghast, and I put my hands on my hips, readying myself for the battle I know is coming when her eyes catch on the diamond perched on my hand. They widen, narrow, then flash up to my face triumphantly.

"I knew I recognized you," she says. "You're engaged to Oliver Fritz."

Ugh. Here we go.

"Yes. I am." I move for the drawer with the rhinoplasty pamphlet in it, pulling one out for her. "Now, it's a pretty straightforward procedure—"

"What's he like? I mean, dreamy is obvious. Rich is another. But wow, I never thought he'd actually get engaged. Let alone get engaged to a nurse, though the papers yesterday didn't mention that at all. They didn't even know who you were. I always felt like we'd see him end up with someone like Captiva Shaw or Alessandra Flores. You know, someone hot and young and famous."

"Uh-huh. So as I was saying—"

"But the two of you looked so in love in those pictures," she continues without missing a beat. "My friend Val and I totally swooned. Gah, I'm so jealous. You have to tell me everything. How did he propose? Did he buy the ring just for you?"

Mercifully there is a knock on the door and then Dr. Sagginalls pops his head in, eying the patient and then me. "Sorry to interrupt, Amelia, but do you have a minute?"

"Yes, we were just finishing up. I'll be right out."

"I'll be in my office."

He shuts the door behind him and then I launch into my rhinoplasty speech, handing her the brochure. I do a quick exam, taking some measurements, and documenting how she says she wants her nose to look after the procedure. I escape the room by telling her to look over all the information I've given her and if she's still interested to schedule a pre-op appointment with Dr. Sagginalls for after the baby is delivered.

I exit the room hastily, speed-walk down the hall, turn left, and then sag unceremoniously against the wall, my head back and my eyes closing. My fingers twist the large, heavy stone on my hand as I take a breather. I knew people loved the Fritz boys, but man, I had no clue about their reach. How obsessed and consumed people are with them.

You'd think they were the Red Sox, for Christ's sake.

Thankfully that was the last appointment of the day and tomorrow we're in the OR—my favorite. Then again, I don't typically spend my office days dodging questions about my personal life, my fake fiancé, or my fake engagement. I used to roll as unnoticed as a butterfly in a pack of elephants, which is how I liked it.

But not anymore.

Now I'm as visible as a streaker running across the field at Fenway. My ass is everywhere.

I need to go face Saggingballs—er, I mean Sagginalls. *Dammit, Layla!*

Prying myself away from the sanctuary of the wall, I turn just in time to plow straight into Kathleen, our receptionist, who is holding a large platter of something that bangs brutally against my chest, impaling me with a sharp jolt. I go flying back, the thrust of the platter giving me an extra push, and whatever she was carrying goes up in the air. My ass hits the floor with a hard thud and what appears to be heart-shaped cookies rain down on me like confetti, smashing onto my prone form, and breaking apart into a crumbly mess.

"Oh, my goodness. Amelia, I'm so sorry."

"Shit, baby, are you okay?"

That voice. That second voice. I sit up, a factory of cookies falling from my head and onto my lap. I'm slathered in pink and red frosting, chocolate chips smearing into the mix because believe it or not, the cookies are still just a touch warm. The frosting extra soft and the chips ooey-gooey perfection.

Just the way I like them.

Now they're ruined.

Oliver crouches down, hovering over me. I gaze up at him in total bewilderment. "What on earth just happened?"

"Should I check your pupils?" He's grinning and that grin could fill a romance novel of swoon specially written just for me.

"Ha. Only I didn't hit my head."

"Then maybe I should check your ass? Thoroughly and for medical purposes only, of course."

I blush like the love child of a tomato and a beet because Kathleen is definitely within earshot, and she definitely heard that. A point she proves by giggling under her breath. Kathleen is about sixty, though she looks more like thirty-six thanks to the ridiculous discount she gets on her treatments and injections. If Kathleen were capable of showing facial emotions and reactions such as humor or embarrassment, I'm sure she would be doing so right now.

"At least some of the frosting matches my hair." I stare down at my scrubs. "I look like something out of a Valentine's Day massacre." I laugh lightly. Pink and red frosting are smeared everywhere.

"But a delicious one. Here."

Oliver grabs one of the cookie pieces from my chest and pops it into his mouth. Then he takes another and offers it to me. I open automatically, allowing him to feed me while I build up to asking what the hell he's doing here and why I'm now covered in a tray of what appear to be custom-made cookies.

I chew on the cookie, and I'm hit with an explosion of flavors that trigger a million lost memories. "My favorite."

His grin grows into an all-encompassing smile as he leans in and licks the corner of my lips. A hot swoosh of sugar-rushed butterflies launches hellfire through my body.

"Chocolate," he explains. "And they were meant to be your favorite. Chocolate chip cookies with frosting, but now both you and the carpet are wearing more than are edible."

"You brought me cookies?"

"Chocolate chip and frosted, the best of both worlds."

I gawk at him. Eyes wide, mouth open. How did he know? That's exactly what my mother used to say whenever we'd bake them together. We'd stand in our tiny kitchen, drinking milk and eating this exact type of cookie, and I would tell her everything. I had no friends. She was it. The best listener ever. Never an ounce of judgment in sight.

Emotion clogs high up in my throat, practically suffocating me as it builds, filling my eyes with unshed tears. I cup his face in my hand, staring into his eyes. "How?"

"Layla," he whispers so only I can hear. "I needed to know your favorite. She told me the story about your mom, and it was such a good story I had to do it. I was hoping these would make you smile."

A strangled sound hiccups past my lungs.

Is he for real?

Does he have any idea how long it's been since I've had any form of positive male attention? How long my heart has been starved of someone doing something thoughtful just for me? I could have worn the same pair of panties daily for years and no one other than myself would have known. Suddenly this man is all up in my business, making waves and splashing the hell out of me until I'm soaked in his ocean.

"Oh, baby." He cups my face in his hands, his eyes searching mine from inches away. "Don't be mad. I couldn't get you any old cookies. Not after she told me that." Now he places a peck on my cheek. He's completely misreading my emotions. Pulling back, his voice grows louder. "I figured now that we're officially out in the open with our relationship, I could spoil you. Only it seems to have backfired."

No. No, it didn't.

"I'm not mad." I'm swooning. Hard. "I just can't believe you did this." For me.

Because fake pretenses or not, he still went to the trouble of getting me these cookies.

Kathleen makes some sort of simpering sound, obviously falling for it all.

I can't decide if I want to kiss him or throttle him. On the one hand, he did his research. Then he went and had these made specially for me, taking the trouble to hand-deliver them. On the other hand, the fucker is playing a card I don't like—the showing up and lying in my workplace one after hitting my emotional trigger button. He's giving off the illusion that what he's doing is real when it's not.

It nearly makes me hate him. And love him. Bastard.

Doesn't he know what he's doing to me? What game he's playing with my heart? With my life? "Oliver—" I want to ask if it's real. I need to know if he did this, stole a memory of my favorite cookies, of a special time with my mother, for show. Or if he genuinely, truly did this for me. Only I never get the chance as my words are cut off.

"What's all the commotion?" Dr. Sagginalls comes bustling out of his office, marching down the hall. "Jesus, this is a mess. Amelia, what happened?"

Now Oliver pops up, grabbing my hand and helping me to do the

same. The carpet is absolutely ruined. It will have to be professionally cleaned and I cringe thinking about the cost of that.

"It's my fault," Oliver says. "I wanted to do something special for
Amelia and this happened." He gestures to me and then the rug. "My
apologies. I'll happily pay to have your carpets cleaned." Oliver
extends his hand at Sagginalls who eyes him like he's a leaking
implant. "Oliver Fritz. Amelia's fiancé. It's nice to meet you finally.
She's spoken so highly of you."

Like a peacock, he perks up at that. "Mike Sagginalls."

"I'm shocked we haven't met before. My friend, Jonah Hughes,
informed me you do pro bono cleft palates for our babies
sometimes."

"You work for Jonah?"

"I do. And at MGH in one of the family medicine practices
because I'm a glutton for punishment, otherwise known as a resident.
At least until July. Again, I'm sorry about the cookies. I just missed my
girl, you know, so I wanted to surprise her with her favorite treat.
Make it known that I was thinking about her."

He winks at Dr. Sagginalls and then turns my face, kissing me
soundly on the lips. Hard. My hands hit his biceps and I push back,
digging my nails into his flesh when he doesn't relent. Finally, he
releases me, a shit-eating grin sprawling lazily across his lips.

Wanker. He knows exactly what he's doing.

He turns back to Dr. Sagginalls. "I'm a lucky man, wouldn't you
say?"

Oh, hell. Oliver, what the absolute fuck?

Sagginalls straightens his spine, glaring at Oliver. "Amelia never
mentioned you or the fact that she was engaged. I read about it like
everyone else. I wasn't sure I believed it. Especially when she recently
told me she wasn't dating anyone."

Oliver laughs like isn't that just the funniest thing ever. His steadfast gaze holds. "Well, obviously she is. Amelia doesn't like to mix her
personal life with her professional life as I'm sure you can understand. She wanted to hide me like her dirty secret when all I've
wanted to do is shout about her from the rooftops. But now that my

girl has my ring on her finger, I assume there will be no more confusion about her dating status or who she is with during her private, afterwork, time."

I stomp on Oliver's foot. He pinches my hip. I dig my nails into his arm. He presses me tighter against him. My gaze threatens blood and mutiny. He smiles at me like the sexiest devil there ever was.

"No," Sagginalls remarks, though his tone is biting. "No, of course not. We're all so happy for Amelia."

Yeah. He doesn't sound happy at all and I have to wonder if I'll end up paying a price because of it. Even though I repeatedly told him I wasn't dating, had no plans to, nor would I ever consider dating my boss. Because that is fucking true. He had stopped asking me out after I made that clear.

But as Layla said, that didn't stop his calls or questions.

Maybe I should be relieved about what Oliver is doing. Maybe I should appreciate his weird form of staking a claim. But he didn't ask. He barged into my work, made a show of it, and is now challenging my boss in a very alpha male display of she's mine, back the fuck off.

If Oliver gets fired from his job, he can find another one. Or hell, he doesn't even have to work. He's a billionaire, for Christ's sake. If I get fired and struggle to find another job—since I've only ever worked in plastic surgery—then Layla and I will starve and lose our home.

Not exactly an even playing field.

"I'll make sure the carpet is cleaned up before your first patient on Wednesday since I know you're in the OR tomorrow."

With that, Oliver takes my hand, brushing me past the mess on the floor, a stunned Kathleen, and an angry Dr. Sagginalls. I grab my purse and follow after Oliver, dazed, confused, and terrified as hell.

Especially when we hit the outside air and Oliver says, "I'm so pissed you didn't get your cookies. But at least now he knows to listen when you tell him to leave you the fuck alone."

I glare.

He grins.

"I don't regret it," he informs me. "I know you're likely furious with me. But you're hot as fuck when you look at me like that."

"That's my job, Oliver. Don't you understand what you just did?"

He twists us around on the sidewalk, walking me back toward the side of the building before getting right up in my face. "Yes. I know exactly what I did. I made it clear that he has no business getting into yours. He's the type of man who abuses his power because he can. That makes him a first-rate piece of shit asshole. The type who gives all men a bad rap. He knows you need this job, so he holds it over your head. He has a reputation for shit like that, Amelia, and I wasn't going to sit around and let that continue. He won't listen to you because men like him don't think women are capable of saying no and meaning it, but he *will* listen to me."

I blow out a breath. It's true. Everything he just said is true, and I know it. I need this job so I don't push back with him as hard as I would anyone else. He does have that power over me. Welcome to the unfortunate world of being a woman. Of being a woman with limited fucking options.

I tell him no and he 'respects' that, but obviously, he doesn't mean it.

"Tell me if it weren't for Layla that you wouldn't have left him years ago."

I lick my lips. "I can't." Behind that truth, I feel both weak and strong. Weak because I stay. Strong because I endure.

"Then again, I'm not sorry and I have no regrets."

"Were the cookies all for show?"

"No. The cookies were for you. Everything else was for him."

A relief I have no right to feel hits me like a bullet to the chest. So, I do what any woman at risk of losing herself would do. I narrow my gaze. "That wasn't fighting fair. I'm trying to keep this uncomplicated."

"I like complicated."

"I'm starting to learn that about you." I sigh. "Oliver. Those cookies. They're..."

"All over you? Yes. But it only makes you more edible." He winks and I can't stop my laugh as it bubbles out of me. Damn him. He makes it impossible not to adore him.

"I'm not going to punish you the way you'd like me to."

His forehead meets mine, his nose brushing back and forth, tickling my own. "Shame. But I'm more into delivering the punishments than accepting them. Just for reference."

"Oliver."

He squeezes my hips. "How about dinner? Takeout for you and Layla? She likes Italian, right? I figure I owe her for the cookie tip. I know just the place. We can pick it up on our way back to your house."

Staring into his green eyes, so close, marveling at the way he looks at me like I'm something so real and precious to him. This man is going to own my heart. He'll never know it either. He'll just be him, going about his life not understanding how impossible it is not to fall for him.

If I wasn't sure before, I'm damn positive now. I have to safeguard my heart, or he'll break me apart.

"What are you doing?" *To me*, I don't tack on.

He shrugs and judging by his expression, I'm not sure if he even knows. "Evidently, I'm a jealous, possessive bastard. Who knew? Certainly not me, but here it is. I also desperately want to have dinner with you and Layla tonight. We can call this date one for the week if that makes you feel better about it."

He's so adorably hopeful. His green eyes piercing mine, his smile almost boyish.

I should argue this. But suddenly, my heart no longer has that particular fight left in me. Maybe it's the cookies. Maybe it's because he stood up for me when no one in my life ever has. Maybe it's the fact that despite knowing I need to safeguard myself; I can't help but be lured by his charm. Whatever the reason, I know one thing for sure.

When it comes to Oliver Fritz, I have no idea how I'll make it through these few months with my heart intact. Especially when it's already starting to crumble like those cookies.

12

Oliver 🖤

All this week it's been a game. A trick of the mind. When to call Amelia. When not to call her. When to text—and what to say—and when not to text. When to think about her and when not to think about her. When to see her and touch her and when to hold back. Never in my life have I put so much damn thought into my actions with a woman as I have this week.

It might be easier if Amelia wasn't so resistant, and I wasn't so persistent.

We make a weird pair like that.

I keep telling myself to back off. To listen to Amelia and keep my distance. And yet I can't seem to stop myself from doing the complete and total opposite. I might not do relationships, nor do I even want any of this to be real, but I've also never held myself back from someone I've wanted either.

And I think at this point it's pretty damn obvious, I want Amelia.

Even if it's just her body. The fact that I absolutely fucking love hanging out with her and Layla is a bonus. An extra special treat to all this. It's not like I actually want Amelia for something else. Something more.

After the cookie incident, I bought her and Layla an Italian feast. I wanted to make sure they'd have plenty of leftovers because I know money is tight for them. I overheard Layla tell my mom at dinner that typically she and Amelia eat light, just sandwiches or pasta for dinner and that Layla gets free lunch through the school she attends.

I'll admit, this confused me because I'm pretty sure Amelia makes a decent living—it's why she puts up with Dr. Saggingballs—so why are they so broke? Other nurses I've gone out with don't seem to have that issue. I mean, they're not rolling in it, but they're able to more than just get by. Hell, even Rina lives mostly off her salary as a nurse and she's always going out with her friends.

I'm missing something, a large piece to Amelia's puzzle, something I know she goes out of her way to hide from me. She brushes me off every time I try to gently or casually broach the subject. It's a gross reminder that despite my ring being on her hand, we're not at the point where I can pry like that.

But because I made her have dinner with me on Monday night, we've already broken our rules or boundaries or whatever you want to call them. Amelia balked when I suggested dinner at my place later in the week prior to our first big night out. I explained that we couldn't go from Monday to Saturday without seeing each other. It would look suspicious.

That's how I was able to feed her and Layla a second time.

Layla then proceeded to kick my ass in Scrabble. I also made the mistake of teaching her how to play poker. Brilliant kid that she is, kicked my ass in that too. I'm thinking I'll have to bring her around for poker night with my siblings so she can hustle the hell out of them the way she likely hustled me.

But tonight, is different.

Tonight, is a date yes, but a staged date. A date out in public at a nice but not over-the-top restaurant. It's a place I've eaten at once before and loved. I'm hoping that despite the fact that I'm pretty positive we'll be photographed, Amelia enjoys it.

Pulling up to the curb in front of her house, I check my hair and teeth in the rearview mirror. My hands tingle and I shake them out, wondering what's wrong with my skin to make it feel like my body is being attacked by fire ants. I suck in a shaky breath, blowing it out slowly.

"You're like an intern on your first day of residency," I tell my reflection. "What the hell, man? Get your shit together."

Grabbing the bag from the passenger seat, I hop out of my Porsche, jogging up the steps to her front door, ready to push the buzzer for her place when the door swings open, and someone comes barreling out. "Oh, I'm so sorry."

I wave the woman off and quickly enter the building, heading up to the third floor, my heart rate growing faster with each step I take.

It isn't until I reach her door that I realize what this is. I'm nervous.

It drags the most bemused smile to my face. I'm nervous. Am I nervous about being photographed, about the fact that we're faking this thing or the fact that it's Amelia I'm taking out? And legit, when the fuck was the last time I was nervous about anything, let alone taking a woman out to dinner?

I raise my fist to knock when I hear Amelia on the other side. "The red one? For real?"

"Yes," Layla says, almost exasperated. "The red one."

"Layla, it's been in my closet since college. I was nineteen the last time I wore this." Then she growls. "It's too tight. He's going to be here any minute and I still don't know what to wear."

"The. Red. One," Layla snaps, punctuating each word in a harsh staccato. "I'm telling you, it's perfect. It's not too tight."

"But my butt—"

"Looks hot in it."

"And my boobs—"

"I can only pray one day I'll grow those. Just don't bend over and you'll be fine. Or do bend over and maybe you'll get a free dessert you can bring home to me."

"Layla," Amelia reprimands. In the week or so this thing has been going down, Amelia does that a lot. Just say Layla's name in that tone. Like a mother would, but not as harsh. Still, I can't help the huge smile on my face just listening to the two of them.

"Do I get an opinion on the dress?" I ask through the door and both girls shriek at once.

"Oliver, haven't you ever heard of ringing a bell, or knocking even?"

"I like having the element of surprise. Keep things interesting."

"I've noticed," Amelia yells through the door. "It's how we got here in the first place."

"I'm going to open the door."

"No! I'm not dressed!" Amelia squeals at Layla.

"You have like five seconds to get the red one back over your head."

"Layla—"

"Five, four, three..."

"Ah, you monster." I hear the locks start to disengage. "No. Stop. It's not on yet."

"One." The door flies open and there is Layla in her Harry Potter pajamas, staring at me with wide blue eyes and a huge shit-eating grin. "Good evening, Dr. Fritz. You may enter."

"Thanks, Sprite. I..." I get a flash of Amelia tugging a skintight red dress down her thighs, adjusting it this way and that. It hugs her body like a second skin, and I seriously hope Layla doesn't look down right now because she'll spot the wood I just sprung for her sister. "Holy damn."

Amelia spins around and now my eyes shoot out of my head. Cleavage. So much cleavage. So much beautiful cleavage. Amelia's eyes snap down to what I'm unable to look away from despite my best efforts.

"Crap." She tugs the dress up, twisting to the side as she adjusts her girls, and I think I just drooled a river on her floor. "Pretend you didn't see that."

"Impossible. Layla, cover your ears, I have to tell your sister something." Layla cocks an eyebrow at me. "Come on. Earmuffs. I want to tell your sister exactly what I think of her in that dress."

Layla giggles and Amelia just rolls her eyes at me.

"Too much? It's too much, right?"

I shake my head, my eyes trailing down every inch of her with painstaking slowness, capturing every detail and committing it to memory. That dress with those heels on my shoulders will star in my fantasies every damn night this week.

"No. Too much is definitely *not* what I was thinking. You're... exquisite." And so sexy it's taking everything in me not to walk across this room and devour you.

And if I thought I was sweating before, this weird pounding in my heart is doubling down on that. It's like someone doused my body in gasoline and set fire to it.

"See," Layla says, doing a little dance that has her shaking her hips and swinging her arms at the same time. "Told you. She looks hot, right? Red hair, red dress, red lips."

"Uh-huh." I can't stop staring. My dick is actively trying to undo my zipper from the inside of my pants. Are her panties red too?

Amelia saunters over to me, patting my cheek and closes my apparently gaping jaw. "You're cute when you drool. Should I get the mop and bucket?"

"Ha." That's all I've got. Because I'm still drooling. And up close, she smells damn good.

"Let's go before Layla gets more ideas about my wardrobe." Amelia points to the door directly behind me. "Layla, I won't be out late, but only one scoop of kernels for popcorn and please, for me, try not to burn down the house this time. If you do set fire to the kitchen, run outside and then dial 911."

Layla rolls her eyes. "Like duh. And last time wasn't my fault. The pot got too hot." She snickers. "I'm a poet and I didn't even know it. But remember how cute that fireman was? The one who kept checking for fire hazards to make sure the house was safe?"

"Fireman?" That brought me back.

Now it's Amelia's turn to roll her eyes at me. "Yup. A whole truck full of them. Don't ask." She gives me a tug, looking back over her shoulder to Layla. "Love you. Lock up behind me. Text or call if you need anything. It's just dinner, but—"

"Yeah, yeah, blah, blah. I know. I'm fourteen, not four. Have fun.

Wave hi to the paps for me. Can't wait to see and read all about your date tomorrow on the internet—"

"Oh, wait," I say, cutting her off. "Sorry. I nearly forgot. I brought you a sub and some candy." I hand the large brown bag to Layla who takes it, staring down at it in awe.

"You brought me dinner and dessert?"

"Yes?" I say it as a question, the look both women are giving me is a touch intense. "Bad idea?"

"Can we keep him?" Layla turns and asks Amelia. "He brought the good stuff. We're talking king-size Twix *and* Twizzlers. There's a party in my tummy, so yummy, so yummy," Layla sings, doing that dance thing again.

"Thank you," Amelia says to me. "That was insanely generous and thoughtful. Twix and Twizzlers are her favorite."

"I know. Like how I know your favorite cookie. I do my research."

Amelia swallows hard, something I can't read passing over her features.

"No, really," Layla says. "I want to keep him. Like a puppy, but bigger and less messy. Likely housebroken too. Thank you, Oliver. You're my new favorite fake almost brother-in-law."

Amelia groans, but we somehow manage to make it out and into my car, driving back toward the city. I reach out and take her hand, something I seem to do when we drive together. Okay, that's a lie. I hold her hand a lot. It's small and always warm and fits perfectly in mine.

I like the way it feels, the way she feels, far too much for anyone's health.

"I wasn't kidding about how you look," I tell her. "I'm a very lucky man to have you as my date tonight. Thank you again for agreeing to this."

"A night out at a restaurant with a gorgeous guy is not exactly what I'd call a hardship. Even if that guy is you." She bats her eyelashes teasingly.

"All I heard is that you think I'm gorgeous."

She scoffs, shifting in her seat in the small interior of my vintage

Porsche, taking my hand with her. It ends up on her lap and I'm not complaining. Not at all.

"Is that all I am to you? Arm candy? What about my stellar personality?"

"You have your moments," she comments dryly.

"Moments?" I'd clutch my chest in agony if I wasn't driving and she wasn't holding my other hand.

"Are we going to pretend you don't know you're gorgeous and can basically get any woman you look at with a snap of your fingers?"

"But what if I only want one?" And why the fuck did I just say that? I don't even know where it came from. That can't be true, can it?

"Until the next one comes along."

I have nothing for that so I fall silent. I can't even deny it. It's absolutely true. At least that's how I've operated since my life became a sad country song titled, "Nora Did Me Wrong."

I'm a player. Nothing to be proud of there, I know. It's certainly not a badge of honor or a moral code. It absolutely disgusts the hell out of my mother and my sister.

But until this very moment, the title never bothered me. It was just how things were. A necessary evil. A safety net against the maelstrom of interested women, women who never knew me or cared to, only hungry for my name as bragging rights and money in the form of what will I buy them before I move on.

Hell, half the time, it's them who use me and not the other way around.

But for some reason, hearing that from Amelia, it sits differently on my chest.

I don't want her to see me that way.

I want her respect. I want her to see *me*. The man beneath the headlines. Not as Oliver Fritz, billionaire playboy doctor, but as Oliver Fritz, her guy. Someone she can talk to and depend on. Someone she can trust. I want her to look at me and know that I'm not just feeding her a line or trying to be smooth so I can end the night in her panties.

She is beautiful. She is smart and deadpan funny and a little awkward and occasionally unsure but yet so goddamn strong. The strongest person I know.

And since I set eyes on her a week ago, I do only seem to want her.

There, I said it. I admitted it.

I want Amelia to like me because I'm unfortunately starting to like her.

We're doing this thing together and none of it is real. I don't even know what she genuinely thinks of me. If she enjoys spending time with me the way I enjoy spending time with her or if she's merely tolerating me because of the deal we made. And not knowing the answer to that is killing me.

13

Oliver

"I 'm sorry, Oliver," Amelia says, breaking the silence, her voice low as she holds my hand tighter in hers. "I didn't mean that. You've been nothing short of wonderful this week. I'm just out of sorts, nervous about what all of this will bring for me. That's all that was. I had no right to comment on your dating life when we're not actually engaged or even dating."

That catches my attention. Was she... was she jealous? Was that what all that was about? God, I hope so. I like the idea of Amelia being jealous. Of her wanting me back enough to be jealous. I let it drop though.

Nothing good can come from asking her that.

The restaurant is in Kendall Square, Cambridge, just over the Longfellow Bridge and has beautiful views of the Charles River and the city on the other side. The sun is just now starting to set in the west, casting the most gorgeous splashes of gold, pink, and purple across the sky as if the color is jumping from puffy cloud to puffy cloud.

"Wow," Amelia breathes as she takes her seat, the host holding her chair for her. "This is gorgeous. I can forgive you for taking me out on a Sox-Yankees night."

I grin at that. The Sox are a half-game down on the Yankees so tonight is a big night. "I requested this table specifically."

Amelia's eyes fly up in my direction, a bemused smirk on her lips as the host goes about setting her napkin in her lap and handing her a menu. The moment he's out of earshot, she leans in toward me. "Did you really?"

I nod. "I wanted you to have the best view."

Her eyebrows bounce. "Well, I'm impressed. Thank you. You certainly put in the effort to wine and dine."

"Not really," I admit, glancing over the menu without really looking at it. "At least not usually."

Her mouth tilts down into a confused frown. "What do you mean?"

Her comment in the car has been grating on me. Her comment just now too. Because I have been putting in effort with Amelia when I shouldn't be. The more time I spend with her, the more I have to convince myself that she's here with me to get Layla into school and I'm here with her to keep my mom happy and save face publicly.

"I don't make reservations at restaurants and I sure as hell don't pick out specific tables," I growl the words, angry. "Usually I pick my dates up, allow them to choose the place since they typically have one in mind they'd like me to take them to, and that's that." I set my menu down, scooting closer to her chair and staring into her wary eyes. "I don't put in effort, Amelia. Most times, dinner is just pretenses to dessert for me, and yes, I mean that in the crudest way possible. But the women I tend to sleep with want to be seen with me, want their faces in online rags, and want a free dinner somewhere stupidly expensive. I haven't cared enough about anyone since Nora to bother with anything extra. You said until the next one comes along—"

"Oliver, I shouldn't have—"

I cut her off with a shake of my head, reaching out and taking her hand. "No, you were right. That is how it's been, and I've been fine with that. More than fine. I haven't wanted to put myself out there again. That's what that's about." I don't know why I'm explaining this to her if for no other reason than I can't stand the thought of her thinking less of me. "I don't view women as disposable or think of them as if there's a million fish in the sea and I want to taste them all. It's just easier to have fun than it is to risk getting hurt again. At the time, Nora's betrayal cost me everything and I've resented both her—and myself if I'm being honest—for it ever since."

And wow, I just said a whole lot of personal shit. A whole lot of personal shit I'm not even sure I've admitted to myself. Not that directly anyway.

Amelia's eyes sparkle, the colors of the sky reflecting off her soft, muted gray making them look like a watercolor painting. She is fire in red, but her eyes have a softness to them as she gazes at me like I've never experienced before. It suffuses my veins with something intoxicating. Like she sees something inside me no one else believes is actually there.

"I understand that, you know."

"You do?"

"I was in love with a guy," she says it so low I have to lean in closer to hear her, placing my hands on the table between us. "I met him in my very first class freshman year. He came and sat down beside me, introduced himself, and immediately asked me out for coffee after class. He was my first boyfriend. My first love. My first... everything. High school was a nightmare for me, and college was the fresh start I so desperately needed. No one liked me in high school. No one thought I was pretty or worth talking to."

"I did," I interrupt. "I thought you were pretty. I noticed you when I was twelve and trust me when I tell you, I liked you."

She smiles at that, but it's sad, her eyes glassy. "Then you were the only one and obviously that didn't get us very far with each other. So when this guy came around, when he liked me, pursued me, I was helpless to resist him. I fell fast, and I fell hard. So hard. And for over a year, our relationship was incredible."

Her words die out as our waiter fills our water glasses, asking if we need more time to decide. I tell him we do, and he scrams. But my heart is in my throat. My stomach in knots. I don't like the direction this story is headed. With Amelia getting hurt. Even if she is opening up to me for the first time.

"Then what?" I ask after she takes a sip of water, placing the glass back on the table.

Her eyes meet mine, holding on, though they're fuzzy, lost in her memories. "We moved in together our sophomore year. Neither of us cared that we were too young. It felt right and we rolled with it. We talked about forever. We talked about marriage and what our kids were going to look like. He had it all mapped out. I would go to medical school, and he could work from anywhere because that's what computer programmers can do. Then my parents died."

She sucks in a breath, her eyes shining with tears, and I reach out, unable to stop it and take her hand. I hold it in mine. I hold it because I cannot hold her here in this stupid restaurant I'm suddenly wishing I had never taken her to. We should be at my place. Just us. And she should be telling me this when I'm able to comfort her.

"Your parents died," I echo.

"They did. I got the call in the middle of the night because that's how it always goes until they can locate next of kin. I rushed home. It was midterms, so he stayed. I didn't think too much about it at the time. My heart, my mind... I didn't think about it. Then two days later he sent me a text. Right before the funeral. It said, I'm not coming. I'm not ready to leave school or become a stepdad yet. I'm sorry, but I have to end this now before your life ruins mine."

I blink at her, staring so dumbly because words absolutely fail me in this moment.

"I'm sorry..." I begin only to trail off. "He said..." Yep, words fail me.

"He did."

"And he did that by *text*?"

She gives me a wan smile. "He did. A few days later, all of my stuff arrived in boxes and that was that."

Damn. And I thought Nora was a bitch. "Is he still alive?"

She doesn't laugh and I don't intend for her to. I'm not kidding. I know people. I'm a Fritz. I could pay for him to be dead in under an hour. No wonder Amelia is such a mess with me. No wonder she's so reserved and afraid. There is more to her situation with Layla. I'm certain of it. She's holding something else back.

But hell, how does a human rebound from that?

From someone they love, who swore love to them, abandoning them at their most dire hour of need? All the while dealing with the grief of losing both parents and having to leave school to come home and take care of their much younger sister?

Fuck. How is she sitting here breathing? But the fact that she's opening up to me? Sharing something with me I know she doesn't ever talk about?

"Amelia..."

"My point behind that story wasn't for sympathy or drama," she says, giving me a withering attempt at a smile. "It wasn't to one-up you. It was to let you know that I get it. I get why you do the things you do, and you do not have to explain yourself to me. I have no judgments even if it sounded that way. That was... jealousy, I guess. Anyway, you date a lot of women because you don't trust easily, and you don't want to put yourself back out there and I hardly date at all for the very same reason. We're the same, yet opposite, both doing whatever we have to do to get by."

Except what has she done? How is she getting by? She's surviving. It's not the same thing. What would I give to rid her heart of all its ache? She's already doing that to mine and she doesn't even know it. Hell, I never even wanted it.

One week and my world has become Nora who and Amelia yes.

"I never thought I'd find someone worth taking the risk on," I tell her. "That's for sure."

She angles in my direction. "What would you call this then? Letting everyone think you're engaged?"

"You and I are different. This situation is different." At least, that's what I keep telling myself. "You're different than the Nora's of the world. And I'm different from your nameless asshole. I wouldn't be here with you otherwise."

Except that's not why we're together at all, is it? Even if it feels like yet another truth I maybe shouldn't have said.

"You are different," she tells me. "*I* wouldn't be here with you otherwise. I'm trusting you with this and you're doing the same with me. It's the trust of everyone else we're putting at risk."

I frown at that. Thinking about my mom. How she's sick. How we're just at the start of a very long road for her. The thought of hurting my mother, of hurting anyone I love, is like knives stabbing into me and twisting around.

The slice and burn of betrayal is not a favor I want to return.

"Would you still want to be with Nora? Married and about to become a father?"

She misread my expression completely, but still, I answer her all the same. "No. I'm glad Nora is gone. I'm glad I'm not married to her."

And this I can say that with ease. I don't miss Nora. I feel like I dodged a bullet when she broke up with me. Who knows the type of man I'd be now otherwise. Probably working in dermatology and carrying her purse whenever we went out shopping. I let Nora hold too much power over me.

A mistake I know I'd never make again.

It's why I've been surviving as the lone wolf. Women want my name. Women want my money. Women want to manipulate and take advantage because I come across as a nice, easy-going, malleable guy.

No thanks. All set with that.

"What about you? Would you still want to be with that guy?"

She thinks about this. And the fact that she has to do that, burns my blood. "No. I only wish I had lived more before I met him and done more after he was gone."

"Is that what you're doing with me?"

"I like to think so. At least that's how I'm selling this to myself. It's insane. So over the top. But it's also something I don't want to look back on and regret not taking the leap with. Even if it's just for Layla."

Amelia *is* different. Just as I said.

The glimmer in her eyes. The stubborn lift of her mouth when she effortlessly calls me out on my shit. The way she looks at me with understanding as if she knows I'm more than the person I show the world. It's all kinda heady. She's not a game player. She's not an opportunist. She has zero fucks to give when it comes to my money.

She's just a woman trying to get by doing the best she can for someone else. A woman who has been hurt, ransacked by life, and come out stronger on the other side. Fuck all if that doesn't make me want to give them both everything simply because I can.

And before I can stop myself. Before I can think about anything else, I cup Amelia's face, lean in, and kiss her lips. Her lips that I'm hopelessly addicted to. Her lips that taste like honey and home.

"If I had married Nora and you had ended up with that guy, I wouldn't be here with you tonight." I pull back an inch, staring into her eyes, my heart thundering in my chest as realization sweeps through me like a drug. "Amelia, there is nowhere else I'd rather be than here with you."

She starts to smile, starts to lean in to kiss me back, only to catch a flash of something out of the corner of her eye. A camera. Narrowing in on the diamond on her hand, she pulls away. Then she frowns, staring at it before finding my eyes like she's searching for the lie beneath my words.

She thinks I said that as part of this thing.

As a line.

Only I didn't and before I can tell her that, we're interrupted by our waiter again and Amelia is gone. Sitting up straight in her seat and staring at the menu and I'm ordering wine for us and that's that. Moment over.

Maybe it's just as well.

A saving grace from the way her story tonight is holding me captive. From the way *she's* holding me captive. A way for me to keep my head on straight and my mind in the game. The game that does not end with me wanting more from Amelia Atkins. No matter how much I'm starting to.

14

Oliver

"How's your fake engagement going?" Carter asks, shifting the cereal around in his bowl. He does this. Come upstairs to my place at random times, eats my food, drinks my drinks, and generally ingratiates himself into my days. He's my brother and my best friend, so I think he feels that gives him permission.

"If we're going by the pictures from the other night," Grace says, "I'd say it's going swimmingly." Grace also likes to just randomly show up. It doesn't help that she and Carter work together as OB-GYNs at the same hospital I now do a couple of shifts a week in as a family medicine resident.

That and I also always have food they both like to pillage.

"I didn't look at the tabloids yesterday," I say, sipping at my coffee.

Both Carter and Grace give me dubious looks, but it's true. I haven't checked. Yes, obviously there is a part of me that's curious, but the larger part of me doesn't want to know. After our somewhat strained start to our date, things got progressively better and better. Amelia relaxed. I did too and by the end of the night, we were laughing and talking so much we lost track of time and practically closed the place down.

But I haven't talked to her since I dropped her off with an awkward hug and a stupid wave. Nothing yesterday. I wanted to call and text her so many times I nearly chucked my phone over my balcony so I wouldn't do it. And like the douchebag I'm turning into, I was disappointed she didn't call or text me.

I finally succumbed to the temptation and texted that I had a good time with her Saturday. She never responded. I have no idea what's happening between us. What's happening to me. Neither the good nor the bad.

"Well, you were all over them." Grace has a smug grin I'm choosing to ignore.

I didn't pay attention if anyone was watching us. I know we were photographed at least once because that's what ruined my moment with her after we bared our souls to each other. Spoke truths I know neither of us ever willingly speaks.

I have no idea how it happens, but no matter where I go in this city, if there is a woman on my arm, I'm photographed. It's the same with all my brothers. Only Rina and Landon escape this. Rina because she's been through enough and made sure to keep a low profile. Landon, because he's a single dad and much like Amelia, he doesn't go out often. Rarely at all. His heartbreak has depth and teeth, sort of like Amelia's, and he doesn't take that lightly.

"Are you going to do the *Boston Magazine* thing?" Carter asks. "Kaplan said they're being persistent with you."

"They are and I haven't decided. I want to talk to Amelia about it."

"It would make Mom happy."

"And make us look shittier when this ruse is over."

"But aren't you two actually dating now or is this really all for show?" Grace pushes, looking forlorn by the idea of this really all being fake.

I stare at Grace, allowing her question to marinate in my brain for a moment. I also think about the sparkle in Amelia's eyes when I told her there was nowhere else I'd rather be than there with her. The words tumbled out. The desire to be close to her strong. The need to kiss her pervasive, like a sickness I haven't been able to stop from spreading.

"No," finally slips from my lips. "We're not." I set my mug down and go about getting my stuff together for my shift, including my stethoscope and ID badge.

"But you should be. She's perfect for you."

"You don't even know her, Grace. You barely knew her when we were in high school."

"I know you liked her back then, and I know you like her now. The pictures say it all."

I scoff at that. "Because tabloid pictures never exaggerate anything or know how to spin a smile to look like love?"

"I didn't say anything about love. You did." She points an accusing finger at me. "I said like. So again, why aren't you dating her?"

Because I do like Amelia. That's why. I want to be good for her and I'm not sure I am. In fact, I'm pretty positive I'm not. Look at the mess I've gotten both of us into. She deserves a better man than me. Someone who has their head on straight. Who doesn't have crazy trust issues and isn't lying to their sick mother.

Only I can't say that because I know Grace and she'll be all over me for that. Yeah, I like Amelia and there is potential there, but I respect her too much to bring her into the mess that is my head and heart and world. I don't stay with a woman past one or two dates. I don't get serious. Never again.

Amelia's not casual. She's not someone I can just fool around with to get out of my system. Hell, one night with her, and I was already craving more, not less. That only seems to grow stronger the more time I spend with her.

But she set a hard limit of no sex. She set a hard limit of boundaries. She doesn't want to confuse what we're doing with something else. The woman hasn't even responded to my text. Given our situation, attempting something like actually being together would be disastrous anyway.

I need her too much right now.

"Not everything is as easy as your heart wants to make it," I say.

"And not everything is as difficult as your brain wants to make it. Sometimes your heart knows better."

For a second, I have no retort. Her words cling to me like an old wool sweater, rubbing me all wrong and yet a little too right.

I clear my throat. "Let it go, Grace. It's not going to be like that with Amelia and me."

Grace huffs, pushing her cereal bowl away with gusto. She opens her mouth, ready to really lay into me when Carter cuts her off. "Drop it, okay? Oliver knows what he's doing. We've pushed him deep into this enough not to make comments on how he plays it."

Grace catches his eyes and I watch as my big brother tells her a whole fucking play's worth of shit with just his eyes. I don't interrupt. They've developed a shorthand of sorts. Maybe it's from working together? I don't know. They have a connection that even Grace and I don't seem to have, and we've been best friends since infancy.

Finally, she acquiesces. "Fine. I'll keep my comments on this to myself. For now," she warns. "We should get going, or we're all going to be late."

**

"Dr. Fritz, we've added on a last-minute patient to your schedule."

I glance up at the nurse who is newish to this practice. "You do realize my schedule is already full and I have three appointments that are already double-booked, right?"

Welcome to family medicine in community health.

She shrugs like she's not quite sure what to do. "She requested you specifically."

She? I inwardly sigh, leaning back in my chair. "What's she here for?"

"She wouldn't say."

Now I want to growl, because it's her job to ask. And typically, patients aren't just added onto a schedule without a chief complaint or reason for appointment. But at this rate, the longer I argue with her, the farther behind I'll be on my day.

"Do I need a chaperone?"

She shakes her head and then shrugs again. "No. I don't think it's that type of appointment."

"You don't think?"

The nurse blushes and looks down at the floor and this time, there is no suppressing my sigh. I'm still strung tight after my impromptu come-to Jesus breakfast meeting with Grace and Carter, and I don't mean to snap but come the fuck on.

"Sorry, but in the future, when adding someone onto my schedule, please find out a bit more about the reason for their visit, so I know what I'm walking into."

"The other nurses said you've been nicer since you got engaged."

Jesus hell. Is that even true? And when was I ever not nice to anyone, let alone the nurses? I am a prince to the nurses. Even when I'm not screwing them.

"They said I wasn't nice before?"

"Maybe nice isn't the word they used? Maybe they said you were different?" She tilts her head as she contemplates this until she snaps her fingers in an ah-ha way. "Oh, they said they liked you better before you got engaged. That was it. But it was Christy who said that, and I think she was more jealous because you never went out with her like you did a few of the other girls."

I have nothing for that.

"Please, just stand by the door in case I need you," I say, trying to check my tone. A woman requesting me specifically isn't something you play with. If I have to, I'll haul an arsenal of nurses and med students in with me.

Dragging my ass out of my chair, I make my way down the hall, the nurse pointing to room 304. I knock and the second I swing the door open; I practically growl out, what the absolute motherfuck? Because that's precisely what I'm thinking.

"You're not a patient here," I tell Nora, who is sitting primly on the exam table wearing a plethora of designer clothing, diamonds and a satisfied smile.

"I am now."

For fuck's sake.

I turn back to the nurse. "Thanks, I'm all set. She won't be staying long."

The nurse gives me a tight grin and shuts the door behind me, closing me in this tiny four-by-five room with a woman I was hoping never to see again.

"What do you want, Nora, since I know you're not here for a physical."

"What if I am?" She tilts her head coquettishly, and that's it. I'm already done. I move to leave when her voice stops me. "You look happy with Amelia."

I spin back around, leaning against the door and squinting at her. "Is that why you're here? To see if I'm as happy as I appear? Because the answer to that is yes. Mission accomplished, now you can go."

"Robbie and I aren't happy," she says, ignoring that last part. Her gaze falls to her lap. "Things have been bad between us for a while. I was hoping this pregnancy would change that, and it hasn't."

I sigh, because that seems to be my thing today, dropping onto the rolling stool, though I press myself against the wall, ensuring I have plenty of space between me and the blonde snake.

I rub a hand over my forehead, trying to rein in my temper. "I'm sorry to hear that."

"No, you're not and I don't blame you. I swear, Robbie only made a move on me to try and show you up. I doubt he ever loved me. But I was lonely. You were always in class or studying. Working so hard we barely ever saw each other."

"Are you kidding me with that?" slips out. "Nora, lest we forget the myriad of sacrifices I made for you." I point at her. "Why the hell else do you think I was working so damn hard all the time?"

She swallows, licking her lips as she nods. "I know. I was stupid and young. I made a lot of mistakes with you, Oliver, but I'll never forgive myself for the way I hurt you."

I stare at her, trying to see through the thick layer of bullshit she wears like makeup. "Is that why you're here? To apologize?"

"Yes. Partially." She shifts on the table, uncrossing and then recrossing her legs, her hands ringing in her lap like she's actually nervous. Only when she's genuinely nervous, she doesn't do that. She taps her nails. "I also had to see you. I miss you. I know you don't believe me because I've given you no reason to, but it's true. Seeing you at the reunion, seeing you with Amelia, it was torture. It made me realize all that I gave up. All that I want back."

I stand abruptly, so disgusted I can't stomach to be in the room with her a second longer. "That ship sailed away years ago, Nora, and no matter what, it ain't coming back. Your appointment is officially over and I have actual patients to see. Best of luck with your pregnancy and the baby."

"She's using you, Oliver," she cries out in desperation as my hand hits the doorknob. "You're not stupid. You have to know that's what she's doing. She doesn't actually love you. Think of who she is. A charity case who got her hands on the winning lottery ticket. She'll get what she wants from you and then she'll be gone."

I blaze with fury, vitriol dripping from my every breath. "You know nothing about Amelia. Or me, for that matter. You and I ended a long time ago, sweetheart. Something I should actually thank you for. Stay the fuck out of my life and I'll do the same with yours."

She folds her arms defiantly over her chest, giving me that self-satisfied grin again. "You think I don't know you anymore, but I do. I know you better than anyone else. Your heart is too big, Oliver. It always has been. You give up so much of yourself for other people and you're doing it now with her because you want to help her. You can't even see the reality right in front of your face—"

The door slams shut, cutting off her words as I storm angrily down the hall, back toward my office. I have patients to see, but they're going to have to wait. Ripping my stethoscope from around my neck, I chuck it against the wall, kicking my door shut so hard it rattles on its hinges.

I don't know why I'm so upset. Why Nora's words cut a little too deep.

I don't give a shit that she claims to want me back. That's her warped, I don't want him, but I don't want anyone else to have him crap. It's the same reason she still calls me to tell me all her bullshit. No, it's the stuff she said about Amelia that's eating at me.

I do give up so much of myself for other people. I always have. It's how I made so many mistakes with Nora in the first place. And I do want to help Amelia. It's why I took all those extra steps to ensure Layla will get exactly what she needs.

It's true, after Amelia gets what she wants from me, she'll be gone. She is using me just as I'm using her, because it's the fucking agreement we designed.

But... I've also started to like her. Seriously like her.

And now she's ghosting me. We had that amazing night out together, an amazing week before it, and now she doesn't call or text or respond. She's placing distance between us when I seem to only want to be closer. I'm using her to help me, but suddenly, it feels like I'm getting played instead.

The way Nora once played me.

I fall into my chair, my hands running over my face and through my hair. My heart was too big. Too trusting. Nora cured me of that, but did she? Am I already falling into old habits with Amelia? Getting swept up in a woman who views me only as a means to an end?

Amelia and I *are* using each other. It's a business arrangement, as she said. I know this. So why does the idea of her getting what she wants, and then walking away make my chest feel like it's caving in on itself? And what the fuck am I going to do about it?

15

I 've spent the last three days completely and totally avoiding Oliver. And feeling like shit for it.

We had a best date ever Saturday night at that restaurant. I mean, once we got past our shaky start, it was everything. We didn't stop talking. We didn't stop laughing. To the point where we actually closed the restaurant down and didn't realize it had gotten that late.

He bared his soul to me. I did the same with him.

Then Sunday morning happened.

The headlines came.

And there we were, splashed front and center across Twitter, Instagram, Facebook, and even TikTok as well as local Boston press on our best date ever. Only now they know exactly who I am. The mystery girl has been discovered and there it was, my life in print with a hint of an unflattering spin.

The poor girl likely taking advantage of their favorite prince.

Layla and I spent more than an hour scrolling through it all and with each swipe, I felt a little sicker.

I know that's why Oliver and I are doing this. So he doesn't lose face with the media after our reunion blunder. So his mom can see us and smile and feel good that her son has met someone to love and is happy while she's going through the hardest thing she'll ever go through.

I know all this, but that date...

That perfect, best date ever...

I wanted it to be real so bad. And it wasn't. It was an act. A charade.

I haven't liked anyone in a very long time. And the last time I did nearly destroyed me. I was not okay for longer than I care to admit.

So imagine meeting this guy. This perfect, perfect guy. Smart, sexy, funny, charming. Everything you've always wanted in a man. But he's a player. A man just as broken as you are. And then you end up trapped in a situation that has you straddling the line between real and fake. You don't know which end is up. What is a lie and what is real. Plus, you start to develop feelings—intense feelings—for the guy when you absolutely positively know you shouldn't. That doing so will certainly lead to heartache and ruin. Again.

I just... I needed space. And time.

Which is why I've avoided him. I needed a few days after that night to rearrange my thoughts. To get my head back on straight. To focus my mind and shut down my heart.

Here we are on day three of Oliver detox and I haven't stopped thinking about him. Not even a little. Not once. I can blame it on the press and the resulting comments and questions. On Sagginalls asking me a zillion questions all through our surgeries today. But my heart knows better. It's saying, girl, is that really what's kept Oliver Fritz front and center on your brain?

My foot presses onto the pedal, water shooting out of the faucet as I go about scrubbing out, our last surgery of the day over. A breast reconstruction, which of course also makes me think of Oliver. Of his mother who will likely have to undergo the same procedure in the not-too-distant future.

"Good work today, Amelia," Sagginalls says, coming to scrub out beside me. "You really have a talent for surgery. It's why I let you do more than most scrub nurses or surgical techs get to do."

I beam at that. "Thank you. That means a lot."

"Is that what you wanted to be? A surgeon?"

"Yes. So this is the next best thing. Thank you for taking the time to train me and allowing me that sort of freedom in the OR."

His head bobs gently as he focuses on washing his hands. "Once you marry Fritz, I hope you don't plan on quitting?"

"What?" I startle.

"He's a billionaire, Amelia. I read the articles on you two. How fast your relationship seems to have come on. Things like that have a tendency to burn fast and hot and die just as quickly. I'd hate to have you throw away a very promising career for something that might not last all that long."

I should be angry at his words, but he's more right than he knows. I meet his eyes. "I have no plans on quitting. I love my job."

And I do. Sagginalls aside, I love what I do. Say what you will about plastic surgery, it's not all as shallow as it seems. We do cleft palate repairs on babies. Scar revisions. Breast reconstruction. We also help people regain a piece of their self-confidence they might have lost or not had to begin with. Even if that's in the form of a different nose, a tighter tummy, or larger breasts.

I have no judgment with it.

We're all just trying to get through the best we can.

"Glad to hear it." He angles in my direction, his dark gaze piercing mine. "Listen, it's no secret he has a reputation. Especially a reputation with nurses. I care about you. I know you already know that. The last thing I'd ever want is to see you get hurt."

That goes for both of us. I swallow hard and jerk out a nod.

"Just be careful, okay? If you love the guy, great. Just make sure you're doing this for the right reasons. The media is having a field day with the two of you, and I'm already reading some unflattering things. They seek out scandal, and you and Fritz are the perfect target."

He finishes up, leaving me standing here, reeling.

"See you tomorrow."

"Yeah," I say absently. "Sure."

By the time I walk out of the hospital, my feet automatically guide me in the direction of the T until I'm getting off at the stop for Oliver's office. Layla is staying late at school to work on a project and has informed me that her teacher is ordering pizza for the group. It's some big, end-of-the-year thing to go along with their graduation from middle school at the beginning of June.

Opening the doors of Hughes Healthcare, I glance from left to right. Boston is known for its stellar, first-rate healthcare and Hughes Healthcare is no exception in that. They have branches all throughout the city and the surrounding areas.

Spotting the registration desk, I head there first. Oliver texted me and I never responded. That was two days ago. The man has no idea I'm in his building.

"May I help you?" the woman behind the counter asks, ever the pleasant smile despite it being the end of what I imagine to be a long, busy day for her.

"I'm here to see Oliver Fritz."

"Do you have an appointment?"

"No. I'm not a patient. I'm his—"

"Oh, I'm so sorry," she cuts me off, her eyes brimming with sudden recognition. "You're his fiancée. I saw you in *Boston Landing* and TikTok the other day. So weird. So crazy. I mean, he's our resident celebrity. You know, because he's still a resident for another couple months and he's most definitely a celebrity." Her eyes widen as she holds up her hands in surrender. "As I'm sure you already know." Her face drops to her hands before she laughs and then stares back up at me. "Okay, I'm just going to let you go through because I'm making a mess here." She points to a door. "I think he has one last patient, but his office is at the end of the long hall, second on your right."

"Thank you. And you didn't botch anything up. Oliver always tells me how amazing the support staff is here." I give her a wink, stealing moves from Oliver and she beams at the praise which was obvious my intent. Making my way through the door and down the long hallway as instructed, I get stares.

A lot of them. Some curious. Some in recognition. A few even in disgust.

But no one stops me, and I quickly find the office with the placard that says, Dr. Fritz on it. Entering his office, I quickly shut the door behind me, take in the meager surroundings and then decide on his chair instead of one of the two in front of his desk.

I sit in silence for a few very long, pointed moments, my thoughts starting to crash down on me. Thinking about the looks I just got walking in here. Sagginalls' words. What the press wrote about me. Now that I'm not moving, I'm thinking rationally.

And with thinking rationally, I'm starting to realize, I likely shouldn't have come.

"I should go."

"Actually, I'm thinking you should stay," Oliver says, and I leap out of his chair, my knees smash into the underside of his desk.

"Ow." That is most definitely going to leave a mark. I didn't even hear the door open.

Oliver approaches, spinning the top of the chair until it's facing him. Then he pushes me back down onto it while dropping to his knees in front of me. Quiet and still, his eyes searching, waiting for resistance, his hands gliding up the bottoms of my leggings until they're up and over my knees.

"Just a little red," he whispers, kissing the tiny red dots on the tops of my kneecaps.

"How long were you watching me?"

He grins, but it doesn't reach his eyes, which are cautious. So unlike Oliver. "A few minutes. You looked a little lost I wasn't sure you were in the right place."

Ow again. But only because of the hurt he's trying to mask. I didn't think he'd care that I was ghosting him, but evidently, I was wrong in that. It hits me right in the chest. So, I say the stupid thing. "I missed you."

He glances over his shoulder, but no one is there. I didn't say it for an audience. I said it for him. Because it's true. I did miss him, and I tried not to. I tried not liking him either and look how well that's turning out. This is precisely what I was afraid of. Exactly what I warned him against.

"I missed you too. I thought you were avoiding me."

I grin, biting into my lip as I sit back, fixing my leggings. He stands up, perching himself on the edge of his somewhat cluttered desk. "I was. I'm sorry."

"Why?"

"You don't know?"

He shakes his head.

"Because I had a really great time on Saturday."

His eyebrows knit together with so much confusion it's almost comical. Oliver Fritz is not used to women ghosting him. That much is obvious.

"So," he starts slowly, almost as if he's testing the words on his tongue. "You had a great time with me and..." He shakes his head. "Yeah, I'm not getting it."

"Come on, Oliver. You're a smart man. Surely you can figure it out without my having to spell it out for you." I giggle lightly at him, and he reaches out, pinching my side until I squeal with laughter, trying to force his hand away. "Stop. I'm ticklish there."

"I know. I found that spot after the reunion when you were in my bed."

The laugh dies instantly on my lips as a blush flows rapidly up my neck and across my face. His fingers track it, starting at the base of it and gliding up until they dive into my hair and he's holding me steady by the back of my head.

This is it. This, right here. This is the reason I've avoided him.

Every time we're together, we combust. Fire and water, we're opposites in so many ways, but when we come together, it's like the laws of nature no longer exist. We coalesce in the most perfect of ways as if this is how it was always meant to be.

The longer I stare into his eyes, deep and brilliantly green, the more I get swept up in him.

Sensing this, he leans in, his grip in my hair tightening until his lips land on mine. He kisses me faster until I let out a moan, my body begging for more as it does every time we do this. Only now it's just us. No show. Rules breaking. Boundaries gone.

And I'm scared.

He kisses me until I'm breathless, tugging on the strands of my hair until my head is forced back and his lips latch onto the sensitive skin of my throat. I gasp as he licks down my neck, goose bumps exploding everywhere.

"Oliver," I whimper, begging him to keep going and to stop.

He groans into me, and I know it's because I said his name like that. It sends an irresistible rush of wet heat through my core.

"I'm cooking you dinner tonight. No cameras. No takeout."

"No," I tell him because I can't go to his place. If I do, I'll never want to leave. "I'm cooking *you* dinner. At my place."

He chuckles into me as if reading my mind completely. "You think you're safe that way?"

He pulls back when I don't reply, a dirty and devious smile curled up his wet and swollen lips. His eyes search mine, reading my fear, and there's a darkness that grows across them like an invading storm.

"Okay," he finally relents. "Your place. But I'm buying the groceries and there are no fucking arguments about it."

"I can buy my own groceries."

"You can do anything. I already know this. But it makes me happy, and since you won't come to my place and do all the wicked things you know I want to do to you, you have to surrender this to me. Just no more avoiding me. That shit really pissed me off."

My heart quakes in my chest at that, my knees along with it, but I manage to rise out of his chair and take his hand.

"No more kissing me," I say. "I can't take the kissing."

"What if I can't keep that promise?"

"I need you to." I nearly beg the words.

"Is that why you've been avoiding me?"

"Yes."

His eyes bounce back and forth between mine and without another word, he leads me out of the building to his car, parked in the garage. We drive toward the supermarket in between here and my place, music is playing in the background, but Oliver is quiet. He's also not holding my hand, something he always does whether he's driving or not.

"You okay?" I ask, no longer able to stand it.

He parallel parks into a spot, turning off the car before he answers me. "Not really. It's only Tuesday and it feels like the longest week ever." He pauses here, looking like he wants to elaborate on that, but doesn't.

"I'm afraid of liking you." As much as I do.

He blinks rapidly at me. "I know. But I like you liking me."

"I freaked out over what the press wrote about me. About us."

"That's why you ghosted?"

"That's one reason. The first thing I mentioned is part of that too. I'm sorry if I hurt you."

"You did, but that's definitely not why it's been the longest week ever."

"Is it because your mom has her surgery on Friday?"

Oliver hasn't talked about this.

Maybe that's just with me, but on the couple of occasions where I asked about his mom or how he was doing with her diagnosis, he clammed up. I know she's the main reason we're doing this, but I also feel like he's partially avoiding her and what's to come. I want him to feel comfortable opening up to me. He also needs to talk about it. It's unhealthy to let something as daunting as a sick parent fester.

He swallows thickly, pain slicing across his face. "That's one reason. I... Luca and Kaplan are both surgeons at Brigham and Women's. My dad too. They've all made sure my mom is seeing the best breast specialist. The best oncologist at Dana-Farber. It's just..."

"She's your mom," I finish for him.

His eyes hold mine. "She's my mom. What was it like losing your parents?"

I could tell him her diagnosis doesn't mean she's going to die, but he doesn't need to hear that from me. He's a doctor. He knows what he's asking me.

I lean back in my seat, staring up through the skylight. "It was like someone punched a hole straight through me, ripping out a vital piece of my insides along with it. One that you know will never heal or grow back. It was devastating. My mom was my best friend. My dad and I were close—he's why I'm obsessed with the Red Sox—but he worked two jobs and I didn't see him as much. He was closer with Layla. That was the other part of it. I didn't have time to mourn. They died and I was suddenly an adult. A single parent, forced to move back home and take care of a kindergartener, all the while switching schools and majors and losing a guy I had thought I was in love with. A guy I thought I could rely on. Some nights I didn't even have the strength or energy to cry. Even breathing or putting one foot in front of the other felt impossible. But I had to be strong for Layla."

His hand cups my jaw, and he turns my face to his. "I wish you'd let me hunt down that prick who broke up with you by text after your parents died and kick his ass."

"He's not worth anything. Layla is worth everything."

"She's lucky to have you."

"We're lucky to have each other."

"You have me too, you know. I know you think you don't. That because the ring on your finger isn't real that the rest of it isn't. But that's not the case, Amelia. I like being with you. I like being with Layla."

My eyes burn with tears, my nose along with it. He just said everything I needed him to say. We aren't dating and I'd do right not to think of us in those terms despite the kissing and hand-holding.

"You have me too," I tell him. "I know you have your siblings, but I'm here for you."

"We've got a couple more months that we're doing this thing, but that doesn't mean I want to lose you when it's over."

"You won't," I promise him.

He's likely saying this as a friend and nothing more.

It would be prudent of me to consider him solely in that way. As a man, I won't have sex with or grow emotionally attached to because we're talking about Oliver Fritz here. There is a reason, other than

Layla, of course, that I ran out on him before he woke up. That I told him no more kissing and definitely no more sex.

But despite my head knowing that, his words just flayed me to the bone. There is so much hope building within my heart and I'm having trouble forcing it to listen to my head.

Truth is, it might already be too late for that.

I came to his office today for no other reason than to see him. Than to be near him. Now he's saying I have him and dammit, I want that to be true. This charade just got a whole hell of a lot more complicated and nothing I do will be able to stop that.

16

Amelia 🖤

My foot taps out an uncoordinated beat, my lip getting a workout between my teeth as I sit here in the plush lounge area and wait. And wait. It feels like forever since Layla went into that boardroom and I was instructed to sit. Whether Oliver can coax a full scholarship or not, she has to get into the school first.

Her grades and entrance exams are exemplary. But let's be real here. It's more than that. Despite my status as an alumnus and our father's as a former employee, they have to like Layla. She has to fit into a certain ideal of what they're looking for in a Wilchester student.

I was quiet. I was studious. Layla is sharp-tongued and has zero issues pushing back against authority. This also isn't just to get her into the school. This is to get her into the gifted student program, which consists of honors classes throughout her four years as well as college credit in her senior year. That will help her get into whatever college she wants if she plays it right.

Possibly even with a scholarship.

Which, let's face it, she needs. I'll never get out from under the debt I've placed myself in when finishing my degree. I've pretty much accepted that this is my life and I'll be in debt, hopefully eventually being able to pay more than the minimum on my loans and credit cards, until I'm about eighty.

But I don't want that life for Layla.

I watched my parents struggle my entire childhood and now Layla watches me struggle, and I'll do whatever I have to do to break that cycle for her. Even if it means using Oliver as Layla's stepping-stone with school.

But first, Layla has to charm the pants off the board.

I don't remember my interview taking this long. Why is her interview taking this long?

Unable to sit another second, I get up out of my chair and walk to the large double window, staring out at the immaculate grounds beyond. I had to take a day off work and Layla had to miss a day of school for this, which is why there are kids spilled all over the campus enjoying the beautiful spring day. Their semester is just about over, their school year finishing the end of May.

What will this place be like for her?

Will she make friends where I never could? Even now it's still a hardship for me, though Rina is making a tremendous effort, having me over for a dinner party last night and introducing me to her group of close friends, all of whom I liked immensely. Luckily Layla is far more outgoing than I ever was. She also doesn't have the horrible glasses and frizzy red curls I did. If being a scholarship kid wasn't bad enough here, I had the image of Little Orphan Annie's way nerdier sister.

And as if my nightmares from the past haven't quite finished with me yet, the door opens and in walks Christa Foreman. She takes a small step back when she catches me by the window, obviously surprised to find me here. A point she proves when she so politely asks, "What the hell are you doing here?"

I spin on my heels to face her, straightening my spine. "My sister is here for an interview."

Christa rolls her eyes. "Oh, fabulous. Another Atkins scholarship."

I tilt my head at her. "What is it you have against scholarship kids?"

Something flashes across her face. Disgust maybe? Anger? I'm not sure. "I have nothing against scholarship kids. It was *you*; I had a problem with. You graduated valedictorian and me salutatorian. The only reason I gave the graduation speech is because you declined doing it and I was also the class president. I spent my entire high school career fighting you to be number one because that's what I had to be and in the end, you won."

I shake my head at that. I had no idea I was fighting anyone for anything other than my daily survival. "So that's why you and your friends were always so nasty to me?"

She scoffs, folding her arms. "No. We just flat out didn't like anything about you. The fact that I had to fight you for grades is why I hated you."

Jesus. Some people, I swear.

"Christa, did you go to college?"

She bristles at that. "Of course, I did. I went to Yale."

"And now? What do you do now?"

"I'm a homemaker most of the time, which is my choice. I also work here three days a week, helping out in the registrar and admissions offices."

"And are you happy with your life?"

She stares at me with cold eyes. "I have no doubt my life is a lot better than yours, if that's what you're insinuating."

"Fine." I hold up my hand in concession. "I won't even argue that, because there is no point. I think it's fairly obvious my shit is way more together than yours since I'm not a hateful monster who enjoys preying on others. But what the hell is actually missing from your life that you think I stole by graduating top of our high school class?"

Blank. The woman's face is blank. Probably because she has no answer. Sometimes it's easier to blame someone else for your own problems when they should fall squarely on your shoulders and no one else's. I get it. Sorta. Maybe not.

She was part of a gaggle of girls who enjoyed sucker-punching the less fortunate because they could. Because they felt better about themselves for doing so.

"Well, it seems now you're about to marry up. Marrying into the Fritz family is about as good as anyone can do. Bravo," she sneers sardonically, setting whatever she had in her hands on the desk and then folding her arms over her chest. "You must be so pleased with yourself that you'll never have to be poor again."

Is it as miserable to be in her own skin as it appears? Such a sad existence. And actually, for the first time in my life, I think I pity Christa Foreman. I may not have much. I may always be poor. But I'll never be like her. Contemptuous. Bitter. Hateful. That alone makes me richer than all the Christa Foremans in the world.

"As I told Nora at the reunion," I say, "I'm not marrying Oliver for his money. It's everything else about him that I want."

That's actually true. It's not even a lie.

It really is everything else about Oliver that I want. Because he's impossible *not* to want. Or like because I'm definitely doing that despite my best efforts. Okay, fine, I admit it, I more than like him. I'm absolutely fluffer-nutter about the man, as Layla would say.

Tuesday night he bought groceries and then we cooked together side by side in my tiny kitchen, making pesto chicken pasta and listening to music, drinking wine, and touching each other whenever possible.

I'll admit, I haven't dated anyone in about a hundred years, but it was never like this when I did. Never this fun or easy. Never this sexy or perfect. I had no frame of reference at the time, but the differences between then and now are glaring.

But that's Oliver, right? He is all of those things. We swing from heavy and intense to vulnerable and awkward to light and breezy and I'm there for it. For all of it. I don't want it to end or to stop. I want to believe him when he says he doesn't want us—whatever the mother-fuck this thing is between us—to end when our arrangement does.

Still, I'm doing my best to keep my distance. To maintain our boundaries. Because, you know, I'm easy prey. I'm lonely, for starters. Oliver is my childhood crush and I'm subject to falling without a net or someone to help take me to the hospital after I've broken every freaking part of my body, including my heart. If that even makes sense. I'm a heartsick casualty waiting to happen and as much as I want to give into Oliver in all the ways, I'm scared.

And for the most part, Oliver is too. Sorta. The man likes to test limits whether he wants to cross them or not, that's for sure.

"Right," Christa snarks. I swear, I almost forgot she was here. Stupid brain. "That's why—"

The door bursts open, cutting her off mid-stream. Like we summoned him here, Oliver comes flying in, harried and restless, scanning the room with wild eyes. They finally lock with mine and he smiles a smile that never fails to make my knees weak and my belly flutter.

He calms as he asks. "Am I late? Did I miss her interview?"

I shake my head, staring at him, suddenly choked up. He came? "What are you doing here? You have patients."

"I wasn't going to miss Layla's big interview. I asked her to tell me when it was the other day with the exact time, and I told her I'd come. I take it she didn't mention that to you?"

I shake my head again, eating my lip.

"Hey," he says, crossing the room and cupping my face, his eyes searching mine. "It's not a big deal I'm here, right? I just had to shift a few patients around. Why do you look so upset?"

Shit! Shit, shit, shit. I can't cry. I can't cry.

I sniffle. Swallow hard. Blow out a breath.

"I'm not upset," I croak.

He grins. "You're upset."

"Am not. I'm happy and so terrified I'm about to cry and pee my pants at the same time."

He laughs, his lips pressing to the corner of my mouth. Then the tip of my nose. "Good surprise then?" he whispers against me and this time, I nod instead of shaking my head because my head seems to be the only thing capable of moving or reacting other than my tear ducts.

The sound of someone sharply clearing their throat startles us apart. Oliver whips around, surprised to find Christa there. "Damn, Christa. You scared me. Sorry, I didn't see you."

He really didn't. He had no idea she was even in here when he approached me and held my face and kissed me. He's not even here for show. He came for Layla. He came for me.

Christa glares at the two of us, then spins on her heels, storming out of the room without so much as a word to Oliver.

"Nice seeing you again, Christa," I call after her. "We're a hot beat away from besties, I think," I finish to Oliver.

"Wow. You have a snarky side I'm only just starting to learn about."

I sigh, sagging into his side. "I don't really. I'm just living out my teenage dream of talking back for once. That woman really hates my guts."

"Lucky us. Imagine if she liked you? I still say we both dodged a bullet getting away from the Christas and the Noras of this world."

I laugh at that, giving myself thirty seconds to enjoy the feel of his body against mine, the incredible scent of his cologne before I force myself away. Trust me when I say it's not easy.

"I made the call already," Oliver says to my back as I walk back to the window. "If she gets admitted, it's full boat including her tablet, laptop, books, uniforms. Everything for all four years. And since we both know she'll get in, it's as good as done."

I gasp. "What? How?" That's definitely not part of any scholarship I've heard of.

"I have connections. Let's just say that."

My insides quiver as my hand meets the glass pane. "Thank you, Oliver. I... thank you."

My eyes close, a tear finally leaking out. But that's it. Only that one is allowed to escape. My heart is attempting to explode from my chest and jump into his, while I do everything I can to hold it back. To compartmentalize. To resist just a little longer.

"Am I allowed to take you ladies to lunch after this?"

"I'm positive Layla will insist on it."

I can practically hear him smile. "Good, because I have a surprise for her that you might not be so jazzed about."

"What's that?"

Before he can answer, the door opens for the third time, only now Layla has returned along with two of the people she interviewed with. She has a triumphant gleam to her eyes and my breath quickens. Oliver goes straight over and shakes their hands, thanking them for their time. I do the same, nearly sagging with relief when they tell Layla they'll see her soon. They tell me they'll be in touch with their final decision shortly and that's that.

We're excused.

But the moment the three of us hit the path that leads to the parking lot, Layla lets out a loud squeal. "I totally rocked it. No joke. I'm in for sure."

Layla does another squeal, launching herself into my arms, and I wrap mine around her, holding her tight. "They haven't fully accepted you yet, but I'm so proud of you. So, so proud. Mom and Dad would be too."

She squeezes me harder with that. "Thank you for this."

I still haven't told her that Oliver is helping to get her a full scholarship instead of a partial. But she's the one who got herself here. Not me. Not Oliver. "You did this, Layla. It was all you."

Oliver joins us, hugging us both, telling Layla that she's kick-ass. She's going to fall in love with him too. She already talks to him like a big brother. Calls and texts him, obviously. I'd say her love for him is something she'll outgrow, but Oliver Fritz isn't a someone you get over or grow past.

Once he's in, he's in. That's it.

I wipe at my eyes and Layla does the same, both of us smiling stupidly at each other. "When you get your admissions letter, we'll celebrate. I'll splurge on ice cream sundaes at that place you like."

Layla lets out a whoop, fist pounding into the air.

"But first, how about a ride on Frosty?"

"What? Are you for real?" Layla asks Oliver, eyes wide. I should have known. This is what he meant when he said I wouldn't be so jazzed. I love Oliver's family. I love his mom. His dad is cold to me, but whatever. I don't fault him for that. But I hate lying to them if I can avoid it and going there means I can't avoid it. But Layla deserves a treat, so I'll keep my mouth shut and smile my way through it.

"I told my mom where I was headed today, and she invited you to come over after for lunch and a ride."

"She has her surgery tomorrow," I say. "Is she sure she wants company?"

Oliver takes my hand, helping me into his car since Layla and I took the bus here. "I think that's exactly why she wants company."

I suppose she needs the distraction Layla presents. I had already taken today off and couldn't arrange for tomorrow because tomorrow is an OR day. But lucky for me, Mrs. Fritz, who makes me call her Octavia, is having her surgery at Brigham, which is where we have our surgeries scheduled tomorrow. I'll be able to pop over and see Oliver and his family on my lunch break. I haven't mentioned it yet because I'm worried I won't get the time if our surgery runs late.

Plus, he hasn't exactly asked me to come.

Yet I can't help wanting to be there for him. The way he is for me. The way he was here today for Layla. It's a little bit dangerous. But despite my crush—because juvenile or not, I will not call it by any other name—I like to imagine that Oliver and I have become friends. That he genuinely cares about me and about Layla.

Same as we do for him.

And maybe I'm also hoping that when this ruse between us is over, he'll continue to seek us out from time to time. Kinda like he said. For Layla's sake, of course. Not for me. No, I need to keep my thoughts about him in check before they get ideas and start sprouting roots and wings and teeth and legs and I find myself growing into something that only exists in my head.

But there's something about him. Something I've tried to fight since the first day I met him when I was just twelve. Something I felt spring to life the moment I saw him again at the reunion. Something that, despite my ardent denial, won't be thwarted. It destroyed me the second he walked into that waiting room today.

I need to get under wraps. Like this very second.

Before I go and do something stupid, like fall in love with my fake fiancé.

Oliver ♥

Tomorrow might become one of the worst days of my life. At least, that's how I'm prepping myself. My mother is undergoing a double mastectomy and partial lymphadenectomy to hopefully excise her cancer. If all goes well, she will stay in the hospital overnight. She will heal from her surgery. Then exactly one week later, she will start a rigorous round of chemo that will strip her of her hair, make her physically ill, cause her to lose weight and her appetite, and there are zero guarantees that any of this will work at eliminating her cancer.

We aren't most families.

We're the Abbot-Fritzes.

Billionaires. Boston icons.

Stupid fucking influencers, as Amelia likes to call us. Healthcare providers. Doctors and nurses, and that's what fucking hurts the most. I'm a doctor and I can't prevent my mom from having breast cancer. I'm a doctor and I can't ensure she survives.

Our mom is our glue.

Our guiding force and light.

We were raised by both my parents, not a nanny or a fleet of hired caretakers. But mainly by our mother. She read to us. Played with us.

Taught us German, French, and Spanish. Educated us on how to exist in the world we were born into. She was tough and fair.

That makes us a rarity in our world. We had staff and nannies. But they were only there when my mother couldn't be. My parents love each other. My parents love us. And because our family is as close and tight-knit as we are, this is gutting us.

Gutting me.

I think that's why I ditched out on work today and went to Wilchester. Yes, Layla asked if I'd come when I asked for her interview details. Yes, I knew Amelia would be there and seeing Amelia, regardless of how fleeting or the circumstances surrounding it is like fresh air my lungs never knew they needed to breathe. Yes, I wanted to ensure that the administration people saw me after the conversation I had with them that will never, and I mean fucking ever, reach Amelia's ears. She must never know what I've done to ensure Layla's placement.

But I also went because I needed an escape.

A distraction that work just couldn't provide me.

A way to shut off my brain, to stop feeling *this*.

I needed Amelia.

I needed her eyes. Her smile. Her warmth. Her fucking sass and reserve. I fall asleep with her on my mind, my cum that belongs to fantasies about her squirting onto my chest. I wake with visions of her eyes. Her fucking eyes haunt me like a sexy dream, just out of reach.

I don't know what's going on.

I definitely can't explain it.

So I can hardly be blamed when I take her hand and guide her up the stairs of the west wing of our house, along the corridor and past my siblings' rooms. All the way down to my room.

"What are we doing?" she asks. "What is this?"

My mom has Layla. My father is working in his study. The staff are all either doing their thing or in the residence. It's just us. "I want to show you my bedroom."

She cocks an eyebrow at me.

"What? Have you ever seen it? It's like a piece of Oliver Fritz history."

"Are there pictures of naked women glued to your walls?"

"Not glued."

"Oliver.

"Amelia. My beautiful fiancée. I want to show you my room." And possibly kiss the hell out of you even though that's against our rules. Maybe go down on you because the taste of your pussy in my memory gets me harder than any naked woman ever could. I want her to ride my face and scream out my name.

I certainly won't be thinking about anything other than her if she does that.

These rules have been killing me. I had one night with Amelia, one absolutely incredible, out-of-this-world night, and I'm not allowed a repeat? Not even allowed to cop a feel?

Fuck that shit.

It's like someone dangling a delicious piece of candy in front of you and telling you you're a diabetic now and can no longer eat it. It's tragic is what it is because she's right here. And she looks sexy as all fuck in her black pencil skirt, cream blouse, hair pulled up, and heels. She's even wearing her glasses today.

She is my sexy librarian fantasy come to life.

My fingers toy with the ring on her finger as I open the door, leading us in. Another unexpected thing. I like seeing my ring on her hand. It's my brand. It says, property of Oliver Fritz, now back the hell off. No other man will touch her while she's wearing it. Again, who knew I was so jealous and possessive? Just the thought of her boss asking her about her weekend plans turned me into a cookie buying monster.

Amelia steps through the door, and I shut and lock it behind me. Why? Because right now, I feel like a teenage boy having her in here. A teenage boy who always had a secret crush on this nerdy redhead. She was the first girl I orgasmed to. Right there in that bed.

Now I want to return the favor by making *her* orgasm there.

She moves cautiously throughout the room, almost like she's

afraid to touch anything, but her eyes are everywhere. They're all over my dresser. My bookshelf loaded with college and med school textbooks and old sports trophies. My walls sans naked women but filled with famous quarterbacks. My bed with the thick blue blanket and matching plush pillows.

Then something catches her eye, and she gasps, walking briskly toward it and reaching out to touch the glass of the framed picture. "This is the 1999 All-Star game at Fenway. Ted Williams came out and Pedro Martinez struck out five of the six batters he faced, earning MVP of the game. I was only six, but I remember staying up late with my dad to watch it. It was a big deal."

I love how much she loves the Sox. I love how she's obsessed because it's something she did with her dad. Stepping in behind her, my hands find her hips, my lips the crook of her neck where I take a deep inhale.

"I was there," I whisper into her.

Another gasp. "You were?"

"I was. My family has a box at Fenway. I'll take you some time," I promise as I lick her neck.

She shivers against me and that right there, that tells me she feels this too. Our night together aside, if she wasn't into me, I wouldn't affect her the way I do. I make her nervous and excited.

I make her tremble. I turn her on. Same as she does for me.

"Oliver." It's a rasp coated in desire.

"Mmmm." My lips trail slowly up her neck, soft, open, kisses that make the rise and fall of her chest go faster. I lick at her carotid, feeling her pulse thrum. My girl wants me.

"We..." Hard swallow. "We shouldn't be doing this."

Needy hands glide up the fabric of her shirt, over her taut stomach, until I'm cupping her full breasts through her thin blouse. "Worried we'll get caught," I husk into her ear. My cock presses into the seam of her ass, my thumbs brushing her hard nipples. She moans, and I thrust into her, unable to stop my reaction to that sound. That fucking *sound*!

"I. We..."

"I want you so bad." Nip. Bite. Squeeze. "You're so fucking sexy, Amelia. I can't get enough. I want to lift up this skirt. This sexy as fuck skirt that instantly got me hard when I saw it. I want to drop to my knees and bury my face in your pussy. Lick you till you gush your wetness all over my face and cry out my name."

She moans again and I growl in return, a goddamn animal where she's concerned.

She spins in my arms, her hands getting lost in the back of my hair as she drags my mouth down to hers. I groan into her, my tongue demanding entrance and just as I get it, she rips herself back. Our eyes lock, loaded with tension and heat, the air crackling between us.

"I said no more kissing. This is a lot more than kissing. We're not supposed to do this."

She takes a step back and I take a step forward, stalking her. I wonder if she's aware she's headed in the direction of my bed. "But we want to."

Her head shakes, some of those beautiful red strands falling free from her bun, framing her face. "We set boundaries."

"That I'm about to break."

"Oliver."

I smirk at her attempt to be reprimanding. "Amelia, do you have any idea the things I want to do to your body right now? The way I want to touch you and taste you and fuck you?" Her breath hitches, her chest heaving as a trickle of red climbs up her neck, landing firmly on her cheeks. "I used to jerk my dick right there," I point to my bed behind her, "thinking about your beautiful tits. Your wild red hair all over me. Your cum drenching my fingers and cock."

Black eclipsing gray eyes beg me to stop.

"Do you really want me to stop?"

Maybe I should. But I want her. I want her like a man obsessed. Ever since she opened up to me at dinner. Ever since she came to my office. Ever since she sought me out. A switch has flipped in me. Now it's her. It's all her all the goddamn time. And if she wants me too... everything else we can figure out.

"I... I don't know."

"How does what I told you make you feel?"

She licks her lips, taking another step back until her knees hit the side of the bed, making them buckle and her body fall, catching herself with her hand so she's not sprawled out for me. Shame.

"Scared," she admits, staring up at me with those eyes, dark and burning like coal.

Stepping into the narrow opening between her legs, I push her until she falls onto her back. My body climbs over her, holding my weight up with my hands, my knees on either side of her hips. I watch her for a moment, just stare into her eyes. She is scared, and the longer I stare at her, the more I understand it. I don't get involved. I don't get attached.

But she's looking at me like she's hoping I'll reconsider.

I see the potential, that's for sure.

For that reason alone, I should get up and walk out of this room. But then I wouldn't have her. And I think I want her more than I don't want to be involved or attached. I could say something stupid like we'll just take it slow or keep it casual. I could tell her the truth: I don't fuck women I can see my future with.

But I can't make the thoughts form. I can't make the words come out.

She's not casual and I'd never be able to take it slow. And my future? The more time I spend with her, the more she seems to hold it in her fist.

By coming to my office, she eviscerated all my doubts. All the bullshit Nora spewed at me. Amelia's just afraid. That's all this is. That's why she was avoiding me. But she's only afraid because she feels this too. I saw it in her eyes that day and every moment I've been with her since. It's not fake. It's not pretend.

This, right here, it's as real as it gets.

"Do you want me?" I ask, my voice husky, suddenly just as scared as she is. A tremor of apprehension rolls up my spine like an icy warning. But still, I don't move. I wait, needing her answer. Needing her more than I need my scars to keep me locked away and sane.

"Yes," she says, voice trembling. "That's why I'm scared."

Her vulnerability destroys me and before I can stop it, I sink down, pressing her into the mattress and covering her lips with mine. "Me too," I whisper into her as my tongue rolls with hers, claiming her mouth in a feverish kiss.

"I don't want you to be charming," she tells me. "I want you to be real."

"Baby, I've never been more real and less charming with anyone in my life."

I'm not sure anyone has ever liked me for me before. Not even Nora. But Amelia does. She looks at me in a way no one else ever has and it's like a tonic to my damaged soul. A drug I never knew I wanted to be addicted to. I never realized how badly I wanted someone to see me, to actually give a fuck until she came along.

A hazy smile curls her lips and then I go back in, deeper, needier, rougher. I grind in an upward thrust between her legs, hitting her in just the right spot that makes her nails dig into my shoulders. Sweet lust tears through my body, my movements wild and frantic.

My mouth trails down her jaw, her neck, my fingers poking at the buttons on her blouse, undoing one at a time when what I really want to do is rip them apart and watch them fly.

I make it to the third one, getting a flash of smooth skin and gorgeous swell, my teeth grazing along the peekaboo of lace when someone jiggles the handle of my door.

Shit. The two of us spring apart like we've been electrocuted. Frantically Amelia sits up, buttoning her blouse and attempting to fix her hair that is in such unfixable disarray I nearly laugh. She's not though. I can tell she finds no humor in this at all.

"Who is it?" I call out.

"It's me," Layla says. "Why is the door locked? Your mom had me come up to tell you that lunch is ready."

"Oh, is the door locked?" I say. "Weird. Hold on." I run my hands through my hair, fixing my clothes and adjusting my harder than steel dick so I don't give Layla the fright of her life. "Take your hair down," I whisper to Amelia as I slowly rise off the bed. I give Amelia a minute as I make my way over to the door, placing my hand on the knob. Amelia is standing now, raking her fingers through her tangled hair, quickly redoing it into a ponytail.

But she won't meet my eyes and I open the door.

Layla stares at me with suspicion. She is fourteen, after all, and no fool by any stretch. "What were you doing in here?"

"Showing Amelia my room. I wanted to show off my football trophies and my big textbooks." I can't fight my grin. "I must have hit the lock button by accident."

Amelia's facing the bookshelf, her face still flushed as hell, but that might also have something to do with the fact that her little sister nearly caught us. Still, she's not looking at me.

Not even as she finally turns around and asks Layla, "How was riding Frosty?"

And just like that, Layla's focus shifts from us to the horse she rode. She launches into a step-by-step account of how she rode Frosty and how my mom taught her to post and said she was a natural. Amelia attempts to race past me, following after Layla, who is still going strong. I try to grab her hand, to pull her back, to get her to look at me, but she shrugs me off, and just like that, my heart plummets.

Shit. I think I just seriously fucked up.

18

Amelia ♥

After Layla nearly caught us making out in Oliver's room, I couldn't get away from him fast enough. It was like a slap to the face. A bucket of ice water I was immensely grateful for was dumped on me. I get lost too easily with him. Lose my head and my focus.

But today is different.

Today his mom is having surgery.

The hospital is actually buzzing with it. The entire Fritz clan is up in the surgical waiting room. And I'm not. I'm stuck in the OR with Sagginalls, who for all his concern for me the other day, has made remark after remark about how I'm not with them despite the fact that I couldn't get the day off.

Trust me, I tried.

I texted Oliver, letting him know I was thinking about him and his mom. That I wanted to be there and that I would try to run over and see him in between surgeries. I didn't get that chance. Sagginalls had it out for me today evidently because he pushed up surgical times for some patients or lingered longer than necessary on others.

I don't know if it was intentional or not, but it felt that way.

Luckily, on Fridays, we end around three and after scrubbing out at lightspeed, I fly down the hall, racing as fast as I can to the waiting room only to smash into someone. I nearly go down but am instead saved as a set of hands grab my shoulders, steadying me.

"I'm so sorry," I exclaim, brushing my hair from my face to find myself staring into a pair of green eyes that match Oliver's. "Rina. Hey. How's your mom? I hate that I wasn't there today. I tried to get off work, but I couldn't. We just finished up and I got here as fast as I could."

Rina waves me away. "It's fine. Relax. She did great. We won't know all the details until the pathology report comes back, but her doctor thinks he was able to excise all the cancer. She's resting comfortably upstairs. My dad is with her, and she kicked the rest of us out. I just came back to grab the sweater I forgot in the waiting room."

I sag with relief. "I'm so happy to hear that. Wow. That's fantastic news."

"It sure is. Were you meeting Oliver? I think he already left with Carter."

I shake my head. "I texted him earlier, but I haven't even checked my phone to see if he replied." As much as I hate to admit it, I'm glad he already left. Otherwise, I'd have to see him. Talk to him face to face. He texted last night asking if everything was okay and I replied back that it was, but it's not. Not at all.

"Perfect. Then you can come with me. I need a drink. And some seriously greasy bar food and I'm guessing you're right there with me on that."

I hesitate because I seriously am right there with her. Layla is sleeping at Stella's tonight.

Landon called me last night and informed me that Stella had already invited Layla over for the night. I told him that with everything going on with his mom, that I would take the girls instead, but he told me it would be a nice distraction having them around, so I relented.

But with everything going on right now, I'm not sure how close I should be getting with his family.

"Let me rephrase," she says, grabbing my arm and tugging me along with her. "We're going to my place, changing our clothes, opening a bottle of wine as we do, and then going out. No arguments. You're coming. I'm meeting Margot, Halle, and Aria at The Hill and I know they're going to want to see you."

***

An hour later, we stagger into The Hill. And when I say we, it's really more me. Rina opened a bottle of wine as she said she would and poured me two-thirds of it. Then she proceeded to style me all up with hair and makeup and clothing and heels—heels that no sane human would ever wear. Oliver texted that he was out with Carter and that he was fine.

That was it.

We've officially hit the strained stage of this arrangement. And it's my fault because I freaked out. I've been telling myself it's the way it has to be, but it has my insides twisting up all the same. I told him from the start that intimacy confuses things. I told him I don't do one-night stands or meaningless sex.

So what the fuck, Oliver? What game are you playing with me?

I will fall for him and then what will he do?

"Oh, good, they're already here." Rina points to a booth along the back wall. Halle Hughes, who is married to Jonah, Oliver's boss, Aria Davenport who is the sister of Rina's boyfriend, Brecken, and Margot Cady, an ED nurse, are waiting on us. They all stand up, hugging me, and then Rina, asking a million questions about her mom.

Rina fills them in as she goes about ordering a round of cocktails for the table, telling everyone tonight is all on her. I don't know if she's doing this for me because she knows I can't afford it—cue the embarrassment—or if because she means it when she says it's good Karma and she needs all she can get with her mom.

All I know is that trays of food and drinks are delivered, and we're all digging in with gusto, toasting to Rina's mom as we go. By the time we're finished with our first round and Rina is ordering the second, I'm rocking a serious buzz.

It's also when Aria gets a wicked gleam in her blue eyes. "Tells us how being engaged to the fabulous Oliver Fritz is going."

They all know it's fake. In fact, the only people who don't seem to know it's fake are Oliver's parents, my boss, and the media.

"Fine," I lie, trying to hide it by taking another sip of my martini that is flowing like water down my throat. Who knew alcohol could taste this delicious while destroying the brain cells I didn't really want to use tonight anyway?

They must read it instantly because Margot says, "Uh oh. What happened?"

"Nothing," only it comes out as a squeak. Kinda high-pitched. A bit slurred.

Halle snorts. "Right. You do realize we all know Oliver. That's his sister—" she points to Rina "—and I work with him, so you're not fooling any of us."

"Sure, I am," I argue. "In case you've missed the last two weeks of my life, I've become an impeccable liar."

"Not so much," Rina chimes in, attempting to nudge my shoulder only to miss and fall into the table, nearly spilling all our drinks. Clearly, I'm not the only one drunk here tonight. She straightens up, rolling her eyes at herself. "Now spill it. Since I nearly just did."

"Um. I'm not sure I should."

"Oh my god!" Aria points to me. "You're blushing. Like harder than Halle ever blushes, and the girl makes a tomato look like an onion." She shakes her head. "Did that make sense?"

"It did," Halle grumbles. "And thanks. But she's still right. You are blushing worse than I do. From one redhead to another, we can't hide anything, so it's best to let the alcohol do the work for you and tell us everything."

They're right. My face is a fireball of embarrassment. "But..." I bob my head in Rina's direction, pointing at her in case they miss my not-so-subtle hint. "That's his sister and the things I need to say are not PG-rated."

"Oh, please," Margot admonishes, waving me away. "I'm engaged to Aria's ex. Rina is dating Aria's brother. Halle is married to her boss. We obviously have no limits here, so just tell us, because now we have to know. Especially the non-PG stuff."

"Wow," I muse, staring at each of them. "You guys are more of a mess than I am."

Rina shakes her head at me, lifting a chip and popping it in her mouth, talking as she crunches. "I seriously doubt that. You're fake engaged to my brother, Dr. Scandalous Nurseizer himself. That should legit be his full name, and I've heard it all before when it comes to him. He's a talker. Anything you tell us that makes me want to throw up and cut off my ears I'll just pretend is about someone else."

I meet her eyes. "You sure?"

"Yes," Aria answers for her. "She's fucking sure. Now tell us and I want all the romance book drama."

"I'm a disaster," I admit, sagging back against the booth as the words tumble from my lips without restraint. "This whole thing is messing me up so bad. I'm sleeping like shit. Having trouble eating. I'm a ball of nerves. I have no idea what's real and what's not anymore. Oliver and I go out and it's great. But is it great because we're clicking as friends? Because we're doing this all for show? Or because something else is actually going on? The media takes all these pictures of us, and they print all these things about me, about us, and my boss goes and says shit. And I'm so confused. Did I already say that?" I scrunch my brows together, unable to remember, before getting over it just as quickly. "Anyway, I really like Oliver. Like a lot and I'm trying so hard not to because he's fucking Oliver, right? I mean, what you said." I point to Rina. "He's Dr. Scandalous. The man who plows through nurses and women like he's playing a game of beat the clock. But then he said some stuff I can't get out of my head and yesterday he pinned me down on his childhood bed and whispered the dirtiest things anyone has ever said to me and got me so hot and bothered I nearly forgot about my rule of no sex. Luckily my sister knocked on the door, interrupting us and saving me from making a huge mistake."

I finish my rant, slightly out of breath and even more upset than when I first started only to find three sets of wide eyes pinned on me, mouths agape, slightly horrified like I just told them they canceled Bridgerton before season two comes out.

Rina is the first to snap out of it, taking a hefty sip of her drink. "I think you need to tell him everything you just told us."

I shake my head. "I can't do that. Because then he'll know I like him and tell me I'm crazy and that it's just some fun he was trying to have. Just how our night after the reunion was only meant to be fun. Oliver flirts. He fucks. He moves on. I can't do that because I won't be able to move on the way he will. It's like my heart is intricately linked to my vagina. Once it's penetrated, that's it and both end up getting fucked."

Margot points at me while staring at Rina. "Did you know she was like this? Like one of us?"

Rina snorts out, stuffing her face with more chips. "Obviously. Why do you think I had her to my dinner party Wednesday?"

"God, I was so like this with Jonah it's crazy," Halle says, her finger running along the rim of her drink. "We had our one-night and then tried to resist, but there was no resisting because we were too hot for each other. You and Oliver are like that. Ready to rip each other's clothes off and hump like bunnies. Not much you can do to stop that once that train gets going."

"Okay," Rina says with an exaggerated gag. "I know I said I'd pretend we weren't talking about my brother, but I think just threw up in my mouth."

"Sorry," I grumble sheepishly.

"Don't apologize," Aria demands, tapping her nails on the table. "She's done way worse to me about Breck. But Rina is right. You do need to talk to him. It sounds like the feeling might be more mutual than you think."

"He's told me he never wants to put himself out there again after what his ex did to him. I'm just setting myself up for the fall if I do that."

"I don't know about that," Halle muses. "I work with him. I see him three days a week and he's a different man since you came along. He doesn't flirt with anyone. He doesn't look at any of the nurses. None. And it's not even like he's playing a part. It's like he doesn't even see them anymore. Other women no longer register. I'm not the only one who has noticed it either. Trust me, it's all the nurses talk about. He also bitched out his ex about you when she came to see him at work."

"What?" I cry out. "Nora came to see him?"

"Yep. On Monday. You could hear him throughout the halls. Then he stormed out of the room, slamming doors, and scaring the crap out of all of us. Oliver never loses his cool like that. She was saying shit about you, and he lost his mind on her. We could all hear it. Unfortunately, the walls are paper-thin, and they weren't exactly quiet."

Monday. That's when I was ghosting him. And Nora came to see him? I can't believe he yelled at her like that. About me. My heart starts to race around my chest, clumsily bumping into my lungs and making it hard to breathe. The things he said to me... could he actually—

"You need to go talk to him," Margot jumps in, cutting off my train of thought. "Like now. This minute. No more putting it off. In fact, I'm ordering you an Uber."

"No!" I exclaim.

"Yes," the others chirp in response, excitement carrying in their voices. "Go to his place. Ask him what's up and then spend the night with him," Halle finishes.

"Here." Aria pushes the remains of my martini closer to me. "Finish that up and then go give that hot doc a piece of your mind. No more games. No more messing around. Time he learned how to be a grown-ass man."

I swivel to find Rina, my body already shaking with nerves as I attempt to build myself up to what they're saying. What I know I'm risking by doing this. My heart won't survive Oliver breaking it. It's already too damaged. Too scarred.

She nods at me, dropping her hand onto my shoulder and squeezing. "They're right. You need to go and figure this out. It's time Oliver gets over what happened with Nora. That was years ago and you're not her. You're nothing like her. Just don't break his heart, okay? He'd never survive that happening to him twice."

Wasn't I just thinking the exact same thing about myself?

God, am I actually considering this? Going to his place at this hour and telling him how I really feel?

And what if he doesn't feel the same way back? What if they're wrong about all this?

I lift the remains of my martini, down it in one swift move, and slam the glass down on the table before wiping my mouth with the back of my hand. I guess there's only one way to find out.

19

Oliver

After the day I've had, I'm in no fucking mood for this. For the incessant banging on my door, that can only be Carter on the other side. No one else would continue to *bang, bang, bang*, despite my not answering. *It's midnight dickwad, and I don't want to hear any more.* He berated me all through dinner and drinks about Amelia. So did my other asshole brothers.

About how I should leave her alone. Stop pressing her physically. Keep our relationship purely platonic and distant so this arrangement stays clean and uncomplicated.

"She's essentially a single mom," Carter had said. "And you don't fuck around with single moms. You respect them enough to do the right thing by them."

I hated every word. Because he was right. I should back off Amelia. I should let her be. And until I figure out exactly how to do that, I'm keeping my distance from her. But that doesn't mean I want to.

So, yeah. No. I don't want to answer the door for round two.

"Go away, asshole," I yell through the door.

The banging instantly stops. Then I hear someone clear their throat. Only that doesn't sound like Carter.

"Sorry," the soft female voice says. "Your doorman just told me to knock and ring until you opened the door. Said that with a place as big as yours, you might not hear me." Then I hear her breath hitch. "I didn't ring the bell though." Her slurred words crack on that last part like she's about to break into tears.

Dammit. What the hell are you doing here, Amelia?

I swing the door open to find her pressed against the doorframe, her eyes red-rimmed and bloodshot with smears of mascara beneath. More of her hair frames her face than is held back in her low ponytail. Her ill-fitting blouse hangs limply off one shoulder and she's holding her heels in her hand like her feet hurt too much to wear them.

She looks so small like this. So nervous and unsure of herself. So fucking pretty my chest clenches. And it's like everything my brothers said tonight, everything I resolved to do where Amelia is concerned, just zapped right out of my brain.

She's here.

"Hi," I say, fighting my grin. She's drunk. If I couldn't tell by her appearance, I can smell whatever sweet concoction she's been drinking on her breath.

She sighs. She also still hasn't looked at me. "Hi," she says to my hardwood floor. "I don't know what I'm doing here."

You wanted to see me, that's what. Warmth trickles through my veins.

"Your sister and her friends put me in an Uber. They told me to come here and talk to you. I listened because it seemed like a good idea at the time."

"Do you want to come in then?"

"Do you think I should?" She tilts her head as if she's actually considering this as a question. Her eyes make a trail up my body, starting at my bare feet, trickling along my legs, over my boxer briefs where my dick is starting to harden, up along my abs and chest. All the way up to my face. "You're naked!" she gasps, pinching her eyes shut, and shaking her head so fast she nearly topples over from making herself dizzy. "I mean, you're like that." She points blindly, waving her hand in my general direction. "I can't talk to you when you're like *that!*"

I can't resist. "Like what?"

"You have abs. So many hard abs. Like six of them. And your transverse abdominis. That's there too. But they're super muscular and indented. And of course. You know. What's lower and in between them."

I chuckle, no longer able to hold it back. "What's lower and in between my super muscular and indented transverse abdominis?"

She blushes more than she was even two seconds ago, her eyes still closed as she gnaws on her lips. But she folds her arms now, trying for indignant. "You know what's there. You don't need me to tell you."

"Oh no, baby. I think I do."

Her eyes flash open, staring directly at the appendage in question that is very happy to see her before snapping up to mine. "This was stupid. I... I'm going now. Sorry to have bothered you."

She starts to turn on wobbly legs, heading for the elevator when I reach out and grab her hand, stopping her. "I can't let you do that. You're drunk. Come inside and I'll make you some coffee and we'll talk. I'll go put on pants if that will make you feel better."

I hear her swallow, her back to me. "And a shirt. You need a shirt too."

Fuck, she's adorable. "And a shirt. Just don't go. Come in and stay." Stay forever, I think and shake it off, tugging her in and locking the door behind her in case she gets any crazy ideas like running out on me again.

With this one, I wouldn't put anything past her.

I take her hand and lead her to the kitchen, sitting her on one of the barstools, making sure she's steady because damn, she's drunk. She drops the heels to the floor with a heavy clunk, resting her face in her hands. Her eyes, so very wary, are following me.

I quickly grab her a glass of water and set it in front of her. She lifts it, taking a slow sip, all the while staring at me like she's not sure what to do or say next. Never did I expect Amelia to show up here tonight, but I'm sure as hell not complaining.

I missed her today.

Today was rough. It was terrifying.

And what I wanted was her there with me.

I'm scared about my mom. About what's going to happen with her. I had my family there, but they're not the same as Amelia. Just being near her makes my heart slow down and speed up. My mind relax and race. She both calms and excites me. Such a fascinating dichotomy that works so effortlessly it's almost preternatural. A high I feed off of and needed today to get me through when there were moments I wasn't sure I could.

I crouch to meet her eyes. "I'm going to change. You okay for a minute?"

She nods slowly, her eyes turning that smoky gray. That color they get when she's turned on.

"Are you going to stay?"

"That's why I'm here."

I smirk impishly. "I thought you were here to talk."

Her eyes hold mine as she says, "That too." And those words just went straight to my dick. Because there was so much suggestion in her low, raspy voice. Only she's drunk. And I won't let her do something I know for a fact she'll regret tomorrow in the light of day. I pushed her hard on my bed yesterday and then she pulled away from me completely.

"I'll be right back."

Bare feet slap loudly against the floor as I jog to my room, flipping on the light and grabbing the T-shirt and gray sweatpants I have still sitting out on the bench at the foot of my bed. I throw them on at lightspeed and then race back out to Amelia, whose head is now down, resting on the stone countertop.

I slow my pace, taking her in as I approach, running my fingers down her long, silky red hair, gently removing the elastic as I do. She's out. Head draped over one slacken arm, breathing heavily, and already drooling a little.

I chuckle. "I guess our chat will have to wait. Probably better since you likely wouldn't have remembered it anyway."

She doesn't make so much as a peep.

Sliding one arm under her knees, the other around her back, I lift my pint-sized woman up into my arms, cradling her against my chest. She shifts, sinking against me, her face falling into the crook of my neck where she emits a content hum.

My lips press into the crown of her head, taking her sweetness in for a moment before carrying her down the hall in the direction of the guestrooms. I pick the closest one with the biggest bathroom and walk us to the bed. She stirs but doesn't wake as I pull back the blanket and adjust the pillow, placing her delicately down and covering her up.

I run and grab the glass of water I had poured for her as well as two ibuprofen and set them both on the nightstand for her. Leaning in, I brush some of her strands back from her face, kissing her forehead. She grumbles something under her breath I can't make out, turning over onto her other side and tucking in the way a small child would.

And for a moment, I can't do anything other than stare at her.

At the woman who has managed to flip my world upside down in such a short amount of time.

"Do you know how much I'm starting to like you?" I whisper into the darkness, knowing she's asleep and doesn't hear me. "Do you know how much liking you like this scares the shit out of me? All of this is supposed to be fake but being with you... nothing has ever felt more real, and I have no idea how to make heads or tails of it."

The only sound is the gentle push and pull of her even breathing. I don't even know why I'm saying this. Why I'm allowing myself to even think it. The more I imagine her like that, the more my feelings for her solidify.

I scrub my hands up and down my face before dropping them to my hips.

"My brothers told me tonight to back off. To give you space and keep things platonic so I don't hurt you. But I think they have that the wrong way around. I should do that, so *I* don't get hurt. So I'm not such a fucking mess when you walk away. And you will walk away," I tell her, absolutely positive in that. "I'm a lot to take on and I see it in your eyes every damn time you look at me. The second this arrangement is done, you're gone." Exactly as Nora said she'd be. "And me? I'm stuck. Hung up on you. A moth to your flame, desperate for your heat and light even if it burns me. So yeah. Maybe they're right about that whole backing off thing."

I take a step back and then another, forcing my words into action.

I need to protect us both.

Amelia is a woman who has been ravaged by the ugly side of life. Who was forced to make choices she had never intended for herself. Even before that, life wasn't exactly kind to her. Or at least the people in her life weren't. Has she ever had it easy? Has she ever had a day when she didn't have to worry or feel scared or trapped? But she doesn't let it diminish her light. She doesn't let it steal her spark.

Maybe that's why I'm so crazy about her.

We're creating a world. A world of lies, yes, but a world for ourselves. A world where I get to see Amelia come to life in ways I'm not sure she ever has before. And in turn, she's dragging me out of a shell *I* hadn't realized I was living in. But is this a world I want to venture into when the shell I was tucked beneath was safe and easy?

I turn on my heel and shut the door behind me before walking across my dark apartment to my room. I strip down, back into my briefs, and climb into bed. Thinking about her. Wondering what made my sister and her friends stick Amelia in an Uber to come here and talk to me at this time of night.

What do you have to say, Amelia?

And what happens if it changes everything between us?

20

Amelia ♥

Until my dying breath, I will never tell Oliver that I wasn't asleep when he thought I was. I heard every word. Felt every ounce of emotion pouring from him. Yes, I was drunk. But his confession somehow sobered me.

It also solidified my resolve.

It was like with all his fears and worries, mine evaporated.

I have no idea if he'll go for this. If he's too set in his ways to risk that level of change. Even for something he clearly seems to want.

Oliver is most definitely worrying enough for the both of us. It tells me he's not going into this lightly. That he's thinking of putting his heart back on the line and wants to do that with me.

I'd be a fool not to run toward him instead of away.

Something I know in the deepest parts of my soul could never happen despite what he thinks and speaks. Yes, he is a lot to take on. His wealth is daunting. It makes me uncomfortable in so many ways. Especially as a woman who has been used to struggling to pay her own way for so long.

But I can't let our differences hold us back. Not anymore.

Even if he requires a push to get him there.

Sunlight streams through the window and across my face,

bathing me in a warmth I want to curl into. My eyes scrunch tighter before slowly blinking open, adjusting at a snail's pace, likely thanks to the alcohol leaving my system. I take in the water and ibuprofen he left for me and smile.

Yeah, Oliver, you're something special worth fighting for.

I drink the water down, complete with pills and use the bathroom, wash my face, and brush my teeth with the spare toothbrush on the counter. Then I pad silently down the hall, already half lost in the size of this place, until I find his room. It's dark in here, the shades drawn, and it takes a second for me to locate Oliver in his massive bed.

He doesn't look like he's wearing much under the covers, and I think that's a fantastic idea. I slip off my leggings and glance down. The blouse I borrowed from Rina is long—she has a few inches on me at least—settling around my midthighs. I toe my panties off too, kicking them atop my leggings and then unhook my bra. Sleeping in a bra is never fun. My breasts gratefully relax, and I nearly moan at how good that feels.

They'll feel even better in Oliver's hands. I already know what those talented things are capable of when it comes to my girls.

Before I lose my nerve, I force one foot in front of the other, my heart thrashing in my chest like a rock band. Oliver either hears me or senses someone in his room because he rolls to his back, rubbing a hand over his face before jerking half up, checking the time on the clock on his nightstand and then snapping over to me.

"Hey," he rasps in a sleepy voice that makes me shiver. He takes in my appearance quickly, blinking several times like he's not sure what to make of any of this. "What are you doing?"

Anxious anticipation seals my lips shut; my words trapped on my tongue. Instead, I draw back the covers and, without invitation, climb in beside him. The bed is soft and warm, and smells like him. Like something spicy, fresh laundry, and sandalwood. It's as if I've entered my own version of sensual heaven with the bonus of the man in it, staring at me with wide, wary green eyes.

"Amelia?" he questions as I slide across the bed until I'm directly beside him. I suck in a shaky breath, proud of how brazen I'm being, and force him onto his back while climbing over him, straddling his stomach.

My shirt covers everything, tucked between my legs, against my bare wet pussy, and I already know I'm going to have to not eat for two weeks so I can afford to buy Rina a new one. Oliver's gaze eats me up, his hands slingshotting to my hips, holding me firmly in place.

He's struggling. I can see it.

He genuinely thinks I'm going to let him get away with keeping his distance for both our sakes. I nearly laugh at that. My hand brushes through the dark strands of his hair, so soft and thick as it trickles through my fingers.

"I need words," he says, voice hoarse, jaw tight. "Every time we've been together like this, you get very silent. I have no idea what's going on in that beautiful head of yours."

He's right of course. Every time I've been anywhere close to intimate with him, I lose my voice, my ability to speak. I've likely always been this way. The eternal wallflower. The quiet, reserved girl, miserably unsure of herself.

Not now. Not anymore.

"I like you," I say, sounding like I'm Layla's age, but not caring in the slightest. "I understand why you think you need to keep your distance from me. But I'm here to tell you I'm not gonna let you do it. I want you too badly to let you try."

I rock against him, his abs hardening, flexing against me at the perfect spot, causing a moan to slip out. I wasn't lying. I want this man fiercely. I want him to explore my body, knowing what it needs better than I do. I want him to seek out my heart, cherishing every thrum as it beats for him. I want him to learn the inner workings of my mind, understanding me in ways even I don't.

I've played it safe for so long and I'm fucking tired of it. What is life without risk? Even if you get hurt in the end? And I already know, Oliver is a risk I will never regret taking. Even if we do eventually end in ruin.

Wild, desperate eyes cling urgently to mine. "Tell me that again."

I smirk. "Which part?"

He licks his lips, eyes flickering to my hard nipples as they poke through the thin material of the blouse before they darkened with carnal desire. Then ever so slowly, they crawl up to mine, so goddamn intense my breath hitches.

"All of it," he demands. "That you want me as much as I want you. That we're done keeping our distance because distance between us is fucking stupid. Tell me you like me because I already know I like you more."

"I'm here, aren't I?" With that, I reach down and slip the blouse over my head, tossing it away, leaving me completely bare before him, on top of him, spread open wide. "I want you, Oliver. I want this to happen. And maybe I should have prefaced myself before I took off my clothes, but this will not end the way last time did. I will not run off, because as I told you that night, I don't do one-night stands. If we do this, we're doing this."

"We're doing this," he parrots, only he's saying it with meaning. A promise. A bond.

And with that, he shoots up, capturing my mouth with his, his hands diving into my hair, grasping the back of my head. My arms snake around his shoulders, feeling hard planes of muscle, learning every inch I was too scared to the first go around.

His mouth ravages mine, hot and needy, messy as hell as we clash with lips, and teeth, and tongues. I'm unraveling around him, unable to think, only able to feel. His hard chest against me. His hands all over. In my hair, down my back, squeezing my ass, toying with my breasts. His cock thrusts up, hitting the juncture between my legs and causing me to cry out in sweet agony. His boxer briefs have to go. The fact they're still on, covering what I need most from him, is driving me mad.

"Patience," he hums into me, grasping my hand and pulling it away from the elastic waist of his charcoal briefs. "I don't want to rush this."

I groan. "Except I only have until noon. That's when Landon is dropping Layla off back at home."

Oliver chuckles against the skin of my neck. "Amelia, it's not even nine yet. We have plenty of time. And then even more time because I will call Landon and have him drop Layla here instead of your place. I want you both to spend the day with me and then sleep over here tonight."

"You do?"

He nods. "Yes, but can we not talk anymore about Layla right now?"

I glance down at his briefs, and he cocks a teasing eyebrow at me.

"Right. Sorry." I give his dick a firm squeeze making him groan. "Better?"

"Much."

My mouth attacks his again, unable to get enough. Rough whimpers tumble one after the other from my lips as he finds my breasts, lifting their weight in his large hands and squeezing them without mercy.

My head falls back, my eyes closing as I succumb to the sweet bliss as he forces me to straddle the line between pleasure and pain. Nipping, sucking, biting on my hard peaks and tender flesh. I grind against him, unable to stop the motion, the ache between my thighs growing almost unbearable.

"Impatient little thing, aren't you?"

"Yes," I cry out as he bites down harder. "Yes. *Please*."

"Tell me what you want," he whispers against me, licking with the flat of his tongue up my neck until I shudder. "Do you want me to sprawl you out on my bed and fuck you with my tongue until you're screaming my name? Do you want me to tie your wrists behind your back and continue to punish these beautiful tits until you're begging for my cock to fill you up? Do you want me to take you over to my window and fuck you against it so all of Boston can watch? Tell me, baby. Tell me and I'll give you anything your beautiful body and mind desires."

I think I just passed out.

I have no idea how to respond. Dirty talking son of a bitch nearly just made me come from his words alone. I can't even. No one has ever talked to me like that. All the times I've had sex before him were in a dark room with little to no foreplay and sex that was over before it even started. Orgasms were few and far between. Dirty words and fantasies never even entertained. And yes, we're talking with the ex who I thought I was in love with.

"I... yes?"

"To which part?"

"Um. All of it?"

He grins against me, pinching and twisting my nipple until I writhe, needing more. "Fuck, you like it rough, Amelia. My crazy, sexy girl who is so prim and proper on the outside is such a dirty, dirty girl on the inside."

I glance down at his smoldering eyes, the darkest of jade green. "Is that a problem for you?"

"Baby, you have no idea how there for it I am. I want to do every wicked, dirty, sweet, and fun thing to you. You're mine now. No one else's. Only I get to do these things with you. Say it," he commands, but there is something else there. Something he's trying to hide but is betrayed in his eyes.

Nora cheated on him and then left him after he gave her everything.

I stare deeply into him, letting him see my soul. "Only you, Oliver Fritz. Only you."

He growls, throwing me back onto the bed and immediately covering me with his body. His mouth comes down in a searing kiss with a hint of sweetness on the back end. The kind of kiss that stays with you long after it's over. The kind of kiss you remember and hold on to because you know it might just be the best kiss you've ever had.

Oliver is greedy for me.

No one has ever been greedy for me like this before.

His lips trail down my neck, between the valley of my breasts, down my stomach until he's staring up at me between my thighs, his hands parting them. "I decided for you," he says with a devious grin. My eyebrows form a V of confusion until his tongue thrusts inside me and my head falls back on a moan. Suddenly it makes sense. He asked me what I wanted and fucking me with his tongue was on that list.

No complaints here.

My eyes close, body falling back, losing myself to a feverish intensity spiraling through my body. Oliver's tongue is relentless, his lips too as he sucks on me. Eating me out like he has all the time in the world. His rough stubble scratches against my sensitive skin as he laps at me, his tongue taking long swipes like a man starving. He circles my clit before plunging back in and my hands fly above my head, grasping the blankets, balling them up in my fists as I hold on for dear life.

Sounds I have no control over escape my lips, tumbling from me as waves of pleasure threaten to consume me. I'm so close and he must sense it because he plunges his tongue in over and over again until I reach the highest crest and then he takes my clit and sucks on it. Hard. I cry out, screaming from the intensity.

My hands abandon the bed, finding the roots of his hair, and I hold on like my life depends on it as sparkling bolts of heat and electricity shoot through me, one after the other in a never-ending assault of erotic bliss.

I fall back onto the bed, my limbs heavy. A dopey smile hits my face along with a bemused laugh. Jesus. "A girl can get used to that."

He chuckles, kissing along my hip bones, over my belly button. "Good. Because you taste fucking amazing, and I plan on doing that again later. Watching you come undone like that is sexy as hell."

"Mmmm." That's as much brainpower as I've got going right now.

"Now onto the rest of my plan."

My eyes blink open to find Oliver above me, his face right there. His wet lips meet mine only to pull back immediately. I lick my own, tasting myself and he grins wickedly. "Why didn't I act sooner? Why didn't I kiss you when I was putting sunscreen on your shoulders at my graduation party? I wanted to. I wanted to do more than that."

I blink, stunned by his words. "You did?"

"Amelia, I wasn't lying when I said I used to get myself off to visions of you. I always saw you. I always liked you. I just thought you were too good for me."

I let out an incredulous laugh. "Too good for you? I was the nerdy scholarship girl. The one no one liked or cared about. You were Oliver Fritz. God of our school."

He hitches up a shoulder like none of that matters. "You just seemed untouchable. Perfect in every way. I never knew how to talk to you, so I didn't."

My mind is reeling at this. His lips meet mine and then he's picking me up, dragging me off the soft, warm bed. "What are you doing?"

"The second part of what I said only I'm not going to tie your wrists. I'll have to do that another time because I'm going to need your hands to be free so you can hold on."

"Hold on to what?"

He places me in front of the large windows in his room and then with the press of a button, the shades slowly rise up, sunlight streaming in inch by inch as does the city surrounding us.

"Oliver?" My voice trembles. He was serious? There are buildings. People, if they looked, could stare right into his window.

He takes my hands and presses them to the cool glass. "You're gonna want to hold on."

The next thing I know, he's pitching me forward, lining his hard cock up with my soaking wet pussy, and then in one hot, deep thrust, he's inside me. My body tumbles forward from the impact, the air fleeing my lungs.

I gasp, fingers digging into the glass, trying to catch myself.

"Take a breath, Amelia. I've only just started."

His hands grasp my breasts, pushing them up and squeezing the hell out of them. His thumbs roll my nipples and then he unleashes himself in me. I try to speak. Try to say something. But I can't. The only sounds I'm capable of are moans and whimpers and cries. His hips piston into me, setting a relentless pace as he uses those strong thigh and ass muscles to fuck me.

His hot breath fans against my ear, the pressure between my legs and on my breasts consuming me. "Open your eyes, Amelia."

I shake my head and I feel his smile.

A rumbling groan hits my neck, his teeth biting into my flesh, and I moan so loud I'm shocked the windows didn't rattle.

"Open your eyes," he growls. "Are they watching you? Are they watching you get fucked so hard the only thing holding you up are my hands on your tits?"

"Oliver," tumbles out of me.

"There it is. I was waiting for that. Do you like this, Amelia? Knowing people are watching you like this? Their dicks hard and pussies wet at the sight of you?"

I shake my head. I can't. I can't... "Yes!" Why the hell that's such a turn-on, I have no idea, but it's driving me higher, taking me closer. My hands press into the glass so hard I'm worried about cracking it. It's all that's keeping me up, that and his hands as he said. My heart pounds like a drum.

"You feel so good, Amelia. So good. I can't get enough of you."

He pumps harder and harder, hitting that spot, that sweet fucking spot inside me. It is so good. So good I can't think. I can't breathe. I can only *feel*. Feel him as he abuses my breasts in ways I never knew I needed him to. As he consumes every inch of my body.

"Oliver," I say again, my voice unrecognizable. "I'm..."

"I know, baby. Hold on. Not yet."

Jesus. I don't know how much more I can take.

Sweat drips from his forehead onto my fevered skin, his cock sliding in and out of me, his hips and thighs never slowing. Not once. Not even to catch his breath which is harsh and ragged against me.

"You ready?"

And without waiting on my answer, one hand flees my breast and finds my clit. It only takes two circles, a tiny amount of pressure, and then I detonate. I soar. I scream, his name and God's name, and I can't stop. Every cell in my body is on fire, my limbs convulsing with the effort to remain upright.

Oliver holds on tighter, grunting and groaning, pressing me

against him tighter as he sinks in as deep as he can go one final time, his body stilling as he spills himself inside me.

"Fuck! Amelia, fuck!"

I shake, the feeling of this man like this inside me, losing his mind, practically pushes me over the edge again. I can't breathe. My heart has never beat like this before. Never.

"Fuck." He whispers it this time, his body relaxing some of its tension. His lips meet my neck, kissing gently. "Are you okay? Was it too much?"

I want to laugh at that, but I don't think I'm capable. "You have a dirty mouth and a dirty mind, Oliver Fritz. Can people actually see us?" Suddenly a wave of nerves takes over. As hot as that was in the moment, I don't think I actually want people to have seen us.

"No. Reflective windows. And I've never had a dirty mouth like this before. You bring out an animal from inside me."

"Good. I like that I bring that out of you. Only me."

"Only you," he says to me, his arms wrapping around my body, his dick still inside of me. "Give me ten minutes and we'll do that again. Only sweeter, slower. I want you, Amelia. I want you all the ways there are."

I close my eyes, allowing his words to sink in. Allowing myself to believe them. To believe in us. Hoping, praying, we can make it through this. Make it through this madness we've placed ourselves in. Needing this to be the start of us when us feels nothing short of impossible.

21

Oliver ♥

"**H**ow is she doing?" I ask my father, holding the phone up to my ear as I pace around my home office in a circle, repeatedly running a hand through my hair and likely making it fall out.

"She's okay. In a lot of pain and being stubborn about taking medication for it. But I managed to get some hydrocodone into her. She's sleeping now."

"And her drains?" I continue, trying to bring myself back to a baseline I can work with. Medicine. "What's the fluid like?"

"Oliver," my father reprimands. "Her drains are fine. She's doing fine. This was all to be expected."

Yeah, but her recurrent cancer wasn't, I want to say but hold my tongue. I love my father, but sometimes he's a bit too pragmatic. Kinda like Carter and Landon in that respect, or maybe they're like him. Whatever. I don't care. My mom being sick isn't something I'll ever be able to tolerate.

"Okay. Just call me if anything changes. I wish I could come—"

"No," he cuts me off. "She was clear about that. No visitors until she's up and feeling better."

I sigh, shaking my head as I continue to work a hole in my floor.

"It's not weak to be hurting and need the help of your family. She doesn't have to be like that."

"But she is. It's how she was raised. Her world is all about appearances, Oliver. Yours is too," he says as a warning. "Which reminds me, how are things with Amelia?"

"Good," I reply, grinning for the first time since I called my father about ten minutes ago, thinking about her this morning. "Really good." She's in the other room with Layla right now, playing Scrabble again since Layla loves to show off that huge brain of hers.

"And the girl? Did she get into Wilchester?"

The girl. That's what he calls Layla. "She hasn't gotten the official word yet, but it's looking that way."

My father huffs a breath into the phone. I haven't told anyone about what I did to secure Layla's scholarship. Wilchester was going to give Layla the full scholarship at my request, but only at the expense of another student. They told me point blank, they do not give full rides. In order for them to give one to Layla, they would have to take away from another student. Obviously, I couldn't allow that to happen, so I paid for the half not covered by the scholarship.

For all four years.

That includes a stipend for uniforms and any technology she'd be required to have.

Amelia has no idea, nor can she ever.

She'd never let that stand, and I know from listening to the two of them talk that a full scholarship is the only way Layla can attend Wilchester. As such, it wasn't exactly a difficult decision. I had promised Amelia Layla would get a full ride and she is. That's me holding up my end of the bargain, just not the way we discussed it.

But in addition to Amelia not knowing, neither does my family. First, it's none of their fucking business. Second, they'd have a lot to say about it, that again, is none of their fucking business. It was my choice, my money, and regardless of what happens between Amelia and me, I have no regrets about it.

Layla deserves this chance. End of story.

"I'm going to ask this again, what the hell are you doing with this woman?"

I grit my teeth, my hand fisting the ends of my hair. "Marrying her," I tell him, because this shit just pisses me off.

"I get it. She's beautiful and smart and different from the women you're used to," he drones in an almost mocking tone. "She doesn't throw herself at you or care about your money. Or so you claim. But how do you know that for sure, Oliver? She's a poor woman raising a teenager by herself, and you wouldn't be the first rich guy to be taken for a ride at the hands of a pretty face and determined mind."

"For the hundredth time, she's not like that. Not even a little."

"I hope you're right, son. I also hope you plan on having one hell of a prenup."

I hate everything my father says about Amelia, but I also know it comes from love and concern for me. Because he's right, there are plenty of men who attract pretty women and get manipulated simply because they're rich. And it's not like I can tell my father the truth of the situation, so all I can do is stand up for Amelia.

"When we get to that stage of this game, we'll figure it out," is my only response because we never will get there. We have a very real and firm expiration date. Something that is now complicated by what happened between us this morning. By the fact that we're now actually dating.

Another thing I'm trying to learn how to stomach and not freak out about.

I can't even ask my dad how he knew my mom was the one because he didn't. Their marriage was essentially arranged. The Abbots and the Fritzes got together and decided their children should wed for financial and power reasons. They only met four times before they said I do and to hear my mom tell it, it took them a long adjustment period to get to know each other and fall in love.

Which they did. Lucky them.

But it's not exactly the story you tell your grandchildren or write into a fairy tale.

"I'm crazy about her, dad. I wish you could be too."

"Once I know the real state of her heart and mind, then maybe I will be." My brows pinch in at that, at the way he phrased it. I'm about to ask him what exactly he means by that when he cuts in with, "I have to go. I think I hear your mother getting up."

"Okay. Send her my love."

"I will. Goodnight, Oliver. I love you."

We disconnect the call and for another few minutes, I continue my pacing, all the while listening to Layla and Amelia go back and forth, shit-talking the hell out of each other the way they do while thinking over my conversation with my father.

At first, when we started this whole thing, I wasn't sure I wanted my parents to like Amelia. I had decided that it would be better if they didn't form any sort of genuine attachment to her when I knew she wouldn't be in their lives very long.

But now... after this morning...

Exiting my office, I make my way down the long hallway to the great room where my girls are playing. I prop my hip against the far wall, watching them unnoticed. Layla is on her feet, doing her victory dance thing she likes to do, all swinging arms and hips.

Amelia is laughing, shaking her head. She's wearing a Red Sox T-shirt that is beyond old and ratty, as well as those pants that are made to look like player's pants. It's the most absurd looking outfit, but Amelia doesn't care in the slightest. The Sox are on, so that's how it has to be.

"I'm going to post you like this on Snapchat," Amelia teases Layla.

Layla scoffs. "Go for it. Tell the world how I whooped your butt at Scrabble. Again. Then I'll take a pic of you and show off how ridiculous you look in that get-up."

"Please, girl. This is a winning outfit, here. Besides, I let you win. How else am I supposed to boost your self-confidence though maybe I've overdone it at this point?"

"Ha! Nice try. No way on earth you were throwing that game. Did you not see that I got equalize and squeeze? Money. Boom." She holds out her fist before opening it like she's doing a mic drop.

"So modest, Layla," Amelia smarts with an indulgent eye roll as she goes about cleaning up the game, putting the letter back into the bag.

"You know if you keep looking like a weird Red Sox bag lady, Oliver won't kiss you."

I hold in my laugh, rubbing at my smile.

"He'll kiss me if the Red Sox win because I'm wearing this," Amelia throws back.

Layla drops down into the chair, helping Amelia clean up. "Now that you and Oliver have updated your status from fake to official, do you think he'd let me makeover my room?"

"We're still not actually engaged. Just... you know... casually seeing each other."

Casually. That word hits me hard.

She's not wrong and I get her saying that to Layla since we literally just decided to take things to the next level this morning, but for some reason, hearing her brush us off like that, stings.

I likely shouldn't be listening in on such an intimate conversation between sisters, but I can't stop myself either.

"So that's a no then?" Layla presses as they fold up the board and close the lid over the game.

"That's a no. We're not moving in here and you need to understand that people date and things don't always end with marriage and babies. I care about Oliver, but I worry about you getting attached to him when he and I might very likely not be forever."

It's like she just confirmed everything everyone has been saying about her. That the moment this arrangement is over, so are we, and she's gone. The thought of that pecks at the soft, gooey parts of me that still roil from Nora's betrayal. I take a step back and then another one, my secret words to her from last night hitting me all over again.

I was going to keep my distance to protect myself. But now, it almost feels too late for that.

"He's not Travis. Oliver won't hurt you the way he did."

Amelia stares down at the now-closed box. "I know he's not," she says, but the turbulence in her voice is unmistakable. Evidently, we both still have a lot of fear and trust we're working on.

"You like him, right?"

My pulse starts to race.

"Yes," Amelia answers Layla. "I like him. I like him a lot. He's an amazing man and I love being with him. But it's new, and like anything new, it's precarious. Especially given the situation we're already entrenched in. I'm just trying to protect us both."

"But you can't protect yourself from falling in love. Love is love, Amelia. It's the greatest thing in the world," Layla protests, her tone indignant, her thoughts innocent if not a little naive. "He's trying to help us. To take care of us. Oliver is your Prince Charming."

"A real princess doesn't need the prince to take care of her, Layla. A real princess does that for herself. Oliver is the best. No question about that. He's someone who will always care about you and be your friend. But if I ran blindly to him without considering the repercussions of something like that, I wouldn't be doing any of us a favor. I want things to work out with him, but you are my first priority, and I will always treat you as such. Does that make sense?"

"Yes," Layla says softly, staring at her sister. "I get it. I just want you to be happy the way you try to make me happy. You do everything you can and don't think I'm oblivious to it."

"Oblivious is a good Scrabble word," Amelia quips with a wry smile, clearly trying to change the topic, and this is when I take my cue to enter the room, having heard everything I need to.

"Who won?" I ask like I don't know.

"Who do you think?" Amelia stands up, taking the box off the coffee table and walking it toward me. "Girl kicked my butt, just ask her." She reaches me, placing her free hand on my chest and staring up into my eyes with so much warmth and concern, I now know beyond a shadow of a doubt I don't stand a chance. "How's your mom doing? I tried calling her earlier, but she didn't pick up."

"She's okay. In a lot of pain."

Amelia frowns.

"My dad is on it. Making her take her pain meds and rest. I don't think she'll let us come visit before she gets her drains out."

"If I can do anything, please tell me. I want to help."

I lean in and kiss her lips. Not even caring if Layla sees. "You can put Layla to bed," I whisper against her so only she can hear.

My thoughts right now are too chaotic, too scandalous to put to rest. I need to lose myself in her, with her. I need to look into her eyes as I sink inside her. I need to feel her body around mine. I need to snuff this fear out of both our hearts.

I need to stop thinking is what I need to do.

"Layla, Oliver and I need to talk. You good to go to bed?"

"Ugh. Gross. You could stop kissing when you ask me that. Oliver, I can't believe you're kissing her in that get-up. All she needs is a bunch of scruffy cats to complete the look."

I laugh, unable to stop it. "Did the Sox win?"

Amelia turns her head toward Layla, pointing her finger. "See! I told you. This outfit is everything."

"Not so sure about that," I say. "But you're adorable in it. Even if you do look like a crazy cat lady."

"Ha! *I* told *you*," Layla smarts, grinning from ear to ear. "Can I watch a movie on your massive setup in your media room?"

"Sure."

"Nothing rated R," Amelia adds.

"*Twilight*?"

"Deal," Amelia agrees. "And no burning the house down with popcorn."

Layla groans. "You keep harping. One time, Amelia. That was one time."

I interlace my fingers with Amelia's and glance over my shoulder in Layla's direction. "Pick up the landline and hit the pound key. Tell the person who answers that you want movie-style popcorn and whatever candy you like. He'll get it from the theater around the corner."

Layla shoots off the couch, fist-pumping into the air.

"Oliver—"

"Amelia, don't talk him out of it. Please." Layla holds her hands in supplication, begging Amelia with full-on puppy dog eyes. "Pretty please."

"Fine. But don't take advantage."

"I won't." She lets out a gleeful shriek.

With that, I drag Amelia behind me, all the way across the apartment. I don't care what Layla orders or if she takes advantage. All I know is right now, I need Amelia beneath me. My body inside hers. The door shuts, and I lock it, much like I did in my childhood bedroom. Only this time, there will be no interruptions. This time, I am going to fuck this woman six ways to Sunday.

"I heard you talking to Layla," I admit because suddenly, I don't like having secrets from her. Well, maybe just this particular secret.

"You did," she hedges, taking a step back and out of my arms. "Oliver, I said those things—"

"You're just looking out for her. For yourself. But it's like I told you this morning, we're doing this. And Layla was right. I'm not that guy. I'd never hurt you like that."

"Right back at you."

I inhale a shaky breath, those words, that promise slaying right through me.

She swallows thickly and then reaches down, pulling off her top. "I want to take us slow. I want to do this the smart way."

"And that involves you getting naked with me?"

"With any hope, regularly."

I grin like the devil at midnight, attacking her awful pants and sexy panties. Naked. Naked is how I like Amelia best. Bare and open and sweet and shy and frisky and dirty and wild and brazen and motherfucking perfect. This girl. This woman. She wrecks me.

Her body. Her mind. Her heart. All mine.

Fuck anyone who tries to argue it, including ourselves.

Two fingers reach down, rubbing up and down along her soft flesh. I tasted it this morning. I screwed her wild up against my window. But I told her I also wanted sweet, and I meant that. I want to look into her eyes. I want to feel her around me.

I want to get lost.

Firm hands grasp the backside of her thighs, just beneath her supple ass and then I'm lifting her, carrying her, placing her down on the bed, and with one swift motion, I'm inside of her.

She's wet. So wet and ready. No foreplay is even needed because I swear to all I will make her come so hard she sees stars. "Eyes on me," I tell her, cupping her jaw with my hand as I start to slide deeper into her, only to withdraw slowly, nearly to the point of leaving her body. "Have I told you about your eyes?"

She shakes her head, her red hair flying every which way.

"I love your eyes, Amelia." Thrust. "They stun me stupid." Thrust. "They knock me senseless." Thrust. "So beautiful." Thrust. "Just like you."

"Oliver." She grasps on to the back of my hair, tugging, holding on for a mercy I will not grant her. I want to feel her come undone. I want to bring her pleasure, so much pleasure there is nothing else. Plus, I think it's already been established that my name on her lips makes me harder than fucking steel.

"That's right, baby. It's just me here. Just me inside you."

My lips fall upon hers, turning our kiss into a caress, a sonnet of crazy-ass shit I have no business thinking at this point funneling through my chest. My body worships hers. My thrusts dominate both of us.

Lifting her up I flip her over, reentering her from behind with deeper, harder, longer thrusts. The headboard slams against the wall, *bam, bam, bam.* Her tits fly, jiggling and swaying, my hand coming down in a hard *clap* against her ass.

"Fuck! Oliver."

"Yes," I hiss, doing it again and again, alternating hands until pink prints are all I can see against her alabaster skin, my cock driving in and out of her. And God, what a fucking sight that is. My cock glistens, coated with her arousal, slipping and sliding into her tight heat. She holds me in, greedy, like she's afraid if I pull out, I'll never dive back in again.

One hand presses firmly into the mattress, the other wraps around her hair, tugging her head and neck back until my lips can reach the skin beneath her ear and along the slope of her neck. This woman makes me feral. Insatiable.

I position her head to the side, taking her mouth that way as I use my other hand to find her clit. She emits a deep, raspy moan into my mouth as I rub her in circles until she's a trembling mess beneath me. A gruff, desperate cry flees her lips that I quickly swallow down.

"I think I told you this was going to be sweet."

She half-laughs. "There's always next time."

"And a next time there shall be."

Moans and whimpers hit the air; her sounds the end of me. My balls draw up tight. My dick ready to explode.

"Harder, Oliver. I need it harder."

Fuck! I clench my eyes, lock my jaw, and breathe out through my nose as I slam into her, over and over, my fingers rubbing her until I feel her body start to lose control. Her sounds echoing off the ceiling. Her fists clutching my comforter, wrinkling it in her fists as her head falls forward on a harsh scream she tries desperately to muffle.

Her pussy convulses around me, milking my own release from my body until blinding spots of light cover my vision. I grunt, my face dropping in between her shoulder blades, my teeth biting down as I explode inside her, shooting out an orgasm like none I've ever had before. I fuck her until I can't, my body spent, my limbs boneless, and then I fall against her, shifting to the side and taking her with me, holding her back against my chest.

"I'm leaking."

I growl, my dick somehow finding life enough to jerk against her. I'm a beast of a man, utterly untamed.

"I like my cum leaking out of you."

"I got that impression."

"I'm possessive. Not gonna apologize for it."

She sighs, sagging back into me, so sweet and suddenly gentle and shy. "I like you possessive. It means you're mine."

My lips meet the crook of her neck. "You're mine too, you know. You and Layla both. I want you, Amelia. I want this." So much so I'll fight for it. Even when the odds seem stacked against us.

22

Amelia 🖤

This isn't what I expected. Not at all. In fact, it's way, way better.

I stand up and stretch out my limbs, the hot afternoon sun blazing down on my face, almost as if it's mocking my fair skin, the sound of the rowdy Fenway crowd loud, music to our ears even from up here in the Fritz luxury box. It's a slice of heaven.

Especially for a girl who has only ever sat out in the bleachers.

"Does anyone want anything?" I ask since we're in between innings. Weird as it sounds, you can't pee in the middle of an inning unless your team is losing and you need to change momentum. "I'm running to the restroom and then I'm re-lathering myself in SPF 50. I'm starting to char out here."

Layla's head pops up, her lips smeared with ketchup as she chews on her bite of hot dog. "I'm good," she grumbles with her mouth full.

"Do you want another beer?" I offer to Oliver just as he polishes off the last sip from his cup.

He glances down at the plastic and then up to me, debating. "Do you think it's bad luck if I switch it up?"

"Huh?"

"This was a Harpoon. And the first sip of it I took, the Sox got a triple and since I've been nursing it, we're winning. But I'm not really in the mood for another beer. I was thinking maybe a Jack and Coke instead."

"I think you get me," I tell him.

He grins. "I do. It's why you're going to pee now instead of before."

God, I think I love this man.

"I think you're fine with the drink switch up so long as you don't move seats. That's what our dad always used to say. The seat is the key to success. If they're losing, you switch it up. If they're winning, you don't mess with it."

Oliver considers this as seriously as any superstitious sports fan does and nods, his gray hat with the large red B on it bobbing up and down. "Right. That makes so much sense I don't know why I never considered that before." He looks to Layla. "Your father sounds like he was a very smart man. I'm sad I never really knew him."

Layla just shrugs a shoulder because she never really knew him either. At least not so much that she remembers. Still, hearing him say that and watching her reaction to it, makes my chest ache.

"So, a Jack and Coke?"

"A Jack and Coke would be great, baby. Thank you." I start to walk away, catching Oliver tell Layla about a time when our father caught him in the locker room marking up the lockers before a big game and how he made Oliver clean it all himself.

The fact that Oliver knew my father at all means something to me. He even knew my mother though he never had her for a teacher in middle school. Oliver and I talked about it, figuring out that we've known each other since we were in sixth grade. He had a crush on me, and I had a crush on him, and yet we never did anything about it.

All these years later, here we are.

Right, fake engaged to a man who is never serious and if he is, he's never serious for long.

I hate to think about it that way, but it's true. Oliver is smart, sexy, devastatingly gorgeous, the most charming man I've ever met. But to say since Nora, he's turned fickle is an understatement.

He doesn't commit.

His career as a serial dater is well established, but it goes beyond that. He's loyal as hell to his loved ones, yes, but he grows bored quickly with every other aspect of his life. I mean, his switching up drinks now is a prime example. Never does he have the same drink back-to-back. He can't stand to eat in the same restaurant more than once or twice and never ever orders the same meal because he's a variety is the spice of life guy. Even in his career choice, he works in family medicine because he likes all ages, from birth to death and everything in between. He wants to treat all different types of cases instead of specializing in one particular field.

I don't know how to compete with that, so I don't try.

I couldn't resist him any longer. I'm the one who showed up at his place. I started this and I take responsibility for that. Despite the mess I made; I wouldn't change a single second of any of it. Still, I can't help but hope I'll be different. That we'll be different. That we'll defy the crushing odds stacked against us.

He cares about me. I know this. He tells me and shows me all the time. We're having fun. The sex is incredible. He loves spending time with Layla and me. It's the absolute best and I'm loving every second of it. Loving every second of him. Even if the reality of our situation sticks to me like gum on the sidewalk.

With Oliver, I have one absolute truth.

I'm head over heels in trouble.

I use the restroom, washing my hands and then generously reapplying sunscreen so my already freckled face doesn't start looking like one giant brown spot. My old hat isn't doing anything to keep the sun off me. I should have agreed when he offered to buy me a new hat the way he did for Layla, but I hate Oliver buying me stuff. I'm a woman who has earned her own way always, and it's a hard thing to adjust to. I don't like relying on others. Especially when people have a tendency to be here one second and gone the next.

I already feel like I'm taking advantage by having him get Layla that full scholarship—especially now that we're sleeping together—so him buying everything for us just makes me feel more indebted.

Exiting the bathroom, I order two Jack and Cokes, one for Oliver and one for myself from the attendant they have here in the booth. That's another thing to adjust to. The wealth and opulence of this family still astounds me. While I wait for him to make them up, I survey the buffet of food they have laid out, trying to decide if I'm hungry at all.

Just then cheers erupt throughout the box and I spin around to find everyone on their feet clapping and whistling. I glance up at one of the televisions in time to catch the replay of a home run over the Monster seats.

"Yes!" I squeal, clapping my hands.

Oliver and Layla are high-fiving, and I watch as he tosses his arm around her shoulder, giving her a playful shake, gleeful smiles plastered over their faces.

He spins around, searching and then finding me, that smile growing the second he does, his full set of white teeth gleaming. "This seat, baby. This seat." He points to me and then his chair. "Let it be known now," he calls out to his entire family minus his parents, who didn't come today, "this is my seat from now on. This is a winning seat, right here. And I'm thinking Layla is my good luck charm and must attend every game I do."

She whoops so loud everyone, including Stella who is sitting in the corner reading, laughs.

"Fantastic," I groan. Now there will be no stopping her.

"They're having a good time," Carter says from beside me. I hadn't even realized he was there.

"They are," I agree, swallowing down the flood of emotions as they threaten to rush up and over me. "I think sometimes Oliver is more of a kid than Layla is."

Carter laughs, finishing off whatever it was he was eating, licking his fingers. "I think his birthing order is to blame for that. He was the baby of the family until Rina came along, but they treated her more like a princess than a baby. Oliver got away with murder. We still know he's the favorite."

"Layla was treated like that too. The princess and the baby. Likely because she's so much younger than me and they tried for

her for so long. Stella doesn't seem to be in on the fun of the game,"
I note.

"Poor Stella got dragged here." He points to his niece in the
corner who is face-deep in a book, completely indifferent to all that's
happening around her. "She hates sports. It's good that you and Layla
like them since Oliver is so into them. He mentioned you're crazy
about the Sox and more superstitious than he is."

"I might be, but if you're going to tease me about it the way Layla
and even occasionally Oliver does, I will deny it."

He laughs. "I'd never dream of ribbing on a fellow Sox fan. How is
Layla feeling about getting into Wilchester?"

"Great," I exclaim, my smile rushing back. We got the letter and
phone call on Wednesday. "I don't think I've ever seen her so excited
about anything."

"She got a full scholarship, right?"

I glance up at him, finding his deep brown eyes pinned on me.
"She did."

"Must be a relief for you."

I swallow and nod. I hate talking about money, especially with
someone who has more than the Queen of England.

"Well, this is certainly a fun way to celebrate it." He rocks back on
his heels, returning his gaze to the field and I do the same, finding
Oliver who has his arm around the back of Layla's chair as they sit
and watch the game, talking with their heads close.

"It was wonderful of Oliver to set this up with everyone. To bring
us here. It's truly a dream come true for us, well, at least for me it is."

Carter chuckles, leaning into me and nudging my shoulder,
almost conspiratorially. "Amelia, I think at this point, it's pretty
obvious Oliver would do anything for you. And for Layla."

My eyebrows pinch in at the way he says that. At his tone. Like
there is something I'm missing. "I don't think that's the case. He was
just excited about her getting in. About her scholarship." I have no
idea what his brothers know about our arrangement. If they know the
terms I set for this fake engagement or not.

"I think we both know that's not all of it."

"What do you mean?" I press, because that tone. Still with that tone. Almost like he's warning me. Like he's about to drop a bomb in my lap and watch it explode.

"I'm thrilled he has you. I truly am." He looks back at me, his expression serious. "You make him happy, and Oliver hasn't been happy in a very long time. Hell, if we're being honest, I'm not sure he ever has been. Not even with Nora though he told himself he was."

"Why does it feel like there's a but coming."

He grins down at me, tall and impossibly good-looking, same as all of Oliver's brothers. Carter looks different from the rest. His hair a bit darker, his eyes brown instead of green. Tall, dark, and handsome.

"Because there is. I like that you're smart and candid, Amelia. It makes this easier for me to say. I've been holding my tongue about it because what's done is done."

"Then say it," I bristle. "I'm a big girl. I can handle it."

"Okay, then." He turns to face me, and I do the same. His smile is warm, maybe trying to calm me a bit. "I won't pull any punches with you because I both like and respect you. I'm worried about what you and my brother are up to."

Me too, I think but don't say. Instead, I go with, "Which part?"

He laughs. "Good question. Well, the business side of this was kind of my idea, so I can't say that. And I still don't regret it. That side of things is turning out exactly as we had hoped and planned. It's everything else that's getting complicated."

He's right about that. Oliver's mom is undergoing chemo. She's already had her first round and so far, she feels okay. I went to see her with Oliver the other day and I could tell it made her happy we were there together. She went on about engagement parties and picking a wedding date and our upcoming *Boston Magazine* interview—since I got talked into agreeing to it—and I felt like shit.

Oliver did too, I think, and when we left, neither of us had much to say.

Lying to her isn't easy and I know it eats at him, but I could also see the joy on his face every time she smiled and focused on us instead of her diagnosis and treatment. He's the baby boy, as Carter said. The people pleaser. The one with the biggest heart I've ever seen.

Sometimes to his own detriment.

The media are also all over us. Still. They follow me and they follow him, and they follow us. They write articles and people post tweets and Instagram photos of us. Everything, thus far, is going exactly as planned.

Layla got into school with a full ride. Oliver's mom is happy. The media too.

But Carter is right. I believe that Oliver and his brothers stepped into this idea with the best of intentions. But now it's complicated. So very complicated.

And I'm the one who complicated it.

"I know," I say. "I knew it was stupid. He knew it was stupid."

"But you couldn't resist each other. That much is clear. It's what happens when you guys get serious that I'm worried about."

"It's only been two weeks, Carter. I think we're putting the cart before the horse, so to speak. Oliver and I are just having fun right now. Nothing serious. We are talking about Oliver, after all." I don't know who I'm trying to convince more with that. Me or him. I don't even believe the damn words I'm saying.

"You don't even believe that, do you?" he says, clearly reading my mind.

"No. But I think it's the safest way to go at this point."

He shrugs up a shoulder, turning back to the game, sipping at the drink in his hand. "If you say so. We had told him not to get involved with you like this, but I think it was inevitable from the start." He sighs, pinning me again with that stare of his. The one that busts through all pretenses and bullshit. "Look, he'll kill me for this, and I don't care. Oliver may seem wishy-washy, but he's not. It's his way of protecting himself. But when he decides on something, he's all in, Amelia. Please remember that. I'm glad Layla got into Wilchester. I'm glad Stella will have a friend there when she attends the following year. I'm thrilled my mom is happy, because that's ultimately what we wanted for her with this. But I was there after everything went down with Nora and I watched helplessly as what she did broke something inside him. I also know how Oliver feels about you."

My eyebrows shoot up at that, and he chuckles, running his hand back through his dark hair.

"What? Don't look so shocked. His face lights up whenever you enter the room. He tracks your movements whenever you're together. He talks about you all the fucking time. Layla too. He's crazy about both of you. Say you won't hurt him. That's really all I want to hear."

I lick my suddenly dry lips, my heart jumping all over the place inside my chest. "I'm crazy about him too and hurting him is the absolute last thing I'd ever want to do."

"That's what I thought, though it looked terrified saying it." He winks at me, and I laugh, some of the tension fleeing my body.

"It was. He's not the only one at risk of getting hurt. Only it's not just my heart I'm gambling with. I worry about Layla's too."

Carter sips his drink, his eyes back on the ball field. "Then maybe you and Oliver need to figure out a way that doesn't happen. For any of you."

"Ma'am," the attendant calls out. "I have your drinks."

I grab them and thank him.

"Better get back to them before Oliver throws Layla over the edge of the booth to try and catch that foul ball," Carter says, nodding in the direction of the outside seats of the box.

"What?" sputters from my mouth, my gaze slingshotting in that direction. Sure enough, Oliver is helping Layla lean over the edge. He's holding on tight, but yep, she's trying to catch a ball headed in our direction. "Oh, Lord."

"Have fun tonight on your special date. Oliver has the whole thing set up." My jaw unhinges, and he smirks at me. "Like I said, he'd do anything for you."

Carter strolls off, over to Kaplan, Luca, and Landon, and I make my way back down to my sister and Oliver. I know Oliver is taking me to the museum this evening, but the way Carter is saying it, it sounds like it's a lot more than that. Still, it's hard to focus on tonight when

Carter's words are living and breathing inside my chest. A flutter of hope giving them wings to fly.

A dangerous and delicious potion I'm only too eager to drink down.

Stepping back out into the open sun, I find Layla pouting and out of breath. "I just needed a few more inches," she gripes. "You're strong. You could have pulled me back up."

"Sorry, Sprite. I think your sister would have killed me if—"

"Yes," I say, cutting him off. "I would have. Plus, I'd have to toss you over the side to go and get her."

"Sounds reasonable."

I hand him his drink and he leans in, kissing the corner of my lips. "Come sit beside me," he whispers against me, causing chills to erupt across my skin at his husky tone.

"It's not like I would have died," Layla grumbles, sitting down in a huff, folding her arms petulantly over her chest like the teenager she is.

"Glad we didn't have to find out," I tell her, pushing down on the brim of her hat to cover her eyes.

Oliver takes my hand, pulling me across them and into the seat on the other side of him. His free hand hits my shoulder as he tugs me closer. "You ready for tonight?"

"What did you do?"

His green eyes sparkle as they take me in, that sexy, self-assured, cocky grin on his lips. "You'll see. Trust me, you'll love it."

23

Oliver

The idea came to me when I was out for a run. I'll be honest, I'm not much of a museum guy. But then Amelia and I watched the Netflix documentary about the Isabella Stewart Gardner Museum, and she commented on how it's her favorite place in the city to go, and then there I was, running right past it.

Best part? It only took one phone call and five minutes out of my day to arrange.

That's what happens when you're a Fritz and the media's favorite darling.

Places that don't typically allow for a completely private rental after business hours suddenly do. Plus, the head curator knows Amelia well.

All I had to do was agree to some pictures out front with Amelia and, of course, a donation. It seems ridiculous now to have photos of us taken. To still be a hot topic. Amelia and I no longer have fake, pre-arranged dates because they're not needed—we're actually dating—but pulling up to the museum and helping her out to the flash and click of cameras and the barrage of questions this feels like one.

I wrap my arm around Amelia's waist, gathering her firmly into my side as we make our way to the entrance of the museum. They ask Amelia why we're here and she informs them it's her favorite place in the city. It makes me fist-pump for being such a good listener and setting this whole thing up.

"Oliver, do you have a date set yet for the big day?"

I glance up to answer the guy asking the question when someone standing beside a tree catches my attention just as a flash goes off in my eyes, momentarily blinding me. I blink, forcing my eyes to readjust, but by the time they do, the person is gone.

Nora.

I'd swear it was her, but in scanning all around, I don't see her anywhere. The troubling part of that is, I swore I saw her outside MGH when I left after my shift last week, and Amelia mentioned something in passing that she saw her when she was headed into the grocery store the other day.

I have no idea if it's coincidence or our imaginations getting the best of us or—

"Oliver?" the guy presses, and I come back from my search, reaffixing my most charming smile.

"Not yet," I answer. "We're focusing on my mother's health at the moment. For now, we're just happy being together. Have a good night."

Entering the cool dark building, we're immediately met by a curator, Alice, who gives Amelia a big hug. "Oliver, this is Alice," Amelia introduces. "She is who Layla's middle name is after."

My eyebrows hit my hairline. "Seriously? You never mentioned that."

"Amelia's mother studied art under me," Alice informs me. "We became very close friends."

I spin to Amelia, stunned. "I thought your mom was an English teacher."

"She was," Amelia says. "But she loved art too."

I turn back to the woman. "Wow. It's so nice to meet you." I shake her hand again, and she laughs at my exuberance.

"It's my pleasure. Please. Come this way." She gives us some history of the museum, explains the current exhibits, and informs me that everything I requested is set up and waiting for us in the court-yard. I thank her, Amelia hugs her, and I take Amelia's hand, leading her away. Then it's just us, strolling through the dimly lit museum, taking in one masterpiece after the other.

"I can't believe you did this," she finally says as we enter a long, narrow room, the room filled with tapestries and furniture, a few of the windows made of glowing stained glass that reflects prettily throughout the space. "Who does this, Oliver? Who rents out a museum after it's closed?"

"Me."

She snorts, rolling her eyes at me over her shoulder, but she can't help her smile. For the amount that she doesn't like me to make a fuss over her, I see how much it means in her eyes. Now it's become a game to me. What can I do next? How can I up the ante? No one has ever spoiled Amelia. Ever made her feel special.

Being the first, the only is addictive.

"You didn't need to do this. Especially when I have the feeling there is more in store."

I wrap my arms around her from behind, kissing her neck. "Plenty more in store." I kiss her again. "And I didn't need to do anything. I wanted to. I wanted it to be just us. Just you admiring all these beautiful old things. All this gorgeous art. If I had brought you during the day, we would have been photographed in here. Well, that and Layla wouldn't have gotten to go to the game today. I don't care about art, Amelia, but I know you do, and I wanted to do something special."

She grows quiet and I squeeze her tighter, already nervous about what else I have planned for us. Already suspecting she might not like it but knowing it won't stop me from doing it. She showed up at my house two weeks ago and told me she wanted me.

And with every passing day, I want her more than the one before it.

I can't stop it. And for the first time, I'm not wanting to. It's a runaway train and I'm in for the ride.

"Thank you," she whispers, spinning in my arms and kissing my lips. "You take special and raise it to an art form. God. You make it absolutely impossible for a girl not to totally crush on you. I'm like a teenager all over again, only this is way better because now I actually have you."

"Am I sweeping you off your feet yet?"

"My feet haven't hit the ground since I saw you again at the reunion, Oliver Fritz. This past month has been nothing short of a whirlwind of interesting and amazing."

"Good. I like you off balance."

I dip down and kiss her lips. She's so short and since we're alone, I lift her up, forcing her legs around my waist in the dress she's wearing. She sucks in a gasp as my tongue plunges deeper, my hard cock pressing against her so perfectly all it would take is a few clothing adjustments and I'd be inside of her.

I want her to live in the moment more. Something I know she struggles to do. Everything about Amelia and her life is planned. Thought out. Held back. She keeps so much of herself closed off and I know it's because she's afraid of just how quickly everything can change. Because of that, she's never able to really let go. Does she even know who she truly is beyond her day-to-day struggles?

In high school, she was bullied.

She had a year and a half of college, pre-med college at that, and then she was forced to become a grown-up overnight. The guy she was with up and dumped her within days of her losing her parents. Since then, she's all responsibility. All worry. Completely closed off. I see glimpses of her. The woman she truly is. The one she showed to Nora that night at the reunion and Christa at Wilchester. The one who sasses me, challenges me, keeps me forever on my toes.

What I would give to watch her petals peel back. To see her fully bloom.

"My mom used to bring me here on weekends," she says as we stroll. "English was her first love—Layla especially gets that from her —but art was a close second. She'd bring a sketchpad and draw for hours while I'd read. My dad would be working since he rarely ever could take time off. Maybe that's why I love the Sox so much," she muses, talking aloud, but almost to herself. "He never had time when I was young and any time he had was with the Sox, so naturally I joined in." She shakes herself. "Anyway, I didn't start to appreciate art until I was in high school. She made me take an art class with her on Saturday mornings. Told me it was therapeutic. I was terrible, but it was fun, just the two of us."

I love it when she opens up to me like this. "Was your mom good at it?"

"Yes. Her sketches were better than her paintings. I still have some I kept, but I never had it in me to have any framed." She gives me a wan smile. "Hurt too much, you know?"

"Maybe one day you will."

"Maybe. I think Layla would like it. But being here, I feel close to her." Her eyes hold mine. "You have no idea how special this is. How much it means to me."

I take her hand, walking us through the museum. We marvel at the empty frames left on the wall from when the paintings were stolen. Room after room, it's just us. And just before we get ready to head out into the courtyard—my heart hammering in my throat—we come upon the last room.

"Jesus Christ," I hiss, my eyes going wide.

She spins around to see what I'm gawking at. "Yep," she muse. "That's him. The big guy right there."

I laugh, shaking my head. "Yeah. He scared the shit out of me. I wasn't expecting that. Jesus on the wall in such... large display."

"Do you think I should steal it? Put it on your wall?"

"You don't want it for your place?"

"Nah," she says. "I don't think I would look good in orange. Messes with the red hair."

"Baby, you look good in everything. Besides, it's all about who you know in this city, and I know everyone. No one is arresting us, and we'd never go to prison."

"That's what Whitey Bulger thought."

"He was on the run into his eighties, not so bad, if you ask me." I grab her hip, spinning her in place and dragging her back to me. "Come on, baby. Let's live on the lam."

"Do I get my own gun, Clyde?"

I grin like a bastard, smacking her lips with a hard kiss. "Whatever you want, Bonnie. We can make Layla our lookout girl while we steal the world."

She laughs, her head dropping to my chest. "Courtyard?" she asks.

"Courtyard."

"Why did your heart just start to race?"

I suck in a shaky breath. "Come on and I'll show you."

Leading her out to the courtyard loaded with flowers and trees, the sky black as it peers down at us through the glass ceiling, I reach into my pocket, clutching the box she has yet to notice hiding there. We meander our way around until she spots the picnic I had set up for us, complete with flameless candles and champagne.

"Oliver," she whispers on an empty breath.

My lips trail up her neck, licking at her sweet skin. "Good surprise?"

"It's beautiful. Like something out of a fairy tale."

"That's me. Prince Charming."

I help her down onto the blanket and then work the cork of the champagne, opening it with a loud *pop*. Pouring her a glass, I hand it to her and then open the picnic basket, loaded with all kinds of things I'm not the least bit hungry for. Why I thought food was a good idea after all the crap we ate at Fenway today is beyond me.

"Are you hungry?"

She shakes her head, falling back onto her hands as she watches me intently, knowing I'm holding something back. Here goes nothing.

"I got you something," I tell her, not wanting to put it off any longer. "I saw it and I thought of you, and I just went in and bought it."

"And that's why you're nervous?" she surmises.

"It's this." I slide the box out of my pocket, and she sits up straight, staring at it like she has no idea what to do with it.

"It's a jewelry box," she deadpans.

"Yup."

"But... we've—"

"I know," I cut her off. "I know. I don't care."

She sucks in a shaky breath, her eyes glassing over with unshed tears. Mine watch her face as I open the box, revealing the large diamond solitaire in a platinum bezel setting on a delicate platinum chain.

"Oliver." It's a gasp.

"Now you know why I was nervous."

She blinks rapidly. Her eyes bouncing back and forth between mine and the necklace, the diamond glimmering against the fake candlelight. "It's... wow. It's... I can't accept that."

I knew she was going to start there. "Tell me why."

"Because we've only just started dating. Because we have a business arrangement. Because—"

"When was the last time someone bought you a present?"

She shoots up off the ground, pacing around in a circle.

"Amelia, when?" I press.

Her hands meet her hips, her breathing hard. So hard I know she's fighting tears. Fighting everything, including me. "I don't need you to buy me presents."

"I didn't do it to prove how I care about you."

"It's so beautiful. I don't want you to think... Why did you buy it then?"

I stand up too, taking the necklace out of the box, holding it in my hand, my nerves now gone. She's simply afraid. A constant I know how to work with.

"When was the last time someone spoiled you? When was the last time someone saw something and bought it for you because they absolutely had to?"

"Jesus, Oliver."

"Jesus is in the other room," I tell her, fighting my grin as a gust of a laugh flees her lips.

"We started this thing, and I don't know what to do now," she rants. "Carter said stuff and now we're here and you bought me that and—"

"You're scared?"

"Yes." She spins around, her eyes wild with fire. "I'm scared. You know I am and that hasn't changed. People come into your life, and you care about them, and then suddenly they're gone and I—"

"I'm not going anywhere."

She shakes her head. "That is not a promise you can ever make. I can't... whoa." She blows out a heavy breath. "This is going so fast. Everything with us has been so fast." Her voice quakes.

It has been. She's right about that. I saw the necklace and I thought... maybe. I thought maybe this time, with this woman, things will be different. No, fuck that. Things are different because she is different. And I know she thinks I'm going to leave her, like everyone else in her life has, but I'm not that guy. I'm not the guy who leaves. I'm the guy who stays.

"I'm scared too," I admit. "I haven't cared for anyone in a very long time and the last time I did, it nearly ruined me. I swore it was not something I would ever do again. But I can't help it with you, and I know you're the same way with me. Being afraid of this only means it's real. This is real, Amelia. You and me."

She puffs out a breath, her body trembling. "I know it is. I feel that too. It's just..."

"Do you like me?"

She snorts. "Are you twelve?"

"That's when I first noticed you, so maybe. You're wearing something fake on your finger and I decided I wanted to give you something real. Something that shows you, that tells *you*, this thing between us *is* real. Even if the engagement isn't. So again, when was the last time someone bought you something just for you? Something special. And I'm not talking about what Layla gets you for your birthday or Christmas. It's not the same and you know it."

She swallows impossibly hard, her eyes glittering at me. She takes a hesitant step in my direction. "I don't know," she says, her voice cracking.

"Yes, you do."

"Fine. Never."

I nod. "Exactly." I take a step toward her, then another, until I'm standing right before her. "I liked buying you this. In fact, you need to start getting used to that now. I plan on spoiling you rotten, baby."

She hiccups out a sob, her forehead falling to my chest. I breathe in her scent, and just like every time I'm with her, something within me clicks into place.

"I'm crazy about you. You can't break my heart. I won't survive it. You're so you and I'm still me and I..."

"I won't break your heart," I promise her. "And I'm crazy about you too."

"We have so much to figure out, Oliver. We're in a real mess of a situation."

"Do you want to stop?" I ask, my stomach churning at the thought.

"No," she says quickly, her eyes desperately catching on mine though her voice skips. "No. I don't. But I don't see how this ends in anything but disaster."

"We won't let it," I tell her, hoping to hell that's a promise I can keep when I'm not sure it is.

My lips fall to the top of her forehead as I loop the necklace around her throat, fastening it behind her neck. I release it and she peers up at me through her lashes as my fingers find the diamond now nestled against her suprasternal notch. It sparkles and I smile, feeling so fucking gratified and complete.

"We have two more months to figure this thing out," I tell her. "Until then, let's promise each other something. We stop overthinking. We stop overanalyzing. We stop sabotaging this before we even get started. We'll just take this day by day, moment by moment. Okay? We'll take the hurdles as they come. Together."

"Okay. I can try. I'm not very good at that. At this."

I kiss her. I kiss her hard. Holding on tight. Then I take her down to the blanket and together, we sip champagne. She tells me more about her mom. About how she used to come here with her and how this is the place she still comes when she needs to feel her mother's presence.

I hold her while she talks. While she cries about her mom—something I haven't seen her do yet. While she absently plays with the necklace. I hold her and we drink champagne and eventually pick at some of the things in the basket. We stay here for hours, just talking, just staring at the beautiful courtyard we're in all alone. Our private oasis.

"I love the necklace," she finally says. "It's my heart on a chain."

Fuck. Now my heart is there with hers. "It's my heart too. For you."

She sighs, her ear against my chest. Against my pounding heart. Something her hand meets, feeling, testing. Another sigh and she says, "I'll always keep it safe."

I know now I never want this to end.

We've only been together a couple of weeks and I already know that.

Live in the moment, I remind myself. Day by day, I force through my skull that's pounding with thoughts I can't allow to escape. But Amelia is right. We are in a real mess, and this could very well end in disaster. Amelia is different. She. Is. Different. Dammit, she has to be.

I want us to have a real shot at this when a real shot feels nothing short of impossible for us.

For the first time since this whole thing began, I wish I had never put my ring on her finger. Because then I wouldn't be so scared of this ending and me losing her when all I'm trying to do is keep her for real.

24

Amelia ♥

It's one of those picture-perfect spring days that, at present, is making me want to throw up. Oliver and I were forced here today like it's a prison sentence. Pictures. So, so many pictures. And questions. So, so many questions, most of them very personal.

So, this picture-perfect day is like mother nature flipping us off while cackling.

Bouquets of fragrant flowers in pink, purple, yellow, and red line the paths of the Boston Public Garden. The trees surrounding the pond are the most perfect shade of green. The sky a cloudless blue. The swan boats majestically circumventing the pond are loaded with locals and tourists alike.

And then there's us.

Stuck taking part in an exposé on our fake engagement.

I pushed back hard against this. The magazine had called me personally no less than five times. More with Oliver and eventually the relentless bastards got his mother involved and here we are.

It's been four weeks since Octavia's surgery. Three weeks since she started chemo.

She's been sick. Feeling the full effects of the treatment. Her hair is gone. Her appetite dwindling. So, for now, there is no saying no to her. There is only making her happy when she feels nothing short of miserable. After all, she is the main reason we're doing these shenanigans in the first place. Something that is growing more and more confusing and complicated as time goes by.

And now I sound like I'm Sam from Casablanca, but you get what I'm saying there.

It's no secret Oliver and I are very much together.

We're as out with our relationship as two people who are dating can be.

Only, we're not just dating, and this isn't any ordinary new relationship.

After the night at the museum, things changed for us. We said day by day and moment to moment, but it was like the second he put that diamond on my neck—which I never ever take off—there was no going back. No slowing it down.

We spend as much time together as possible. Sleep at his place most nights since his apartment is closer to Layla's school than ours, and let's be real here, the man's place is a mansion in a building with concierge service. Layla has her own bedroom and bathroom and occasionally Stella comes over and the girls have sleepovers.

We're the definition of a new couple tumbling fast into serious-town complete with the hot sex and romantic dates. If this were a rom-com, we would have officially hit the music montage of our story.

But it's not a fucking rom-com.

This is real life, and Oliver and I can only be described as a fledgling romance. How does that work when you're also selling a lie that you're engaged? What happens when we decide it's time to call off the engagement side of things? Does our relationship go with it? Or do we say, hey, guess what, we like each other and want to keep dating, we just don't want to be engaged anymore? Impossible, right?

But it's more than that.

Being with Oliver is more than that.

It's like he took the shell I had been hiding in all these years and not only cracked it open but shattered it. He's brought me back to life.

A life I'm not sure I ever lived until I met him. A life filled with beautiful, wonderful things.

The best of which is him.

I can be myself with him. He sees me for exactly who and what I am, and he actually likes what he sees. Nerdy glasses, crazy red hair, weird Red Sox outfits and insane superstitions, single parent, broke—well, he doesn't know the extent of that and that's how I intend to keep it. But I'm falling. I've fallen. And I have no idea what to do about it.

Especially the deeper this engagement goes.

First step is engagement photos and articles in major publications. The next is an engagement party—we're fighting that one tooth and nail. Then there's, you know, actually planning the fucking wedding. Something Octavia keeps asking us to start doing. Something I absolutely cannot under any circumstances allow to happen.

This was supposed to be a three-month business arrangement and only six weeks into it we're already setting so many fires I have no idea how we'll ever put them out.

The one bright shiny silver lining to all this, other than how amazing Oliver is to go out with, is that Layla got into Wilchester's honor's program, not just the school, which we already knew she was accepted into with her full scholarship. Oh, and Sagginalls has completely backed off. He's now the model of professionalism.

It's what I cling to in moments like these.

"Yes, that's perfect," the photography director says. "Oliver, keep your hand on her back like that and stare into her eyes. Amelia, tilt your head back just a touch. I want the sunlight to catch your hair. That's it. Beautiful." *Click, click, click.* "After this, will take some more on the bridge and then down by the pond. Oh, maybe some on one of the swan boats."

"Orgasms," I grumble through closed teeth so only Oliver can hear, making sure I maintain my smile. "You owe me lots and lots of orgasms."

He grins wider, a Cheshire Cat leaning in and breaking the pose so his lips can skim my ear. "Whatever my fiancée wants, my fiancée gets. Can we play doctor tonight? I'm dying to give this body a full exam." His hand covertly skims the side of my breast and my breath hitches, a fresh blush springing to my cheeks.

"Oh, Yes. I think we have to. I haven't been very good to my body, Doctor. I need you to examine me closely."

Click, click, click.

I groan. Moment over.

"Tell us how your family took the engagement, Oliver," the interviewer asks, tablet and stylus at the ready. "After all, you and Amelia hadn't been dating very long when you popped the question."

Well, that's loaded. Thankfully Oliver takes it in stride.

"They love, Amelia. From the moment I introduced her to them, they were even more enamored than I was. They were overjoyed when I told them I proposed."

"Liar," I hiss.

He whispers in my ear, "Do you know what's getting my dick hard right now? Making you come with the vibrator I just purchased for you."

"You what?"

"You walked into this park in this dress, and I just knew I had to fuck you in it. Lift it up over your ass and sink inside you while taking your new toy against your clit. The second this bullshit is done, I plan on taking you home, slipping you out of these pretty flowers you're wearing, and then seeing how many times I can make you scream."

"Oh, god," I moan against him.

"Such a greedy little girl, Amelia. A naughty woman who needs her doctor to give her a full exam."

Dying. I'm dying. Oliver Fritz is impossibly dirty, and it seems I can't get enough of it.

"Amelia, are you okay? You're all red?" the journalist asks.

"And wet," Oliver rasps in my ear. "I'd bet my inheritance your pussy is wetter than sin, just waiting for me to dirty it up."

"I'm fine," I reply. I'm not fine. I'm nowhere close to fine. I elbow Oliver in the side, making him chuckle. Bastard knew exactly what he was doing with all that. "Just. You know. Allergies?" Yes, that comes out as a question.

"Oh, so sorry to hear that," the photography director says. "Then maybe let's move closer to the pond and finish this up?"

"Works for me," the journalist states, scrolling through her tablet, presumably reading over her notes as we walk down in the direction of the large pond that spans this corner of the park between Arlington and Boylston.

"Oh look," I remark, walking to the edge of the pond and peering in at the mass of twigs, branches, and debris. "Is that a nest?"

"I think so," Oliver says. "They do have swans here."

"Cool. I don't think I've ever seen a swan's nest."

"Just be careful. You don't want to fall in."

"Ha!" I laugh. "I'm not that clumsy." But I do take a step closer because I think those are eggs in there.

Squawk! A loud sound to my right startles me so bad, I nearly do fall in the pond. I turn in time to see a very angry swan, her long white neck angled in my direction, her black beady eyes narrowed. *Squawk!* She honks at me again, only this time louder, and I take a step back because though swans are beautiful, they're notoriously mean.

"I'm sorry. I'm not going near your nest. I was just looking." I hold my hands up in surrender, taking another step away.

Squawk!

"Oh boy, you really pissed Mama Swan off now," Oliver muses, coming to me, his hand outstretched like he's about to grab me and pull me to safety when the swan yells at him as if to say, *back off, pal, this one is mine.* "Damn, you seriously made her mad. Come here, Amelia. Slowly though, I think."

"I'm trying," I tell him out of the corner of my mouth, hoping she doesn't hear me and catch on to what I'm planning.

A few more loud squawks with every step back I take, but the more I retreat, the more she advances, waddling her ass back and forth, until she lunges for me like she's going to try and beak me to death.

"Ah!" I scream, jumping out of the way just in time. I turn and take off running. "I said I was sorry!" I call over my shoulder, only the damn swan is chasing me now, up away from the edge of the pond and back over toward the bridge. "What are you doing? I was an ugly duckling just like you once. We're kindred spirits. Stop chasing me!"

Oliver is in stitches with laughter, practically doubled over and splinting his side. The photographer—along with plenty of bystanders—are taking pictures and likely videos and yet this damn swan is still in hot pursuit, yelling swan profanities at me as she picks up speed.

"Very heroic, Oliver!"

"Hey, didn't you tell Layla that a princess has to save herself?"

I did, didn't I? Crap.

I leap over a small bed of flowering bushes, landing not so gracefully all the while the swan just plows through them. "What do I do?"

"Try reasoning with her," Oliver suggests, and now the reporter and the photographer can no longer hold back their own laughter.

I circle back around a tree, heading in the direction of Oliver and her nest, hoping she'll return there if we get close enough. Unfortunately, my heeled foot hits a patch of soft earth and I go slipping and sliding, my arms flailing, before falling back onto my ass into something soft and cold and wet.

The swan sees this as her moment and goes to strike. I toss my arms over my head, letting out a scream, but just as she springs, Oliver picks her up from behind, walking her back to the water, and gently tossing her in the direction of the nest.

"Alright, you've had your fun," he says to her. "Go back to your babies, they're getting cold without your ass on them."

Speaking of asses, I have a very bad feeling mine is covered in mud. Unfolding myself, I try to stand, only to slip some more and quickly give up. "Ugh."

Oliver, the valiant hero who looks a little too pleased with himself, saunters in my direction. "I don't know what your problem is with her. She listened to me."

I glance around him and find the swan back on her nest. "The only thing to make this better would be if a bird pooped on my head."

"Isn't that considered good luck?" the journalist asks.

"How is anything pooping on you ever good luck?" I retort and she shrugs like she's actually considering that.

Oliver crouches down in front of me, using the hem of his shirt to wipe at something on my face. His smile is so big and so bright it could light up the darkest of skies.

"You okay?"

"Grand." Only I'm laughing now too because I was just chased by a swan in the middle of a photo shoot about my fake engagement. If that isn't the most ridiculous thing ever, I don't know what is.

He leans in, kissing my lips and that's when we hear more click, click, clicks going off.

"Did you get it?" Oliver practically growls in annoyance. I don't even hear what they're saying. He drags me up by the arm, checking me over. "You're a mess. Let's get you home."

He glances over at the photographer, director, and journalist. "The interview is over," he announces.

We thank them and then get the hell out of the park, running down the street, my dirty dress and crazy hair flying behind me. "I can see the headlines now; Fritz's fiancée gets taken down by swan."

"Too boring. They'll come up with something much better than that."

"Lovely," I deadpan. "I definitely need a shower, some clean clothes, and a large glass of wine."

"Done. Oh, and did I mention the vibrator I bought for you is waterproof?"

"No. But you'll have to show me."

25

Oliver ♥

We're not even three seconds into my building's elevator and I'm lifting up the hem of her dirty dress, peeling back layers of tulle to find her panties. To say I'm insatiable when it comes to Amelia is an understatement. It's so much more than I can't get enough of her. It's a visceral craving so deep-seated I know in my gut there will be no limit or end.

Never in my life have I felt comfortable letting my hunger out.

With Nora, I was too young. She was the only girl I had ever been with.

With the subsequent women, well, they were fillers. Temporary placeholders. Fluff I never trusted nor dared to let my guard down with.

Amelia has awoken a beast I scarcely knew existed inside me and now that I've found him, allowed him to come out to play, I have no intentions of corralling him or forcing him back into hibernation.

Best of all, Amelia is right there with me. So unexpectedly wonderful, open, and uninhibited, it's the opposite of how she can be in real life. I like to imagine it's me. That this trust we've placed in each other is a two-way street. We're bonded by this lie we've created and in forging that bond, it's connected us in ways I had no clue you could be connected to someone.

Still…

"Oliver," she rasps, her head falling back against my shoulder. "Someone could see us. Not to mention, I feel filthy and not in a hot way."

A smile spreads my lips. "You were attacked by a swan."

She laughs. "I sure was. I don't think that's the engagement interview your mother had envisioned."

"No. Probably not. But it's a way better story."

She stares woefully down at her dress. "Another piece of clothing of Rina's I'll have to replace."

"You borrowed this from Rina? Why? I would have bought you something if you had wanted."

"I know you would have. It's why I didn't say anything."

I shake my head, bothered by that. She's proud and determined and I get it. I respect it. At least, I think that's what this is. Sometimes, I'm not so sure. Sometimes it still feels like she's keeping something from me. But I have money. So much money. More than I could ever spend in a dozen lifetimes. Doesn't she understand I'd give her anything she could ever want? That being with me means she doesn't have to worry?

I want to spoil this woman and she doesn't let me.

"I hate that you had to borrow a dress."

"It's fine. Things tend to get tight by the…" She trails off, almost as if she caught herself admitting something she didn't want to admit.

"Why do things get tight?"

She huffs. "Just drop it, please. I don't want to talk about this."

She never does. Ever.

I don't know if it's because she's still cautious with me, about me, or if this is just how she is because she's having trouble adapting. But I'm an all-or-nothing guy. Once I'm in with something, I'm in for it. And that's where I am with her.

I know my money makes her uncomfortable, but there's nothing I can do about having it and wanting to spend it on her. I need her to open up to me—and she has, in so many ways—but she's definitely holding something back.

"Remember what I said about wanting to spoil you?"

"I know. And you do. It's just... I'm used to paying my own way. It's important to me. Especially when I know people already believe I'm with you for your money. You have no idea how much that bothers me."

Hard to argue with that, so I let it drop for now.

The elevator doors open on my floor, and I spin her around to face me, my mouth attacking hers as I walk her backward in the direction of my door. I unlock it, letting her enter, and then spinning her back around, pressing her dirty ass against my hard dick.

"Go into the bathroom and get naked," I whisper into the shell of her ear. "Wait for me."

I give her a nudge and she sets off for my bedroom, throwing me a dark glance over her shoulder. I make you nervous, Amelia. Good. I push your limits. And I don't just mean in the bedroom. Excellent.

We have a lot to figure out, and this is still so new, but I want her.

I want her big, stubborn heart. All of it. A brutal reminder I still have one I should be cautious with.

Grabbing the small box that was delivered this morning, I walk it into my bedroom. Amelia is waiting for me in the bathroom and since I know my girl can be an impatient one, I'm going to make her wait just a bit longer. Build her suspense and anticipation. The dress she borrowed from Rina is hanging over the back of my chair, dirt side up, and I take a quick look at it.

YSL.

Shit. Rina won't care, but Amelia will, so I make a note to talk to Rina about what happened so she can let Amelia off the hook. I'm happy to buy a new dress, but I know Amelia will fight me on it.

Removing my clothes, I kick them to the side and then go for Amelia's new toy. I switch it on, feeling the vibration against my palm, grinning like a deranged fool. It's sleek and purple, and I can't wait to watch her skin glow and her body tremble against it.

I enter the bathroom to find a naked Amelia perched on the

corner of the vanity, her legs crossed and arms folded over her breasts, an impatient scowl on her face. I set the vibrator down beside her and wordlessly turn on the shower, getting it hot and turning on the steam function.

Amelia is holding the toy, her eyes dark as she caresses it making my dick jerk in her direction as if to say, *don't forget about me, I need love too.*

"Come here, pretty lady." Before she can move, I scoop her up into my arms and carry her into the shower, sitting her down on the bench while kneeling before her. I spread her legs, loving how her breath always catches when I do that, and then lean in to place an open-mouth kiss against her sweet pussy.

Her hands immediately dive into my hair, gripping me hard. "Oliver."

There it is. She's primed.

I turn on the toy, the sound vibrating loudly against the running water and marbled walls and floors. "Do you know what I really want to do with this toy?"

"What?" she asks, her voice breathy and hoarse.

"Fuck your pussy with it while I take your ass."

"Jesus, Oliver."

Her head falls back against the tile.

"I haven't done that before. Anal. Life of a playboy and an unadventurous girlfriend before it doesn't really lend itself to that. Do you think that's something we could try?"

"Now?" Her eyes are wider than a full moon and just as luminous.

"If you're game, I am."

She starts to pant, her chest rising and falling in rapid succession. "I've never... you know... either."

"Don't move."

I press a kiss to her lips and quickly hop out of the shower, wrapping a towel around my waist and heading for my nightstand, where I retrieve a bottle of lube. In a flash, I'm back in the shower, setting it beside her on the bench.

"Oliver."

I love it when she does that. When she gets nervous and loses her words, but always starts and ends with my name. It says I'm all that's on her mind. The one thing she can make sense of and wants the most. At least, I hope that's what it means because I think I'm falling for her. I think I fell for her that night at the reunion. The moment those gray eyes looked up, and she stunned me breathless with her beguiling beauty.

I turn the toy back on using the remote, pouring some of the lube onto it, but unable to remove my gaze from hers. She's mesmerized. Nervous as hell, but so far, very willing to try whatever I have in my head if the look in her eyes is anything to go by.

"Do you know why I purchased this specific toy?"

"No." She can barely catch her breath.

"Because it can do this..." Slowly, with my eyes on hers, I rub one side against her opening while the other finds her clit.

"Oh shit!" she yells, jerking back into the wall, her hand flying out to my shoulder where her nails dig in. "Oliver. Oh my god!"

"Is it too much?"

"What setting is it on?"

Settings. Right. I press a button on the remote and the vibration sound instantly lowers. "Better?"

"Yes. Holy hell, I think I nearly died a second ago."

I laugh, leaning in and kissing her. "Sorry. Can we try again?"

Reaching between us, she covers my hand holding the toy and brings it back to her, moving it around, showing me what she likes. It's the hottest, most erotic thing I've ever seen and I'm about two seconds from coming like a teenager watching his first porn.

"Mmmm," she moans. "Like that. I like that."

Holy fuck. This woman. This goddamn woman. She absolutely owns me.

Her hand falls to her side, her head back, and her eyes closing as I slip one side of the toy inside her hot, wet channel, the other angling up and tickling her clit.

"Good?" I rasp, clearing my throat. For the first time with her, I'm the one at a loss for words.

"So good."

My mouth crashes against hers, needing to taste and feel her moans and whimpers as they climb from the back of her throat. Her back arches and she grinds into my hand, fucking the vibrator. God, she's so beautiful. My lips find her breasts, sucking hard on her nipples. Her skin is red and wet, her body slipping the closer she gets to her release.

"I want to feel you," she gasps. "I want more of *you*."

I squirt some lube onto my fingers, finding her tight ring at the back. She jerks against me, her eyes snapping open, her mouth agape. I increase the pressure, slipping my lubricated finger in and out of her ass as the toy continues to work her pussy.

"Good?"

She nods, her breath stalled in her throat.

I look down, entranced, watching the toy, watching my finger, watching her body.

"You're going to leak all over my fingers when you come on this toy." I slip another finger in her, stretching her, feeling how tight she is, the way her muscles fight, and I groan, so turned on and ready I can hardly stand it.

"Oliver. Holy hell. I-It's a lot. A lot of pressure. I'm so close."

"Don't come yet."

She lets out a strangled laugh. "Are you kidding?" she pants, her hand gripping my shoulder like a vise. "I have to. Oh, my god. I have to. *Oliver!*"

I continue to stretch her, scissoring my fingers back and forth as the toy continues to fuck her. A scream pierces the air, reverberating off the hard surfaces as she convulses around me, scratching her nails into my flesh.

My mouth claims hers, whispering every thought as it enters my head into her. Telling her how beautiful she is. How amazing. How sexy. How I can't wait for my cock to replace my fingers, which it will the second she's done coming. On and on her orgasm goes and when she finally sags against the wall, her breathing ragged, I pick her up and drop myself onto the bench where she was just sitting, positioning her on my lap instead.

I turn off the toy, setting it beside us, knowing I'll likely use it again in a moment. Amelia is limp against me, but I know she feels what I'm doing. I know she hears the lube as I squirt it onto my hand and coat my dick with it.

Her breath hitches and she stiffens against me.

"I'll go slow. Just remember to breathe and relax. I'll go slow," I promise her again, adjusting her as I start to gently toy with her sensitive clit, using my other lubed hand to play with her asshole. "Did it feel good, baby? Did it feel good having my fingers inside your ass while the toy was inside your pussy?"

"Yes." A whisper.

I start sucking on her neck, kissing and licking her, working her up with my fingers to the point where she's needy once more. Writhing and ready for me. And then, I lift her hips, positioning my cock against her forbidden hole while ever so slowly sinking myself inside her.

She shifts, rocking her body as she tries to adjust, the feel so damn tight, stars erupt behind my eyes. My lungs empty as I go in and out, each time sinking in just a little deeper, moving past her tight ring of muscles.

"You doing okay?"

She's silent again. Other than her heavy breathing, she's not talking.

"Amelia?" I pinch her nipple, bringing her back.

"Yes. I'm okay. It's... it burns a little."

Reaching over, I grab the toy, turning it back on to a gentle hum and rubbing it against her clit. "Focus on that. Focus on me filling you up. On how good it feels."

"Okay. Keep doing that."

Deeper and deeper, I go until I'm fully seated inside her. She takes the toy from my hand, using it to play with herself, and I bend her forward, grasping her hips while fucking her, watching how my cock slides in and out. She starts to bounce with me, moving in time with my slow thrusts, and when she inserts the toy inside her, I nearly explode, feeling the vibrations through the thin membrane.

But God. This feeling. How tight she is. How deep inside her I am. How crazy, sexy, fucking beautiful she is. How bold and brave and trusting she is. My hand wraps around her hair, twisting the wet strands around my fist and jerking her head back so I can kiss her.

This woman... this woman is my absolute everything.

Never in my life have I felt like this with someone, so connected, so a part of them.

We continue to move, to kiss, to fuck all the while steam and water surround us. But it is just us. There is nothing else. No outside world. No media or lies. Nothing fake.

She picks up her pace, her thighs trembling the closer she gets, and I know I won't be able to hold off much longer. She feels too good.

I pump harder and harder, deeper and deeper until she grips my cock so tight, I bellow, gritting my teeth while she comes harder than I've ever seen her come. Violent and thrashing, I abandon her hips, holding her against me so she doesn't fall, toying with her breasts which only seems to drive her higher.

The second she's done, I pull out of her, jerking my cock and coming all over her back and ass in thick white ropes, yelling out an orgasm so deep it consumes every cell in my body, taking over time and space. Shattering me to pieces before rebuilding me whole.

Just like Amelia.

"Christ. That was..."

"Mmmmm."

That's all either of us has left after that.

I wrap her up in my arms, holding her impossibly close, making sure she's okay. That I didn't hurt her. That she loved it as much as I did. She kisses me, reassuring me that she's good and that she did love it too. And then we get up, my hands washing her hair and body, still needing to touch her, to be close to her.

Hoping she's as deep into this with me as I evidently am with her.

It's hit me like a tidal wave. It's crazy. The way she makes me feel. The things that are happening between us.

How do I keep her when everything we've outwardly been doing has been based on an outlandish pile of lies? How do I convince her I'm sincere when nothing we've done up until this point is? And what happens when our arrangement ends, and I can't let her go?

26

Oliver

"I have a problem," I announce, leaning back into the leather of my sofa, dragging my bourbon with me because it's one of those nights. Well, one of those days really. Step one in any addiction is admitting you have a problem. Right? I mean, that's what we learn in med school. So that's what I just did.

Still, all I can think about is fucking Amelia's ass yesterday. Is how badly I want to do it again. I'm obsessing over the idea of her sitting on my face, so I can eat her pussy out and she can say my name the way she always does. I think at this point, calling it a problem is a disastrous understatement. It obviously goes way beyond my sexual need for her. But again, I get lost and hung up in a bubble of desire the second I picture her.

Now that's a problem.

"Agreed," Grace says with a scowl as she glares into the jar of crunchy peanut butter. "This is almost empty. How am I supposed to stress eat an entire row of Oreos if I don't have crunchy peanut butter to eat them with? Do you have any idea what an OB-GYN residency is like? You're done with your residency in six weeks and already have multiple job offers. I have two more years left on this bitch and let me tell you, birthing women are no joke. Plus, my attending is a dick."

"Hey," Carter snaps. "I am not. And for the record, Oreos with crunchy peanut butter is fucking nasty."

Grace shoots him a glare that threatens to murder him where he sits.

I groan, stopping this before the two of them really get going. "Grace, it's like you don't even know me. I have a fresh jar for you up in the cabinet. It's the organic non-stir, just how you like it. I also have fluff, and if you're really having a bad day, sour gummy worms."

Carter makes a gagging sound at that last one. The man can't stand anything gummy.

My best friend smiles a smile at me that says I get her and her weird food addictions. "You're a prince among mere mortals. Now tell me about your latest problem and I'll do what I can to help."

I open my mouth, ready to launch into a tirade over the fact that I'm starting to fall for Amelia—that alone is a problem given how much I hate on love—and there's the whole fake engagement thing to work out now that we're together, when my front door bursts open. Brecken Davenport, Rina's boyfriend, comes strolling in like he lives here, his eyes on his phone.

"Nice of you to show up," I deadpan. "We finished the pizza an hour ago."

"I walked Rina into work," he says, slipping his phone into his jeans pocket and taking a seat beside me on the couch, helping himself to an empty glass and filling it with bourbon from the bottle I have out. "I hate it when she works night shifts. I know she loves them because she says that's when shit really goes down in the ICU, but with her working nights and me working days, I don't get to see her." He lifts the lid of the empty pizza box. "You really didn't save me any? Not even a slice?"

"Evidently we're stress eating," Carter says, winking at Grace who again looks like she's ready to flay him alive. I have no idea what happened between them today at work, but clearly, it was something.

"Dick," she mutters at him under her breath.

"Right," Brecken says with a scowl. "So..."

"There's a sub in the fridge if you want to eat it. Chicken parm. I had gotten it for Amelia, but she stayed home to have a movie night with Layla."

Brecken slaps my shoulder, hopping off the couch and heading into the kitchen to heat up Amelia's sub.

"You said something about a problem?" Carter questions against the sound of slamming cabinets and fridge doors.

"He's in love with Amelia," Grace calls out as she reaches up to grab the tub of marshmallow fluff.

"Am not," I call back before turning to Carter. "I might be."

"Does she not feel the same way back?"

Carter is confused and I kinda get that. Kinda, but not really. "I have no idea. We haven't talked about it. We've only been fake engaged for six weeks, actually dating for four. It's new and we're trying to not put any pressure on ourselves. That was my idea, actually and it's not working out so well for me at the moment."

"I'm not understanding," he admits.

"Oliver's worried about what happens to the relationship when the engagement side of this ends. Again, he's in love with her and has no idea how she feels in return because he's too much of a pussy to use his words and talk to her. Given his past, he's jumpy like a woman with PID (pelvic inflammatory disease) getting a pelvic exam."

"Thank you, voice of God. Believe it or not, Grace, I can speak for myself without you having to read my mind and do it for me. And can we not talk about pelvic exams. Work is done for the day."

"Just moving things along."

I flip her off and she laughs, returning with her arms loaded with more sugar than I can even begin to think about.

"How do you eat all that and still stay so small?" Brecken asks her, his sub on a plate as he reclaims the seat beside me while Grace sits on the floor in front of the coffee table so she has better access to her buffet.

"If you're under stress, calories don't count."

Brecken snorts out a laugh around his bite of food. "Is that your scientific opinion, doctor, or just wishful thinking?"

"It's fucking scientific," she declares. "When you start delivering babies and doing surgery on lady parts, Brecken then you are free to comment but not before. Keep eating your sub and be thankful I don't like chicken parm, or that would be my next victim." She huffs, dropping her elbows to my coffee table. "Why do I hang out with you losers? And why isn't Rina here to buffer any of this?"

"Because Rina is working, and we're way more fun to be with than Tony is. Plus, I feed your addiction," I tell her. I like Tony, I just don't love Tony. He's a piece of dry toast. If starving, you'll deal with it, but otherwise, you'd pass. Why she's engaged to him, I'll never understand.

"Wait, can we backtrack?" Carter interrupts, sipping his drink and wiping away a residual drop from his lip with his thumb. "What's wrong with your engagement? For as sick as Mom is with the chemo, it's giving her something to focus on and be happy about. The media is obsessed with the two of you, especially Amelia. She's become their Cinderella. You've never looked so good in their eyes, and you were always their favorite of us. What am I missing?"

"Our engagement is set to end in six weeks."

He shakes his head. "Why? Does it have to?"

"If they stayed engaged, eventually they'd have to plan a wedding," Brecken jumps in. "And since they've crossed the line they shouldn't have crossed and are together, it complicates things further."

"Right." I point at him. "What he said. Mom will never let me have a prolonged engagement. She's already all over us to at the very least plan an engagement party. She's mentioned that a winter wedding at the compound would be magical."

"So," Carter continues, "you need to end the engagement without ending the relationship and your relationship is too new to stay engaged and make it real because that means you'd have to plan a wedding and actually get married?"

"Something like that," I say.

"Are we forgetting the fact that he's also in love with her?" Grace chimes in.

"Quit it with the in-love stuff," I groan. "It's not helping anything. Can we focus on the engagement ending thing?"

Carter leans back in his chair, taking another pull of his amber liquid as he mulls this over. "Yeah. I can see how this a problem."

"Thanks, big brother. Always there for the obvious. What do I do about it?"

He hitches up a shoulder. "Don't look at me. I was in love with a woman for years and did nothing about it until it was too late. I'm the last person you should seek relationship advice from. But as I recall, we told you not to mix business with pleasure. You're the one who couldn't keep his dick in his pants. Though if you're genuinely asking, Amelia is great and I think she feels the same way about you, so just see what the next six weeks bring and go from there."

"Except he's falling for her?" Grace goes on, ignoring my dropping the whole in love piece of this pie. "He's in love and this is Oliver. A man who swore to never fall in love again," Grace protests because she's a woman and women love love. Men can take it or leave it, and the leave it side has pretty much been my life for the last seven years. But now, I'm starting to creep over to the dark side, and I don't know what the fuck to do about that.

It's only adding to this mess.

"I should have used you as my fake fiancée," I say to Grace.

She starts to laugh only to choke on a gummy worm. Carter reaches over, patting her back until the item dislodges and she can breathe again. "Thanks," she grumbles, reluctant to thank him for saving her life. Damn, what did my brother do to her? "And thanks to you, asshole, for making me choke," she snaps at me. "No one would ever believe I would be engaged to you."

"Why? You're engaged to Tony and I'm way better looking, not to mention cooler than he is."

Grace groans. "Leave Tony out of this. And you're the least good-looking of your brothers."

"Is that your way of saying you think I'm hot?" Carter asks her.

Her eyes roll, but she otherwise ignores his question.

"You're only engaged to Amelia because you stepped in to play the hero for her at the reunion. You're Oliver Fucking Fritz. You should have expected people to go bananas over you being engaged when all you did before was create scandal and broken hearts. Be that as it may, you need to talk to Amelia. Tell her how you feel."

I shake my head adamantly, polishing off the rest of my drink before pouring myself another two fingers' worth. Like I said, it's that kind of night. "It's too soon. She's not there yet and I know it. It will only freak her out and make her run and I don't want her to run."

Want to know something else?

I miss her.

The woman left only twenty-four hours ago, and I fucking miss her already. I miss Layla too. I would have rather spent the evening with them at their place, watching teenage romance flicks and listening to their back and forth than sitting here with my friends drinking expensive booze and eating garbage. I don't know what's happening to me. All I know is that I can't seem to stop it.

Then again, I haven't exactly tried very hard.

Any time I consider holding off or pulling back or resisting or whatever smart thing I should do, I end up doing the complete and total opposite. I'm running full steam ahead into serious relationshipville and like the fool I am, I might be doing it alone. I have no fucking clue where Amelia's head is with us.

None.

My reticent girl tends to not give much away.

I know she cares about me. I know she's worried I'm going to break her heart—I ditto that sentiment. I know she's scared about what happens with us in six weeks—same as I am. But I'm in love. Totally. Completely. Unconditionally. No turning back now in love.

Not only am I screwing things up with this fake engagement business deal, but I could very well end up getting my heart pounded on. Again. Only Amelia will do it with explosives and blow it to smithereens because I already know I like her way more than I ever liked Nora, and I was ready to marry that woman. For real.

"She won't run," Carter declares. "She's in this with you. I know it. She told me as much at the Sox game and that was weeks ago now."

"Just tell me what to do about the engagement side of this mess," I grumble, my mood turning south the more I think about the predicament I'm in. I'm not ready to tell Amelia how I feel. I don't even like admitting it myself.

Love is scary. It's wild and unpredictable. It holds unmatched power over lives and hearts. And when it grows restless or temperamental, it annihilates them.

Everyone is silent, exchanging wide-eyed, fuck-if-I-know expressions. Awesome.

"I think Carter is right," Brecken finally announces. "I think all you can do is continue on like you're doing and see what the next six weeks brings. Maybe something will happen, and the situation will naturally sort itself out."

Yeah. With me going through the shredder.

27

I 've never felt like such a fish out of water before. Almost literally.

"Do I need a life vest?" I ask Oliver as he holds my hand, leading Layla and me down the dock of the harbor.

He laughs. Actually laughs.

Does he not understand I've never in my life stepped foot on a boat before?

"No," he tells me. "You don't. We're not going on the sailboat. My mom was worried the motion would make her nausea worse."

At the mention of his mom, I'm reminded of what I'm really more nervous about his family. But I push that aside and focus on what he just said about the boat.

"I don't understand," I admit, and Layla starts chortling.

"Dude, we're going on that thing." She points straight ahead at the big fucking thing at the end of the dock.

"*That*? We're going on that? It's a cruise ship."

"It's not a cruise ship," Oliver corrects me.

"Oliver, that thing is larger than a football field." I'm not even joking.

"Honestly, I'm not sure how large it is. It's my mother's baby and one day it will be Carter's since he asked first. Weird how that happened, but whatever. My dad's sailing yacht is the really fun one to go on. I'll take you on that this summer, but we'll need Kaplan to help us sail it since he's the one big into sailing along with my dad."

"Jesus," I hiss. "And what crazy thing are you hiding?"

"If you're asking if I own a yacht, or an island, or something else fun, the answer is unfortunately no. But I do have a villa just outside of Positano, Italy, that I own with Luca. Besides that, I haven't had time to really explore my options. Life of a resident and all that."

All I can do is shake my head. And roll my eyes because Oliver is not a typical resident, that's for sure. These people and their money.

"Cool," Layla says, excitement lighting her blue eyes. "Can we go? I'm dying to see Italy. Imagine the food." She groans, clutching her stomach in a food orgasm way.

"Not today, Sprite. Today is all about the water. Our first boating trip of the year. You'll love it."

He's right, of course. The yacht is amazing.

We're led up to what I guess is a sun deck, greeting the captain, Tom along the way. A steward takes our bags, informing us he'll put them in our cabins. This ship has eight guest sleeping cabins and Layla is set to bunk up with Stella. We're sailing out to Martha's Vineyard for the long Memorial Day weekend, where they have a house and a private beach.

The weather is hot and sunny, absolutely perfect.

Cool wind whips up off the Atlantic, blowing my hair from my face as I walk around the spacious deck. This is the back of the shift or the stern, as I think it's called. There are two levels back here, this one which has a small whirlpool/dipping pool surrounded by chaises and built-in benches as well as a shaded eating area that looks like it can accommodate ten. Beneath us is a lower deck that's more like a landing bay for a smaller speed boat and jet skis.

The front of the boat also has a large open area and in the center of it is the main living space that flows three tiers up as well as a few below deck. It's overwhelming and beautiful and insanely cool. Never in my life did I ever expect I'd be aboard a luxury mega-yacht.

Layla is already splashing in the pool with Stella when we're greeted by Oliver's father. He gives me a cool, barely polite nod, his eyes swiping over me before hugging his son. "Glad you could work this out," he says to Oliver, completely ignoring me.

"We wouldn't have missed it," Oliver replies and his father frowns at the word we. Oliver makes a point to raise our joined hands, kissing the finger with the ring on it, and that frown quickly morphs into a scowl.

I think it's safe to say his father hasn't warmed to me in the two months we've been pulling this charade off. While his mother can't get enough of us, his father hardly acknowledges my existence, and whenever he does, it's with disdain. I don't know what to do about it. Oliver says he just needs time to adapt, but I think it's more than that.

The man genuinely dislikes me and everything I represent.

When this all first began, I wasn't sure I wanted them to like me. Now I want them to love me. I'm in love with their son and I have no parents of my own. I miss my father. I miss my mother. I wouldn't mind having surrogate parents. People who love me.

"They're here," Octavia announces, walking up to us with outstretched arms before she wraps both of us up into a hug. "This is the absolute perfect weekend. My entire family in one place." She looks at me as she says this, like I'm one of her family.

And instantly, I'm choked up.

It's like she just read my heart's and mind's desire.

With each passing day I'm with Oliver, that seems to be more and more of what I want. Falling for Oliver, loving him, it's becoming as natural as breathing. Terrifying and nerve-wracking, but nothing short of splendid and soul-quenching. It's not something I thought I would have like this. I keep waiting for the other shoe to drop.

Any second, because that's how it always goes.

The moment everything feels absolutely perfect, just so right, that's when the rug inevitably gets pulled out from under you.

She must read this on my face because she grabs my hand, gingerly yanking me into her side. Her movements are careful, her frame slighter than even the last time we saw her a few days ago. It breaks my heart, but hopefully once the chemo is finished, she'll be stronger than she ever was.

"Come with me, Amelia," she says, grinning conspiratorially. "Let's let the boys play and we'll sit in the sun, catching some Vitamin D."

"No wearing the red bikini until I can see it though," Oliver says, and my face heats six ways to Sunday. My mouth falls open, and he laughs, leaning in and kissing me, right here in front of his parents. "Just wanted to see that pretty blush. Have fun." Another kiss, this one to my cheek and then Octavia is dragging me along.

"Oliver mentioned you've never been on a boat before," she states, leading me over to the build-in bench along the side of the yacht. "It makes me glad we're on this one and not the sailboat. We won't be going fast so you'll hardly feel the movement on a ship this size."

"That's good to know. I was worried about feeling queasy," I admit, matching her position with my face upturned toward the sun. It's still early in the day, but the rays instantly seep into me, warming me through in the most splendid of ways.

"This was my father's ship," she goes on. "When he passed, I inherited it along with everything else from the Abbot line. Over the years, we've made some upgrades, but I spent most of my childhood on this ship, sailing around the world with my parents who were never happy in one place. Or with each other for that matter." She winks at me. "It feels as much like home to me as anything else."

"It's lovely. Did you enjoy growing up that way? Obviously not with parents who didn't enjoy each other." My face hits my hands. "Sorry."

She squeezes my forearm. "You're perfect. My parents were arranged, similar to Dr. Fritz and me, though it worked out far better for us than them. But do you mean traveling the world?"

"Yes. That's what exactly I meant. It sounds incredible. I haven't been anywhere other than Massachusetts and New Hampshire where I went to school for a couple of years."

"I did and I didn't." She crosses and then uncrosses her legs, waving her hand about the ship. "It's a big, beautiful world and in traveling, I learned and saw a lot. Both the good and the bad side of what this life can do to people. But it was also lonely. I was an only child, as is Dr. Fritz, which is why we both wanted a big family. Well, after we decided we liked each other, that is." She winks at me again, and right now, I see so much of Oliver in her charm.

I laugh at that. "A big family you got. I can't imagine what raising five boys was like. I'm having enough trouble with one teenage girl and Layla is amazingly easy."

"It was challenging, I won't lie about that. I liked doing a lot of it myself, but I was desperate for a girl, so we kept going. Believe me, I didn't intend on having six children. I likely should have stopped after the twins, but I don't regret a second of it."

"I'm grateful you kept going for the girl."

Something about me saying that has Octavia's expression sobering. She sits up, her cold, bone-thin hand wrapping around my forearm, drawing me away from the sun to meet her eyes.

"You really love him, don't you."

It's a statement, not a question, but I swallow thickly and nod all the same. And I'm not even doing it to maintain our ruse. I'm telling her a truth I haven't admitted to anyone. Certainly not to Layla or Oliver. Hell, I've scarcely allowed myself to think in those terms.

Without a word, she wraps me up in her arms, holding me tight. "I'm so grateful for you, Amelia. You've brought my son back to life. Back to love. And his heart is too big and beautiful to be lonely and empty. It needed a match. Someone who would love him back with all the passion and fire he deserves."

And now I'm crying. I can't speak because if I do, I'll sob for sure. I'm definitely trembling against her.

I clear my throat. "He did the same thing with me. I was going through the motions, day in and day out until Oliver came along."

"That's what happens when it's right. Suddenly you have no idea how you lived before them because it was all colorless and flat."

"Exactly. That's exactly how it's been."

I can't stop my tears. Thinking about what she just said. About how my heart soars with it. But my tears are also the tears of a woman on the edge of uncertainty. We have only one more month of this deal, and then what?

We haven't talked about it.

And I don't know what to say.

How do you maintain a relationship when its foundation is a mountain of lies? How do you build a future when you're already pretending at one? How do you tell yourself everything will be okay when it never has been before?

She pulls back, wiping at her own emotion, but managing to smile through it when I'm incapable.

"It's all I've ever wanted, you know," she tells me. "For my children to find love and happiness. My own marriage was arranged as I know you know, and while I wouldn't trade any of it, I love Dr. Fritz very much. It could have very easily gone in a different direction."

"Like your parents?"

"Yes," she says. "Precisely that way. I never want that for my children. Neither does Dr. Fritz. It was the start of what drew us together. Seeing our children settled in love is my greatest wish. And watching Oliver, my baby boy, with you, being engaged to you has been my greatest joy."

And now I think I'm going to throw up.

Another tear hits my cheek, one I'm miserable to stop, and I turn instantly, locking on Oliver who I felt watching us, his eyes boring into me. He's dripping in concern, staring as more tears helplessly fall.

"You okay?" he mouths and I don't have it in me to answer him.

Am I okay? No. Not exactly. I want to stay lost in this. I want to pretend just a while longer. I want to laugh and smile and be with Oliver.

With my eyes on his, I say to Octavia, "I would never do anything to intentionally hurt him or any of you."

It's my simplest truth. And maybe it sounds bad. In fact, I know it does.

But suddenly, perpetuating this lie doesn't sit well with me.

Her greatest joy is a lie.

I should end this. I should end everything. Because inevitably, someone *will* get hurt. Eventually, if Oliver and I continue, we will have to come clean about our lie. And then what? His mother will be devastated. His father will hate me for it—more than he already does.

There will be no path forward after that.

A frown slices my features in two, the weight of my thoughts crushing me from the inside out.

No matter what, this ends. One way or another, when the fake engagement ends, so do Oliver and me.

28

Amelia ♥

"**P**edal, pedal, pedal!" Oliver yells as he runs beside Layla's bike, one of his hands on the bottom of the seat, the other holding one of the handlebars.

"I am!" she screams back, but the laugh in her voice and the smile on her face tells me she thinks this is hysterical. I do too. I haven't stopped laughing once.

"You're not pedaling fast enough."

"Come on, Oliver," I call out, cupping my hands around my mouth. "Run faster. You're not a very good teacher."

His eyes shoot over to mine, narrowed like he wants to spank my ass for that comment, and I laugh harder. He's trying to teach Layla how to ride a bike so we can go into town that way to the ice cream shop Layla has been desperate to try. Poor, deprived city kid that she is, doesn't even know how to ride a bike. The last thing she rode had training wheels, and that was when my parents were still alive.

"Balance your weight," he tells her, practically gritting his teeth as Layla swivels and sways around the huge driveway of the Fritz's Martha's Vineyard home.

"Can't we just take the Jeep?" I ask because whether she learns how to ride it or not, I don't exactly feel safe with her riding into town.

"That's giving up," he says.

"No, it's smart," Layla retorts. "I'm done. I don't feel like getting hit by a car."

And with that, she hops off the bike, practically while the damn thing is still moving, and Oliver is still running. The bike falls to the ground and Oliver huffs out a tired breath, his hand on his hips, sweat slicking his forehead.

"Aw, Sprite. I'd never let a car hit you," he promises. She folds her arms defiantly over her chest. I do the same, and he growls in defeat. "Fine. No bikes. We'll take the Jeep."

"You can teach me how to drive," Layla offers. "Amelia has no car, so I'm SOL there."

"SOL?" he questions.

"Shit out of luck."

"Hey, mouth."

She rolls her eyes at me. "That's why I said SOL." She turns back to Oliver. "What do you say?"

"You're only fourteen."

She smiles at him, batting her eyelashes. "Please," she begs, holding her hands up in supplication. "Pretty, pretty please. With a cherry on top? This might be my one and only chance."

He fights a grin, trying for stern and failing. Oliver, I don't think knows how to say no to Layla. All the girl has to do is smile at him. I'm thinking that's going to be a chronic problem for him.

"What say you, big sister?"

I shrug. "I don't see the harm as long as it's just the driveway."

"Yes!" Layla squeals, jumping up and down and then hauling me in for a hug before abandoning me just as quickly and doing the same with Oliver. "You're the best. Let's do this!"

Layla runs toward the massive garage off to the side and Oliver strolls over to me, tossing his arm around my shoulder and kissing my temple. "I never thought I'd be twenty-eight and teaching a teenager how to drive."

"But now you're her hero."

"I like being her hero. It's fun getting to do big brother-type stuff with her."

I wrap my arms around his midsection, pressing my cheek into his chest, listening to the steady beat of his heart. His lips fall onto the top of my head, breathing me in and out. This man... God, he really is something else. Something so incredible. Something I never want to let go of. Ever.

"Come on, you two," Layla yells. "You can hug and kiss later. Daylights burning and ice cream waits for no one."

I laugh, pulling back to peek up at Oliver. "You ready to teach her how to drive, hero?"

"No. But let's do it."

A few minutes later, Layla is sitting in the driver's seat and my heart is already pounding. Oliver might not be ready to teach a teenager how to drive, but that goes for me too. Layla, while very much a teenager, is still young. And I'm, well, yeah, the years have gone by a little quick.

"Alright. First thing is, you adjust your mirrors," Oliver says, his voice calm but firm. He's way better at this than I would be. I'd be a nervous wreck. Oh wait, I already am. My heart is beating like a damn jackrabbit and we're only in the driveway.

"Done," Layla says as she finishes with the side mirrors. "Next?"

"Next is you make sure you're in a good position. You look around. You take in your surroundings. Then, when you feel comfortable, press your foot onto the brake, and put the car in drive."

The car is already on since Oliver had to back it out of the garage —something he would not allow Layla to even attempt.

"Okay. Here we go. Eeeek!" Layla shifts the Jeep into drive and then, naturally, hits the gas way too hard and we go flying only for her to freak out and slam on the brakes with a scream. "Crap. Oh my god. What did I do wrong?"

Oliver glances over his shoulder at me, a harried look on his face.

"Does this thing come with a harness back here? I don't feel like this seat belt is enough."

"Amelia," Layla yells. "Don't tease me."

I hold my hands up. "You're right. I'm sorry. But next time, maybe ease onto the gas instead of pressing down with all your weight."

"Oh. Okay. Good call. Can I plug in your phone so I can set up my music?"

"No music, Sprite. You have to concentrate."

"But I need my tunes. How am I supposed to get my head on straight if I'm not rocking out."

Oliver rubs at his lips, his hand reaching back and squeezing my knee. I think Oliver has officially bitten off more than he can chew. "Sorry, no music. Come on, you can do this. Just as Amelia said, ease onto the gas at an even weight, hands on the wheel and focus on where you're going."

Layla throws him a dubious look.

"You've got it," he encourages. "I know you do. That was your first time. That happens with everyone."

"Does it?" she turns and asks me, gnawing on her lip.

"Definitely. Dad sprung his first gray hairs the first time he took me driving, and I was a lot worse. I nearly hit a telephone pole. This is all driveway and grass. Just don't hit the house."

Layla groans at my teasing tone, but she's smile, more relaxed. "Okay." She wiggles her ass on the leather seats and starts off again, this time much slower on the gas. Almost too slow, but that's fine.

"Good," Oliver praises. "That's it. A little more. Perfect. Now that you feel that point on the gas, focus on your steering. I want you to go down the driveway in a straight line, then we'll turn around and head back for the circle."

Layla takes us down the long driveway at a snail's pace, her posture more rigid than I've ever seen.

"The first time my dad took me driving, he brought me out in his old Porsche."

"Like yours?" Layla asks.

"Like mine. A stick shift. That's much harder to learn on, but an important skill to have all the same. When you're older, a little more experienced, I'll take you out and we can try that."

"In your Porsche?" Layla practically squeals, incredulous.

"Does that mean I get to drive it then?" I quip. "I have my license."

"Can you handle a stick?"

He quirks his head over his shoulder, his dirty eyes filled with mischief.

"Oh, I'm sure I can manage. Especially with the right teacher."

"You wanna drive my Porsche, baby?"

I can't fight my smile. "Absolutely. Any chance I can get."

"Why does it sound like you're talking in code?"

Oliver and I both start cracking up, the car jerking forward only to speed up one second and nearly stop the next. At this rate, we'll all have whiplash and need urgent care instead of ice cream.

"This is the end of the driveway. Do you want to try turning around?"

"Um, yeah. Did you see how awesome I was? Totally drove straight. I've got this. I don't know why you have to wait until you're sixteen. I'm a natural."

"And modest too."

"No backseat drivers, Amelia. My fake brother-in-law is teaching me, not you."

She points a stern finger at me in the rearview mirror and I make a motion to zip my lips.

"Now you're going to want to turn the wheel and before you get to the edge, you'll want to brake and then go in reverse, turning the wheel in the opposite direction. Does that make sense?"

"Um. I think so." She glances at Oliver, turning the wheel around and around. "Like this?"

"Yes. Now slow on the gas. Good. Good. Now stop, foot all the way down on the brake before you put it into reverse and—"

"Ah!!" Layla and I scream at the same time as the Jeep goes flying at top speed, hurdling over the side of the driveway and down into the thick grass. We're thrown back into our seats, wind whipping all around us as it comes in through the open top.

"Brake, Layla," Oliver barks urgently, trying to stay calm. "Hit the brake."

"I'm trying!" she screams, panicking. "It's not working."

"You're hitting the gas! That's the gas. Shit, turn the wheel or we're going to hit that tree."

The Jeep lurches and swerves back and forth as Layla frantically starts spinning the wheel this way and that, all the while we're still barreling toward the tree. My hands white knuckle the seat, my mouth open on a silent scream because I'm worried if I do scream—the way I'm freaking desperate to—I'll scare Layla more.

"Lift your foot off the gas. Now. Do it now as you turn the wheel to your left only. Slower. Don't jerk it, or we'll spin out. Good. That's good. Now press your foot on the other pedal. The one on the left."

The Jeep comes to a screeching halt, all of us flying forward with the momentum of the car, narrowly missing the tree.

"Oh my god," Layla cries as we all pant for our lives. "We almost died. I almost killed us."

That's when she breaks down. Her face hits her hand as she's consumed with sobs. Oliver throws the car into park, unbuckles his seat belt, and crawls over the console to hug Layla. His arms capture her small body, and he pulls her to him, unbuckling her seat belt and practically dragging her into his chest. She grips his shoulders fiercely, holding on for dear life as she absolutely loses it on him.

"Shhh. It's okay, Layla. It's okay. We're fine. No one got hurt. Shhh. Don't cry, Sprite. I've got you."

"But... but... I could have. I could have hurt all of us."

My hand finds her hair, stroking the blonde strands as she sobs uncontrollably into Oliver's shirt, likely soaking it through though he doesn't seem to care.

"Layla," I whisper. "This car has airbags."

"What?" she sniffles, unwilling to release Oliver.

"The Jeep. It has airbags. Mom and Dad's car didn't. It was very old, and it didn't have airbags. That's why they died. If their car had been newer and had airbags, they very likely would have lived."

She starts to pull away from Oliver's chest, her face absolutely soaked in tears and snot. Oliver goes to the glove box and grabs some tissues, wiping under her eyes. "It's just a car, Layla," he tells her, smiling warmly at her. "If you had crashed it, we would have gotten it fixed. Plus, this is a Jeep. A big Jeep. We would have been fine."

"Are you sure?" she asks, her chin trembling, her eyes still watery. "I'm so sorry. I panicked. I meant to hit the brake, and I pushed harder on the gas instead and then I didn't know what to do."

"You listened to me when it really mattered," he explains. "You did exactly what I told you to do, and we didn't hit the tree."

She swallows hard, bobbing her head up and down before twisting to find me. "Is that really why they died?"

I unbuckle myself now that my heart rate has slowed, and I once again have control over my basic motor function. Because holy Jesus, I don't think I've ever been that scared in my life. It's a wonder I didn't pee myself.

Scooting up, I cup her face in my hands. "Yes," I tell her, staring into her blue eyes. "It was a bad accident, and they likely would have been hurt either way, but part of the reason it was so bad was the car. Any car you drive now, you'll be much safer in. And honestly, today you just learned a valuable lesson."

"What's that?"

"The importance of trying not to panic, even in a scary situation and treating driving with the respect it requires. Because unfortunately, we did learn the hard way that it's not all fun and games. But Oliver is right, you listened, and you were able to stop the Jeep."

"You alright, Sprite?"

She turns back to Oliver and gives him a wan smile. "I think so. I'm so sorry about the grass."

Oliver waves her away. "It'll grow back. How about I drive us to get some ice cream now. I think we could all use it."

"And a shot of tequila," I tease, winking at Layla who giggles lightly, hopping down from the Jeep to switch places with Oliver. They meet at the front end of the Jeep, the two of them exchanging something that I can't hear before a smile lights up Layla's face. She gives him another hug and my heart explodes in my chest.

I knew they had gotten close. It was easy as day to see.

But the way he held her just now in the car and the way he talks to her...

I want that for her. I want that so badly I can hardly breathe. I want her to have an Oliver in her life. A big brother who will always have her back and take care of her when she needs him most. I just hope I can keep him with us. Forever.

29

Oliver ♥

From the moment my mother finished her conversation with Amelia on the boat on the way out here, I knew shit had gone down. I also knew Amelia would be a mess about it. I was right. She was quiet for the entire rest of that day, hardly eating any of her food, and then that night, she laid silently awake while she thought I was asleep.

It took a lot of specially designed torture to get her to talk. A lot of tickling and licking and sucking—in the precise spot designed for optimum pleasure without delivering the big O until she promised to spill all. Only once she did, did I let her see stars.

She told me what my mother had said, and I very nearly replied with, I could have told you that. My mother has never been coy about telling each and every one of us what her greatest wish is for us. To find love and be happy. Truth, I think that's likely top on most parents' wish list for their kids, so it isn't exactly like any of us gave it a lot of thought until this whole fake engagement thing got started.

But Amelia doesn't have parents to tell her that stuff. That they want her to be happy and in love. I think that's why Amelia is struggling so hard with the lie. She loved her mom. She misses her mom. And not just does she hate lying on principle, but I know deep down she's worried that by lying to my mom, she'll lose her before she ever has a chance to truly win her.

At least that's what I inferred was bothering her from what she said. Sometimes it's impossible to tell if Amelia is holding out on me. The problem was, that night, I didn't have it in me to convince her that what we were doing was right. Because even though my mom is happy, the heavy and looming end of engagement deadline is taking small slices out of me with every uncertain thought.

I've contemplated every angle. Every possible approach.

And short of fessing up or actually asking Amelia to marry me—something I'm pretty positive she would say no to but find myself actually considering all the same—I don't know what to do.

Which brings me to tonight.

Our last night on the vineyard.

It's been the perfect weekend. Lots of sun and beach. Shopping in town. Ice cream and bike rides. A near car accident. Tonight, we had a lobster bake and a bonfire on our beach, which is where we are now. The sun has just set, sinking into the dark, turbulent ocean that matches my insides, the pink, purple, and gold collage of colors draining from the sky along with it. The breeze turns from pleasantly warm to the slightest bit chilly, and my thoughts are fragmented.

One more month.

Then it's three weeks. Then two. Then one. Then over.

The worst sort of perpetual countdown on an endless stream through my head.

One by one, my family packs it in. My parents first, my mother's waning energy barely managing to hold on through dinner. She takes the girls in, getting them ready for bed and my father silently broods as he follows after to help. Next are my brothers, who are hell-bent on having one last night in town out at the bars. Luca in a particularly crappy mood as our lovely Raven Fairchild, daughter of our house manager, for lack of a better title, didn't come out this year. She hasn't in years, not since he broke her heart, so I'm not sure what he was expecting this go around.

Rina and Brecken stroll off hand in hand down the beach,

heading for who knows where. Brecken, I think, is getting ready to pop the question in the next few weeks. Something I wish he had done sooner, though at this point, nothing could have prevented the trajectory Amelia and I find ourselves on.

"It's so beautiful here," Amelia says with a light sigh. Despite the difficult first night on the boat, she's been nothing but smiles and laughter all weekend. She's had a fantastic trip, we've had a fantastic time together, and I don't want this weekend to ever end.

"Do you want to go swimming?" I tease as I take her hand and lift her up until we're both standing, ambling toward the water's edge as the tide rolls in to meet our bare feet.

"Isn't that how Jaws started? Right here on this very island?"

"Oh, so you were thinking about skinny dipping?"

The water leaps up over our feet and ankles, splashing along our calves and she lets out an *eeek*. "No!" It's a gasp. "Holy mothballs, if I was before that thought just died along with the feeling in my toes. That's freaking freezing."

"We'll come back in August. The water is much warmer then. Maybe we'll even find Jaws."

"Har, har," she mocks. "We're gonna need a bigger boat."

"Understatement of my life there, baby."

Now she cackles. "I seriously doubt that. Your bigger boat is parked offshore somewhere because it wouldn't even fit in your marina."

I take her hand in mine, spinning her around in a circle, the dwindling fire not even fifty yards from us burnishing copper against her red hair and pale skin.

"What if I want to take you and Layla somewhere? My residency ends in July and then I don't start my attending position until August. I have a whole month off with nothing to do and Layla doesn't start Wilchester until September."

Her breath catches just as I force her into my chest, my hands wrap around her lower back, hers around my neck as we stare into each other's eyes, lost. Damn, I'm so fucking lost in this woman.

"A trip? Where would we go? Your villa?"

She thinks I'm kidding. I'm not.

"We could, you know. It's hot and sunny, but the Mediterranean that time of year is incredible."

She blinks up at me. "You're serious?"

"I am."

She considers this for a moment. "I want to say yes. I want to say yes to everything. A trip like that with you would be a dream come true. But I don't know how we can. I know you're going to argue with me, but I don't have the money for a trip like that and I can't allow you to pay for us."

My forehead drops to hers. I knew she was going to say that. "Can we pretend?"

"Pretend?" she parrots, staring straight at me.

"If you could pick the perfect vacation, where would you go?"

"I'm not sure. I never allowed myself to think about it all that much. I'd love to go to Italy. All over Europe. All over the world."

"Can we bring Layla with us?"

A smile splits her lips. "You grew very close with Layla this weekend."

"I'm crazy about her." I'm crazy about you. Why can't I make the words come out? Why can't I tell her that I never want us to end? "So, is that a no to Italy?"

"Oliver, we seriously need to figure out where we'll be in a month."

I shake my head at that. I don't want to figure that out. I don't want to be practical. I don't want to think about anything serious at all. I just want to be with her. Because being lost in her is a hell of a lot easier than attempting to deal with reality.

She has no clue what she's done for me. To me.

I love her. So very much. And it's not something I ever imagined I'd feel again. Not only that, what I feel for her is infinitely stronger than anything I ever felt for Nora.

"We're not ending in a month, Amelia. It will simply be an adjustment in our plan."

She smiles. The most breathtaking of smiles. A smile that holds the key to my heart. In this moment, I'd do anything for her. Anything to keep that smile going. Because that's exactly what she's done for me. She's brought me back to a life I hadn't realized I had given up on.

When love hurts you in the cruelest and most deceiving of ways, it's easy to turn your back on it. Hell, it becomes a natural instinct. A method of self-preservation.

Amelia lost her parents, a guy she thought was her future, and then sunk her life into raising Layla. I got backstabbed by a woman I was planning on marrying. A woman I thought was my end game and when it turned out she was all things rotten, I became a one-date wonder.

But now I don't just want one date or twenty. I want all the dates. I want all the moments. All the sunrises and sunsets. All the tears and smiles. I want Amelia and I'm pretty fucking positive I want her forever.

"What kind of adjustment?" she asks, cocking an eyebrow in my direction. "I'm hoping you have an idea because I've got nothing."

"Well, you could marry me. For real."

Her laugh tells me everything I need to know and the words, I love you so fucking much I can hardly function with holding it in a second longer, dies on my tongue. She thinks I'm joking when I'm not sure I actually am.

"Don't joke about stuff like that. There has to be a real way to do this."

She thinks I'm joking when I'm not sure I actually am.

Too soon?

Yeah, I know.

Insane?

Very likely.

Do I care?

Not really.

Problem is, we're both hiding things. Me what I did to get Layla her full 'scholarship' for school. Her... well, I have no idea what she's keeping from me, I just know it's something. Her heart isn't an open book. She may have laid part of it in my lap for me to pick up and hold beside mine, but she clutches the other half possessively, offers it cautiously, even as she loves selflessly.

"If you have a solution, I'm all ears."

She shakes her head, her eyes glassing over. "I don't want to talk about it anymore tonight," she says on another sigh, this one heavier than the one before it. "I just want to be with you and enjoy our last night here."

"We can do that."

I dance with her against the rising moonlight, the sounds of the ocean on the shore our music. I hold her and we sway, sort of how we did at the reunion, lost in ourselves, in a moment. I close my eyes and my face dips into her neck. Breathing her in, I clutch her just a bit tighter, already feeling this slipping away from me.

Like I'm about to lose everything again.

But instead of it making me want to run, it's making me rebel. Fight.

"I'm not letting you go," I tell her.

"I don't want you to let me go. Ever. But I'm not about to let you destroy your reputation with the media nor break your mother's heart either."

"Why is it one or the other?"

"Tell me how it's not?" Her voice is almost pleading. "Tell me how we fix this. How we're together and not engaged without telling your parents? I'll do it, Oliver. I swear, I will. I'll do anything."

I open my mouth, and nothing comes out. No sound.

Because even though she's brought me back to life. Even though she's taught me how love should truly be. I can't tell her I love her. I can't tell her I need her. I can't tell her anything because even though my mind is quick to forget, my heart isn't. It reminds me of how badly we've been damaged.

"I don't know, Amelia. I don't know. I just have to imagine we'll think of something."

She doesn't look so sure we will. "I thought we said no talking about this tonight," she goes on, forcing me to dip her back until her fingers glide through the soft grains of the sand.

"How about I just dick you instead then?"

"What?" she snaps, bolting upright at my harsh tone.

"I'm thinking you could use a deep dicking. Might help things out. Get your mind straight where we're concerned."

Her eyes sparkle with life and challenge. "You think I need that?"

"Without a doubt," I tell her, grinding into her.

"And what exactly do you think I need my mind straight on?"

I press into her. Deeper. Harder. My face mere inches from hers, I let her see the wild in my eyes. The fucking extremes floating uninhibited through my crazy.

"That you're mine." And that's where it ends because I shut up any bullshit retort with my lips. I kiss her like the devil. Like a demon. Like a thief. "Argue it, Amelia. I fucking dare you."

"The hot thing about badass bitches, Oliver, is that we don't have to argue it. We might like that shit you alphas breathe down our throats, but we all know it's us who own both you and your dicks."

And that's when I die. Almost literally. I absolutely collapse into the sand, dragging her down with me until she's locked on top of me. My legs around hers. Arms around her back. Lips layered with hers.

"Where the fuck have you been, Amelia Atkins?"

She smiles like the first burst of morning sunshine after a week of rain. "Right here all along. Waiting on one particular alpha dick to find me. I am yours, Oliver. But you're mine too. Don't forget it."

I laugh, utterly deranged. "You're goddamn brilliant. I'm hard as a rock from that."

"Good. Then you know I mean business."

I roll us, pressing her into the sand. "Then you know I do too. When I tell you you're mine, choices left the building along with common sense and better judgment."

A giggle rolls through her, the water's edge lapping up to meet us, soaking half our bodies in its cold kiss. "I swear I've heard that before."

"Nah, baby, that's all me. Oliver Fritz, super alpha dick. But it sounds sexy, right? Totally got your panties wet?"

"It's not just my panties that are wet as hell. But I think you're onto something there."

I groan. Then I laugh. Because yeah, we're both soaked. And cold. Damn, this ocean is frigid.

But her eyes. Her eyes are like stars. Luminous. Alluring. Home.

I'm home with her.

And no matter what comes our way, I'm not letting her go. No fucking way.

30

Amelia ♥

"Amelia, our last patient of the day got canceled," Sagginalls says as I finish off the last bite of my peanut butter sandwich. No jelly this time. Things are way too tight right now for that.

"How come?" I ask, wrapping everything back up and tucking it inside my lunch bag.

"She came down with a cold and a fever. We'll have to reschedule her."

"Oh. Okay." That's seriously the best news I've had in a while. That means we're done for the day.

As if reading my mind, he says, "Are you going to head out, or are you going to shower first?"

"I think I'll just grab my stuff and head out." I'll shower at Oliver's, whose shower is infinitely nicer than the locker room showers here.

"Okay. I'll walk you out."

I follow after him, through the halls of the day surgery wing, scooting into the locker room and throwing him a wave goodbye as I do. Instead of changing, I just grab my bag, tossing it onto my shoulder, but when I exit the locker room, Sagginalls is still there, waiting for me.

When he said walk me out, he clearly meant it.

We continue on in silence until I think he gets to the point where he can't take it anymore. He slows his pace and I wonder if it's because we haven't spent much one-on-one time since Oliver came into the picture. Before that, he used to try and eat lunch with me, even when doctors never ever do that here. Or corner me for 'patient' conversations in the hall.

All that has stopped and now it's like he has no idea how to interact with me.

"Am I allowed to ask what you're doing this weekend?"

I inwardly grin at his tone. For such a cocky and arrogant man, he tucked tail and ran pretty quickly. Why it took a man entering my life for that to happen, I have no idea.

"Nothing all that much," I say. "I'm going to Oliver's tonight and then I'll probably do something with Layla tomorrow."

He pivots to face me. "You still don't live with Oliver? You've been engaged for nearly three months now."

I blanch at his that's kinda weird expression. "Not yet. I wanted to wait until Layla was done with the school year before we moved in."

"Right," he says, but his entire demeanor changes. "Didn't she finish school over a week ago?"

I swallow thickly, looking down at my feet. "Yes."

He smiles now. Like he knows my engagement is bullshit, and he's back in the game.

A fact he goes on to prove when he continues with, "Well, if you and Layla are interested, my niece, Clara, is in town, and I was thinking about going to the Museum of Science with her. Might be fun to go together. She's fifteen and I'm sure she and Layla would get along well."

"Um." I have no idea what to say. "That sounds great, but Layla and I went pretty recently."

"Think about it," he pushes, a sparkle to his eyes. "Since you don't have plans tomorrow with Oliver, I think we could have a lot of fun together."

We step out into the hot Boston afternoon, the rush of the

hospital flowing around us. He shifts into me, a lot closer than I'm comfortable with, and I step back. He's undeterred. Fabulous. His head dips down, his grin impish.

"Have a good night, Amelia. I hope to see you tomorrow."

And with a flirtatious wink, he strolls off. I puff out a breath, knowing I'm going to have to deal with him again like this. Especially when my engagement is set to end in two weeks. Something Oliver and I still haven't figured out yet.

Shaking my head, I spin around only to slam directly into someone. "I'm so sorry," I say, stumbling back a step and brushing a few strands of hair from my eyes.

"That's alright, I've been waiting on you."

I blink up, fighting the bright afternoon sun as I take in Dr. Fritz, Oliver's dad standing tall before me.

"You were waiting on me?" is my only response.

"Yes," he says, ushering me off to the side of the building, his hand on my upper arm as if to prevent me from getting away. "I saw on the OR schedule that your last patient got scrapped. I figured I'd wait out here for you."

"Oh. Is everything alright? Is there a problem with Octavia?"

He stares down at me, his brown eyes as cold as they always are when he regards me. "Octavia is fine. She's at home resting after her chemo yesterday. No, I came here to talk to you and that's not something I wanted to do in the hospital."

"Alright. What can I do for you, Dr. Fritz?"

"I know about your debt," he says without any preamble.

I jar back at that, utterly stunned. An uneasy knot forms in my gut, making my half-digested sandwich feel like a lead weight. "How did you—"

"I have my ways," he cuts me off. "It wasn't exactly hard to find though. Anyone with half a brain could have. You're in quite a bit of trouble, aren't you? Barely making your minimum payments on your credit cards and student loans."

I turn away from him at that, seething. I grit my teeth before I force myself to suck in a calming breath. It doesn't help. I'm pissed.

Nearby, a car honks its horn. People are on their phones, walking past us, and right now, it feels like my world is falling apart while everyone else's goes on. Just another Friday afternoon for them.

"You had absolutely no right to—"

"I had every right," he snaps, coming in closer, shifting me against the brick building. "You're engaged to my son. You're wearing my family's heirloom on your hand. Another diamond on your neck. You're taking advantage of my son."

"No," I bark, adamantly shaking my head. "I'm not."

He laughs cruelly. "You expect me to believe that? I know about what Oliver did for Layla."

"What?"

"There are no full scholarships at Wilchester, Amelia. I know you're aware of that. I know what Oliver did for Layla to get her 'full scholarship'?" He puts air quotes around the word.

I shake my head, confused. "I don't know what you mean. They made an exception."

He glares at me like I'm stupid. "They don't make exceptions. Not for anyone. Not even for Oliver. No, he paid for the other half of Layla's tuition for all four years. Or are you pretending you didn't know that or ask him to do it?"

"What?" I gasp. "No. He wouldn't. That's not... I didn't know he did that." I didn't fucking know that at all. Ire heats my blood, my face no doubt matching my hair.

I'm furious.

How could Oliver do something like that? How could he pay for her like that? That wasn't the deal. That wasn't any part of the goddamn deal we made.

He has to know I would have never accepted that. And he did it anyway. Why? For Layla or so that I would keep up my end of the deal and stay his fake fiancée? Plus, he lied to me. The bastard lied about all of it.

"Don't you dare lie to me," he snarls. "You expect me to believe you dating my son and getting him to propose after only a couple of months—during which time he never mentioned you to us once—is happenstance? True love?" he scoffs. "Please, Amelia. I am not a stupid man. You might have blinded my son into thinking you're in love with him and you might have charmed my wife and children, but you have not fooled me for a second. I know a gold-digger when I see one. You're in so much debt there is no end in sight, and now Oliver is paying for half of Layla's high school tuition. His heart is simply too big and trusting to even entertain the idea that you're using him, but the facts are what they are. It was only a matter of time before we learned the truth about you."

Tears prickle my eyes as my fists ball up. "I'm not using him," I grit out. "Oliver knows nothing of my debts, and I had no idea what he did for Layla."

He glares at me, his features wooden. "Right. Of course," he says sardonically. "Because Oliver naturally would have just paid for Layla's tuition without being asked to." He practically rolls his eyes at me, and I clench my teeth. "As for your debt, I believe you that Oliver doesn't know about it. You're smart. You had to know that if you had told him, it would have set off all kinds of alarms for him. No, you just figured you'd wait until you were married. Then pay them off when you have access to his money."

Indignation flares through me, but I try to rein in my temper, hold my tone steady and calm. "Dr. Fritz, I understand your position on this, and I appreciate you looking out for Oliver's best interest, but I can assure you, everything you are saying about me is wrong. Yes, I have a lot of debt I accrued after my parents died and I was trying to take care of Layla and earn my degree. Yes, it is a struggle for me to pay this off. But that debt never is something I would allow Oliver to be responsible for nor pay off for me. It is my responsibility and mine alone." I suck in a breath here, because I can't tell him about the arrangement with Layla and school. "As for Oliver paying for Layla's tuition, believe me when I tell you I will not allow that to stand. I do not want him paying for her education."

"So you care nothing for Oliver's money?" he challenges, incredulous.

I hold my head up, staring defiantly into his eyes. "Nothing."

"And you love my son?"

"Yes," I tell him because I do. "With all my heart." Even as it destroys me. Even as what Dr. Fritz is saying about me breaks my heart. Even as everything inside me shatters and dies.

"And if I were to give you this?" Reaching out, he thrusts something at me that I reflexively take.

Unfolding it, I gasp, nearly choking on my own bile as it climbs up the back of my throat.

It's a check.

A check to buy me off.

A check to get me to walk away from his son. To get me out of their lives for good. Never in my life have I felt lower or more disrespected, and yet, I can't hate him for it either.

He's trying to protect his son. His family.

And I'm just the poor, parentless girl who tricked and manipulated his son. The gold-digger as he said.

I'm holding two million dollars in my hand. Two million dollars that would change my life. Eliminate my debt. All my fears and anxieties along with it. Pay for Layla's education—college included.

I crumple the check up in my hand before pressing it into his chest. "No thanks," I tell him, releasing it and forcing him to catch it before it falls to the ground. "I don't want your money; Dr. Fritz and I don't want Oliver's. I don't belong in your world." My breath hitches high in my throat as I say that, the truth behind my words practically gutting. "If I didn't already feel it, you just proved that to me. I will never be accepted by you." I take a step back as the first of my tears burn my cheeks.

I'm devastated. Heartbroken. Angry. Humiliated.

I was foolish to think I could be part of their family. That I would be loved or accepted. That Oliver and I would be able to find a way for this to work.

No. At the end of the day, I was never going to be one of them.

This always had to end, and now it's ending ugly.

Sooner or later, everyone leaves me. Whether by choice or force of nature. The moment I start to allow myself to depend on others is the moment I'm most likely to be disappointed. It's a lesson I've learned the hard way but evidently needed a refresher on.

Dr. Fritz watches me, almost as if he has no idea what to do with me now that I rejected his offer. "Amelia," he tries, his hand with the check in it reaching out as he takes a step like he's going to follow me.

I shake my head, my gaze narrowed at his offending hand. He drops it instantly and suddenly; he looks so very unsure of himself. Like he knows he fucked up.

But it's too late now.

The damage has already been done.

"I knew it all along," I say, almost as if I'm talking to myself. "Nothing good ever lasts."

At least not for me.

31

Oliver

The second I get out of the shower, the doorbell rings. With a groan, I grab my towel, wrapping it around my waist sprinting across my apartment to answer the door. "Come in, baby," I call out to Amelia as I nearly bust my ass, slipping all over the place with my wet feet.

The door opens, the smile on my face dropping along with my stomach. "What the hell are you doing here?"

Nora looks me up and down, her eyes feasting on my wet, naked chest and abs, and I clench the towel tighter at my waist.

"We need to talk," she declares breezily, a smirk now on her ruby-red lips. A color I've never seen her wear like that, and I have to wonder if it's because Amelia does.

"I have nothing to say to you. Get the hell out."

She makes a tsking sound. "I bet you'll change your mind after you hear what I have to say. See what I have to show you."

Fuck. Just fuck. How the hell did she get up here?

"By all means, stay like that," she continues. "Or better yet, drop the towel."

I laugh at that. "Honey, even if I did drop the towel, it would take a vat of Viagra to get me hard. My dick has never been less interested in anyone than it is in you." I spin around and take off for my room, knowing my psycho ex won't leave until after she tells me whatever the hell she has to tell me. "Touch anything in my house and I will have you arrested. Test me if you don't believe me."

My bedroom door shuts behind me, and I click the lock into place, texting a WTF to the doorman. I towel off in record time, tossing on a pair of briefs, some shorts, and a white T-shirt, and in under a minute, I'm back, not even caring if my hair is all over the place and will dry like that.

Folding my arms over my chest, I glare at the woman who is now perched on a barstool in my kitchen. The same barstool Amelia sat on when she showed up drunk at my place two and a half months ago. It only aggravates me further.

"I know you've been following me," I say, standing on the opposite side of the island so she can't touch me or get too close. "You've also been following Amelia."

She shrugs, not even bothering to deny it. "And look at what my following her around has gotten me." Her phone slides across the counter, but I don't bother to glance down at it. I'm sure I won't like whatever it is. She wouldn't be here otherwise.

But first things first...

I steeple my fingers, pressing my elbows onto the counter as I look into her blue eyes. Blue eyes I used to think were the prettiest things ever. Until a pair of gray eyes blew all others out of the water.

"Nora, as much as I hate you being here, I will confess, I'm a bit worried about you."

She shifts in her seat, tilting her head ever so slightly. "I'm not the one you should be worried about. You're the one you should be worried about."

"You're missing my point here. You're pregnant and you're stalking people. Rather ruthlessly, actually. I appreciate that during pregnancy, hormones can change and alter the way you think and feel and react to certain situations. But I am concerned for your mental health as well as the health of your child once you deliver it if you're unable to gain control of the situation. Have you spoken with your OB? With a therapist about any of this?"

She rolls her eyes derisively, folding her arms over her chest. "Don't patronize me. I'm absolutely fine and I know exactly what I'm doing."

Except she's clearly not and I'll have to talk to Grace about this since I think she's her OB.

Nora glances down at the stone countertop, her shoulders slumping forward. "I could handle it when I knew the women meant nothing. When I knew it wouldn't go anywhere." She breathes out a heavy breath and meets my eyes once more, suddenly dejected, and I'm getting whiplash from her mood swings. "I can't stand to see you with that gold-digging whore. Look at my phone, Oliver. You need to see it."

She reaches out, tapping her phone until it illuminates again before she unlocks it. Holding it up, she practically shoves it in my face. It's a picture of Amelia and my father standing outside what looks to be the hospital. She starts swiping until I'm stuck on a picture of my father handing her something. The next image is Amelia holding a check.

What the fuck is this? My father is trying to buy her off?

Why would he do that? Goddammit, why would he do that to her?

"Did you know your charity case is in quite a bit of financial trouble," Nora goes on, misreading the fury as it dances across my face. "It's no wonder she latched herself onto you so tightly."

I shove her phone away, not wanting to see or hear any of this.

Nora smiles like the cat who ate the canary. "Right now, she's holding onto about eighty thousand in debt. A debt that only increases with her monthly interest." She taps her bottom lip. "Hmmm. I wonder how poor Amelia Bedelia was ever going to be able to get the kind of money it would take to eliminate that sort of debt? To people like us, that money is nothing. To people like her, it seems she'd go to any extremes to get it. Using you. Taking money from your father."

Nora keeps going, but all I can think about is the eighty grand.

No wonder Amelia struggles the way she does. No wonder she never liked to talk about her situation. No wonder she needed the scholarship so badly for Layla. She never told me about it, and I understand why.

My father must have known. If Nora knows about it, my father must as well.

"Oliver, did you hear me?" Nora snaps, and I turn back to her, realizing I'm gripping the hell out of my counter.

"No. I stopped listening to you because I don't care about anything you have to say. Why are you still here?"

She stands up, striding around the island in my direction, attempting to be sexy and seductive. It makes me sick to my stomach. It makes me sad for her. What must her life be like that she's going to these extremes? Does her husband have any clue how unstable his pregnant wife is?

She stops before me, her hand meeting my abs before sliding up my chest, her eyes following. "I love you," she whispers, now trying for sweet and contrite. I swear, could she be more mercurial? "I've always loved you. I screwed up. I know I did, but you're it for me, Oliver. We're it for each other. We have been since we were kids, babe. I never should have left you. Please, I want you to marry me. I want you to be the father to my baby. I want you to be with me. Not her."

Dear Lord in Heaven, give me strength.

I open my mouth to tell her just how flipping off the deep end she is with that when my words get cut off.

"You really shouldn't touch another woman's fiancé," Amelia says.

Nora twists around, taking a possessive step back into me. I shift around her, moving away. Closer to Amelia, though she's not looking at me and something feels very wrong. Her entire disposition is off.

"We know about the check you took from Oliver's father," Nora hisses. "All about your debt."

"Goodie gumdrops on you," Amelia deadpans, unimpressed. "Nora, I'm going to say this once and then it will be done. You need to get the fuck over Oliver. You need to move on with your life. You need to seek professional help because stalking is no joke, and it speaks to you being unstable." She takes a step and then another until she's in Nora's space without touching her. "But know this, pregnant or not, if you ever come near me, my sister, or Oliver again, I will call the police and file a restraining order. I will make sure it goes public. I will drag your name through the mud in ways you have never even begun to imagine. Think of what will happen then. Think of what happens to your baby if the state gets involved. Do yourself and your baby a favor, leave now and get your shit together."

Nora scoffs, but there is fear in her eyes and in the tremble of her voice. "Oliver would never do that to me."

"Oh, you can bet your ass I would," I tell her. "I've already told you this more times than I can count, but because I'm getting the impression your mind is warping shit all wrong, I will spell it out for you again. You and I are done. I do not love you. I do not want you back. I am happy with Amelia. And yes, if I ever see you again, if you ever try to meddle in my life, Amelia's life, or the lives of any member of our families, I will take you down. It's a fucking promise. Now get the hell out of my house!" My voice booms as I point to the door because the woman still looks like she wants to argue it.

Finally, after what feels like the longest moment of my life, she tosses her hair back, squares her shoulders, and saunters to the door, closing it behind her like she hasn't a care in the world. I can only pray she doesn't push me because as much as I'd hate to do that to a pregnant woman, I will.

"Christ, I thought I'd never be rid of her," I say, walking over to hug Amelia only to have her step back. My arms fall to my sides as I study her. And for what feels like the first time ever, I can't read her. "Amelia?"

"Don't you want to ask me about the check?"

"Nora said my dad offered you money." I watch her closely, her posture rigid. It never even occurred to me that she would take it. "I'm sorry he did that," I mumble, my voice not my own. I can see what's coming. I can feel where this is headed.

"Two million dollars. That's what I was worth to him to get rid of me."

Shit. That fucking asshole.

"Amelia..." I don't even know what to say. "He had no right to do that."

"Don't you want to know if I took it?"

I shake my head. "I know you didn't."

"Even now that you know about my debt? Are you so sure I wouldn't do something like that?"

I am sure, so instead I go with, "Why didn't you tell me about your debt?"

"Because it was none of your business. Just like it was none of your father's business or Nora's."

"You could have told me. Opened up to me."

"No, Oliver. No, I couldn't have. You would have tried to pay it off. Just how you paid Layla's tuition and then lied to me about it."

Shit. So that's what this is.

"Come here," I plead because I need to explain myself to her and I need to do that with her in my arms.

She doesn't come.

Altering her stance, she shifts her weight from one foot to the other, and I'm done with this. I can't talk to her like this. My hand snatches hers, dragging it away from her chest, and walking her into my family room. She pulls her hand from mine, sitting on the chair instead of the sofa, and that right there tells me everything I need to know.

She's done.

I sit on the couch, my elbows dropping to my knees, my head to my hands. I give myself a minute. A minute for that to sink in. For the panic and heartache to start to take over before I push them all down. I said I would never do this to myself again and I won't. Even as the emotions threaten to rebel and take over, I don't let them.

I clear my head and look up, meeting her distant eyes, a dark charcoal gray. Cold. Lifeless. But beneath that, broken. Flayed. A shadow of the woman I've fallen in love with these past few months. What did my father do to her?

"Wilchester was willing to give Layla the full scholarship," I start. "But it would have been at the expense of another child, and I couldn't do that. I couldn't take away from one to give to another. So I paid it. I had told you Layla would not have to pay for anything at Wilchester and I kept my end of the arrangement."

"But you never told me, Oliver. You lied to me about it."

"I never told you I got her a scholarship."

"Bullshit you didn't. You had them write me a letter saying that's what she got. It never once mentioned private funds. You had the school lie to me just as you lied to me."

I push up off the sofa, storming over to the window. "I didn't know what else to do. You and I made a deal, and I didn't want you to back out of your side of things."

She sucks in a rush of air, and I spin around to face her. Her eyes are glassy, heavy with tears. "So you did it for the arrangement."

It's not a question, but still, I know I have to defend myself.

She's right. I did lie. And I had the school lie for me. It was wrong and yet I don't regret what I did. Only that Amelia is upset about it.

"What else was I supposed to do? You would have never accepted me paying for the other half. Never. Just as I know you didn't accept my father's check today. You're stubborn and proud and refuse help. Layla deserves that program, Amelia, and I was going to do whatever it took to get her into it."

She stands up, fire in her eyes. "Layla is my responsibility. Not yours. You should have talked to me. Told me the situation and we could have worked it out together. I can't let you pay for that, Oliver. It's too much."

A growl sears past my lips. "Yes, you can. Yes, you fucking can. Please, Amelia. Don't do this. Don't ruin Layla's future over something like money. Over something like pride. You're right, I shouldn't have lied, but you shouldn't have kept things from me either."

"My debt is not your business and Layla's education is not your responsibility."

"Yes, it is! Because you are!" I yell at her, storming over and grabbing her arms so she can't run or hide from me. "You are my responsibility. You are my business. You are mine."

"If I let you pay, I'm everything they say I am. A gold-digger."

I shake my head, even as I understand her thinking on it. "You're not because I know you're not. That's all that matters. You're mine!" I say again. "So why does it feel like you're trying not to be?"

Tears slip from her eyes, trailing down her cheeks. "Because I don't belong in your world. I don't belong with you. This was always going to end. In two weeks, this was going to end."

I stare at her, stunned, my heart thrashing around my chest. It's exactly what I feared all along. That the moment our deal was over, she'd walk. Just as she's doing now. My mind is telling me to retreat. To pull back. To close ranks and protect what's left of our forces.

But I can't do that because doing that means I'm allowing this to happen.

"You don't have to do this. Amelia, don't do this."

More tears fall and I reach up, cupping her face in my hands, wiping them away with my thumbs, begging her with my eyes.

"Oliver, it was never going to work," she sobs. "What your father did and what he thinks of me aside, in the months we've been together, we haven't figured out a solution. Probably because we both knew the reality, we just didn't want to face it or believe it. This has to end. And now, after what happened today, we have the perfect excuse."

My throat closes in on itself as I watch her eyes solidify with determination.

I love this woman and she's walking away from me. Just like that. No fight. Yeah, she was pissed about the scholarship. Hurt over what my father did. But... at the end of the day, she doesn't love me back. Does she?

"What if I told you, I love you?" I ask. "That I'm in love with you? Does that change any of this for you?"

Her face crumples, her body trembling so hard she falls into me, her hands clutching my back. "I love you too," she whispers against me, her voice cracking. "So much. But I can't let you pay for Layla, and I can't lie anymore. Sometimes loving someone isn't enough to overcome the reality of life."

I don't know what to say. What to do.

With a final squeeze, she steps back, her face soaked in tears, her eyes red-rimmed. She's as heartbroken as I am, which is why I don't understand her walking away. Except I do. She thinks she's saving me from her. From what she does to my life. From what the truth would do to my world.

She doesn't feel worthy. Always the poor girl. The bullied girl. The one who doesn't belong. And if she was unsure about that before, my father just nailed it home for her.

Not only that, she doesn't trust. Neither did I until she came along. Now look.

All her life she's been left by those who love her, forced to pick up the pieces because no one else was there to. Even now, she can't put her faith in me. In us.

"You're scared," I challenge. "You're leaving because you're scared. Stay with me. We can figure it out together."

"Don't you understand? There is no figuring this out. If there was, we'd have done it weeks ago. I'm doing this to protect you."

She takes off her ring, setting it down on the coffee table. The necklace next, and all I can do is stand here and watch, heart in my throat and chest empty.

In the next breath, she's gone. Just like that. Like she was never here to begin with. Our fake engagement was always going to end. Our relationship along with it. And now I'm left with nothing.

32

"**W**ake up, dickwad, you're a fucking mess," Luca barks in my face, only to slap it twice when I don't respond with anything other than a groan.

"Go away."

"How much has he had?" someone else asks. I think it's Carter. "Please tell me this bottle wasn't full."

"I think it was." Landon. How many goddamn people are there in my house?

"I'll make some coffee." Rina. Why is Rina here?

"Yes. I'll help. Muffins. I'm going to make some muffins. Muffins will absorb whatever he's been drinking. Do you think we should start an IV? I brought stuff to do that. He has to be dehydrated as hell."

"I hate muffins," I tell Grace.

A cold hand meets my cheek, and I open my bleary eyes to find Grace hovering over me. Blazing, blinding sun shoots razor blades into my eyes and I wince, instantly shutting them back up.

"No, you don't," she whispers softly. "I make amazing muffins. I'll even make you chocolate chip because I love you. But first, you need a shower. You look and smell awful. Then I'm going to start an IV or have your sister do it."

"I love you too. Now go away. All of you. I don't need this."

"I tried the gentle approach," Grace says. "Now he's all yours."

Her hand leaves my face and then suddenly, I'm hoisted up in the air. At least I think I am because my head spins and my stomach roils as it lands against a very hard shoulder, my body getting ready to spew out whatever I put in it last night. Blanton's, I believe it was. Single barrel. Smooth on the way down and likely to burn like hell on the way up.

Good. Bring it on.

"Come on, baby brother. The lady is right. You stink. I get heartache, but it's certainly not worth killing your liver over."

"Your Boss Baby-looking ass has never been in love," I snarl at Kaplan.

"True," he says, ignoring the Boss Baby comment. "And from the looks of it, I think I'll keep it that way."

"Wanna tell us what happened?" Brecken asks. "Why we walked in to find you passed out on your sofa?"

"It's morning. People sleep on their sofas all the time."

"It's twelve-thirty and we've all been calling you for hours."

Oh. "I turned my phone off last night."

My father kept calling. He kept calling and Amelia wouldn't pick up and I couldn't take it anymore.

"We realized that," Kaplan mutters dryly. "Dad called us."

"Fuck him."

Two seconds later, I hear the shower starting, and then without warning, I'm tossed in clothes and all, falling hard onto the marble floor, instantly drenched from the freezing spray. That's when I start to throw up. Dragging myself up onto all fours, my stomach empties and empties and empties until I'm nothing but dry heaves and misery.

"Did you really drink the whole bottle?" Luca asks, crouching down and brushing my wet hair back from my forehead. He checks my pupils and a few of my cranial nerves, ever the neurosurgeon.

"Looks that way." Feels that way.

But for real, what the hell else was I supposed to do? Amelia wouldn't call me back. She wouldn't answer my calls. She would reply to my texts. I'm a broken man. This is nothing like it was when Nora betrayed me. This is visceral. A plague. Abject despair.

I never tried to get Nora back. I was done the minute she walked out of that restaurant.

But I can't do that with Amelia.

She didn't betray me. My dad made her believe she didn't belong with me. In my world. That she was nothing more than an opportunistic gold-digger. Things she's already been made to feel all her life because prep school kids with too much money are real assholes to kids without it.

I don't blame her for walking away.

She's right. We never were able to come up with a solution to our problem.

But so fucking what?

Falling back on my ass, my head hits the wall behind me, my eyes closed, as I let the water run over me. It's still cold, which shockingly enough, I appreciate.

"What do I do?" I ask, not even knowing if anyone is still in here with me or not.

"You really love her?" Landon. A man who, too, has seen the ugly side of love. Who has been betrayed by it. Who turned into an absolute wanker of a man because of it. A grump whose only soft spot is his daughter.

"Would I look like this if I didn't?"

"Okay. So what are you going to do about it?"

What am I going to do about it?

"I refuse to let her go."

"Then you need a plan."

I need a plan. Yeah. That sounds good.

But before I can get there, I need to do a few things first.

I slither my way up the wall until I'm standing. Then I strip out of my clothes which miraculously clears the room pretty damn quickly.

The shower gets turned to hot and after I'm clean and dressed, I have Rina start an IV—always have the nurse start the IV—of lactated ringers for me while I devour two piping hot chocolate chip muffins.

And once I'm completely sober and fully rehydrated, I kick everyone out of my place and drive over to my parents' compound. This isn't something I ever wanted to do. But now it seems I'm without a choice. If I want Amelia back, I have to fight for her. If I want Amelia back, I have to prove to her that she does, in fact, belong in my world.

There is no other place for her to be other than by my side.

The moment my tires come to a halt and my Porsche is in park, my dad is waiting for me on the front steps. He looks like shit. His dark salt and pepper hair is all over the place, like he's been running his fingers through it. Strained, wary eyes with purple stains beneath them hold mine as I amble out of the car.

I've only seen him like this once before and that was after Rina's psycho ex kidnapped her.

"I've been calling you," he says, taking the three steps down to meet me in the circular driveway. I'm guessing he doesn't want my mother to hear any of this.

"I had nothing to say to you on the phone. Everything I have to say needs to be done in person."

His hands meet his hips, and he lets out a weighty sigh, but his dark eyes hold mine. "I'm sorry, Oliver. I hurt you and I know I hurt Amelia. But I had to know for sure."

"My word wasn't good enough? You couldn't have talked to me first? You had to go and do that to her? To make her feel that way? Do you have any idea what you've done?"

He glances back over his shoulder and then back to me. "Take a walk with me."

I'm not given the choice as he grabs my arm, twisting me around and leading me in the direction of the tennis courts.

"I was in love with a woman before I was forced to marry your mother," he starts, and my eyes explode from my head. I've never heard this before. "I met her in college, and it was pretty damn close to love at first sight. I was crazy for her. Blind to everything and everyone else. I knew my marriage was going to be arranged for me. I knew I was going to marry Octavia Abbot even if I had never met her. Your grandfather was very old-school. Very traditional, and this was just the way it was.

"I told him I was in love. That I wasn't going to get engaged or married to anyone else. I had planned to propose to the woman I was in love with and have us elope. And the night I went and attempted to do that, she asked me one question. 'What happens to your money if we do that?' In the four months I was with this woman, a woman who I would have sworn on my life was as in love with me as I was with her, never once did I realize what she was really after."

"Your money."

He nods his head, his expression sad. Broken. "My money. The moment I told her I would be giving up my inheritance, that I'd have to take out loans to pay for medical school, but we could be together, she was gone. Just like that. Six months later, I married your mother, and it was the best decision I was ever forced into. But when I learned of your engagement, of how quickly you and Amelia got together, I panicked. I saw you repeating my old mistakes and I couldn't allow that to happen. I knew about what you did for Layla at Wilchester. I learned of Amelia's debts. And I was positive, in my heart, that you were being played."

"Except you were wrong."

He licks his lips, stopping us just before we hit the path for the tennis courts, just on the edge of the driveway and garage. His hand meets my shoulder, squeezing. "I was wrong. I was so, *so* wrong. I expected Amelia to take the money and run, just as that woman would have done if she had ever been presented something like that. But Amelia didn't, and in her eyes, I saw what my assumption did to her."

I glare at him. Hurt for Amelia. Furious for what that must have been like for her.

"Did you know she was bullied all through middle and high school? Made to believe that because she was a scholarship kid, she didn't belong? That she wasn't good enough? That she never fit in and was ridiculed by everyone?"

He takes a step back, his eyes falling to the ground as his hands meet his hips once more. "No. I didn't know that."

"Because you never tried to get to know her!" I bellow. "You never gave her the benefit of the doubt. Instead, you nailed home every single doubt and insecurity that was ever drilled into her. Amelia didn't know I paid for Layla's tuition. I did that on my own because she would have never let me pay for her to attend Wilchester. She also never told me about her debt because she knew I'd want to pay it off. And I would have. Because Amelia deserves the fucking world, Dad. She had to drop out of college at twenty. The guy she was with for over a year ended their relationship over a text, and she came home to take care of Layla who was only six at the time because her parents were dead. She had to switch up her entire life including her desired profession and she did it all without complaint or second thoughts. Just because she's poor doesn't mean she only cares about money."

His gaze flickers up to mine where they lock. "I owe you and especially her an apology."

My eyes narrow at that, so incensed and heartsick I can hardly stand here without going crazy. "Except she's gone, Dad. She left me."

He starts at this, his eyes bouncing back and forth between mine in confusion and regret. "Oliver... I... Why would she do that? Because of me? Because of what I did?"

"I have something to tell you and Mom." Without another word, I turn and storm back to the house. My father quickly catches up, tracking my side. The house is quiet, dark, and overly warm, which I imagine is for my mother's comfort. Typically, my parents spend the majority of the summer at the house on the vineyard, my father doing pro bono work at the hospitals there and on Cape Cod.

But not this year.

My mother is sitting in the solarium, a book in her hand though her focus is out the window, staring out into the gardens beyond. She hears us enter and instantly puts a smile on her face. It's forced and it hurts to see. She has three more chemo sessions and then some scans and then we'll know more.

"Oliver," she exclaims, some of the light returning to her eyes. "What a lovely surprise. Come sit with me."

I do and I can tell by her expression that my father never told her what he did with Amelia. That's his sin to confess. I have my own to cleanse myself of.

My mother scoots her legs over and I sit on the edge of the long plush chaise, taking her hand in mine. It feels like ice, and I instinctively use my other hand to adjust the blanket over her legs.

"Stop fussing," she admonishes. "I'm fine, but I can see you're not. What's wrong?"

I glance quickly up at my father and then return to my mom. "Mom, the engagement with Amelia was fake."

"Fake?" my father echoes, obviously not expecting me to say that.

"Yes," I answer, still staring at my mother. "Fake. Amelia and I didn't reconnect again until the night of the reunion. I had stepped in to save her from some nasty comments and then both she and I got to talking. Neither of us wanted to go in there and face our pasts, so we decided to do it together. I wanted her to feel confident. To have the people who had bullied her, including Nora, eat their words. I had the ring in my pocket, and I slipped it on her finger. We spent the evening together and I think, in truth, I fell in love with her that night. By the morning, our pictures were everywhere."

"And I started calling about it," she says, leaning back in her seat, holding my hand just a bit tighter.

"Yes. We were worried about you. You were just diagnosed and about to undergo surgery and chemo. We wanted you happy and you were happy that I was engaged."

"So you lied to us? To the world?"

I look up at my father and nod. "Yes. We did. I asked Amelia to pretend to be my fiancée for three months and in exchange, she asked for Layla to get a full scholarship to Wilchester. She told me flat out she didn't want my money. Just a scholarship. All she asked was for me to pull some strings. It was meant to be a business deal."

"But you fell in love with her," my mother says.

"But I fell in love with her."

"Then I ruined it," my father jumps in, sinking down into a nearby chair.

My mother turns sharply to him, though she doesn't ask questions yet. No doubt that will come the moment I leave. She purses her lips at him and then her eyes meet mine and that scowl turns into a warm smile.

"I knew the engagement was fake, Oliver."

My jaw hits the floor. "You did? How? When?"

She laughs lightly, almost like I'm a fool for not realizing this sooner. "Of course, I knew. You may be secretive about your dating life with us since Nora, but that doesn't mean I don't know you. I'm your mother. I didn't know the details until now, but I understood why you were doing it."

"But..." I'm flabbergasted. "You never said anything. Never hinted at anything. You were pushing us down the damn aisle."

"Because I knew you always had a thing for Amelia. Even way back when you were with Nora. Any time I would pick you up from school, you would make me wait to leave until Amelia left the building and then you'd watch her until she got on the bus."

I belt out an incredulous laugh. "I did? I don't even remember doing that."

"So when I saw the pictures of the two of you, the way you kissed her, the way you looked at her, I knew Amelia was your one. Even if you hadn't yet. Also, the poor girl can't lie to save her life." She snickers, hitching up her shoulder, and my smile is all over the place. She knew. All this time we were lying to my mother, trying to make her happy, and she was pulling a bait and switch on us.

"Jesus, Mom. I feel like such an asshole."

"Language," she admonishes even as her eyes sparkle at me with mirth. "You shouldn't though. Fake or not, seeing you with her has filled me with endless joy. Just like seeing Rina happy with Brecken has. But why are you telling me she's gone?"

My father launches into an account of what he did, my mother silently listening though she looks as though she's ready to grab a kitchen knife and cleave him to death with it. When he's finished, her eyes fall back on me.

"Oliver, you have to fix this. You have to find a way."

"I know. I had to tell you first."

She nods, thinking. "Well, now that you have, what are doing here? Go get your girl back."

33

Amelia 🖤

My head aches. My eyes burn. My stomach churns. And my heart... my heart is dead. Dramatic? Probably a bit, but that's how this feels. After Travis ended things with me, I didn't feel like this. Maybe I was too heartbroken over the loss of my parents. Over the loss of the future I planned. Whatever the reason, leaving Oliver feels like the end of me.

Even if it was the right thing to do.

Sagginalls texted me twice already today after calling three times yesterday. I haven't even told him Oliver and I are over, but it's like he knows. I told him yesterday Layla and I weren't going to the museum with him, but that hasn't stopped him from trying other things.

I'm finally fed up with it.

With everything.

I've been searching for new jobs all morning and my options aren't great. Any OR or hospital nursing jobs require night and weekend rotating shifts and with Layla, I can't exactly do that. I can't leave her home alone all night multiple nights in a row. I can't be away from her for entire weekends. It's just us and she'll be starting a new school.

Any outpatient jobs with better hours don't pay enough.

And I'm going to need all the money since I emailed Wilchester Friday evening when I got home and explained that we cannot accept the Oliver Fritz scholarship. That I will have to work out some sort of payment plan with them instead. I still haven't heard back, and I don't know what to do.

If they say no to that, I'll need to figure something out and do it fast.

Maybe I can sell one of my kidneys, oh, or my eggs.

Just as that thought springs to mind, my phone rings. I don't have it in me to get up and check it. It's either Sagginalls or Oliver, and I'm ignoring both. I can't talk to Oliver. If I do, I'll cave, and I don't want to cave. Yes, I'm angry he lied to me. But that's not why I left.

I left because I had to.

I left because if I didn't do it then, I might never have had the strength again.

His father hates me. Thinks I'm poor, gold-digging trash, and not nearly good enough for his son. And I'm so fucking tired of people thinking the worst of me. Of everyone thinking I'm lacking because I'm poor. I'm done with it. I don't want to be around people who see me that way and it's obvious he'd never accept me. I can't be part of a world I know I don't belong in.

Then there's the fake engagement that was set to end.

A situation we were never able to figure out.

Like everything, Oliver and I were always going to end. We were never meant to be. Soon he'll get over it. He'll move on and restart his player, bachelor existence.

It's for the best. It is.

Still doesn't stop the incessant aching that feels like the flu in my body.

"Amelia, pick up your damn phone," Layla yells.

"No."

"It's not Oliver, and it's not Saggingballs."

Oh. Shit. I fly off the sofa and run for it, catching it in midair as Layla tosses it at me. "Thanks," I mutter to her just as I swipe my finger across the screen, answering the unknown number before it can go to voice mail. "Hello?"

A voice clears on the other end. "Hi. Amelia?"

My eyebrows knit. "Speaking."

"Amelia, this is Christa Foreman."

I'm impersonating a goldfish. "Hi, Christa. What can I do for you?" I spin around in a circle, finding Layla, who is mirroring my expression though she's mixing it up with a gaping jaw. I walk back over to the couch and sit.

"I saw your email to the registrar, and I wanted to talk to you about it."

"Um. Okay."

Great. This is going to hurt. My eyes close and my forehead meets my hand. Why, of all the people who had to call to talk to me about this, did it have to be Christa Fucking Foreman? Haven't I suffered enough?

"Well," she starts. "First, you should know that we do not offer payment plans for tuition. It's all or nothing."

Great. That's pretty much what I was expecting. "Alright. Thank you for telling me. I'm sure I can—"

"Are you really turning down Oliver's money?" she asks, interrupting me.

I pinch my eyes shut tighter. "Yes. I was not aware that what I thought was a full scholarship was actually him paying for half her tuition."

She clears her throat. "Amelia, the reason I'm calling you on a Sunday is because I wanted to discuss an opportunity with you."

"An opportunity?"

"Yes. You're a nurse, correct?"

My whole face is scrunched up. Only now it's in confusion. "Yes."

"Friday morning, our school nurse informed us that she was retiring. This came on rather suddenly as we believed she had a few more years, but she evidently changed her mind. We will, of course, begin a formal search for her replacement, however, I wanted to mention this to you first."

I fall back against the sofa, bringing my knees up to my chest with me. "You did? How come?"

"Because if you work here, then the second half of Layla's tuition is covered as part of your employee benefits. Same as it was for you when your father worked here."

Holy shit. Ho-lee-shit!

I slingshot off the couch, pacing a circle around our worn coffee table that creaks against the carpet with every pass I make.

"Christa..." I'm actually at a loss for words.

"I realize you likely already have a job, but—"

"Yes!" I practically scream it into the phone. "Yes, please. I'd love to be the school nurse there. You have no idea how absolutely positively perfect that would be for me. What do I have to do?"

Christa laughs and I think that's the first time she's ever done that with me instead of at me. In fact, I'm positive it is.

"Just send me your resume with a cover letter and I'll push you through to the top of the pile. It being summer, the administrators do not want to have to go through the ordeal of surveying resumes and starting a lengthy interview process. They like their summers off. So if you can get it to me today, I will make sure they see it first thing tomorrow."

I think I'm having a stroke. I freeze, standing immobile in my family room with my phone pressed to my ear. This is too good to be true. Which makes me think...

"Christa, please don't take this the wrong way, because I am so grateful for all you're offering me, but why are you helping me? I thought you hated me?"

I hear her breathe out into the phone and for a moment, she's silent. I gnaw on my lip, worried I just fucked this whole thing up.

"Nora called me Friday afternoon. She told me you had just accepted two million dollars from Oliver's father and then lied about it to Oliver. She told me you were a thief. She said she wanted to ruin your life the way you were ruining hers. She asked if there was something I could do to get Layla kicked out of school. She threatened me, actually. Told me if I didn't do it, she'd reveal something I wouldn't want people to know about."

I gasp, my hand covering my mouth before the words, that fucking bitch leak out.

"I listened to her and nothing she was saying was making all that much sense. First, how could you take a check and then lie about it? Second, I have no idea what she could possibly have on me. Then I saw your email," she continues. "And I knew something must have happened. I read over Layla's file, and I read your email where you stated you didn't know what Oliver had done, and I knew I couldn't let this go. You were right. My life has never lacked for anything and any competition and hatred I felt toward you was really a reflection of myself. I don't want to be like that anymore. Now I'm trying to do the right thing."

Jesus Christmas.

"Christa, if I could hug you right now through the phone, I would. Thank you. Thank you so very much. You have no idea what this means to me."

"I'm glad. I truly am. I hope one day you can forgive me for the way I've treated you and we can be friends."

I'm smiling. I'm crying. "You are forgiven. I forgave you the day of Layla's interview, actually. And yes, I'd love to be friends."

"Wonderful. Thank you for that. I'll let you go now, but please get me your resume as soon as you can."

"Will do. Thanks again, Christa."

She disconnects the call and I spin toward Layla, belting out a scream and jumping up and down. "You're going to Wilchester with a full scholarship, and I won't have to sell off a piece of my liver to get you there."

Layla climbs off the barstool in the kitchen, stopping when she's right in front of me, her expression as serious as I've ever seen it. "I heard. Are you sure you want to do that? Won't you be bored as a school nurse? And what about the income drop?"

"No. It'll be awesome. You and I will have the same schedule and I can pick up per diem shifts during school vacations to make up the extra income. Also, it's only for four years, then I can do something else if I want."

"So no more Saggingballs?"

I grin. "No more Saggingballs. No having to rely on others for your tuition. We don't even have to stay in the city anymore. We can get a place closer to the school, where the rent is cheaper and lord baby Jesus, one with air conditioning."

Layla stares at me, her eyes all over my face. "And what about Oliver?"

I puff out a breath, all my sparkly happiness deflating like a hot-air balloon crashing to the ground. "There's nothing more to say there, Layla."

"He loves you. You love him."

"I do. And sometimes, when you love someone, you make sacrifices for them. You do what's best for them, even if it hurts you."

"But you're hurting him too," she protests, and I can't have this fight with her again.

"His mom is sick, Layla. I don't want her to know that we lied to her. I don't want the press to hate him because we lied to them. Besides, it wouldn't have worked out in the end. His family wouldn't have truly accepted me as one of their own."

"You're dumb. Your reasons are dumb."

Maybe, but they're all I've got and right now, they don't feel dumb. They feel necessary.

There are only so many times a person can handle being left before it breaks them past the point of repair. The fact that Oliver never came up with a plan for us for after the engagement side was over tells me everything.

He never wanted anyone to know the ruse we were pulling on them. Especially his mother. Maintaining the lie was more important to him than anything else. Including me.

That's not something I can tell Layla because I don't want her to hate him or be angry with him. He chose his family, and I chose myself while giving him the out he needed, and that's how this has to go. Even if everything about it feels wrong.

34

"**E**xcuse me, Dr. Fritz," one of the nurses hesitantly approaches me, hovering by the doorframe like she's afraid I'm going to lash out at any second. I might. I have been all damn day. "I'm sorry to bother you, but we've had to add another patient to your schedule."

Yup. I'm going to lose my mind in three... two...

"She asked for you specifically."

I spin around in my chair to glare at the poor, terrified nurse whose name I can't even remember right now. The last time that happened, it was Nora. And I swear to God, if it is Nora in that room, no one in this place will be safe. I obviously can't wring Nora's neck, she's pregnant after all, but the need to throttle someone is real.

"What are they here for?" I snap.

She bites her lip. "She's a new patient who wants to be part of our system here."

That tells me absolutely nothing helpful.

"Fantastic," I growl, standing up and shucking on my white lab coat, followed by my stethoscope around my neck. Fucking fantastic. It's probably Nora, which means I can yell at her at least because I can't yell at Amelia because she won't pick up my fucking calls.

Not one.

Short of stalking her ass down, which will only piss her off more. What the hell am I supposed to do? I talked with my mom. I talked with Rina. I talked with my brothers.

All of them told me to give her some time. That if I keep trying, eventually she'll come around.

Bullshit.

Don't they know how stubborn my woman is?

No, I have to do something drastic. Something dramatic, probably. I debated coming clean to the press about it, but me aside, they will drag her name through the mud. They will say a hundred horrible things about her, and I cannot let anyone else do that to her. Never again.

So no. That's out.

But I need a plan and everything I conjure up feels wrong.

"Come with me in case I need a chaperone," I tell the nurse before plowing past her as she yells out a room number to me. I can hear her squeaky shoes scurrying a solid five feet behind me as I storm in the direction of the patient room, thrashing an angry path down the hall.

Everyone skitters away from me. Everyone except Halle and Jonah, who stand by the nurses' station with identical folded arms and scowls that say, *get your shit together, you're at work.*

Right. I'm trying.

Okay, I'm not trying. Not at all.

I throw my hands up at them. "I'll try," I promise them.

Halle cocks an eyebrow that says, *you better,* and then spins around on her heels, her red hair flying around with her, and I miss my redhead. I miss her so much I can't stand it anymore. It's only been a few days, and it's just getting harder and harder.

I'm going to show up at her house tonight. I have to. I'll force her to listen to me. I'll tie her down if I have to. It's what any sane, rational man would do in my situation. I'm sure Layla will even help me.

I open the door to the patient room and Layla jumps off the table, hands held out, eyes wild with nerves. Speak of the devil.

"Don't get mad. And whatever you do, you can't tell Amelia I'm here."

Ah, hell.

"Layla, what are you doing here?"

"I need to talk to you."

I twist back to the nurse. "I'm fine. You can go."

The nurse leaves the room, and I shut the door, pressing myself against it, my head tilting as my arms fold over my chest. I stare expectantly at Layla with a raised brow that typically gets my teenage patients to fold like a flat sheet, but not this one.

"I want to go on the pill."

Now I choke. On nothing.

She laughs. "Ha, gotcha."

"Layla!"

She laughs harder, head thrown back, full-on cackling now. She points at me while slapping her thigh. "You should totally see your face. Damn, that's priceless. I should TikTok it. I bet I'd get like ten million views."

"You're cruel."

She shrugs with a sorry, not sorry expression.

"What are you even doing here?" I go on. "Aren't you supposed to be in your summer science program thing?"

"I am, but I needed to talk to you, and I can't do that with Amelia around. Hence the whole you not telling her I'm here thing. I mean, I'm a patient of yours now. So, you like, can't tell her anything. It's doctor-patient confidentiality, right?"

"I can't tell her anything now that you said the magic word." Her brows pinch together. "Birth control is the magic word. It places you securely within the confidential space despite your minor status. Thankfully you didn't go with sexually transmitted infections, or I think I would have stroked out for sure."

"Oh. That would have been even funnier than the pill thing."

"Yes," I say warily because I have to tread carefully here. "It would have been. So what's up? Are you actually here as a patient?"

I fall onto the rolling stool, ready to pull up her chart before passing her off to another provider if she says yes. She jumps back up onto the table, swinging her legs back and forth.

"Amelia is miserable," she starts and wow, that was a perfectly aimed sucker punch. The effect has my lungs emptying.

"Miserable?" I parrot.

"Yes. She's been doing nothing but moping around for the last few days. She didn't change out of her pajamas or even shower until this morning before having to go to work."

I sigh. And sag. And feel like someone is poking at my chest with an eleven blade. "I tried calling her, Layla. She won't talk to me."

"Because she thinks she's doing you a favor or something. I don't know. It all sounds like bullshit to me."

"Language," I warn, knowing full well I sound like my mother. And Amelia.

"Whatever. It's true. She loves you. She told me. Then she gave me this whole long excuse thing, but I think the truth is, she's scared. Scared of loving you and having you leave her like everyone else has."

I stare at the young woman on the table. "Layla, where did you learn something like that?"

She rolls her eyes at me, and just like that, she's a kid again. "From books, duh. I read plenty of romance novels and watch plenty of movies. I know how this all works. Amelia is scared. She doesn't think she belongs with you and she's afraid you'll realize that and leave her."

I stand, crossing the room and hopping up onto the table next to her. Tossing my arm over her shoulder, I draw her into my side. "I love your sister, Layla. I love her more than anything in the world. I love you too, and I want all of us to be together. Scared or not, she won't talk to me. I was actually going to show up at your place tonight and demand she listen to me."

"Dude, she'd freak at that. She's too stubborn."

Tell me about it.

"Plus, Saggingballs was calling her all weekend."

I glare down at the lanky child. "Are you trying to make me postal?"

She laughs. "No. She's quitting actually. Christa Foreman called her and offered her a job at Wilchester as the new school nurse. By doing that, the other half of my tuition is covered as part of her benefits."

Damn. That... has me smiling for so many reasons. Goddammit, Amelia, is there anything you can't do? She doesn't need me. She never did. But hell if I don't need her.

"Christa Foreman? You're sure?"

"Positive. She said she felt bad for the way she treated Amelia all those years. She also told her Nora tried to get me kicked out of school. Tried to blackmail her into doing it while lying about Amelia."

And just like that, my smile is gone.

I fly off the table, heading for the door only to spin around and march back in Layla's direction. That was it. The final fucking straw. Pregnant or not, she went too far with that. Hell, she had already gone too far, but that? Trying to ruin a kid's future?

How fucking crazy and vindictive can one woman be?

"I'll deal with Nora," I tell her. A phone call to Rob. A phone call to Grace, who is in fact her OB. A possible phone call to the police. We warned her that if she didn't back off, we'd take action. Well guess what, that's exactly what I'm going to do now.

No one messes with my girls. No one.

"Awesome. But I don't care about Nora. I'm not getting kicked out of school and now I have a full scholarship. Yet another thing Amelia is doing to sacrifice herself for me. I have to make her happy, Oliver, and the happiest I've ever seen her is when she's with you."

I join her again on the table, hugging my little Sprite. She has no idea how much I needed to hear that. Hear that Amelia loves me as much as I love her. Hear that I make her happy.

Everything else we can manage. All that matters is that we're together.

And if she's too stubborn to see that, then I'll have to prove it to her.

"I need you to help me get your sister back. If she won't talk to me, I don't know what else to do."

Layla's cornflower blue eyes light up. "Oh, I think I know the perfect way to do that."

35

Amelia ♡

I t's been a week since I've talked to Oliver. A week where I've second guessed everything I've done with him. Right from the very beginning. Especially since he's stopped calling. Three days of calls and texts and then gone.

I guess I can't blame him for that, I never picked up or wrote back.

Still, it hurts more than I should probably let it.

I knew this was who he was. A man who moved on. A man who never let a woman hold him back for long. A man who was adamant about never getting involved again. I walked away from him. I gave up on him.

And the moment I was ready to pick up the phone, he stopped calling.

Now I just feel broken.

Sad. Dejected. Mournful. Stupid. So fucking stupid for doing what I did. For thinking I was protecting him when what I was actually doing was protecting myself.

There has been no news about us. If Oliver told the world we were no longer engaged, I haven't seen it anywhere. I have no idea what, if anything, he's said to his parents. I haven't even heard from Rina, so I guess that friendship is gone along with Oliver.

At least I only have two more months of Sagginalls who was not happy about letting me go. He tried to get me to stay. In fact, he offered for me to keep only my OR days, which I would have done since I love the OR if it weren't for Wilchester needing me there full-time. I figure I can go back to the OR when Layla is done with high school and off to college.

I promised to stay for the summer and help him train whomever the new person he decides to hire is. No doubt she'll be young and beautiful and have zero nursing experience.

Until then, I'm shopping for a place for us closer to Wilchester and excited about this new venture for Layla. For us. I'm excited too. Though it's impossible to get excited about anything when it feels like your heart is missing from your chest.

"Come on," Layla whines at me, grabbing my arm and tugging on me. "I'm bored. I'm sick of sitting in the house. You refused to go out with me at all this week, fine. But you need a shower. And a change of clothes. And to stop eating the popcorn we made last night because it has to be stale."

I glance down at the large red bowl on my lap. The popcorn is stale, but I don't care. It was here, and I was too lazy to make myself breakfast. Layla's right. I am a mess. And this isn't exactly the best lesson in heartache or how to be a good big sister/guardian.

"Okay," I relent. "What do you want to do?"

"I want to get some new books because I've already done all of my summer reading and the library has nothing I want."

I need to get Layla a Kindle or some type of e-reader. The cost of all these paperbacks is killing me. "Two books," I tell her because I seriously cannot afford more. Not if we're going to be moving. Moving is expensive as balls.

"Fine. Two books. But they'll have to be thick at the rate I'm plowing through them."

That's it. I'm saving every penny I earn and getting her a damn e-reader for Christmas.

I stand, setting the bowl of popcorn down with a regretful sigh. It would have been good with chocolate chips in it even though I don't have any and I don't particularly like chocolate. Another sigh flees my lips. I think I'm starting to lose it.

"Alright. Give me twenty minutes to get ready and we'll go book shopping."

Thirty minutes later—evidently it takes longer to brush through your hair when you haven't brushed it in a week—we head out into the balmy summer day. Normally we hoof it up there since it's only about two miles to the Barnes & Noble at the Pru, but it's too damn hot so we hop on the E-line and take it up to Huntington, getting off at Prudential and then walking through the long mall, soaking up the air condition as we go.

"Why don't you just call him if he's not calling you," Layla suggests, eyeing the phone in my hand. "You're going crazy without him. Kinda literally since you've put off almost all basic hygiene until today and have taken to eating junk food you hardly ever eat."

"I wasn't checking to see if he was calling me," I lie. I absolutely was.

"Sure. Yeah. That's why your face was so pinched up it looked like you were sucking a lemon."

I nudge into her, evidently a bit too hard, because my skinny as a rail sister goes flying into one of those fake hair extensions stands and the woman running it thinks Layla is in the market for a new look when she has to grab on to a black wig to stop herself from falling to the ground.

"Sorry," I apologize sheepishly, helping Layla up and handing the woman back the wig. "You okay?" I ask Layla.

"I'm fine," she huffs, fixing her shirt that got twisted. "But next time you try to deny something we both know you're doing, please do not take it on my body."

"Deal. Come on, let's go get you some books."

"There's this new vampire romance I want to get," she starts as we head into the B&N. "But it's not in young adult. It's in romance."

I cock an eyebrow. "Is it clean romance, or are you trying to sneak in some sexy vampire love?"

Layla's cheeks pink up and she turns away, taking particular interest in the signs that indicate which section is which, though she knows the layout of this store by heart.

"I'm not sure. It's probably a lot like Twilight."

"Layla," I start, but she just grabs my hand and drags me along, all the way to the romance section. A section I do not want to be in.

Stupid romance. Look where you've gotten me.

"Just look for yourself," she begs, trying to get me with her large puppy dog eyes.

"Fine. But if I find any explicit sex, or even not so explicit sex, I'm cutting you—"

"Hey, don't I know you?" someone asks behind us, and I spin around only to choke on my tongue. "We went to high school together. And middle school."

Oliver steps forward until he's directly before me, his eyes all over me, his sexy, confident smirk right there, front and center.

"You sat beside me in math," he continues when I'm unable to speak. "That was the first time I noticed you. I was twelve. Then after that, I didn't stop watching you. Something my mother told me just the other day. Apparently, I used to get into the car after school, but I wouldn't let my mother leave until I saw you leave the school and get on the bus."

Emotion clogs my throat. I look up into his oh so green eyes. I can't believe he's here. He's actually here.

For me.

I glance over at Layla, and she's smiling like the devil. Probably because she is the devil. Or my angel. She arranged this whole thing; it's written all over her face.

"Is that so?" I ask, trying to fight my smile as I turn back to him.

God, how I've missed him. The scent of his cologne, all sandalwood, and spice. The heat of his body, how it engulfs mine the moment he's nearby. His smile that never fails to have my body flutter with butterflies.

"Funny," I remark. "I'm not sure I remember you."

His arms wrap around my waist, dragging me into his chest. I fall helplessly to him, restraining myself not even a thought in my head.

"Is that so?" He throws my words back at me. His voice dips as does his head, his eyes now feasting on my lips. "I guess I'll have to remind you then. How about I buy you and your sister lunch here in the mall?"

I blink at him because that is not what I was expecting him to say, or do for that matter, but then it clicks.

All of this.

Barnes & Noble at the Prudential. Him coming up to me and saying he knows me from high school. Him offering to buy us lunch.

This is how our fake relationship started. What we told everyone was our meet-cute.

I loop my arms around his neck and that smirk of his erupts into a full-blown smile. One that lights up his entire face.

"I guess we could do that."

"Thank god," he whispers, his face inching in even closer, the tip of his nose gliding back and forth against mine. "Because after lunch, I was thinking we could spend the afternoon together. And then I could buy you dinner. And then make you breakfast tomorrow morning. And then maybe you and Layla can move in with me. Or better yet, we can find a new place together."

"Oliver." It's as far as I get, but he doesn't care. He likes that I just said his name. He always has.

Reaching into his pocket, he pulls out my necklace, slipping it back around my neck and securing it with the clasp.

"Mine," he says against my lips. "And I'm never letting you go again."

Tears blur my vision, making it hard to see, my nose burning as I fight them back. "But, what about your parents? The media?"

"I told my parents everything. My mom already knew, believe it or not."

He laughs at my gob smacked expression.

"She was onto us from the start, baby. My dad is another matter. He is desperate to talk to you and apologize. He's a mess about it actually, which I'm kind of enjoying. As for the press?" He shrugs up an indifferent shoulder. "They can say and print whatever the hell they want. I don't care, Amelia. I don't care about any of it. I only care about you. You belong with me. In my world. By my side. Always."

The first of my tears hit my cheeks just as his lips crash onto mine, stealing my breath and quelching my sob. I kiss him with everything I have, standing high on my tiptoes and not even caring that Layla is watching.

We are in the romance section, after all.

His forehead presses to mine. "I love you," he says, lips layered with mine. "I love you so much. I was so scared to tell you for so long and now that just seems so ridiculous. I should have told you about it from the start. I should have never let you walk away from me. I can't tell you how much I've missed you."

"I love you too. I'm sorry. I'm so sorry I ran out on you."

"Don't be. I understand why you did it. But Amelia, no more running." He raises an eyebrow at me in warning. "I can't handle you running from me, baby. You're going to have to learn to trust and depend on me. Just as I will have to do with you."

I kiss him again, telling him without words just what that means to me. Just how much I love him. How I never want to be separated from him again.

No more running. No more fear. Just us. Always, as he said.

"Just us," I agree.

"So we can move in together? Find a place closer to Layla's school?"

I shake my head, incredulous. "You're serious about that? About us, the three of us, living together? Moving out to the suburbs?"

He scrunches his nose. "Maybe someplace in between is more our speed. We can figure it out together. But, baby, you're going to have to get used to me spending my money. Spoiling my ladies. Taking care of us forever."

I shake my head at that. I don't know if I'll ever be comfortable with his money or the way he likes to spoil us.

"I'll work on it," I promise. "Just don't overdo it and nothing crazy."

"Yes, ma'am. I'll try, but I make no promises with that. I can be impulsive every now and then." He winks at me, and I giggle.

Ain't that the truth.

"No more lying to me, and I won't hide anything from you. From now on, we're open and honest with each other."

"There is no other way." His hand takes mine, kissing my knuckles one by one and then frowning when he reaches my fourth finger. "I miss my ring here. I don't like how your hand looks without it."

I laugh lightly at that. God, everything in me is light. All that heaviness of the last week gone.

"I felt naked without it all week." I did. It was the weirdest sensation. I used to hate how uncomfortable having that ring on my hand made me feel, and then once it was gone, it was like I was missing a piece of myself.

A piece of him.

"Can I put it back on? Even if it's just a placeholder for the future?"

I think about that, completely unsure how to answer.

"Yes," Layla snaps, answering for me with a nudge to my back, shoving me harder into Oliver. "Yes. It's not fake anymore, Amelia. It's all real. Oliver wants us and we want him."

"We're not engaged though," I reply to her before turning back to him. "Won't that be weird?"

"Nah," he says, taking the ring from his other pocket and slipping it back onto my finger. I stare down at the large, sparkling diamond, my heart so full it's ready to explode. "This was always meant to be yours. My heart. My love. My life. My forever."

EPILOGUE

Oliver ♥

Two weeks later

"I SPOKE TO GRACE TODAY," I tell Amelia, holding her hand as we walk through the quiet Chestnut Hill neighborhood, past the large houses that line this street. "She's officially placed Nora on a seventy-two-hour psych hold."

Amelia gasps, squeezing my hand tight. "What? How?"

"She was a danger to others. She evidently threatened the police officer who came to speak to her. Threw something at him. She's lucky he didn't arrest her."

"No."

I nod. "Yes. That, in addition to the complaint we filed—the one stating she not only stalked us but threatened the safety and situation of a minor—sealed the deal. The state's involved now and Grace said that Rob had filed for divorce over a month ago."

"Jesus," she hisses. "What will happen with the baby?"

"That depends on Nora. If she gets the help she needs and does a good job proving to the state that she's not only changed her ways but is a capable, safe mother."

"I'm relieved she's getting help. Both for her and the baby. I still can't believe all the lengths she went to just to get her hands on you." Amelia winks, falling into my side.

"I'm quite the catch. Boston's most notorious bachelor."

"Nah uh," she says. "Not anymore. You're officially off the market."

She holds up her other hand, the one with my sparkly diamond on it. The sparkly diamond I nearly wish I hadn't put back on her to if for no other reason than when I do actually propose to her, it might seem anticlimactic. Not as special.

"Does that mean you'll marry me?"

She laughs. "Not so fast, hotshot. Let's start by finding a place to live together and see how that goes."

"You mean something like this then?" I stop, taking our joined hands and pointing to the large brick house set back off the street on over an acre of land—which for this part of the city—is nearly impossible to find. She twists to face it, staring up at it. "It's big enough for all of us and then some."

"It's beautiful," she says on a heavy swallow. I know that look. I know the fear in her eyes. The dollar signs ringing through her head. It's why I had to take things into my own hands.

"Let's go in and check it out."

I give her a small tug and she reluctantly follows after me, silent. She's trying. I know she is. In two weeks, we've looked at ten places, but none of them were right for us.

Pulling a key from my pocket, I unlock the door and hold it open for her. She gives me a funny look. Her eyebrows knit, and her lips quirked.

"No lockbox? And where is our realtor? Wait. How did you get the key?"

"Just go in and look around."

I get an eyebrow, but she does as she's told, stepping into the completely renovated eighteen-hundreds mansion.

"Oliver." My name is a hushed whisper. Her hand sliding along the smooth railing of the stairs as she walks through the foyer.

"It has six bedrooms. Eight and a half bathrooms. A media room. Two offices. An exercise room. A sunroom and a bunch of other things."

Her shoes tap quietly along the dark-stained oak floors, her eyes wide and her lips sealed as she moves from room to room on the first floor until she reaches the kitchen in the back. Her hands press onto the quartz counter, her eye gazing out the window, taking in some of the grounds.

"You bought this already, didn't you?"

I come in behind her, placing my hands on top of hers and intertwining our fingers, my chest to her back. My mouth dips down to her ear and I say, "I might have."

She sags back into me, her head along with her. "I should have known you'd do this."

"I already told you, I want to take care of you. What's mine is yours. There is no shame in letting me provide for us. It doesn't take away your power. It doesn't make you less strong. And it's certainly not taking advantage. This is our home, Amelia. Hopefully our home forever. The home we'll raise our children in. Throw Layla a sweet sixteen and a graduation party in."

"I love it."

"You do?"

She laughs. "Yes. You sound surprised."

Now I laugh. "More like shocked out of my skull. I was gearing up for an argument."

"I heard it. It was a good one."

I spin her around in my arms and hoist her up, dropping her onto the countertop. Our countertop. The countertop I'd make love to her on if that were an option in this moment.

"I love you."

Her legs and arms wrap around me, dragging me in as close as I can get. "I love you more. I love you in ways I never knew it was possible to love someone. I trust you. I trust you with my heart. With Layla. With all of it. Thank you for buying us this home."

My lips meld to hers, taking in her breath for my own. Our tongues dance, play, tease, our hands tickling, touching, caressing. "I'm going to make love to you in every room, on every surface."

"How about we start now," she rasps into me, going for the button on my jeans.

My hands catch hers, stopping her along with a shake of the head. "We can't yet. There's something else I want to show you."

She groans. "There's more?"

"There's definitely more." Grasping her hips, I help her down, taking her hand and playing with my ring on her finger. "I bought the house two days ago. All cash. It was a flip sale, the house redone by a contractor who gutted it and completely restored it. Including the swimming pool."

"Pool?" she squeals. "Layla will go batty for that."

"I know it. She already did."

"Huh?"

I open the back door, and everyone is already there, waiting on us. Layla and Stella. My parents. All of my brothers. Rina and Brecken. Even Grace is here. My family. Her family.

"Oh my god," Amelia shrieks, covering her mouth, her eyes welling up with tears. "What is this?"

"A surprise, duh," Layla says, making everyone laugh. "We live here now, Amelia. Can you believe it? Oliver said we can move in as early as next week."

The smile on my Sprite's face is priceless as she comes forward to hug both of us. I squeeze them tight, holding them against me. My heart. My life. Never have I felt this complete.

Amelia and Layla whisper things back and forth to each other, both of them a teary mess, but it doesn't last long. Their smiles and laughs quickly take over as everyone begins to funnel in, congratulating us. Wishing us well.

Including my father, who strides toward Amelia with determined steps. Shortly after Amelia and I got back together, my father showed up at her house. He asked her out to coffee and apologized profusely. He explained his actions, why he felt they were necessary.

Since then, they've become close.

He still feels guilty. I know he does.

My father is not used to being wrong.

"Welcome home, sweetheart," he says to her, stealing her from Layla and hugging her fiercely. "I know you'll all be so happy here together."

Pretty soon we're all eating—takeout since there was no other option—sitting on the floor of the back deck and patio—because there is no furniture—enjoying the night. Layla and Stella are running around the grass, splashing each other with pool water. Amelia watches it with a contented smile hanging on the corner of her lips. A smile I don't think I've ever quite seen on her before.

"Hey," I say, whispering in her ear. "You know, I still don't know your middle name."

"What?" She lets out a bemused laugh.

"The first night at the reunion when I proposed, I said, Amelia I-don't-know-your-middle name Atkins. Well, I still don't know it."

Her gray eyes meet mine, sparkling against the setting sun. "Sarah. My middle name is Sarah."

I take both her hands in mine. "Amelia Sarah Atkins, will you do me the incredible honor of moving into this house with me? Helping me decorate it. Furnish it. Make it our own?"

She gulps down a heavy swallow. "Yes."

An unstoppable smile hits my lips, my forehead falling to hers. "What do you think about a dog?"

"Don't tell me you already bought us a dog too?"

I chuckle, kissing her sweet lips. "I haven't, no. I thought that might be overkill."

"I think a dog would be fun. A rescue dog. One hopefully already housebroken."

"You can pick out whatever you want."

"No," she says. "We'll pick it out together. With Layla too. That's what a family does."

Never has anything sounded so sweet.

EPILOGUE 2

Carter

THE SECOND MY pager goes off, I know it's going to be bad news. Nothing good is ever paged at the end of your shift. I stop in the middle of the hall—my back sore and my neck stiff after fourteen hours on my feet—to check the pager when a nurse comes barreling down the hall.

"Dr. Carter, they need you in the ED stat. They have a thirty-three-week pregnant woman with severe painless vaginal bleeding."

"Previa?" I question, reading through the page that says the exact same thing she's telling me.

"Don't know. She's not our patient."

"Tell them I'm on my way."

Without another word, or even so much as a complaint since my shift technically ends in ten minutes, I run for the elevator, hitting the button. Just as the doors open and I step on, Grace Hammond, my resident—and my younger brother Oliver's best friend—steps on beside me.

"You got paged too?" she asks, her voice soft and slightly melodic the way it always is even after a long day of delivering babies and performing surgeries. She leans back against the wall, folding her arms over her chest.

"Yep," I reply, shifting slightly so I'm not so close to her. So the scent of her floral, coconut shampoo doesn't infiltrate my senses. I hate being so aware of her. Still I can't help but surreptitiously take her in. Grace's blonde hair is wrapped up in a tight bun; her blue scrubs a shade darker than her luminous eyes that never seemed dulled by the grueling hours or the fluorescent lights.

I look away, chastising myself for the tenth time today.

"I thought you were off at seven."

"I am," I tell her. "But I got paged, so that's how it goes."

"Previa?" she guesses, clearly having the same thought I was. Heavy, painless vaginal bleeding in a pregnant woman in her third trimester can be signs of a lot of things, but a placenta previa—where the placenta covers the cervix—is usually at the top of my differential diagnosis.

"Probably, but we'll see once we get in there. She's not a patient on our service."

Just then, the doors to the emergency department open and we're immediately greeted by Margot, my sister Rina's best friend and a nurse here in the ED. She starts talking a mile a minute, setting off at a good pace as she updates us on the patient while we head toward the trauma room.

"Thirty-year-old thirty-three-week pregnant woman, G1P0 presented complaining of heavy, painless vaginal bleeding. Vitals so far are stable, but she's losing blood as quickly as we can give it to her, and her heart rate is tachy in the one thirties. Her blood pressure is a little low but holding at 96/62. Stat ultrasound confirms baby is not in any distress, but the placenta presents very low. Likely the cause of the bleeding, but since we can't do a transvaginal ultrasound, difficult to tell if it's a full previa. Patient reports no prior knowledge or diagnosis of a previa."

"Alright," I say, as we approach the trauma rooms. "Have you notified the OR yet?"

"Yes. They're already on standby and so are peds and the NICU. They're just waiting on you."

"You look a little flustered, Margot," I comment dryly, noting her flushed cheeks and messy dark curls. "All going smoothly down here?"

She flips me off without missing a step. "It's July, Carter. Do you know what that means?"

I laugh under my breath as does Grace. "New interns," Grace replies, because yeah, we have them too, though Grace seems to like her newbie, Dylan. I hate July. And August, for that matter.

"Yes," Margot expels dramatically. "New fucking interns who think they're God's gift to medicine and that nurses are placed on this earth to do their bidding. I had to literally smack one of their hands away because he was about to attempt a pelvic exam on this woman. Can you imagine?" She looks to each of us, horror in her brown eyes. "Did he not realize that sticking his hand into a bleeding vagina with a high likelihood of a previa could possibly cause a placental rupture?"

This is why Margot is a kick-ass nurse.

"Obviously not," I comment. "He'll quickly learn that nurses save lives that interns attempt to collect. Thank you for that." And I mean that genuinely. I can't count the number of times nurses have not only saved my ass, but the asses of fellow doctors.

"Any time. Though I highly doubt it will be the last today I have to stop one of them from doing something stupid. The patient is in here." She points to the door, and we stop in front of the trauma room. "Her name is Marissa, and she's scared shitless. Her husband was at a conference, and we were finally able to get through to him. He's on his way now."

"Thanks," Grace says, spinning around pushing open the door of the trauma room with her back as she talks to Margot. "You still coming tomorrow night?"

"I think so. I have to see what time I get off. Rina will be there for sure though. Same with the other girls."

Grace gives Margot a wink and then we plow through the doors, straight into action. I nearly have to shove two interns out of the way —Margot wasn't kidding with how fucking inept they are—and then Grace and I get to work. We assess the mother's condition as well as the fetus's. Within minutes we determine that yes, she's losing too much blood from her previa to be stopped down here or even at all.

We have about ten minutes max to get this baby out of her before the mother goes into shock from blood loss and the baby goes into distress.

"Marissa," Grace soothes, coming right up to the patient's face, hovering over her and gently squeezing her shoulder. "We're taking you up to the OR now. You're going to deliver the baby."

"No," Marissa cries through her oxygen mask. "It's too soon."

"Unfortunately, we don't have a choice. We need to do what's best for both you and the baby, and that's delivering it. I know you're scared, but we'll be with you every step of the way. Don't worry, we're going to do everything we can for you both. You're in excellent hands."

Grace gives her that warm smile, the one that always gets through to patients, and then we're moving. Margot and another nurse are pushing the gurney as we all head for the elevator at a quick pace.

"You scrubbing in on this or is someone else taking over for you?" Grace asks me.

"I'll take it. I've come this far." We all step onto the elevator, the doors shutting. "What are you doing tomorrow night with my sister?" I question softly as my eyes cling to the glowing numbers as we ascend.

"Girls' night. We even managed to force Amelia to come."

Amelia is Oliver's girlfriend. Oliver and Grace have been best friends since infancy. And forever, people just assumed they'd be a thing, but it never happened. They view and treat each other as siblings.

You'd think that would have made Grace an unofficial part of the family and I guess in a way it has. But not for me. I went away to college and then medical school. Did my residency down in Virginia Beach, only returning to Boston last year as an attending.

So I wasn't expecting it. *Her*.

It had been years and years since I had seen Grace.

I wasn't expecting her to be... fuck, everything that she is. Smart. Beautiful. An insanely talented doctor. Funny. Sarcastic. Beautiful. I might have mentioned that once already, but hell does it bear repeating. As someone who has already been down the road of wanting someone you know you can never have, craving her the way I do is like a kick in the teeth.

On a daily basis.

"And Tony doesn't care that you're having this girls' night?" I try to keep all the bitterness from my voice. I try very hard, but Margot's head flies sharply in my direction, her gaze discerning as she cocks an eyebrow, so I'm not sure I quite hit my mark.

Tony is Grace's fiancé, so yeah, again, never gonna happen between me and her.

"He's got some dinner work thing he's going to."

"Right. Of course he does. Can't make partner without putting in all the hours."

Grace rolls her eyes at me, but it's true. The bastard is never around. At least not that I've noticed.

"Uh-huh. What time did your shift end this evening, Doctor? Fifteen minutes ago, is it now? And you're, oh look, heading into surgery."

"Different. Medicine is a noble profession. Chasing ambulances and then going after the doctors who saved the life of the injured isn't."

Before she can lay into me for that, the elevator doors open and now we're back in game-on mode. We race down the hall while the OR nurses take the patient and prep her for surgery. By the time we walk into that OR, she'll be under anesthesia because we don't have time to wait for an epidural or spinal block to take effect.

Grace and I don scrub caps and boots before going about the process of scrubbing in.

"Do you feel you're ready to take point on this?" I ask, lathering my hands with antiseptic soap, washing every inch.

"Without a doubt," she answers confidently, scrubbing vigorously beside me and refusing to meet my eyes.

She's pissed at me for the Tony comment, but I don't care. I don't have to. I'm the attending and she's the resident and that's how our dynamic works. If we weren't in the hospital, she'd mouth off back to me until her face was red, but not here.

"I can have that baby out in under ninety seconds."

"I'm going to time you."

Now she meets my eyes, glaring blue fire into me. I smirk before I can stop it, thankfully she can't see it behind my mask.

"You do that, Carter." She presses her foot onto the pedal, rinsing off the soap.

"If you can do it safely in eighty seconds, I'll buy you something special for your birthday."

She shakes her head, her arms bent at the elbow, sterile hands held up and out in front of her. "You're such a condescending dick," she murmurs under her breath as she plows past me, headed for the OR.

"What was that? I'm not sure I heard you correctly."

"I said you're such a considerate doctor," she yells at me over her shoulder, and now I can't stop my laugh.

But the second we meet the OR floor, all humor is gone from my lips.

"Hi, Dr. Fritz," Angelica, one of the nurses, says to me, batting her long lashes up at me flirtatiously as she goes about tying my gown and helping me with my sterile gloves. "I'm *so* glad you're in here performing this surgery. I know the patient is in the best of hands with you as her doctor."

"Actually, I'm the one doing the surgery, Angelica," Grace

smoothly interjects. "Dr. Fritz is simply here to supervise me. So, if you're ready to get back to work, I'd like to start." With the patient fully prepped and ready, Grace gets into position, holding out her hand. "Ten blade, please."

The scrub nurse obliges, and all other commentary ceases as Grace sets to work while I watch on, here to jump in at any time if needed, but I already know I won't be. Grace, while only heading into her third year of residency, is as competent as any fourth year or attending. She's by far the best OB-GYN resident in the hospital.

Just as she makes the incision, the pediatrics and NICU teams roll in. The patient is holding her own, getting another unit of type-specific blood while Grace works diligently and methodically to get the baby out. That's actually the easy part. The fastest part. After that is where the real work for us begins.

Especially with a case like this. We have to remove the placenta without causing more damage or further bleeding.

"How's my patient doing, Larry?" Grace asks the anesthesiologist just as we get a couple of beeps on the monitor.

"Blood pressure dipped a little, but I'll get it back up."

"That would be greatly appreciated." Grace locates the fetus, working with skilled, precise movements. "If you're not too bored over there, Carter, maybe you could cauterize that bleeder for me?"

"I've got it," the nurse says, doing her job.

"I think *Dr. Fritz* is well beyond cauterizing bleeders," Angelica simpers. "I've seen him perform the most complex of surgeries with ease."

"Hey, Larry?" Grace cuts in once again, completely ignoring Angelica who has always been a flirty kiss ass. "Did *Dr. Fritz* ever tell you why he decided to become an OB-GYN when the field is predominantly female providers?"

"Here we go..." I mutter.

"Yes. Here we go." Grace extracts the baby, blue and wet, handing him directly to the waiting pediatric team. They immediately start working on him. "Time of delivery, nineteen-thirty-two." She glances up at me. "Seventy-eight seconds, Carter. I believe you owe me one hell of a birthday present."

"I'll let you use the robot in my next surgery."

She shakes her head. "No way. I want something better from you, Doctor. Something real I can sink my teeth into."

So do I, I think and then quickly shut that bitch up. "A steak then?" I offer. "Since we know Tony won't be around to take you to dinner."

I get a death glare for that.

"Wait, back up," Larry jumps in, before Grace can unleash more of her wrath. "Why *are* you an OB-GYN, Carter? You that into pregnant chicks and pussy?"

Grace, as well as every nurse in here, throws Larry a scathing look.

"I'm going to pretend you didn't just say that, because it makes you sound like a total misogynistic asshole," Grace barks while she goes about removing the placenta and tying off any active bleeding vessels. "But no. He actually walked in the room when his mother was in the throes of delivering Rina and after that decided birthing babies was his life's calling."

I hate that story.

It always makes me sound like such a pussy—pun intended.

Plus, Rina works in this hospital as an ICU nurse, so I know this will somehow funnel back to her, which never fails to make her laugh at my expense.

Speaking of... all the nurses, right on cue, start oohing and awing, humor dancing in their eyes. The NICU team who have an umbilical line placed and are giving the baby—who is pinking up and half crying—oxygen to help him along, are also joining in on the dig my resident just took at me.

She's not dumb either. Grace has to know I'll punish her for this. Professionally speaking, of course. I'm not actually allowed to punish her the way I'd like.

My comments about Tony must have really pissed her off this time.

Still, when you're engaged to a total dipshit, douchebag who takes you for granted and is never around, you should learn to get used to people making disparaging comments about him. Even Oliver can't stand the guy and Oliver generally likes everyone.

"That true, man?" Larry inquires, not bothering to hide his chuckle.

"Yes, it's true, and now I'm one of the top surgeons and OB-GYNs in Boston that you" —I point at Grace— "have the pleasure of learning from and watching in action. Just wait till you see what I have in store for you tomorrow, Dr. Hammond."

Grace peers up, likely to say something else that will boil my blood when pediatrics cuts us both off. "Five-minute APGAR is six. We're moving the baby up to the NICU. Have someone page us when mom is awake."

They roll out and we finish our surgery, everyone quiet as the team works, the tension in the room so thick you could cut it with a scalpel. Just as Grace finishes the last stitch, I turn and march out of the room, tearing off my surgical gear and going straight for the sink to scrub out.

Then I slink back, tucked in the corner along the shadows.

Two minutes later Grace comes out, glances around and when she doesn't spot me, she sighs. In relief or regret, I cannot tell, but she goes for the sink, rolling her neck until it pops as she begins to scrub out. And when her hands are lathered in soap, and she has nowhere else to go, I move in behind her, towering over her with my height. I take a deep inhale, marveling how she still manages to smell sweet and clean after a day spent in the hospital and my cock twitches in my scrubs.

She feels me behind her, not touching her but merely inches away, and she stiffens. "I thought you'd gone."

"Not quite yet," I whisper, my lips dipping down till they're hovering by her ear, watching as goose bumps dance across her neck. "Pull another stunt like that and I'll have you running scut along with the interns for the rest of your residency. As it is, tomorrow you're on postpartums. No surgeries."

"Carter—"

"The proper response is *yes, Dr. Fritz.* Anything else is completely unacceptable."

"Yes, Dr. Fritz," she grits out through clenched teeth, and I grin, making sure she feels it on my lips. That's how stupidly close I am to her right now. So stupidly close I feel her sharp intake of breath and quickly force myself to get control and step back.

I shouldn't have done that.

Each time I give in just an inch, I lose ground on forcing her into her neat and tidy role in my life. Brother's best friend. Resident. Engaged.

Off-motherfucking-limits.

"Good work in there, Doctor. Keep it up and I will take you out for that steak."

With that, I turn and leave the hospital, needing to clear my head. Clear it of her.

Because that's all I can ever do with her. Even when the desire for more is growing increasingly unbearable.

The End

WANT to get your hands on Carter's and Grace's epic love story? Get your copy of Doctor Mistake now!

And keep reading for an excerpt of The Edge of Temptation to meet Oliver before he got his HEA. Boston's Billionaire Bachelors is a spin-off of The Edge series so you will see many familiar faces!

ALSO BY J. SAMAN

Wild Love Series:

Reckless to Love You

Love to Hate Her

Crazy to Love You

Love to Tempt You

Promise to Love You

The Edge Series:

The Edge of Temptation

The Edge of Forever

The Edge of Reason

The Edge of Chaos

Boston's Billionaire Bachelors:

Doctor Scandalous

Doctor Mistake

Doctor Heartless

Doctor Playboy

Doctor Untouchable

Start Again Series:

Start Again

Start Over

Start With Me

Las Vegas Sin Series:

Touching Sin

Catching Sin

Darkest Sin

Standalones:

Just One Kiss

Love Rewritten

Beautiful Potential

Forward - FREE

END OF BOOK NOTE

Dear reader! Thank you SO much for taking the time to indulge in the Oliver and Amelia's story. I've had this couple, this series, in my head for two years and I'm so excited to finally get it out there.

First, a thank you to my family. My girls and my guy. You're the best. My heartbeat. My life line. My love. I am eternally grateful for all that you are.

My betas, Patricia and Danielle... you rock! This book would never had turned into all that it did without you! And to Joy Westerfield for throwing in a helping hand!

I love Oliver. Let's just start there. He first showed up in The edge of Temptation and then grew a bit more in The Edge of Chaos. He's my super hero. My ultimate alpha boyfriend. And Amelia is just sort of along for the ride. A lot broken and scared. Scarred. Oliver is too, but Amelia's battle wounds run deep.

I had trouble softening Amelia. I wanted her to be strong and independent. A woman who is battle-hardened and has grown from the bullied girl. But I wanted some of that bravery to carry over into her love for Oliver.

Layla might have been one of my favorite characters to write and we will definitely see more of her in future books.

I hope you'll stick around for Carter's book, coming January 2022!
Much love!
XO,
J. Saman

THE EDGE OF TEMPTATION

Halle

"No," I reply emphatically, hoping my tone is stronger than my disposition. "I'm not doing it. Absolutely not. Just no." I point my finger for emphasis, but I don't think the gesture is getting me anywhere.

Rina just stares at me, the tip of her finger gliding along the lip of her martini glass, her expression saying she's got me right where she wants me. "You're smiling. If you don't want to do this, then why are you smiling?"

I sigh. She's right. I am smiling.

But only because it's so ridiculous.

In all the years she's known me, I've never hit on a total stranger. I don't think I'd have any idea how to even do that. And honestly, I'm just not in the right frame of mind to put in the effort.

"It's funny, that's all." I shrug indifferently, playing it off. It's really not funny. The word terrifying comes closer. "But my answer is still no."

"It's been, what?" Margot chimes in, her gaze flicking between Rina, Aria, and me like she's actually trying to figure out the mathematics behind it. She's not. I know where she's going with this and it's fucking rhetorical. "A month?"

See? I told you.

"You broke up with Matt a month ago," she continues. "And you can't play it off like you're all upset over it, because we know you're not."

"Who says I'm not upset?" I furrow my eyebrows, feigning incredulous, but I can't quite meet their eyes. "I was with him for two years."

But she's right.

I'm not upset about Matt.

I just don't have the desire to hit on some random dude at some random bar in the South End of Boston.

"Two *useless* years," Rina persists with a roll of her green eyes before taking a sip of her appletini. She sets her glass down, leaning her small frame back in her chair as she crosses her arms over her chest and purses her lips like she's pissed off on my behalf. "The guy was a freaking asshole."

"And a criminal," Aria adds, tipping back her fancy glass and polishing off the last of her dirty martini, complete with olive. She chews on it slowly, quirking a pointed eyebrow at me. "The cocksucker repeatedly ignored you so he could defraud people."

"All true," I agree. "Matt was the absolute worst sort of human."

I can't even deny it. My ex was a black-hat hacker. And while that might sound all hot and sexy in a mysterious, dangerous way, it isn't. The piece of shit stole credit card numbers, and not only used them for himself but sold them on the dark web. He was also one of those hacktivists who got his rocks off by working with other degenerate assholes to try and bring down various companies and websites.

In my defense, I didn't know what he was up to until the FBI came into my place of work, hauled me downtown, and interviewed me for hours. I was so embarrassed, I could hardly show my face at work again. Not only that, but everyone was talking about me. Either with pity or suspicion in their eyes, like I was a criminal right along with him.

Matt had a regular job as a red-team specialist—legit hackers who are paid by companies to go in and try to penetrate their systems. I assumed all that time he spent on his computer at night was him working hard to get ahead.

At least that was his perpetual excuse when challenged.

Nothing makes you feel more naïve than discovering the man you had been engaged to is actually a criminal who was stealing from people. And committing said thefts while living with you.

I looked up one of the people the FBI had mentioned in relation to Matt's criminal activities. The woman had a weird name that stuck out to me for some reason, and when I found her, I learned she was a widow with three grandchildren, a son in the military, and was a recently retired nurse. It made me sick to my stomach. Still does when I think about it.

I told the FBI everything I knew, which was nothing. I explained that I had ended things with Matt three days prior to them arresting him. Pure coincidence. I was fed up with the monotony of our relationship. Of being engaged and never discussing or planning our wedding. Of living with someone I never saw because he was always locked away in his office, too preoccupied with his computer to pay me even an ounce of attention.

But really, deep down, I knew I wasn't in love with him anymore. I didn't even shed a tear over our breakup. In fact, I was more relieved than anything.

And then the FBI showed up.

"I ended it with him. *Before* I knew he was a total and complete loser," I tack on, feeling more defensive about the situation than I care to admit. Shifting my weight on my uncomfortable wooden chair, I cross my legs at the knee and stare sightlessly out into the bar, still feeling ridiculous in ways I wish I never will again.

"And we applaud you for that," Rina says, nudging Margot and then Aria in the shoulders, forcing them to concur. "It was the absolute right thing to do. But you've been miserable and mopey and very . . ."

"Anti-men," Margot finishes for her, tossing back her lemon drop shot with disturbing exuberance. I think that's number three for her already, which means it could be a long night. Margot has yet to learn the art of moderation.

"Right." Aria nods exaggeratedly at Margot like she just hit the nail on the head, tossing her messy dark curls over her shoulders before twisting them up into something that resembles a bun. "Anti-men. I'm not saying you need to date anyone here. You don't even have to go home with them. Just let them buy you a drink. Have a normal conversation with a normal guy."

I scoff. "And you think I'll find one of those in here?" I splay my arms out wide, waving them around. All these men look like players. They're in groups with other men, smacking at each other and pointing at the various women who walk in. They're clearly rating them. And if a woman just so happens to pass by, they blatantly turn and stare at her ass.

This is a hookup bar.

All dark mood lighting, annoying, trendy house music in the background, and uncomfortable seating. The kind designed to have you standing all night before you take someone home. And now I understand why my very attentive friends brought me here.

It's not our usual go-to place.

"It's like a high school or frat house party in here. And definitely not in a good way. I bet all these *bros* bathed in Axe body spray, gelled up their hair, and left their mother's basement to come here and find a 'chick to bang.'" I put air quotes around those words. "I have zero interest in being part of that scheme. Boring conversations with half-witted men who wouldn't know a female orgasm if it came in their face."

"Well . . ." Rina's voice drifts off, scanning the room desperately. "I know I can find you someone worthy."

"Don't waste your brain function. I'm still not interested." I roll my eyes dramatically and finish off my drink, slamming the glass down on the table with a bit more gusto than I intend.

Oops.

Whatever. I'm extremely satisfied with my anti-men status. Because that's exactly what I am—anti-men—and I'm discovering I'm suddenly unrepentant about it. In fact, I think it's a fantastic way to be when you rack up one loser after another the way I have.

Like a form of self-preservation.

I've never had a good track record. Even before Matt, I had a knack for picking the wrong guys.

My high school boyfriend ended up being gay. I handed him my V-card shortly before he dropped that bomb on me, though he swore I didn't turn him gay. He promised he was like that prior to the sex.

In college, I dated two guys somewhat seriously. The first one cheated on me for months before I found out, and the second one was way more into his video games than he was me. I think he also had a secret cocaine problem because he'd stay up all night gaming like a fiend. I had given up on men for a while—are you seeing a trend here?—and then in my final year of graduate school, Matt came along.

Need I say more?

So as far as I'm concerned, men can all go screw themselves sideways. Because they sure as hell aren't gonna screw me!

"You can stop searching now, Rina," I suggest. This is getting pathetic. "I have a vibrator. What else does a girl need this day and age?"

All three pause their search to examine me and I realize I said that out loud. I blush at that, but it's true, so I just shrug a shoulder and fold my arms defiantly across my chest.

"I don't need a sextervention," I continue. "If anything, I need to avoid the male species like the plague they are."

They dismiss me immediately, their cause to find me a "normal" male to talk to outweighing my antagonism. And really, if it's taking this long to find someone then the pickings must really be slim here.

I move to flag down the waitress to order another round when Margot points to the far corner. "There." The tenacious little bug is gleaming like she just struck oil in her backyard. "That guy. He's freaking hot as holy sin and he's alone. He even looks sad, which means he needs a friend."

"Or he wants to be left alone to his drinking," I mumble, wishing I had another drink in my hand so I could focus on something other than my friends obsessively staring at some random creep. *Where the hell is that waitress?*

"Maybe," Aria muses thoughtfully as she observes the man across the bar, tapping her bottom lip with her finger. Her hands are covered in splotches of multicolored paint. As is her black shirt, now that I look closer. "Or maybe he's just had a crappy day. He looks so sad, Halle." She nods like it's all coming together for her as she makes frowny puppy dog eyes at me. "So very sad. Go over and see if he wants company. Cheer him up."

"You'd be doing a public service," Rina agrees. "Men that good-looking should never be sad."

I roll my eyes at that. "You think a blowjob would do it, or should I offer him crazy, kinky sex to cheer him up? I still have that domination-for-beginners playset I picked up at Angela's bachelorette party. Hasn't even been cracked open."

Aria tilts her head like she's actually considering this. "That level of kink might scare him off for the first time. And I wouldn't give him head unless he goes down on you first."

Jesus, I'm not drunk enough for this.

"Or he's a total asshole who just fucked his girlfriend's best friend," I protest, my voice rising an octave with my objection, my hands flailing outward like a chicken who has lost her way. I sit up straight, desperate to make my point clear. "Or he's about to go to prison because he hacks women into tiny bits with a machete before he eats them. Either way, I'm. Not. Interested."

"God," Margot snorts, twirling her chestnut hair as she leans back in her chair and levels me with an unimpressed gaze. "Dramatic much? He wouldn't be out on bail if that were the case. But seriously, that's like crazy psycho shit, and that guy does not say crazy psycho. He says crave-worthy and yummy and 'I hand out orgasms like king-sized candy on Halloween.'"

"Methinks the lady doth protest too much," Aria says with a knowing smile and a wink.

She swivels her head to check him out again and licks her lips reflexively. I haven't bothered to peek yet because my back is to him and I hate that I'm curious. All three ladies are eyeing him with unfettered appreciation and obvious lust. Their tastes in men differ tremendously, which indicates this guy probably is hot.

I shouldn't be tempted.

I really shouldn't be.

I'm asking for a world of trouble or hurt or legal fees. So why am I finding the idea of a one-nighter with a total stranger growing on me?

I've never been that girl before. But maybe they're right? Maybe a one-nighter with a random guy is just the ticket to wipe out my past of bad choices in men and make a fresh start? I don't even know if that makes sense since a one-nighter is the antithesis of a smart choice. But my libido is taking over for my brain and now I'm starting to rationalize, possibly even encourage. I need to stop this now.

"He's gay. Hot men are always gay. Or assholes. Or criminals. Or cheaters. Or just generally suck at life."

"You've had some bad luck, is all. Look at Oliver. He's good-looking, sweet, loving, and not an asshole. Or a criminal. And he likes you. You could date him."

Reaching over, I steal Rina's cocktail. She doesn't stop me or even seem to register the action. I stare at her with narrowed eyes over the rim of her glass as I slurp down about half of it in one gulp. "I'm not dating your brother, Rina. Any of your brothers for that matter. That's weird and begging for drama. You and I are best friends."

She sighs and then I sigh because I'm being a bitch and I don't mean to be. I like her brother. I like all of her brothers, but Oliver and I are tight. He is all of those things she just mentioned, minus the liking me part. But if things went bad between us, which they inherently would, it would cost me one of my most important friendships. And that's not a risk I'm willing to take.

Plus, unbeknownst—or maybe just ignored—by Rina, Oliver is one of the biggest players in the greater Boston area.

"I'm just saying not all men are bad," Rina continues, and I shake my head, unwilling to budge on this. "We'll buy your drinks for a month if you go talk to this guy," she offers hastily, trying to close the deal.

Margot glances over at her with furrowed eyebrows, a bit surprised by that declaration, but she quickly comes around with an indifferent shrug.

Aria smiles, liking that idea. Then again, money is not Aria's problem. "Most definitely," she agrees. "Go. Let a stranger touch your lady parts. You're waxed and shaved and looking hot. Let someone take advantage of that. And by take advantage I mean I mean take advantage. You need sex, Halle. It's been a hundred years since your orgasms weren't self-produced."

"And if he shoots me down?"

"You don't have to sleep with him," Rina reminds me, cutting a glare at Aria who clearly doesn't agree. "Or even give him your real name. In fact, tell him nothing real about yourself. It could be like a sexual experiment."

I shake my head in exasperation.

"We won't bother you about it again," she promises solemnly. "But he won't shoot you down. You look movie star hot tonight."

While I appreciate the sentiment from my loving and supportive friends, being shot down by a total stranger when I'm already feeling emotionally strung out might just do me in. Even if I have no interest in him. But free drinks . . .

Twisting around in my chair, I stare across the crowded bar, probing for a few seconds until I spot the man in the corner. Holy Christmas in Florida, he *is* hot. There is no mistaking that. His hair is light blond, short along the sides and just a bit longer on top. Just long enough that you could grab it and hold on tight while he kisses you.

His profile speaks to his straight nose and strong, chiseled, cleanly shaven jaw. I must admit, I do enjoy a bit of stubble on my men, but he makes the lack of beard look so enticing that I don't miss the roughness. He's wearing a suit. A dark suit. More than likely expensive judging by the way it contours to his broad shoulders and the flash of gold on his wrist that I catch in the form of cufflinks.

But the thing that's giving me pause is his anguish. It's radiating off him. His beautiful face is downcast, staring sightlessly into his full glass of something amber. Maybe scotch. Maybe bourbon. It doesn't matter. That expression has purpose. Those eyes have meaning behind them and I doubt he's seeking any sort of company.

In fact, I'm positive he'd have no trouble finding any if he were so inclined.

That thought alone makes me stand up without further comment. He's the perfect man to get my friends off my back with. He's going to shoot me down in an instant and I won't even take it personally. Well, not too much.

I can feel the girls exchanging gleeful smiles, but I figure I'll be back with them in under five minutes, so their misguided enthusiasm is inconsequential. I watch him the entire way across the bar. He doesn't sip at his drink. He just stares blankly into it. That sort of heartbreak makes my stomach churn. This miserable stranger isn't just your typical Saturday night bar dweller looking for a quick hookup.

He's drowning his sorrows.

Miserable Stranger doesn't notice my approach. He doesn't even notice me as I wedge myself in between him and the person seated beside him. And he definitely doesn't notice me as I order myself a dirty martini.

I'm close enough to smell him. And damn, it's so freaking good I catch myself wanting to close my eyes and breathe in deeper. Sandalwood? Citrus? Freaking godly man? Who knows.

I have no idea what to say to him. In fact, I'm half-tempted to grab my drink and scurry off, but I catch Rina, Margot, and Aria watching vigilantly from across the bar with excited, encouraging smiles. There's no way I can get out of this without at least saying hello. Especially if I want them to buy me drinks for the next month.

But damn, I'm so stupidly nervous. "Hello," I start, but my voice is weak and shaky, and I have to clear it to get rid of the nervous lilt. Shit. My hands are trembling. Pathetic.

He doesn't look up. Awesome start.

I play it off, staring around the dimly lit bar and taking in all the people enjoying their Saturday night cocktails. It's busy here. Filled with the heat of the city in the summer and lust-infused air. I open my mouth to speak again, when the person seated next to my Miserable Stranger and directly behind me, gets up, shoving their chair inadvertently into my back and launching me forward.

Straight into him.

I fly without restraint, practically knocking him over. Not enough to fully push him off his chair—he's too big and strong for that—but it's enough to catch his attention. I see him blink like he's coming back from some distant place. His head tilts up to mine as I right myself, just as my attention is diverted by the man who hit me with his chair.

"I'm so sorry," the man says with a note of panic in his voice, reaching out and grasping my upper arm as if to steady me. "I didn't see you there. Are you okay?"

"Yes, I'm fine." I'm beet red, I know it.

"Did I hurt you?"

Just my pride. "No. Really. I'm good. It was my fault for wedging myself in like this." The stranger who bumped me smiles warmly, before turning back to his girlfriend and leaving the scene of the crime as quickly as possible.

Adjusting my dress and schooling my features, I turn back to my Miserable Stranger, clearing my throat once more as my eyes meet his. "I'm sorry I banged into you . . ." My freaking breath catches in my lungs, making my voice trail off at the end.

Goddamn.

If I thought his profile was something, it's nothing compared to the rest of him. He blinks at me, his eyes widening fractionally as he sits back, crossing his arms over his suit-clad chest and taking me in from head to toe. He hasn't even removed his dark jacket, which seems odd. It's more than warm in here and summer outside.

He sucks in a deep breath as his eyes reach mine again. They're green. But not just any green. Full-on megawatt green. Like thick summer grass green. I can tell that even in the dim lighting of the bar, that's how vivid they are. They're without a doubt the most beautiful eyes I've ever seen.

"That's all right," he says and his thick baritone, with a hint of some sort of accent, is just as impressive as the rest of him. It wraps its way around me like a warm blanket on a cold night. Jesus, has a voice ever affected me like this? Maybe I do need to get out more if I'm reacting to a total stranger like this. "I love it when beautiful women fall all over me."

I like him instantly. Cheesy line and all.

"That happen to you a lot?"

He smirks. "Not really. Are you okay? That was quite the tumble."

I nod. I don't want to talk about my less than graceful entrance anymore. "Would you mind if I sit down?" And he thinks about it. Actually freaking hesitates. Just perfect. This is not helping my already frail ego.

I stare at him for a beat, and just as I'm about to raise the white flag and retreat with my dignity in my feet, he swallows hard and shakes his head slowly. Is he saying no I shouldn't sit, or no he doesn't mind? Crap, I can't tell, because his expression is . . . a mess. Like a bizarre concoction of indecision and curiosity and temptation and disgust.

He must note my confusion because in a slow measured tone he clarifies with, "I guess you should probably sit so you don't fall on me again." He blinks, something catching his attention. Glancing past me for the briefest of moments, that smirk returning to his full lips. "I think your friends love the idea."

"Huh?" I sputter before my head whips over my shoulder and I catch Rina, Aria, and Margot standing, watching us with equally exuberant smiles. Margot even freaking waves. Well, that's embarrassing. Now what do I say? "Yeah . . . um." Words fail me, and I sink back into myself. "I'm sorry. I just . . . well, I recently broke up with someone, and my friends won't let me return to the table until I've re-entered the human female race and had a real conversation with a man."

God, this sounds so stupidly pathetic. Even to my own ears. And why did I just admit all of that to him? My face is easily the shade of the dress I'm wearing—and it's bright motherfucking red. He's smirking at me again, which only proves my point. I hate feeling like this. Insecure and inadequate. At least it's better than stupid and clueless. Yeah, that's what I had going on with Matt and this is not who I am. I'm typically far more self-assured.

"I'll just grab my drink and return to my friends."

I pull some cash out of my purse and drop it on the wooden bar. I pause, and he doesn't stop me. My fingers slip around the smooth, long stem of my glass. I'm desperate to get the hell out of here, but before I can slide my drink safely toward me and make my hasty, not so glamorous escape, he covers my hand with his and whispers, "No. Stay."

Want to find out what happens next with Halle and Jonah? Grab your copy of The Edge of Temptation now and get lost in the world of hot doctors and spicy romance!

CPSIA information can be obtained
at www.ICGtesting.com
Printed in the USA
BVHW050025161122
651985BV00008B/287